ZEROES

ALSO BY SCOTT WESTERFELD

Afterworlds

Uglies
Pretties
Specials
Extras

Leviathan
Behemoth
Goliath
The Manual of Aeronautics:
An Illustrated Guide to the Leviathan Series

ZEROES

SCOTT WESTERFELD
MARGO LANAGAN · DEBORAH BIANCOTTI

Simon Pulse
New York London Toronto Sydney New Delhi

This book is a work of fiction. Any references to historical events, real people, or real places are used fictitiously. Other names, characters, places, and events are products of the author's imagination, and any resemblance to actual events or places or persons, living or dead, is entirely coincidental.

SIMON PULSE
An imprint of Simon & Schuster Children's Publishing Division
1230 Avenue of the Americas, New York, New York 10020
This Simon Pulse hardcover edition September 2015

Jacket designed by Regina Flath
Interior designed by Mike Rosamilia
The text of this book was set in Adobe Garamond Pro.
Manufactured in the United States of America
2 4 6 8 10 9 7 5 3 1
Library of Congress Cataloging-in-Publication Data
Westerfeld, Scott.
Zeroes / by Scott Westerfeld, Margo Lanagan, and Deborah Biancotti.
p. cm.
Summary: Told from separate viewpoints, teens Scam, Crash, Flicker, Anonymous, Bellwether, and Kelsie, all born in the year 2000 and living in Cambria, California, have superhuman abilities that give them interesting but not heroic lives until they must work as a community to respond to a high-stakes crisis.
[1. Ability—Fiction. 2. Interpersonal relations—Fiction. 3. Adventure and adventurers—Fiction. 4. Superheroes—Fiction. 5. Science fiction.] I. Lanagan, Margo, 1960– author. II. Biancotti, Deborah. III. Title.
PZ7.W5197Zer 2015 [Fic]—dc23 2015001667
ISBN 978-1-4814-4336-4 (hc)
ISBN 978-1-4814-4338-8 (eBook)

For everyone with a power—
whether or not you've found it yet

So many powers.
So few heroes.

CHAPTER 1
SCAM

"MORE COFFEE?"

Ethan jumped. It'd been a long night. "Okay."

The waitress wasn't even listening, the coffee pot dipping toward Ethan's cup. Which was fine. The coffee was crap and he was already wired, but it gave him an excuse to keep sitting there.

He'd spent the last two hours hunched in a back booth of the Moonstruck Diner, staring out the window at the Cambria Central Bank. It was right across the street, and it opened at eight.

"Want anything else?" the waitress asked.

"I'm good. Thanks."

He drank some more coffee. Still crap.

At least the bitter java gave him a reason to seem jumpy.

Nobody would look at him and say, "Hey, that kid is real jumpy. Must have something to do with the army-green duffel bag under his feet."

Nope. Nobody would blame the bag.

He glanced around the diner. Everyone was wrapped up in their own six a.m. thoughts. Nobody was even looking at him. Okay, one girl was looking at him. But she glanced away like she'd been caught staring. So apart from that one cute girl at the front of the diner, nobody was looking at him.

Besides, this was the middle of Main Street. Nobody would come rolling in to seize Ethan and his bag and haul them both out into the dawn. Nothing bad ever happened here in Cambria, California, population half a million during a college term.

The diner was filling up with delivery guys on breaks, respectable citizens in suits, and the occasional group of clubbers winding down. All Ethan had to do was watch the bank and wait for the doors to open.

Easy. As long as the waiting didn't kill him.

"More coffee?"

"Seriously, it's been five minutes. Can you stop with the coffee?"

The waitress looked stung.

"Sorry," Ethan said. But she was already gone.

He pulled the duffel bag up and wedged it into a corner of the booth like a makeshift pillow. Which was pretty funny, given what was *in* the bag. It was the stuff *in* the bag that was keeping him awake. That, and the people looking for it.

He'd always known the voice would do this one day—get him into serious trouble. The voice didn't care about consequences. The voice didn't weigh up the pros and cons and then say, "Hey, Ethan, this is how you can get what you want." The voice wasn't sentient like that; it wasn't smart. It didn't negotiate. The voice just went for it. It lied and lied, and most of the time Ethan didn't even know where the lies came from when they poured out of his mouth. How did the voice know half that stuff?

But Ethan had always known that one day he'd pay for all those lies.

Right now he was hoping today was not that day.

CHAPTER 2
SCAM

THE EVENING BEFORE HAD STARTED WELL.

A date with a beautiful woman, a pre-med student from the north side. Ethan put on his best shirt, a pin-striped button-up his sister had bought him last year, promising it would drive girls crazy.

The pre-med girl was way out of his league, even with the shirt, but the voice had talked her into it. He could see her trying to understand it herself. She was at least four years older than him, way more sophisticated, and much hotter. But every time she seemed uncertain, Ethan would draw her back in.

Or, rather, the voice would.

It would say just the right thing about the midnight art-house film they'd seen, or the obscure pre-med stuff she was into, or Ethan's plan to study at the Sorbonne one day. Whatever the hell the Sorbonne was.

But then it got late and exhausting and frankly kind of expensive. He'd used up all his cash buying movie tickets and caramel popcorn and drinks from a wine bar so divey that Indira had called it "quaint." The wine was fifteen bucks a glass. Ethan didn't even like wine.

If it'd been up to him, he would have scammed his way through the night. The voice was great at getting stuff for free. But Indira clung to Ethan's side, watching his every move like he was some exotic breed she'd never seen before. A teenage kid from the wrong side of town. She probably thought he was quaint too, in a divey way.

It was pretty clear that the voice could never convince Indira to do anything more than talk and smile and cling. A nice girl from the north side, she probably wouldn't even make out on a first date.

So the voice switched itself to mute while Ethan worked out what he wanted to do next. When he decided all he wanted was to go home, the voice sorted that out too.

He left Indira standing by her car in front of the art-house cinema. She seemed to glow, lit by the marquee lights announcing a lineup of classic films. Her long summer dress billowed in the night sea breeze. She looked confused by his sudden departure. Maybe a little hurt.

"This blows," Ethan muttered to himself. In his real voice.

He hated how sad she looked. But he didn't have the energy to turn around. It was all the fault of that stupid art-house film. Who knew it could be *that* boring? Watching it had sucked the life out of him.

As Ethan walked away, he rubbed his jaw with the palms of both hands. His muscles always felt weird after a long night of letting the voice talk for him. Like he'd been speaking a foreign language. It left a taste in his mouth too. Oily charm with notes of bullshit.

The worst part was, he had no way home. He was totally out of cash, so a cab was out of the question, and buses didn't run this late. Indira would've given him a ride, but of course the voice had spun some crap about his vintage Jaguar parked a few streets away, just to get rid of her.

The voice sucked at planning ahead. The voice just knew when Ethan wanted out.

It also liked to twist the knife sometimes. It had claimed the Jaguar was a present from his dad. Yeah, right.

Luckily, it was summer and Cambria's nightclub strip was still in full swing. There were plenty of people to hitch a ride with on Ivy Street. Ethan followed the thudding drumbeat until he reached the crowd. Light spilled from canopied doorways, and people shouted at each other, deafened by music that rebounded from the pavement and warehouse walls.

The voice could talk Ethan's way into one of the clubs. But once inside, no one would hear him over the music. He'd be just another gawky seventeen-year-old with a mousy buzz cut and too many freckles.

No, what he needed was somebody here outside.

A muddle of tribes skirted each other on Ivy. Hipsters and scene kids, crumpled coked-up suits from the stripper bar, a few raver wannabes in summer outfits showing lots of skin. They were mostly older than Ethan, which meant they mostly had cars. Somebody could be talked into giving him a lift home.

Just ahead of him, a guy exited one of the clubs from a side door. Which probably meant he was staff and sober enough to drive.

Ethan sped up.

The guy walked with a steady purpose. He had an army-green duffel bag over one shoulder. Ethan let himself drift into the guy's way until the bag slapped against him.

"Hey, watch it!" he said in his own voice.

The guy spun to face him. He was a few inches shorter than Ethan, but twice as big across the shoulders. And he had no neck. The sort of guy who could crush you with an annoyed glare. His right hand dropped into a jacket pocket, like he was ready to pull a knife.

"Whoa." Ethan backed away. "My mistake. Sorry about that."

The guy scanned Ethan. His eyes were piercing, way too blue. Almost electric. But a moment later he smiled, eased his hand out of his pocket, and gripped Ethan's shoulder. It was like being held up by a wall.

"Sorry, man," the guy said. His voice was calm and low. "Did I hit you?"

"No problem. You missed, actually," Ethan sputtered, fear beating in his chest. All he wanted was to be on the same side as this guy in his next fight. He let the voice take over. "Taylor sent me over to help you out."

That was one of the voice's specialties. Names.

The big guy paused, looking him up and down. Not smiling anymore.

"Taylor sent you?" An edge of disbelief in the low rumble of his voice. "How's a squirt like you gonna help?"

Ethan hated when this happened. The voice would get him into situations that only the voice could get him out of. Then he was stuck, listening and waiting. Letting it talk.

"Taylor said you were bad off last night. Wasn't sure you'd remember the way to his house." The voice sounded like it was making a joke, so Ethan tried to smile.

The guy stared at him another moment, then laughed. Abruptly, like that was the stupidest thing he'd ever heard. "What a dickhead. I worked off that hangover in the gym this morning. How do you know Taylor?"

"My sister's in his old army unit," Ethan heard himself say, and cringed.

Thing was, his sister really was in the army. Stuff could go really wrong when the voice told the truth. What if the guy asked for his sister's name? What would the voice say then?

But the guy relaxed, like he understood everything now. "So you're family. Taylor wants you to join the team."

Ethan nodded, because it seemed like the right thing to do. "He said I should learn from the best." The voice twisted his throat, like it was imitating someone. "'Nobody better than the Craig.'"

A low thunder of laughter spilled out of the Craig, who reached over and took Ethan's shoulder again. The weight of his hand almost buckled Ethan's knees.

"He tell you to say that? What a dickhead." He shoved Ethan, sending him stumbling a few steps backward. "Come on. Car's this way."

The Craig headed for a side street. Ethan took a breath and followed.

Hell, maybe he could still get a ride home out of this.

CHAPTER 3

SCAM

THE CRAIG OWNED JUST ABOUT THE CRAPPIEST car Ethan had ever seen. It was an old beat-up Ford sedan. Either it was brown or it was covered in enough dirt to make it look that way. It was hard to tell.

The Craig saw his expression and laughed that sharp, abrupt laugh again.

"Lesson one, kid: Skip the fancy cars. Too easy to spot. Don't let your ride make you an easy mark. Someone sets up on you, they'll be looking for a fancy car."

Ethan shrugged. There was a kind of paranoid logic to what the Craig was saying. Plus, his right hand had sunk into his pocket again, and Ethan still couldn't decide what was in there. A gun? A knife? Even at four a.m., it was way too hot to be wearing a jacket.

Craig noticed the direction of his gaze. "You're not carrying, are you?"

Ethan clenched his jaw, not trusting the voice. He shook his head.

"Good." Craig looked both ways up and down the street, then opened the Ford's back door and slung the duffel bag across the seats. "For now, your job is to keep your eyes open."

Ethan nodded mutely. A trickle of cold ran down his spine. He was about to get into a car with a strange man—a *really* strange man—who was armed and probably a criminal, with a duffel bag full of who-knew-what, and head for someplace unknown.

He opened his mouth to let the voice take over. It could say whatever it wanted—lie, plead, beg—as long as the Craig let Ethan walk away, back to Ivy Street, where he could charm some clueless raver into a ride home instead.

But the voice didn't say anything. Which meant there was nothing to say and no way out of this, not without raising Craig's suspicions. Ethan wasn't sure what would happen if Craig called Taylor and found out that everything he'd said was a lie. But nothing good, that was for sure.

So Ethan shut his mouth and got into the car.

CHAPTER 4
MOB

KELSIE NEVER WANTED NIGHTS LIKE THIS TO END.

When the nightclubs closed at four a.m., she wasn't ready to leave. But the crowd was breaking into groups of two or three, looking for a way home or some other kind of fun or . . . whatever else they were looking for.

Kelsie hated it when the throngs of dancers shattered into lonely pieces, like the gears of some wonderful machine broken beyond recognition.

She found Mikey leaning against the wall outside the Scheherazade. He looked beat, but he still managed to pull off that lazy-rock-god attitude—knee out, one foot on the wall. He had a cigarette pinched between finger and thumb, and he was watching the crowd through his own exhaled smoke.

She called his name.

His eyes rolled toward her. "Hey, little sis."

She wasn't his sister, but Mikey liked to remind Kelsie that she was too young to hang out in the clubs.

"Wanna get some pancakes?" she asked.

"Sure."

"We should find some people," Kelsie said. "You know, get a crew together."

Mikey took a drag of his cigarette, said in a roiling stream of smoke, "Don't you ever get sick of crowds?"

Kelsie laughed. "Mikey, it's me you're talking to."

He grinned.

She found Remmy next. He was trying to pick up a girl—two girls, actually—and when one of them announced that she oh my God *loved* pancakes, Remmy came with. That made five, including Kelsie. Five was okay, but six was better.

As they headed up Ivy, Kelsie spotted her friend Ling coming out of the Buzz.

She swept up behind her, linking arms. "Hey, girlfriend!"

Ling jumped and spun. When she saw it was Kelsie, she gave her hand a squeeze. "I'm both wired and tired. Is that weird?"

"Too wired and/or tired for pancakes?"

"Never."

That made six, and Kelsie relaxed.

A group was forming around her, like an engine whose last part had clicked into place, ready for the power switch to be thrown.

She knew that if she guided them toward a common purpose, she could keep the group going the rest of the night. At least until the sun came up. The stupid sun always broke up parties.

Kelsie had needed this, the crowd, as long as she could remember. The boom and beat and *feel* of a group. Since the time when she was six and had run away from home, following the pulse of something in the distance.

She'd asked Lee, her mom at the time, what it was she could feel. Was there a flood coming?

"No, darling." Lee had been watching TV, sprawled on the couch. "We don't get floods round here."

So six-year-old Kelsie had walked out of the house in search of answers.

She remembered it clearly. She'd opened the door and stepped into the dark street without the slightest fear, because she had to find the rumble and hum that made her fingertips tremble. She had to follow it to its source.

It'd turned out to be a high school football game. Though it wasn't the game that had called to her; it was the crowd. The temperature and pressure of their excitement had rolled across her like a wave.

The parking-lot security guard had found her an hour later. Sitting on the hood of a pickup, eyes closed. Feeling the sweet, nervous thrum of the home team running down the clock for a win. The home team, she was told later, hadn't won a game in ten years. Kelsie had never felt anything like it.

When the guard asked her what such a tiny thing was doing there all alone, Kelsie had said, "Floating."

And she was floating now, savoring the dregs of the night's energy in the little group she'd gathered. It was like riding an echo, a ghost of the dancing that had swept her away for long hours before.

They headed for the Moonstruck Diner on Main Street. She wanted this. She wanted the group to stay together, because life outside a group was boring. The good stuff only happened when she was part of something bigger than herself.

And Kelsie was all about the good stuff.

CHAPTER 5
SCAM

"YOU PART OF THAT SCENE?" THE CRAIG HOOKED a thumb over his shoulder, back at Ivy Street.

Ethan answered for himself, without the voice. "Me? Not really. Too loud."

"Yeah, I hate *doof-doof* music." Craig drummed on the steering wheel, hissing like a techno high hat. "No wonder they all have to get high. Well, the Craig is here to help with that."

Ethan didn't answer, just glanced over his shoulder at the duffel bag in the backseat. The Ford's windows were open, letting in lashes of wind that set the green vinyl of the bag shimmering.

"Relax, kid," the Craig said. "That stuff stays in the club. We just move the profits."

"So that's money, huh?" Ethan asked in his own voice.

"Course. Taylor told you that, right?"

"He was kinda light on details."

Craig chuckled. "That's Taylor for you."

Ethan made a noncommittal *hmm*ing noise and kept his jaw clamped against the voice. At least they were headed toward his neighborhood on the outskirts of Cambria. Maybe this wasn't a total disaster.

But the Craig was looking at him now. His too-blue eyes glittered in the reflections of the headlights from the occasional traffic shooting past. "Say, what unit's your sister with?"

Ethan tensed. Direct questions were easiest for the voice to answer, but they were the most dangerous, too. "Hundred-and-First Airborne, Three-Twentieth Field Artillery, Second Battalion."

Yup. That was the damn truth again.

Craig smiled, satisfied. "A girl in the artillery? That's badass. Those shells are *heavy*."

Ethan agreed. It was true: His sister was hard-core. Even if she was a Humvee mechanic and never went near any ordnance.

Jess had shipped out a month ago, leaving him alone with Mom. His mother worked pretty much all the time. Which was great during the summer. It meant he could stay out as late as he wanted. Still, Ethan would've preferred to have Jess around.

"Hey, that's . . ." Ethan almost raised a hand to point at the end of his street, but stopped himself just in time. The last thing he wanted was a guy like Craig knowing where he lived. He figured he could walk back from wherever Craig was taking him.

"That's what?"

Ethan shook his head. "Thought I saw somebody I knew at the turnoff back there."

"You must have good eyes, kid." Craig frowned at the rear-view mirror.

Ethan stayed quiet.

The Craig went back to drumming on the wheel, humming some formless tune. They were leaving Cambria now. On one side of the car was a row of suburban houses, spaced far apart. On the other side it was just trees. They hadn't gotten on the highway, though, so at least they were headed someplace local.

But the walk home was getting longer with every mile.

Ethan opened his mouth again, hoping the voice had something up its sleeve, some perfect story that would get Craig to stop the car and let him out.

Nothing. No sound came out. The voice was on mute again, which meant there were no words to get him what he wanted. Ethan had learned to hate the quiet.

Five minutes later the car began to slow.

They pulled onto a dirt road that led into the trees. Craig turned off the headlights, taking the winding turns carefully.

"You don't want the lights on for this?" Ethan asked.

"Don't want to spook anyone. They see the lights, they

might think it's cops and start shooting." In the darkness the Craig's voice was grim.

Ethan's stomach knotted tighter. What the hell had he gotten himself into?

Gravel popped and crunched beneath the tires. The blackness was broken only by flickers of moonlight filtering through the trees.

"What's your name, anyway, kid?"

Ethan was too freaked out to think. He let the voice choose. "Axel."

"Cool name. Your parents Guns N' Roses fans?"

Ethan wondered what guns and roses were. "You bet."

This answer seemed to please the Craig. "I'll tell Taylor you did good. You had my back the whole way."

"Thanks, Craig." The voice sounded calm, but Ethan was half paralyzed with fear. If Taylor himself was at the end of this gravel road, there was no way the voice could convince him he'd sent some strange kid to help move a bag full of money. The voice would remain silent while Ethan was beaten to death.

The Ford slid to a halt. Through the darkness Ethan made out an old cottage among the trees. It was run-down and ancient, like something from a slasher movie. A black Jeep sat next to it, a gun rack against its back window.

None of this made Ethan feel any better about his chances of getting out of here alive.

Craig saw him staring. "You never been to Taylor's before?"

"Sure I have. Just never at night." The voice sounded calm, but inside, Ethan was screaming. This was it. Time to act. Sometimes if he improvised, Ethan could force the voice to do *something.*

Craig switched off the engine, but before he could pull the keys from the ignition, Ethan grabbed his arm.

"Wait!"

"What?" The Craig froze. His gaze swiveled out toward the darkness. His hand dropped into his jacket pocket again.

"Uh, I saw something." Ethan pointed out the front window, wanting with all his heart for Craig to be as terrified as he was. "In those trees."

"What did you see?"

"A cigarette flare." The voice had taken over now, spurred by Ethan's desire. "Guy had a goatee, maybe? That mean anything to you?"

"Are you serious?" Craig pulled his hand out of his pocket. He was holding a big gleaming cannon of a gun.

"You don't think it's Alvarez, do you?" the voice asked.

"Damn! Stay down!"

Oh, yeah. Ethan was staying down.

Craig opened his door and slipped out, crouching low behind the front end of the car. Ethan scooted over to the driver's seat and pulled the door closed. The car keys were right in front of him, dangling from the steering column.

Okay, time to go. The voice could do no more.

Ethan reached for the keys, but he needed a noise. Something to divert Craig from the sound of the car's ignition. He leaned onto the horn as hard as he could. At the blare of noise, Craig hit the ground. He might've even screamed.

Lights popped on in the scary little cottage.

Ethan twisted the keys and turned over the engine. Then he slammed the Ford into reverse, shoving the accelerator down as far as it would go. The tires roared as the car swerved backward through the darkness, sending up a shower of gravel.

He wished the voice would take over his whole body, turn him into some secret agent who could drive as well as he could lie. But it was just Ethan now, clinging to the wheel and hoping he wasn't about to crash into a tree.

The car headlights were still off, but big security floods mounted on the cottage roof suddenly burst to life, spilling through the night.

Ethan whispered a short prayer as the car catapulted backward into the dark. He waited for a shot to ring out, for the windshield to become a spiderweb of glass under a storm of bullets. But Craig, facedown in the driveway in front of the cottage, was still pointing his gun into the trees. Probably he thought Ethan was just some panicky wannabe thug, not an impostor.

Sometimes being a mousy seventeen-year-old could really pay off. Not often, but in those rare moments while stealing a car from a bunch of drug-dealing hoods and not wanting to get shot? Then yeah, definite payoff.

The car reached an opening along the trees and Ethan spun the steering wheel hard, sending the tires skidding until the car pointed back the way he'd come. He switched the headlights on and accelerated.

A moment later he was headed toward the public road, the Ford spitting gravel in its wake.

Finally the wheels hit asphalt. Ethan turned hard left, back toward home. That was when he remembered the duffel bag full of cash in the backseat.

In a way, it only seemed fair. He'd practically earned it after everything he'd been through that night. But he had to put the bag someplace safe. Then he'd dump the car a long way from home so no one could trace it back to his house.

Which meant that, after all this, Ethan still needed a ride home.

He drove hard, the night air whipping through the open windows. Craig and Taylor would be following in that black Jeep soon enough, and there'd be no talking them down. Trouble was, if Ethan kept speeding like this, a cop would pull him over and inevitably check the bag in the backseat.

He nearly missed the turnoff home, he was thinking so hard. But at the last minute he spun the wheel and took the corner wide, fishtailing until the back tire bounced off the curb.

He was about to pull up at the front of his house when he saw lights on in the living room. Damn, his mom was actually up.

Ethan kept the car moving.

Okay. There was no way to dump the bag without her noticing. She'd ask what was in it, and Ethan would be dead meat. He'd been scamming for as long as he'd been able to speak, but by now Mom could tell when it was the voice doing the talking. She'd slap him before he got two words out.

He could try hiding it in the garage, but she was always snooping through his stuff, and—bonus—she worked for the district attorney's office.

"Okay, stupid voice. What do we do now?"

The voice didn't answer, of course. It never spoke directly to Ethan. He could never get it to just *tell* him what to do. But it loved to talk to other people.

He hit the accelerator. That was the key: other people. People could be charmed, reasoned with, and convinced to do what you wanted.

The voice might be deranged sometimes, but in the presence of a listener, it always knew what to say.

He headed back to town. Maybe he could get the voice to tell *someone else* what he should do next.

CHAPTER 6
MOB

AFTER AN HOUR AND THEN SOME OF WANDERING the quiet streets of Cambria, the six of them headed to an all-night diner in the middle of town. An unlikely group, all from different scenes, but connected by the leftover energy of dancing.

The unwind, Mikey called it. The part that came after the clubbing-for-hours. They were tired, but no one was ready for the party to end. Not even Ling, who looked like she might actually be asleep, slumped against the red leather of the booth. Kelsie could feel Ling's connection to the group, the sizzle of the coffee she'd drunk before nodding off.

Kelsie sat with her back against the window, letting the rising sun warm her. Her shadow across the table hardened as the dawn drew on. She'd start every day this way if she could.

If only the Cambria clubs always stayed open late like they did in summer.

Mikey gave her a smile. "Did you have a good night, little sister?"

Kelsie nodded. "Yeah. You?"

"Sure. When I see you coming, I know it's going to be a good night. You always know how to pick the right club."

"Or maybe I *make* it the right club."

Mikey laughed. "Is that why they always let you in?"

Kelsie felt herself blush. She doubted anyone else could spot it under her makeup. She always wore makeup to go clubbing. Without it, she looked too young. Of course, by now the bouncers all had standing orders to let her in. Most nights she even got a few free drinks.

They might not understand how, but the owners and managers knew she brought a good time.

As the sun rose, though, the faces around her grew sleepier. Coming-down, coming-out-of-it faces. Remmy was playing with a saltshaker and staring at the girls across the table. Kelsie had thought they were sisters when she'd met them, but in the dawn light they just looked like two girls who dressed the same. And who were, right now, ignoring Remmy while he tried to find a way into their conversation.

One of the girls said, "The DJ was awesome tonight."

"Totally," Remmy said.

Both girls pretended not to hear. One turned to Kelsie.

"The guy on the door told me Driver's playing tonight. You like Driver?"

Kelsie nodded. She liked any music that got the crowd psyched, got them bonded, ready to dance and dance.

Remmy said, "I like them."

Flat, blank stares from the girls.

Kelsie realized it was coming on fast, the moment when the group would begin to fracture and fall apart. No longer united by a common goal—to dance, to move—their thoughts were beginning to turn in other directions. To real-life jobs and how can I get that girl to talk to me and, ultimately, getting home.

It felt as though her heart were shrinking.

A waitress approached, both arms loaded with plates that steamed in the sunlight. "Slim super stack?"

Food got them energized again. The flash of anticipation, the buzz of hunger around the table, made Kelsie smile.

Mikey pointed at the empty space in front of him. "Right here."

He had to push the dozing Ling off his arm to eat his pancakes. Ling sat up and rubbed her eyes, making black tears of her mascara. Her long hair was a messy tangle, strands of it still clinging to Mikey's sleeve. Ling couldn't help but be beautiful.

The waitress put another steaming plate in front of Kelsie, who claimed the syrup bottle and let it run until square pools formed in the crisscrosses of her waffles. After a long night of dancing, she needed sugar and carbs. She poured syrup until she had to eat her waffles with a spoon.

One of the two new girls sniggered. At Kelsie or her waffles or both. Kelsie didn't care. Remmy always went for the wrong kind of girls. Which was a shame, because he was a decent guy when you got to know him. Right now he was pushing his fork sideways through his stack of pancakes and dropping butter into the holes. He seemed to have forgotten about everything else.

Kelsie let her gaze slide over his shoulder, hoping there was some other group of leftovers from the clubs. Maybe someone she knew, a table she could hop to when this one fell apart.

Half a dozen tables were occupied in the diner, but most of the customers were office workers getting breakfast, or truckers in the middle of a long haul. The only clubbers were couples. Couples were no fun.

There was one guy at the back who looked like he'd been awake all night. He had a buzz cut and was dressed in a nice pin-striped shirt, like he'd been on a date. The shirt was crumpled now, though, and he was alone.

He sat with a hand clamped around his coffee cup, his eyes fixed on the window. As Kelsie watched, he downed the contents of his cup in a convulsive swallow, then tried to get the waitress's attention. The waitress was ignoring him, like he was an ex-boyfriend or something. He half stood, holding up his coffee cup like a white flag. He must really need a caffeine kick. Most people didn't go for seconds of the coffee in this place.

The waitress finally relented and brought the coffeepot over. The kid slid back into his booth. There was a green duffel bag in the booth beside him, which probably meant he was a hitchhiker.

Kelsie wondered who would pick up a guy who managed to look hunted, edgy, and exhausted all at the same time. The buzz cut didn't help. He was too young to be any kind of off-duty soldier, so maybe he was some kind of military wannabe.

She shuddered, feeling how alone he was.

"What is it?" Mikey asked.

Kelsie slid her gaze over to meet his. "Nothing."

As soon as their pancakes were done, the two girls Remmy had brought along went home. They left barely enough money to cover their food, with no tip or tax. Everyone gave their pile of crumpled bills dirty looks, but no one said anything to Remmy. They all felt sorry for him.

"Great night, huh?" Remmy said.

Kelsie nodded. An ache began to settle into her body. Not the sweet muscle ache of having danced all night, but the dull pain of isolation.

She glanced over at Mikey. He was chewing on a bent-up straw and staring at nothing, lost in his own thoughts. Ling had started in on Mikey's pancakes, leaning against him, her long black hair rolling down his shoulder like a scarf. Remmy was restless, changing seats every few minutes.

The two girls might have been annoying, but with them gone, the group was over.

No point delaying the inevitable, Kelsie figured. She dug into her pocket and pulled out her last twenty-dollar bill. She dropped it on the table and flattened it out with the palm of her hand. Mikey leaned over and slid it back toward her.

"I got this," he told her.

Kelsie grinned. She'd learned a long time ago that there was no arguing with Mikey. "Thanks."

"Weird." Ling gestured at the window behind Kelsie with a forkful of stolen pancake.

Kelsie craned her neck. All she saw was the empty street, the dawn light beginning to paint the pavement in a soft glow. Cambria Central Bank squatted on the opposite corner, the park beside it in shadow from the wide trees. There wasn't a shred of traffic anywhere. For a moment it looked like the whole town had been abandoned.

Then a blue car went past, driving slow.

"There it is again," Ling said.

"There's what again?" Mikey asked.

"I swear that same car's gone past three times."

The car turned in front of the bank, heading away down Central.

"Meth heads," Mikey said. "Driving in circles till they crash."

"Which kind of crash?" Remmy asked. "Drug or automotive?"

Mikey laughed, but Kelsie watched the car disappear in the distance. "Wouldn't tweakers get bored driving in circles?"

"What would you know about tweakers?" Mikey asked with an older-brother frown.

Kelsie smiled up at him, trying to look innocent. Mikey didn't know her family history. Her father had never done meth, but a couple of his girlfriends had, back when Kelsie was a kid. One had lost a tooth in the kitchen sink one day. It had fallen like a ripe fruit from a tree. *Tink.* Kelsie had asked if the tooth fairy would come that night, and how much she'd leave.

The girlfriend had just shrugged and washed her tooth down the sink.

"They're probably lost," Ling said. She was pulling paper napkins from the metal dispenser on the table, wiping the syrup from her fingers.

They all watched the street, a silent vigil to see if the strange blue car returned.

It didn't.

"Anyone going to the Jones tonight?" Remmy asked.

"Sure." Kelsie turned back to the table. She had no idea who was playing, but she knew she'd be on Ivy Street again until the clubs closed.

Sometimes she wished summer would last forever so she never had to go to bed before dawn again. It was late June already, only a week till Cambria's big Fourth of July bash, which meant summer was a third gone. But at least there were two months left. The thought of dancing filled the empty space left by the end of the night.

"Okay, there it is again," Ling said quietly.

Kelsie turned to the windows. The sun was warm on her face, bright in her eyes. But she could see the blue car gliding down the street, this time from the direction of the highway.

"You think we should call the police?" Ling asked.

Mikey laughed. "And tell them what? That we've been out clubbing all night, completely free of the effects of alcohol, drugs, and sleep deprivation, and would like to report some suspicious personages?"

No one answered. The car rolled past the diner. Its windows were up, but Kelsie could make out three people inside. She squinted, trying to see their faces. Just then the guy in the backseat turned to glance at the diner, and Kelsie drew back with a start.

"Oh my God," she muttered.

Dad?

CHAPTER 7

SCAM

HE MUST HAVE SPACED OUT, BECAUSE ONE MOMENT the bank was shuttered and dark and the next a line of people was streaming in.

Ethan stood and hoisted the duffel bag onto his shoulder. He left money for the check, then added another twenty bucks from the bundle he'd shoved into his pocket.

The bag had no drugs in it, just like the Craig had promised. Only rolls of money wrapped in bright blue rubber bands—wads of used-looking twenties and tens, all smelling of beer and sweat.

Ethan hadn't counted the bills, but it was more than he'd ever seen. He got a funny thrill from not waiting for his change. Suddenly twenty bucks seemed like nothing.

Besides, he owed that waitress. Apart from the fact that he'd been a jerk to her, she'd helped him decide what to do next. When he'd ordered his first coffee, the voice had asked her what she'd do if someone gave her a big stack of money. Just outright asked her, like that. *Say, what would you do with a big ol' stack of money?* And she'd said, "Put it in the bank, I guess."

Not very imaginative, but it was all he had right then. Put it in the bank. Get it out of sight. Ditch the green duffel bag.

Ethan's legs were rubbery from sitting so long. And from nerves.

He left the diner and crossed the road, checking the shadows of the park beside the bank. No black Jeep, no sign of the Craig. Taylor and him were probably busting heads somewhere, trying to discover how some kid knew so much about their operation.

The good thing was, they'd never figure that out.

Inside the bank there was already a short line of people waiting for tellers. Ethan hesitated. He wasn't stupid enough to deposit this much cash into an account. What if Mom found one of his bank statements?

Forget it. He'd get a safe deposit box. Then he'd have plenty of time to figure out what to do next.

He joined the back of the line. Maybe he could get his own apartment, away from the prying eyes of his mother. Maybe take a road trip. Leave Cambria behind for a couple months. Ethan eased the bag onto his other shoulder. This could be a great summer.

The line edged forward slowly, like a glacier receding. The gallon of coffee he'd consumed was wringing every nerve in his body. He kept waiting for the Craig to come through the door and beat him to a pulp.

A security guard sat in a corner of the bank. He caught Ethan looking at the door every few minutes and gave him a flat, blank stare. He didn't seem like he'd be up to stopping an assault from the Craig. In fact, he seemed more interested in Ethan. Probably wondering why this seedy-looking teenager was so jumpy.

Ethan tried to give the security guy a reassuring smile. The guy continued to stare.

The duffel bag grew heavier with each passing minute. Ethan dropped it to the floor in front of him and nudged it along with the toe of his shoe. He'd be glad to have all that cash safely stored in the bank's basement. Then he could relax.

"What's taking so long?" he muttered.

The girl in front of him half turned his way. She had short, straight hair, the tips dyed in a pink sawtooth pattern. Weird but kind of cool. She was wearing a crisp blue-and-white uniform, like she was about to start a shift as a flight attendant. Back in the fifties. She held a phone in a sparkly case, and pink headphone cables disappeared under her hair. She bobbed in time to whatever she was listening to, sending her glossy hair bouncing.

The next time the line shuffled forward, Ethan kicked his

bag so it bumped the girl's ankles. She turned a blank expression toward him. Her eyes were unnaturally green, her mouth painted into a cute little pout.

Ethan smiled at her. Suddenly what he wanted was to be in familiar territory. Not driving stolen cars or getting shot at—just charming someone.

"I like your hair," he heard the voice say.

She frowned and pulled out one of her earbuds. "What?"

"I said I like your hair."

"Thanks." She turned the rest of the way around, looking him up and down. She was wearing a name tag: MARJORIE.

"You don't look like a Marjorie," Ethan's voice said.

She made a puzzled face, glanced down at her name tag, and shrugged. "They recycle these things. Like, for decades."

"That explains it. You look more like a Sophie."

She smiled. "Close. Sonia."

Ethan nodded. The voice always guessed girls' names *almost* right. Maybe it figured that exactly right was creepy.

"Wait. I get it now," the voice said. "Your hair. *Low Brow.*"

Sonia's eyes widened. "You know Patty Low?"

"I *so* know Patty Low." Ethan had never heard of Patty Low in his life, but he could feel his muscles relaxing as he spoke. Like someone who knew all the answers. "I even know that photo, the one you based your hairstyle on."

"No way," Sonia said.

Ethan gave her a confident smile. "Not the cover of *Low*

Brow, but the special booklet that came with the acoustic versions."

"Oh, wow." Sonia nearly leaped into the air. "I can't believe you know those! That's, like, her most obscure stuff."

"I know all her stuff." The voice knew everything, after all.

Sonia was ecstatic now, launched by his lies into her own little reality. "That's so awesome. I got this stupid job just so I could buy *Low Brow*. You get the joke on the cover, right?"

"Sure! Where she's posing with Jay White—" The sound of the name in his own mouth made Ethan sputter to a halt. "Wait. *The* Jay White?"

Sonia frowned. "What? Of course."

"Ah, man." Ethan hated Jay White. Producer and pop supremo White's crimes against humanity numbered in the thousands. One for every tune he released. Rumor was he could record twenty a day. Before breakfast. "The guy who ran over a couple girls while he was high?"

That was his real voice talking. Ethan tried to slip back into the passive role, the listener. But he was too exhausted, too wired from coffee and anxiety. The ache from speaking with the voice was back now, as if the Craig had socked him in the jaw.

"He was in a bad place then," the girl muttered, turning away.

"Sure." For a moment Ethan wanted to reconnect. But Sonia's pout was back in place, and it was beginning to annoy him. "I mean, those two girls were probably having a crappy day too. Especially after they messed up the paint job on his SUV."

She turned back to him, her expression one of complete betrayal.

Ethan hadn't said that last part; the voice had. He'd only wanted her to stop talking to him. But the voice always gave Ethan exactly what he wanted.

Sonia did exactly that, of course: stopped talking and turned away. She cranked her music until a tinny Jay White–produced tune was spilling out of her skull.

Great. Now he felt like crap. He hated when the voice insulted people. It was hard to take that stuff back. And the awful thing was, half the time he didn't even remember exactly what the voice said. They weren't *his* words, after all.

Last summer he'd lost his three best friends in a single spray of insults. He'd been so angry, wanting those guys to hurt, *really* hurt. Wanting them to leave him the hell alone. And, just like Sonia, they had.

Those three were the only people who really knew what Ethan was. They had their own powers to deal with. They understood.

The Zeroes, they'd called themselves as a joke. Like heroes, but not. They'd even tried to act like superheroes, with stupid training exercises and code names. But at least they'd all been friends.

Until he'd let the voice lash out. None of them had spoken to him since.

The line inched forward.

He tapped Sonia lightly on the shoulder. "Hey."

She turned and glared at him, head still bopping to the music.

"I'm sorry." He mouthed the words clearly.

Sonia hesitated, her eyes narrowing. Finally a half smile crossed her face. After all, he was a fellow fan of Patty Low. At least, she thought he was.

She pulled one earbud out, like she was about to say something. But then her gaze swiveled to a point over his shoulder and she froze.

Ethan turned. Three guys with very big guns had entered the bank. They wore all-black clothes and white hockey masks. One of them lifted his rifle and shot it directly into the ceiling.

The world flew apart into dust and noise.

"Ladies and gentlemen," the gunman said through the ringing echoes of the boom. "Get your asses down on the floor!"

CHAPTER 8
MOB

KELSIE HEARD THE MUFFLED GUNSHOT THROUGH THE bank wall, but mostly she *felt* it—the sudden focus of everyone inside, that wave of heat that came from a group of people united by a surge of adrenaline.

There was a flood, a tsunami of energy from the customers—fear, shock, disbelief. All of it spinning together, strong enough that for a moment it was beyond Kelsie's control. It threatened to drown her, to drag her over into panic. But then her instincts kicked in and she pushed back, fought her way to the top to ride the wave.

It was like blocking a fire hose with her hands. The spooked crowd was a geyser of energy, hot and furious. But she drew them up, up, *up* into her own calm place. She channeled them into peace. She fed them stillness. Numbness. Quiet. And she held them there.

They all wanted the same thing—to be safe. That unity of purpose kept Kelsie in charge. It was all going to be okay.

As long as no one got hurt. As long as nobody hurt her dad.

She backed away from that thought, which threatened to spill over into the crowd. Of course it was all going to be okay. *Of course* it was.

Kelsie had been waiting in the park by the bank since breakfast, trying to look inconspicuous. Just a bored kid, killing time before the mall opened. The blue car had returned right after she'd gotten rid of Ling and Mikey, telling them she wanted to walk home. This time the car had pulled up right behind the bank.

Three men had gotten out, wearing hockey masks. She'd recognized her dad from his walk. The limp that he claimed was a knife wound but was really from the time he'd blown out his knee stealing a two-hundred-pound poker machine.

For all his screwups, Dad had never done anything like this before. He'd never robbed a bank. As far as she knew, he'd never even held a gun. So what on earth did he think he was doing at Cambria Central Bank wearing a hockey mask and carrying that shotgun?

She'd tried to call out, to stop him. But all alone, without a group around her, she'd never have the guts to accost three men with masks and guns.

"Damn it." Kelsie rested the back of her skull against the

bank wall and closed her eyes. It helped her stay connected to the storm of emotions from the crowd inside. She couldn't find her dad in the sickly wash of fear. She'd never been able to pick out individuals once a group took on its own identity. This one was like a big, scared animal with all its nerves jangling.

She kept channeling the fear, replacing it with calm. The sooner this was over, the sooner everybody could go home. And that included her dad.

Something was blinking, flashing above her. On the corner of the bank building, way up high, a blue light was pulsing. It made no sound, but it was bright enough to bleach the early morning daylight.

Someone inside had triggered the bank's silent alarm. No doubt another alarm was pulsing at the central police station a few miles away. The cops would be here soon, and they'd take her dad away. After a screwup as big as this one, maybe he wouldn't come back.

Kelsie felt herself seizing up with panic.

She hauled herself from the wall, breaking the connection she had with the crowd inside. The last thing she needed was for her fears to spread into the people in the bank.

"Come on, Dad. Get out of there."

There was nothing she could do now but watch.

CHAPTER 9
SCAM

"LET'S GET THIS OVER WITH, PEOPLE," THE GUNMAN was saying. "We all want a nice quick job here, right?"

He sounded like he meant it.

Ethan stared at the man in the hockey mask. He felt anesthetized. The shock of the gunshot was wearing off, replaced with a wave of numbness. Like someone was pumping liquid valium into his veins. He knew he should feel more panic, but all he could think about was that he really wished he'd taken a leak before leaving the diner. All that awful coffee, plus lying facedown on a cold marble floor, was doing no favors to his bladder.

He shifted his head to see the rest of the room. The whole place had fallen to its knees in one movement. People had screamed when the first shot went into the ceiling, and yet still dropped. Like they couldn't wait to get to the ground. Even the security guard, who'd had a gun pointed right at his face until he'd tossed his own aside, seemed weirdly calm.

The quiet felt unreal.

Ethan looked at where Sonia lay, one cheek against the floor. She seemed as spacey as he felt. Her phone was clutched in her hand like a talisman, something bulletproof. She gazed back at Ethan, her eyes shiny in the morning light that streamed through the bank. He tried to give her a reassuring smile. She didn't smile back.

He took a wary glance at the men with guns. Far as he could tell, none of them was the Craig. These guys were all too skinny. In Ethan's mind, Craig's neck had taken on epic proportions. Like maybe it was the thickest part of his entire body.

Okay. So this whole robbery thing had nothing to do with Ethan's stolen duffel bag full of money. It was just an amazingly shitty coincidence. The perfect end to his night.

He eased the bag closer to him, willing it to disappear against his body.

The gunman was talking again. "We all want to get out of here safely and enjoy the rest of our lives, don't we?"

Ethan found he did—he really, really did. Still, it was kind of of perverse for a guy to keep talking about safety while he was carrying the biggest gun Ethan had ever seen. If the gunman hadn't unloaded that thing so convincingly into the ceiling, it might've passed for something out of a cartoon. Plaster was still drifting through the air like fake snow in a crappy school play.

The two other gunmen were behind the tills, scrambling through cash. Funny how they were the least calm people in the room. With their hockey masks and frantic movements, they seemed to belong to some separate, insectoid branch of humanity. The sort of creature that didn't care about getting home safely.

Ethan felt a spasm of fear low in his gut. But then, just like that, it was gone again, smoothed over by the valium in the air.

"The vault's shut!" one of the gunmen shouted. "Someone pushed the panic button!"

He started swearing. He seemed to swear for a long time without breathing.

The guy with the giant gun lowered his aim, till the barrel was pointed at his own toes. Ethan reflected calmly how that seemed like a really bad idea. That same gun had taken out a sizable part of the ceiling, and the guy was already limping. He probably couldn't afford to lose a foot.

Now he was tapping the rifle muzzle against the marble floor. Glaring at the customers like the locked vault was their fault.

Ethan tried to become one with the marble.

Beside him Sonia let out a whimper.

"Time to move," Big Gun said. "Bag the cash. I'll see what I can scrape up from the civilians."

The other two scrambled into motion. They began stuffing wads of cash into the canvas bags they'd brought with them. A bill floated down and landed a few feet from Ethan's face. A fifty.

He was in no way tempted to reach for it.

Big Gun was walking through the crowd slowly, his hockey mask swinging left and right. He was sizing them up, maybe trying to work out who had the most money in their pockets. Ethan's hand tightened on the straps of his duffel bag.

Suddenly Big Gun knelt. There was a muffled shriek from an elderly woman in a patterned dress.

"It's okay," Big Gun said. "Just taking your watch, ma'am."

At least he was polite. Which only made him scarier. The woman let out small sobbing noises, but she let him have the watch.

Ethan shut his eyes to stop himself from staring at the duffel bag.

Footsteps came toward him across the marble floor, keeping time with the pulse going off in Ethan's neck.

Big Gun was nearby. "Nice ring, little girl."

"It's nothing" came Sonia's voice, defiant.

"Then you won't mind if I take it."

Ethan opened his eyes. Sonia's hand was wrapped around her phone. On her middle finger was a ring with two concentric circles overlapping. Like owl eyes.

When the gunman reached down, she drew back her hand. "They're not real diamonds or anything. They're totally fake."

The man seemed to hesitate.

"Just give him the ring!" Ethan hissed.

"Do what your boyfriend says," Big Gun told her.

Sonia glared at Ethan. "He's so not my boyfriend!"

But at least she pulled the ring off and sent it rolling across the floor. The gunman swept it up.

He stayed on one knee, his hockey mask hanging in the corner of Ethan's vision.

"Hey, kid. What you got in the bag?"

CHAPTER 10
SCAM

ETHAN GAVE HIMSELF OVER TO THE VOICE. HE DIDN'T care what it said, as long as it distracted this bank robber from the duffel bag.

It came out low and raspy, like nothing Ethan had ever heard from his own mouth before. "You know this is all going to hell, don't you, Jerry?"

The gunman froze. "How do you know my name?"

Ethan shut his eyes, but the voice didn't stop talking. "That's a great question, Jerry. You should think about that. How does some kid with his face on the floor of the biggest bank in Cambria know your name?"

Jerry didn't answer.

The voice was taking one hell of a chance, talking to an

armed robber like they were old friends. And, just like always, there was no turning back.

But then that feeling like liquid valium was pouring back into the room, the tide of fear pulling out again. Ethan marveled that he could feel so calm.

"While you're thinking about that, Jerry, ask yourself: If *I* knew you'd be here, then who else did?"

The gunman's words came out with exaggerated calm. "Tell me what you know, kid."

"Everything. Like why the silent alarm went off ten seconds after you showed up." A strained little snort forced its way out of Ethan. The voice wasn't very good at laughing. "It all has to do with Nic over there."

Jerry's hockey mask swung up toward his two armed colleagues.

The voice continued in a whisper. "Remember his drug charge back in March? The one that went away for no good reason?"

Jerry was quiet. Ethan figured he probably did remember.

"And ever since, Nic's been telling you about this bank job. How easy it'll be. How he wants you to do all the talking, because you're such a nice guy who'd never hurt anyone. People trust you. Then he gives you the biggest gun. How am I doing so far, Jerry?"

The two gunmen behind the tills were done gathering up the cash. Now they were making their way through the customers spread across the floor. As long as they didn't come over here. The voice struggled if there was more than one person to convince.

"Listen, Jerry. I like you," Ethan heard himself say. "You just want what's best for Kelsie, after all. Poor kid still misses her mom. And a guy like Nic, who makes deals with the cops, is a problem for everyone."

"No," Jerry muttered. "No, no, no."

The tip of the rifle was in front of Ethan's face, and it was shaking. Jerry's hand on the butt trembled. It didn't look like fear was making his hand shake, though. More like rage.

Ethan shut his eyes, as if that would protect him from bullets. "Nic hasn't been in town that long, has he? Maybe he's the kind of guy who'd lead his buddies into a trap just to get out of a bullshit possession charge."

"Sirens!" one of the other gunmen called. "We gotta go!"

"Damn it!" Jerry stood and swung his gun up, all in one movement.

Ethan had a moment to breathe freely, a moment when he thought that the voice had done its work and he was free. Jerry had forgotten all about the duffel bag, and now the gunmen were about to make a run for it.

But then Jerry shouted, "You *knew* they'd be here, Nic! *You son of a—*"

And then the shooting started.

CHAPTER 11
MOB

AFTER THE SHOOTING INSIDE WAS OVER, A NEW crowd formed.

It didn't feel like a dance club or a party. It was closer to the rubberneckers after an accident, drawn by the flashing lights, the police tape fluttering in the morning breeze. They milled around in the street, mostly directionless except that everyone kept glancing at the bank doors. They were in there interviewing everyone, and it seemed to be taking hours.

Kelsie was waiting too. For her dad.

They hadn't brought him out yet. Because the first guy out was someone in a body bag. And it wasn't her dad, because . . . well, it just wasn't. No way her dad was dead.

Right behind that was another guy, this one on a stretcher. He was alive, at least. Two paramedics carried him out while a third ran along beside holding a drip high in the air. One of the cops lifted the yellow police tape so they could duck underneath and load the guy into a waiting ambulance. Then the ambulance sped off, and no more paramedics went in.

Everybody else inside had to be alive and unhurt, right? Kelsie doubled over with relief, hands on her knees. She took a long breath. She wasn't an orphan. Not yet.

Somebody asked if she was okay, and Kelsie straightened. She gave the stranger a tight smile and moved away to the edge of the crowd, trying to reconnect with the people in the bank.

When the handful of shots had been fired, there'd been panic. A few minutes later the police had stormed in, and there'd been a swell of relief. Then nothing. Their emotions were scattered, the crowd beast broken into individuals.

A new ripple of energy passed through the people outside. The bank doors opened, and two cops came out, half dragging her dad in handcuffs. He looked dazed and suddenly ancient. But at least he was unhurt.

Kelsie felt relief and grief and anger all at once. He was going back to prison. Every day for the last five years he'd promised he would never disappear again.

The crowd turned its attention to the man in handcuffs, like a herd focusing on a predator. Not a lot of bank robberies in Cambria. Everyone wanted a good look at his face so they could tell the story when they got to work late.

You wouldn't believe this guy. Limping, skinny, burned-out-looking. Robbed a bank and shot two people.

Kelsie couldn't help it; she was part of the crowd now. She felt her grief begin to roll outward, tangling with their curiosity. And not just grief: her anger, too.

How could her dad have risked all those people's lives? Hadn't he felt the fear he'd caused? He'd shredded all the trust Kelsie had ever put in him.

She tried to rein in the emotion. To squeeze it all back inside her own body. But it was too late and she was too exhausted.

Of everything he'd done over the sixteen years of Kelsie's life, nothing had been this wrong, this *selfish*. Maybe he hadn't meant to hurt anyone—she was sure he hadn't—but he'd still done something awful. He'd destroyed their future together.

"Bastard!" a man beside her shouted, and a stir went through the crowd.

The cops looked confused. They had a job to do, and couldn't feel Kelsie's anger winding its way through the crowd.

People began to press against the phalanx of police. They'd turned from docile onlookers into something hostile, something wrathful and righteous and dangerous.

They were becoming a mob.

Kelsie saw the look of terror on her father's face.

"No, no, *no*," she breathed, trying to reel it all back in, to break the connection between her own energy and the crowd's. She'd done this, molded a single entity from the spectators and given her own anger form.

She took a dozen sharp quick breaths, making herself hyperventilate. Dizziness cut her anger. With her influence gone and with the police shouting terse orders, the mob dissipated.

The crowd ebbed, but her dad still looked scared and lost.

For the first time, she felt tears burn.

Her father was pushed into a police car, which was soon nosing its way through the onlookers toward the clump of tall buildings at the city center.

At last the customers from the bank were led out. They stepped into the daylight, blinking and in shock. She felt them click into their own little tribe, united by what they'd been through. Kelsie could feel their shaken confidence that the world made sense. The seeds of a thousand nightmares were taking hold in their minds. They went down the stairs clinging to each other.

Except one guy.

He wasn't in black clothes like the robbers, but two plainclothes detectives were guiding him toward a police car. He wore a pin-striped shirt and carried an army-green duffel bag. He had a familiar expression, too, tired and strung out.

The guy from the diner.

What on earth did *he* have to do with all this?

He wasn't handcuffed, so he was probably just a witness.

Kelsie pulled out her phone. She had to get to the police station and make sure her dad was okay. She hoped Mikey was still awake. She needed a ride.

It was barely ten in the morning. This was going to be a long day.

CHAPTER 12

SCAM

"OKAY, TERRENCE, LET'S GO OVER THIS AGAIN. IS this really your address?"

Ethan didn't answer aloud, just nodded.

He was sitting across from two detectives at the Central Cambria Police Department. He had no idea what the voice had said wrong back in the bank, but he didn't want it screwing up again.

One moment it had all been going smoothly, the voice reeling off a fake name and address and a few generic reactions to the robbery—no, he hadn't seen much, too busy hugging the floor, and oh, how about that, he must have left his ID back at his leafy, north-side home where he lived with his dad. The uniformed cop had looked ready to move on to the next interview.

But suddenly this detective wearing a grim expression had

appeared out of nowhere, and Ethan had been politely but firmly hauled out of the bank. Duffel bag and all.

They knew something, but Ethan had no idea what.

It wasn't about the duffel bag, which was on the floor beside him, ignored and unopened. He'd considered leaving it behind in the bank when they'd dragged him here. Just walk away and pretend it wasn't his. But what if he'd left fingerprints on it? Or DNA? People were always being busted by their DNA on cop shows. So he'd taken it with him.

Plus, the money was *his* now. He couldn't just leave it.

And anyhow, he had bigger problems.

He snuck a glance around. The detective's desk was in the middle of a busy floor full of cops. What if someone who knew his mom recognized him? She was down here at the police station all the time, doing her deputy DA work. With a bank robbery under investigation, she might even be here right now.

Ethan hunched down in his chair.

The detective continued, "And you don't have a phone number yet, right, Terrence? Because you just moved here?"

Ethan nodded. Why the voice had gone with Terrence was beyond Ethan. Sometimes he figured it was just trolling him.

"Do you mind answering out loud?" the other detective asked. She gave a sympathetic smile. "Just so we're clear."

Ethan sighed, letting the voice take over again. "Yes, I moved here from Chicago. That's my new address, right there."

He gestured toward the yellow legal pad on the desk between them.

"And your dad doesn't have a cell phone?"

"That's right, Detective King."

The voice was good at stuff like that, remembering to call adults by their names.

King was kinda nice. She had short hair and brown eyes that were just darker than her skin. She smiled when he called her by name. Her partner, Detective Fuentes, didn't look convinced by anything the voice said. He was taller, wider, and meaner-looking. Ethan shifted his gaze back to King.

"And your mom?" she asked.

"Don't have a mom," Ethan said, too quickly. He reminded himself to let the voice handle this.

"Your dad got an e-mail address?" Fuentes asked.

"He's old-fashioned. Doesn't trust the internet."

King nodded and smiled, as if not trusting a bunch of wires made sense. "Why were you in the bank, Terrence?"

"To open a new account. We don't have a bank here yet. But then these three guys came in. With guns. Really big guns."

"Yeah," said King. "You told us that."

"They were going to rob the place but then they shot each other. That's all I remember. It was pretty traumatic, you know?"

"So you keep saying," Fuentes said. He had the kind of frown that looked like it wasn't going anywhere soon. "None of them spoke to you?"

"They shouted at us to stay down. Then they said they were going to rob us. This girl beside me, they took the ring right off her finger."

King asked, "You didn't know any of these guys?"

"How would I? I'm seventeen, for crying out loud! And I just moved here. Where would I meet guys who rob banks with shotguns?"

"Semiautomatic rifles," Fuentes corrected him.

"Like I'd know what kind of guns they had!" The voice sounded nervous, but Ethan had read that innocent people get nervous when they're interviewed by cops. Only criminals had the patience to stay calm and wait it out.

"Which high school you at?" Fuentes asked.

"I'm not enrolled yet. My dad was thinking of Palmdale Academy."

Ethan had to fight the crazy urge to laugh. He had about as much chance of getting into Palmdale as he did of a career with NASA.

But the lie had done its work. For about a microsecond King looked impressed. Then she gazed down at her notes. "So you've never met Jerry Laszlo before?"

"Who?"

She looked up. "You didn't call one of the bank robbers by name?"

Ethan shifted in his seat, but the voice sounded certain. "That's crazy."

"Isn't it?" Fuentes leaned forward on heavy forearms. "And yet we got you on video, talking to them."

Ethan blinked. They'd already seen the bank's security footage? That was fast.

He gave the voice free rein. "One of the robbers talked to us, yeah. The guy that took Sophie's ring."

"Sonia," King corrected him.

"Right." Great. They'd spoken to Sonia. Of course they'd spoken to Sonia. She'd probably told them about the weird conversation he'd had with Jerry Big Gun. "She wouldn't let him take her ring. I told her to just give it to him! You know, so she wouldn't get killed."

As the two detectives looked at each other, Ethan rubbed his jaw, which felt like he'd spent six hours in a dentist's chair. The worst thing about the voice was that it felt like someone else was operating his mouth. Pulling it open and snapping it shut in time with all the lies coming out of it.

His ears were starting to itch from listening to himself lie so much.

Fuentes said, "We spoke to Sonia Stoller at length, Terrence. She said you knew the guy. Said you had quite the conversation with him."

A stifled sort of laugh escaped Ethan, but inside he was cringing. He should never have insulted that pop-trash guru, Jay Stupid-Face White. He wished he could take it all back, the whole damn morning and, come to think of it, the night before, too. This was turning into a lousy summer after all.

Just like last summer. If the voice hadn't gotten rid of all his friends, maybe Ethan wouldn't have been wandering around Ivy Street without a ride.

The voice stayed smooth. "Yeah, I talked to the guy. I just wanted him to chill out, you know? So I was chatting like we were buddies. But it's not like I *know* him. Sonia was being crazy, not giving up her ring. I just wanted to make sure nobody got shot."

Fuentes said, "The way you tell it, you're quite the hero."

"I did what had to be done." The voice almost sounded modest.

King smiled. "What's funny is, she didn't seem crazy when she talked to us. She seemed like a very composed and articulate young woman."

Fuentes nodded like his partner had just revealed a universal truth. "Yeah. She kept her head pretty good, for someone in the middle of an armed robbery."

Detective Fuentes pulled out a phone with a sparkly case and pink headphones. A smile finally cracked his face.

"You want to watch a video?"

CHAPTER 13
SCAM

ETHAN FELT THE BLOOD DRAIN FROM HIS FACE.

That was the problem—*one* of the problems—with the voice. It couldn't control his expressions except when he was talking.

Both the detectives were smiling at him now.

Fuentes held the phone out so Ethan could see the screen. "You got a clear view of this, Terrence?"

"Oh, yeah," Ethan muttered.

A video began to play on the little screen. It was a shaky point of view from close to the marble floor of the bank. Feet scrambling, blurs of motion, a tiny flash of Sonia's face, all over the distorted sound of shouting through the tiny speakers of the phone.

The view swung around and there Ethan was, hugging the

floor, his expression more spacey than terrified. He remembered the weird, disjointed calm he'd felt after the first shot had been fired into the ceiling. That feeling like he'd swallowed too many painkillers. He really wished the Ethan in the video looked more scared. Or that he had some of that miracle calm right now.

He watched the video in silence while the detectives watched him.

There was Jerry Big Gun looming, his hockey mask filling the frame as Sonia argued with him. Ethan fought a surge of admiration. Not only had Sonia defied an automatic-rifle-wielding criminal over her worthless ring, but she'd been *videoing* the whole thing.

Mental note: Check out this Patty Low sometime.

Fuentes pressed the screen with a thumb, halting the video on a frame of Ethan's too-calm face. "It sounds like you just said 'Jerry.' Did you catch that?"

Ethan nodded slowly, like he was thinking, and let the voice loose.

"Jerry, yeah. One of the other guys said it when they came in. Geez, I hadn't even remembered that, Detective Fuentes. Guess I was running on instinct."

Fuentes rolled his eyes.

"Play the next bit," King said.

Fuentes obliged, and Ethan heard his own voice clearly. "You just want what's best for Kelsie, after all."

Fuentes froze the video again. "So, who's Kelsie?"

"I have no idea." Ethan tried to match a shrug with the voice's innocent tone.

"Funny thing," Fuentes said. "After you mentioned Kelsie, that guy turned around and the shooting started. Which makes you about the most interesting person in this whole station right now."

To Ethan, it seemed like the actual *gunman* would be way more interesting. But this didn't seem like the right moment to argue the point. "I have no idea why he started shooting. Maybe you should ask *him*."

"We did," Fuentes grunted. "He's not talking."

Ethan sighed, almost wishing he was back in the car with the Craig. At least then he'd had a chance to grab the keys and drive away. But here in the middle of this crowded police station, there was no escape.

"I didn't even know what was coming out of my mouth!" Ethan said this in his own voice, utterly honest for once.

King shook her head sadly, like she was hearing bad news. "Best you just tell us everything you *do* know, Terrence. Tell us how you made that guy turn on his friends in the middle of a hostage situation. With a skill like that, maybe we could use you on the force."

Fuentes laughed—which surprised Ethan, because he hadn't thought the big man could. King gave Ethan a conspiratorial smile, halfway between amusement and pity.

Ethan opened his mouth and prayed the voice had something.

"Right. I remember the robber said something about stealing Sonia's ring because he wanted to give it to someone called Kelsie. I mean, the audio's pretty muffled right there, but it kind of jolted my memory."

Ethan had to stop himself from letting out a sigh of relief. The voice was right about the audio. Jerry *could've* said something the detectives had missed.

But Fuentes's gaze only sharpened. "Funny thing. You said you were in that bank to open an account."

"Yeah?" Ethan was wary.

"How you going to do that without any ID?"

"Didn't know I'd forgotten it." Thing was, Ethan almost never carried ID. It was totally unhelpful to carry ID if you were going to lie about yourself all the time. "So is there anything else, Detectives?"

King shrugged. For a second Ethan thought maybe he'd gotten away with it. All of it.

But then Fuentes said, "So what's in the duffel bag, kid?"

Ethan's brain sputtered almost to a halt. He could think of nothing except how wrong it had all gone, starting with his date with Indira. He slumped, letting the voice say whatever it would take to distract them from the bag. "I just realized something, Detectives."

Fuentes smirked. "That it's time to come clean?"

"That you can't question a minor without the permission of a legal guardian."

Both detectives were still, so Ethan figured it must be true. Score one to the voice. Then King smiled that friendly smile again.

"But you aren't a suspect, Terrence. You're a witness. And we're just having a friendly chat. What do you need a guardian for?"

"Yeah," Fuentes chimed in. "I'm sure you want to help us out, don't you?"

"I'm a minor," the voice said with absolute certainty. "So an adult of some kind must be present during questioning. And although my father is unreachable, I just remembered the number of our lawyer here in Cambria."

King nodded slowly. "You did, huh?"

"His name is Scamiglia," the voice said, then rattled off a phone number.

The moment the first few digits were out of Ethan's mouth, he tried to stop himself, but he was too tired, too beaten down by fear, and the voice had been in control of his tongue too much lately.

It was the number of an old pal of his—an ex-pal, really. The head of the Zeroes, who had an ability that was a hundred times more insidious than Ethan's voice. A kid so condescending and imperious that even his best friends called him Glorious Leader.

And thanks to what the voice had said last summer, Ethan was no longer his friend at all.

Detective King scribbled the number down on a pad. “Finally we’re getting somewhere. Can’t wait to see what this Scamiglia guy has to say about you. How do you spell his name? *S-C-A-M*-something?”

“Four letters is all you’ll need,” Ethan said in his own exhausted voice. “Just call him. He’ll send someone right away.”

CHAPTER 14

FLICKER

"WHEN WAS THE FIRST TIME YOU REMEMBER YOUR sister reading to you?"

Flicker kept her expression neutral. This sounded a lot like Dr. Bridges' favorite topic, hidden inside a new question. She answered warily: "I don't know how old we were, maybe six? But I remember the book. It was about slugs."

She heard the squeak of leather, Dr. Bridges shifting in his chair.

"Slugs?"

"They wore clothes and lived in houses. Lily described all the pictures to me." Flicker let herself smile. It had been a very silly book, full of squishy sound effects.

She could hear Dr. Bridges scribbling on his legal pad, and was tempted to peek but didn't. She was *trying* to be good.

"And your sister reading it to you, that was important?"

"Sure." More important than she could say, at least to her shrink. It was while Lily was reading to her that Flicker's power had revealed itself for the first time. She hadn't understood back then, of course. The spindly insects of letters had simply appeared in her head, skittering back and forth with the motion of Lily's eyes.

Flicker sometimes missed those long-ago days, when her power hadn't worked with anyone but Lily. Back then they'd thought it was some kind of twin magic, like the private language they'd shared in the crib. It had almost felt like a betrayal when Flicker started seeing through the rest of humanity's eyes.

"It makes you feel like part of the family?"

Flicker sighed. It *was* the same old issue, the thing that brought her into this office every Friday, along with the neuroses of her overachieving parents.

So she didn't feel bad about peeking. Dr. Bridges' handwriting was a disaster, but he was staring straight at his pad. He'd written *family narrative* in big letters, and his pen was drawing circles around the words now, as lazy and patient as a shark.

What the hell did *family narrative* mean? That she and her sister loved to share stories? Or that Dr. Bridges thought Flicker was making something up?

His gaze lifted from the legal pad, and she saw herself—the bright orange summer dress for visibility in crowds, her brown hair spilling across the dimpled leather of the patient couch.

She smiled, just to see it.

"Is something funny?" Dr. Bridges asked.

"Lily's a part of me, whether she reads to me or not."

"Ah." He took the bait, and his eyes went down to the pad again, where his pen was already scrawling the words *twin bonding*. Dr. Bridges was so predictable. He had a serious shrink boner for the fact that she and Lily had shared a womb. "But what if you learned to read for yourself? How would it change things between you and your sister?"

"It's not that I can't . . ." Flicker bit off the rest of her answer.

This was the never-ending issue, the reason her parents sent her to a shrink: Why had she stopped reading braille? Why did she stay so dependent on her sister? How could her parents, with three doctorates between them, have raised an illiterate sixteen-year-old?

Of course, all those questions were based on bullshit assumptions. Maybe one in ten blind kids bothered learning braille these days. Her parents didn't understand that braille meant big clunky books that marked you as different, while audiobooks lived invisibly on your phone and text-to-speech gave you the whole damn internet.

Besides, Flicker could read perfectly well. Just not with her own eyes.

And there was something important that happened when her sister read to her. The stories became more real, more magical, the way stories had been when Flicker was little, before she could see at all.

"Can't what?" Dr. Bridges prompted.

Flicker strained into the corners of his vision until she glimpsed the timer on his desk. Good. Her fifty minutes were almost up.

"It'd take more than thirty seconds to tell you," she said.

His eyes went to the timer, then widened a little.

"I still don't know how you do that." She heard his smile.

"Blind-people powers."

He wrote those words down, and then his left hand waved around, like he was trying to think of what to say.

"I can hear it in your voice," she said. "When the session's almost over."

"You don't have to worry about me, Riley. This is *your* time."

Flicker sighed again, more at her real name than anything else. Real names were stupid, especially when you had one that your friends had given you. One that made perfect sense.

She stayed silent until the timer softly chimed.

Dr. Bridges straightened in his squeaky chair. "Next time, I want to talk about independence."

Independence? She'd come here downtown all on her own, just like every week. No parents waiting for her in the parking lot. No service dog. But her power needed other people to work, and that was fine with her.

Flicker swung her legs off the couch and stood. In a few swift steps she was at the door, her hand finding the knob without any help from Dr. Bridges' eyes.

"You'll think about that this week, Riley?" His voice followed her. "About things you can do to be more independent?"

Flicker turned to face him and threw her vision into his to admire her own expression. Enough of a smile not to be rude, but one mocking eyebrow arching behind dark glasses.

"Sure thing, Doc."

Out on the front steps she turned her phone on, and it chirruped with annoyance. Her shrink's office was a black hole of No Phones Allowed, not even in the waiting room, to allow patients to "center themselves" before their sessions. It was a law of nature that the week's most interesting messages always arrived during those fifty minutes.

Flicker started walking, one hand sliding along the iron rail in front of the medical building, her other thumb moving across the haptic keys of her phone. A moment later Nate's voice was in her ear: "Crazy news, Flick. There was a bank robbery this morning. And Scam's at the police station downtown, in custody."

Flicker came to a halt, despite the downtown crowd flowing around her. That name still set off stink bombs in her stomach.

"I'll call the others," Nate was saying. "But . . . it's *Scam*. Maybe no one shows up, you know?"

Flicker did know. With a snap of her wrist she unfolded her cane. Here in the crowded streets of downtown, she didn't need it. But the red and white made people get out of her way.

"Call me when you get this," Nate finished. "And head for downtown."

She was moving already, the cane sweeping the pavement in front of her. For the moment she kept herself blind. It was easier to think, and her shrink's office was only a few blocks from the CCPD. No need to rush.

Not for Scam, anyway.

What bank robbery? And why would *he* need to rob a bank? The guy had been born to weasel people out of their cash.

She held down her phone's voice-dial key and said, "Glorious Leader."

Flicker still called him that, out loud when he was being annoying and in her head always. It was only half ironic, because no other pair of words suited him better.

"Flick!" he answered. "It's shrink day, right? Tell me you're already downtown."

"Just like every Friday. Why the hell did Scam rob a bank?"

"Him? Please," Nate said with a laugh. "The detective said he was a 'material witness.' His mouth must have gotten him in trouble."

Something was approaching from behind her on the sidewalk, the metal clicks of a coasting bicycle. Flicker cast her vision into the rider's eyes just as the guy spotted her cane.

The view swerved away, bumping down the curb and back onto the street.

She let herself go blind again. "And he called *you*?"

"Because he's got so many other friends? He told them I was his lawyer, but the detective wouldn't let me talk to him. Whatever's going on, they don't think he's an innocent bystander."

"Weird. His voice must be slipping."

"Scam's power has always been . . . shaky. Tell me you're coming, Flick."

She sighed. "Wouldn't miss it. Where should I meet you?"

"I'm staying away. The cops have my number. I don't want to be anywhere close, just in case Crash decides to help. No telling what she'll do to a police station."

"Wait. She might actually show up?"

A pause. "No answer. She probably hasn't checked her phone yet."

Flicker sighed. After Scam's outburst at Crash almost a year ago, even the charms of Glorious Leader might not convince her to help. Of course, what Scam had said to Nate and Flicker had been almost as cruel.

There was a pause on the other end, like Nate was thinking the same thing.

But then he said, "Stay outside the station, in case it gets messy. I'll conference you in when I have everyone."

Everyone? she almost asked, meaning her and Crash? But

then a trickle of memory reminded her that there was someone else. That other Zero.

The tip of her cane caught on a sidewalk crack, jolting the thought away.

"I'll have eyes inside the cop shop in ten minutes." She'd slipped into the way they'd talked back in the old days. All those training missions, shepherding crowds around a shopping center while listening to Glorious Leader's orders in their earbuds. Always pretending there was a fire or a terrorist attack, when it was really just Crash letting loose.

Flicker had always thought the missions were silly, Glorious Leader trying to forge a superpowered posse for his own mysterious purposes. But after Scam's little outburst had broken the group, she'd dumped her real name and become Flicker all the time. Maybe that was a sign that she missed that energy, that focus.

"Tell me when you hear from Crash."

"Roger that. Be careful, Flick"—and Nate was gone.

As always, there was that abandoned feeling of his glorious attention moving away from her. His power didn't work through the phone, of course, but the reaction was hardwired in her now.

Separation anxiety. That's what Dr. Bridges would call it.

She took a deep breath and flung aside the feeling, sending her vision flicking through the crowd. A hundred different perspectives went through her head—from a passing cab, a gliding skateboarder, an upstairs window—each for a fraction of a second. Her orange dress tugged at them, a single point of reference for all those jittering, moving eyeballs. She oriented herself, then flung her gaze out farther, casting it down the street toward the center of downtown.

A moment later she had it—a view through the eyes of someone gawking up at the stone facade of the Cambria City Police Department.

It gave Flicker a moment of pleasure to think that Scam was trapped in there, stewing in his own lies and probably wondering if any of his former friends would bother to dig him out.

CHAPTER 15
CRASH

CHIZARA PLUGGED THE BOOM BOX INTO THE WALL and switched it on. The power ran straight in and did what it was supposed to, grabbed the radio waves and pumped the music out into the shop. It had been tuned to a trance station.

"Woo-hoo," said Bob mildly from the other workbench. "It's a-li-i-ive."

Chizara smiled. It was a good feeling, bringing an appliance back to life. It was slow and clunky, arranging the metal and plastic pieces by hand, soldering things together, testing individual connections. But it was *restful*, because ancient devices like the boom box weren't smart enough to turn around and bite her.

That was why she was here; that was why she'd begged Bob for a job. *I'm always fixing stuff,* she'd flat-out lied. *People say I have a knack.*

People said no such thing, but she'd been prepared to develop a knack, with pure willpower and asking a truckload of questions. Her mother's favorite proverb was "She who asks questions cannot go astray."

It was worth lying to be allowed to work in Bob's fix it shop full of vacuum cleaners and toasters. Here in the Heights the nearest networked thing was two shops away, no more painful than a mild ice-cream headache.

Chizara clicked through the radio presets and let the owner's selection of bass beats and street chants thunder out for a few seconds. Bits of the casing rattled in time with it. She pulled the plug and stood up.

"Oh, and I was enjoying that so much," Bob said with a roll of his eyes. He only liked old-school jazz. He was working on a disassembled laptop—the best kind, as far as Chizara was concerned. Computers were rare visitors to the shop—most people in the Heights didn't own one. "You gonna sew her up, Doc?"

"Stretch break first. My head hurts."

Bob understood the need to walk away from close-in work every now and again, but he pretended to be disappointed in her. "I don't know, Chizara. Job's not done till it's done."

"Yeah, but I'm young and flighty. You have to make allowances."

Bob gave a little grin. His pale fingers scrabbled after a tiny Phillips-head screw that had rolled away across the benchtop.

"Go on, then. Take your break. You can close it up when you get back."

Chizara went out into the alleyway behind the workshop. They got along, she and Bob, and they were getting along better the more names for things she learned. He was teaching her the words that maker geeks used: "resistors" instead of "hiccups," "fuses" instead of "blurt catchers." She was learning the ancient history of the things that hurt her, seeing them for how they worked and what they did, piece by piece, before they'd all been shrunk down and melded into microchips. And she was also picking up how to seem normal, how to fake her testing, as if she couldn't simply see the pulsing veins inside the machines.

Hiding her ability was an old habit, but if Chizara ever wanted to use her power in a real job, she needed to develop a full set of geek-compatible camouflage. Bob's shop was a slow start, but it was a start. And he paid her to learn, which was more than school ever did.

She tipped her head back to soak up the sunshine for a few seconds, then crossed the alley into the shade. She pulled out her phone, steeled herself, and switched it on, checking her messages as per the agreement with her mom.

I don't care if it niggles you, Mom always said. *I need to know where you are.*

How had mothers managed, before everyone carried these machines that chattered in Chizara's head, sang in her bones, itched under her skin? How had they not gone crazy with worry?

Chizara leaned against the cool of the brick wall and rubbed her face, which was all atickle from the phone, or maybe from the repeater tower nearby. She could see it above the roofline of the shops, throbbing out its signals at her.

Her thumb was poised to power the phone off when it buzzed and beeped and zapped her hand again.

The screen said: *Glorious Leader*.

Chizara held the phone at arm's length for a few seconds, rubbing her scalp with her other hand. What did Nate want? Another mopey nostalgia session about the Zeroes with her and "Flicker"?

She tapped the message open.

Our old buddy Scam is a guest down at CCPD. Any chance you could help us get him out?

Chizara laid the phone on a ledge of brickwork and walked a few steps away from it, crossing from sun shadow into signal shadow to give herself room to think.

"Our old buddy"? That was Nate trying to be chummy and ironic, which worked great when he was right there in front of you, his power focused and amplified. But now?

Why should she care one way or another what mess that little turd "Scam" had gotten himself into? Why should any of them care?

And this was a *work*day. Nate wouldn't understand that—he didn't have to get a job over the summer, did he? And Bob had so much for her to fix right now. That nice antique toaster that lady had brought in, and the little transistor radio that Chizara wanted to see the insides of.

And yet . . . the Central Cambria Police Department. Her mouth was watering. An engraved, personalized invitation to check out some serious tech up close, and maybe bring some of it down—to do exactly what she spent her whole life holding back from. Not too much, of course—no one would get hurt or anything, if she was careful. And she always was careful, right?

The phone buzzed again, and she darted back across the alley to grab it. Another text from Nate: Flicker was on her way into town, and so was "Anon."

Right, Anon. She knew that guy. She couldn't quite dredge up his face, but he came along on Zero missions sometimes, didn't he?

Chizara shook the thought of him out of her head. Damn, they were really going in. Riley would be doing her Flicker thing, with her vision spilling through the building. And the CCPD! Chizara scratched her scalp all over, baring her teeth from all the itches and indecisions.

She ambled back toward the shop. How could she spin this to Bob?

Well, she'd already said she had a headache. It had gotten her out of school plenty of times. Why not work, too?

But she didn't want to lie. . . .

Of course, it wasn't exactly lying. *Lots* of things gave Chizara a headache.

Whatever she was going to do, she had to hurry, to get downtown before the others fixed this without her. The thought of that, of missing out completely on an inside look at CCPD, made Chizara's mind up. She replied *OK* and stuck the phone back in her pocket without turning it off. It pulsed there, a literal pain in the ass, but she was going to need it soon.

At the shop's dented metal door, she pulled her face into a squint and hunched one shoulder. She went in, making herself walk a bit unsteadily up the little passageway past the bathroom, even dragging her shoulder against the wall.

"Hey, Bob?"

He grunted. He was powering up the laptop. Any second now it would start feeling around for wifi.

"I'm getting warning signals in my eyes," she said. "Just checked my phone, and I guess that set me off. And the sunlight out there."

Bob looked up at her. The laptop squealed and scratched at Chizara's skull, looking for connections. It was fixed, all right. Plus her own phone vibrated right then—that would be Riley, opening up a conference call. Nate's training protocols were suddenly back in Chizara's head.

"Thought you had meds for those migraines."

"I do. I can see them, right there on top of the refrigerator at home." Some detail always made a lie more convincing.

"You ain't gonna make it, are you?" Bob knew she lived too far away to outrun an oncoming migraine. "You want to hide out in the supply closet for the afternoon? Nice and dark in there."

"If I catch a bus, I'll be fine." She picked her bag up from the bench, pawed in it for her sunglasses case.

"Call me if you get stuck, okay? And it'd be good to have you back in tomorrow, the way stuff's piling up." They both eyed the "in" shelf, crowded with broken appliances.

"I know. I'm sorry to leave you in a hole, Bob. I'll be back tomorrow for sure."

"Move it, girl. Catch that bus." He really was a nicer boss than she deserved.

Chizara scuttled out through the shop, past the pinpoint of irritation that was Bob's little wireless security camera. She stepped out into the sunny street and hobbled along for as long as the camera could see her through the glass. Then she dropped the hunch and the squint and sprinted toward downtown.

CHAPTER 16
CRASH

AS SHE RAN CLEAR OF THE STRIP MALL, CHIZARA tried not to remember, but it ran through her mind anyway: Scam, the cornered rat in Nate's home theater—the debriefing room—taking the Zeroes down. He'd moved from one to the next, each of them crumpling from what came out of his mouth.

Yeah, but what can he say to me? Chizara had wondered. *What awful secrets do* I *have?*

She ran faster, trying to leave the memory behind. *CCPD,* she reminded herself. She'd always wanted to crack that place. Even just to get in close and check it out. And now Scam was handing her an excuse not only to see what made it tick but to see what happened when it *un*ticked.

It was going to hurt—a *bunch*—but it'd be worth it to get a look at what was inside.

The only real drawback was rescuing Scam, rat Scam, a.k.a. Ethan.

You should see your face when you crash things—

"Shut *up*!" Chizara ran faster still. It was good to be outside, away from Bob's screeching laptop. Sure, there were networks in the apartment buildings on either side of the street, but they were behind walls and mostly up high. There were also phones and GPS systems in the vehicles cruising past, but there wasn't too much traffic yet. It would all get worse the closer she got to downtown; she could feel them foaming against her face even now, all those connections.

You think you're so in control, Scam had said.

She *was* in control. There was no way he could undo her.

But you love to break shit, Chizara. Melting a million phones, zapping a roomful of computers? You get off on it.

"Shut *up*, I told you!" She slowed to a walk, dug earbuds out of her bag, pulled out her phone, and plugged herself into the conference call.

And there was Flicker's voice: ". . . right on the front steps with everyone walking past, staring at me."

"This is Crash." Chizara used the stupid code name automatically.

"Crash?" That was Nate. She had to remember to call him Bellwether, even if Glorious Leader was what they called him behind his back. "Excellent! Are you downtown yet?"

"Passing Ivy Street now. What've you got, Flicker?" The

code names fell into place. And the attitude: calm, sharp, a bit smart-assed, maybe. "What's up with our old friend?"

"He's sitting across the desk from two detectives," said Flicker. "The way they're looking at him, they're dying to lock him up."

"Then why don't we just let them?" Chizara had a vision of Ethan, vicious and triumphant: *You're a demon. You're a walking massacre waiting to happen!*

"Well, that's a good question," said Flicker in her ear. "And yet here I find myself on the steps in front of the CCPD, and you're running to help."

What had the little rat said to Flicker? Something about Nate and her hooking up. Chizara hardly remembered. The words "walking massacre" had wiped out all Scam's other insults.

She was in control. And none of them knew how hard that was.

Among the buildings of downtown, with a million microprocessors and networks all around her, she felt the irritations cluster on her skin, burrowing into her bones. Alongside her, in the traffic rolling along Clark Street, another swarm hummed and stung. Each shop had its clutch of appliances and alarms, and each office's LAN overlapped and tangled with the others', then fed into the rumbling stream of buried fiber-optic cables. All this gnawed slowly but determinedly at Chizara's brain.

Underneath that were everyone's phones. The crowd here

was whiter and wealthier than in the Heights, and everyone seemed to have a networked phone—some carried an extra one, or a tablet or a sleeping laptop. The itches built and built, and she tried not to cringe under the attack. She gritted her jangling teeth and squashed down the temptation to slap people. Why did they need so much painful *stuff*?

"I'm turning onto North Bride," she said. "I can see the place."

The CCPD building sat there like a big wedding cake, every tier full of sweet, forbidden, maddening mysteries.

"Ha, and I can see *you*. Cross over now, and you see next to Ted's Donuts? The cop shop's side entrance is in that alleyway. Because you're a cleaner. From Ultraclean Office Services."

"You worked all that out already?" Chizara stood at the crosswalk, waiting for the light to change. For a moment she wondered if this mission were a setup. Some elaborate ruse of Glorious Leader's to get the Zeroes back together, with Flicker, as always, tagging along.

"I was at my shrink's, down the street," Flicker said. "I've got eyes everywhere. Hey, Bellwether, is what's-his-name inside? You know . . . that guy?"

"Anonymous." Nate sounded long-suffering. "Yes, he's there. Speak up, Teebo, if you can."

"Sure I can," said a deep voice, one she didn't recognize. "It's pretty busy. There's no chance of anyone noticing me."

Chizara frowned. *Teebo,* right. But the guy's real name

wasn't spelled that way—it had a whole lot of silent letters, like some Nigerian names. But he was . . . French?

Pedestrians built up around Chizara at the crosswalk, half of them fiddling with their phones, unable to endure five undistracted seconds. All that wireless fizzed in her muscles. Her own phone in her back pocket was making her butt bones ache.

The doughnut-fat smell from Ted's hit her from half a block away. "What am I doing once I get inside?"

"Chaos production," Nate said. "Distraction. Knocking things out, carefully."

A demon with porn-face. Like you're having the biggest orgasm in the—

"Do I get to knock *Scam* out?"

"Let's stay focused on hauling him out of there," Nate said. "We don't want his voice deciding to tell the cops about the rest of us."

Chizara's step faltered. Right. It would be just like Scam to blurt out everyone else's secrets to take the heat off himself.

She turned into the alleyway, trying to look as if she wasn't under siege, wasn't as excited as all hell. She tried to breathe normally and not shake under the electronic onslaught.

A few uniformed police officers and a dozen or so ordinary people were cutting through from Usher Street. But mostly she was aware of the big, messy, complex fact of the CCPD right there beside her, with all its pulsing temptations. This was going to hurt *so much*. It was already hurting. Her whole skeleton was beginning to ache.

All of Nate's training exercises were coming back to her. They had taught her to not panic, to put off the satisfaction of bringing systems down. To endure the pain and to wrap herself in barefaced confidence and calm as she walked in places where she wasn't meant to be.

She *knew* how to control this excitement, to go beyond the joy of crashing to the brainier thrill of being in among the systems, in the flow. She could shut off the yowling-with-pain part of her while she traced the paths and discovered the nodes, worked out the interrelations and the triggers—calculated how much buzz she was allowed, how much fun, how much relief.

As Nate said, there was an Ultimate Goal to every mission, and each person on the team was putting their talents to serving that. You couldn't just indulge yourself.

The other trick was knowing how the *people* would react when their toys started to fail. The human brain was where the real crashes happened.

"That door coming up on your left, Crash."

"I see it." It had creeped her out the first few times Flicker had looked through her eyes, but now it felt natural.

She walked past the door and leaned against the wall, one foot casually propped on the brick. The blurred signals of the building throbbed and tantalized her through bricks and mortar.

"What's inside, exactly?"

"On your left there'll be an Ultraclean cart. You can stop there and get ready. There's an apron on the handle. Maybe look for some rubber gloves and garbage bags? Don't take the whole cart; it'll only slow you down."

"Apron, gloves, bags. And then?" Chizara closed her eyes and screwed up her face to hear Flicker through the grinding of the CCPD systems.

"Go up the first stairs you find. Nothing but card-key locks in your way. They've got Scam on the second floor, right in the middle of a bunch of cops."

"That sounds tricky." Just standing here was tricky enough.

"Don't worry. It's crowded and noisy, and there are *lots* of overflowing trash bins that need to be emptied." Riley sounded so calm and certain. Of course, the whole building wasn't sinking ice picks into *her* head.

"Okay." Chizara took a breath, watched a white cop come out through the door. "And once I find him?"

"Whatever it takes," Nate cut in. "Lights, computers, fire alarms—give them something bigger to worry about than Scam. Then you both can just walk out. He's not under arrest, as far as we know. Anonymous will help you."

"Not that I'll notice, right?" You only ever found out later that Anon had done something vital. "Tell me the escape route, Flicker. I need the whole plan from *A* to *Z*." Crash had fried her own phone in the middle of a mission more than once, and she didn't want to be left hanging.

"The main stairs are in the middle of the building. They'll take you down to reception and out the front door."

"Got it." For show, Chizara took out her old school ID and swiped it across the card reader. At the same time she reached through the magnetic sensor, in and in and farther in, in a microsecond's flash, to the vigilant source waiting for a signal to read. With her mental fingertip she knocked it out, like flicking away a stick beneath a spinning plate. The fall, and the crash, sent a small, clean, hot, *good* feeling in through all her tangling pains.

Porn-face, that little shit had called it. *A massacre waiting to happen.*

The door clicked. Chizara pushed, and it opened. She stepped out of being Chizara and into being Crash, and strolled straight into the CCPD as if she had a perfect right to be there.

CHAPTER 17
CRASH

IT FELT JUST LIKE THE ZEROES' TRAINING MISSIONS, all those exercises where Nate had tested the limits of their powers. But on this mission, for the first time, there was a real Goal.

Crash stood by the cart, tying her cleaner's apron, trying to look like someone gearing up for another dreary workday. At her very center the mission calm formed a solid core. But outside of that she was more awake than she'd ever been, concentrating hard through the excitement—she was here, in the *CCPD*. And her outermost layer was all scalded flesh and howling bones, wanting to bend and groan, wanting to curl up on the floor under the pressure.

The tech was part of her. It was extra nerves pushing out beyond her skin's limits. It was enormous, *heavy*, intricate antlers coming out of her head. The CCPD was way more wired up than any of the malls or shopping centers Nate had set their training exercises in. A thousand network connections were dotted through the place, lamps hanging burning from the antlers, planes in holding patterns shouting, *Crash me, crash me!*

All the phones in the building formed a swirling galaxy of glowing coals in her mind. They waved around in people's hands, darted about in pockets, lay ignored on desks and in drawers and purses. Each one was a tiny claw clamped on her brain, each sending out a signal, painfully high-pitched. All of it itched in her skin and jerked in her muscles.

As she pulled on the disposable gloves, her hands shook from the effort of holding back, of not tearing down the wall between herself and silence, painlessness—the perfect peace of a big crash.

She accessed her mission-calm center again, tried to keep control. The cameras had to go, along with what they'd already captured of her and of Scam. She focused on the little eye staring down at her from one corner of the hallway, felt around behind it for the strands that led to the pulse of other cameras like it, to the chips that held the gathered images. In the middle of the noise storm, the itch storm, she allowed herself the tiny relief of letting just that mini system drop, getting that mini itch scratched.

There. Neatly done. Now the cops would only have the memories in their own heads, or—

"Have they taken Scam's photo?" she muttered.

"A mug shot?" came Flicker's voice. "He's not handcuffed, so I doubt it. But don't take too long. Those two detectives don't look happy with him. On your right, Crash. There—straight up that hallway."

Crash didn't move and didn't reply. Flicker would see why in a second: There was a fizzle of phones and radios outside the alley door, which meant cops coming in. At the moment they were probably waving their cards at the blank reader. In a second they'd realize that the lock wasn't working and push on through.

She waited by the cart, stealing these moments to acclimatize a little more. It was a gorgeous, painful mess in here.

When the cops came through the door, one of them nodded to Crash, and she nodded back world-wearily.

"I see you!" giggled Flicker. "You totally look like a cleaner!"

Maybe to you, white girl, thought Crash drily. The cops continued on up the hallway while she pretended to check things on the cart, trembling from the close encounter. She was a little out of practice.

So Glorious Leader wanted chaos? It was *already* chaos in here, everything she'd dreaded and dreamed of. New buildings like Cambria Town Hall, she could figure those out at a glance: All the cabling had been done in one hit, and everything was brand-spanking-new and rationally organized. The CCPD was different, its nervous system stuffed into a heavy last-century skeleton where no one wanted to drill through the masonry. Everything had been forced to make way for everything else over years of departmental reorganizations and technological shifts. The IT was thrillingly massive, but it was a jumble. New systems were spliced and piggybacked onto old—the server array stashed near the holding cells downstairs was like a museum of computing, legacy machines lined up there pumping stuff back and forth so slo-owly! If only she had time, and quiet, and no pain, no maddening muscle itch, she could browse through everything and work out some *really* subtle strategy.

But she didn't have time, and she needed to keep the lights working for now.

The air-conditioning could go, though. That would take a little load off, give her a bit more clarity—which would contribute to the Ultimate Goal, wouldn't it? And a little warmth wouldn't hurt anyone.

Crash marked off the parameters and released it. The bliss of dropping that cumbersome chunk of temperature sensors and fan motors lifted her onto her toes. The system groaned through all its ducts, and its white noise died to silence.

Yeah, that would make the cops jumpy. Or sweaty, anyway.

Smoke detection? Alarms were always handy for instant chaos, so she'd save them until she needed noise. Crash sniffed around the radio dispatch center—yes, she could isolate it so the cops still got their emergency calls.

Like a hospital, this was a place to do no harm. Or at least not *too* much harm. For example, those doors to the holding cells downstairs. Lucky they'd turned out to be on a separate circuit from the locks she'd just knocked out. That would've been bad.

All those PCs and servers—she looked at their swarming ant nests of data and mentally rubbed her hands. She could choose her moment with them, too, time the chaos. Blow all the lights at the same time, maybe.

Crash swept a trash bag out of the box on the cart and walked up the hallway, reaching through the stinging bee swarm of systems for more things to sacrifice.

Here were the stairs. She headed up them to the second floor.

"To your left, through that half-glass door," Flicker said.

Loads of people up here. In case anyone was watching, she did a pretend swipe with her school ID before pushing the door open.

Some cops were clustered around a desk, yelling about the air-conditioning, arguing about who they were supposed to contact for a fix. No one spared the cleaner more than a glance.

"On your left," said Flicker.

"I see him." The sight of Ethan—of *Scam*, since this was a mission—sent a new trickle of annoyance down Crash's spine. Not like all the little itches of tech, just the ever-present need to punch him in the face.

Two cops were with Scam, one sitting and one standing. He sat all fake casual in an office chair, his expression alternating between his own scared teenage self and that smart-ass who did the talking for him.

Crash checked out the rest of the room—for obstacles and pathways, sure, but the wiring was the thing, the signals pouring through it and being split and transformed and channeled. Lots of people around her meant better focus, wider reach. She tried to keep her eyes open as she felt along her extending antlers, her lengthening mind fingers.

Flicker interrupted, her voice a little nervous. "Everyone still looks pretty calm, Crash. Pretty business-as-usual."

"Not for long." Crash reached into the smoke detector in the ceiling above her, careful not to knock out the whole system—there was no point if it just died quietly. She had to hold back *so much* of herself, and just make the tiniest adjustment to cut the connection between those two plates *there* . . .

She jumped at the shriek of the alarm, loud even through her earbuds. Everyone around her ducked and covered their ears as if they'd just been dive-bombed, then stared up in shock. *Hoo-ee*, what a noise!

The problem was, she could barely *think* now. How was she supposed to keep the rest of this place working?

Crash steered toward the desk where Scam sat. Flicker was a tiny, tinny voice, cheering and shouting in her earbuds.

"Whatever, I can't hear you," Crash murmured, stepping back as a uniformed woman rushed past, swearing a streak. Lots of men were striding around now, but Crash slipped through them, invisible because she had brown skin, and was a girl, and wore the cleaning-company apron.

Nearly everyone in the office had their hands over their ears. Some were up out of their chairs shouting suggestions. Others kept working away at screens, hunched under the pressure of the noise. One of Scam's detectives, the big guy, had turned away and thrown up his hands. The other, a woman, sat there waiting calmly, fingers in her ears.

From between them, Scam's eyes lit on Crash. His flash of recognition turned to hope, then nerves and flat-out fear as she scowled back at him. He looked away again, self-consciously casual even with his hands over his ears.

Crash stood back to let some cops scurry for the door, then slipped between two desks, where she wouldn't be disturbed, and started sorting out the different layers of tech. She put out her feelers through the shifting galaxy-cloud of phones, through the more stable, tethered thrumming of the computers, to the sweet simplicity of the lighting system.

She crashed it—such a tiny treat, such a little shiver up her spine, when this giant chocolate box was open in front of her. But it was *good*—that whole swarm of stingers finally switching off. Her skin purred for a moment with gratitude. Shouts went up, as if the people in the office were cheering her on.

But then an emergency lighting system kicked to life. No, no, Crash wanted none of that. She dug deeper to its source and allowed that to fail too, and the room dimmed again—

only a couple of frosted windows in the far wall let in sunlight. More cops sat back from their computers and looked around bewildered.

Scam stared at her; then he glanced at the two detectives standing there like gatekeepers in front of him. Semidarkness and a bit of noise weren't going to shift them.

Right, then. Stay calm. Crash's head was beginning to spin from what she'd done and what she might still do. She knelt to reach for a small trash can, an excuse to hold on to something.

On her knees and stable, she let her mind go, and like a small but potent tornado it swept through the building, crashing this and that, all the minor things, all the unlucky subsystems, on its way in toward the roots of the server array. She kept her face down so Scam wouldn't see how good this felt.

"Holy shit." Flicker's voice was tiny in her ears, then suddenly altogether gone. Broken cell-phone connections fluttered around Crash, like streamers from a departing cruise liner.

Something big and important flailed and died in the basement. She'd meant not to crash that, she thought vaguely. But it was too late now.

The storm she'd called into being had its own logic now, its own demands. Was it her or the storm itself whispering through her lips into the chaos? She couldn't hear the words, but she felt them like fire in her bones . . .

It's time to do some damage.

CHAPTER 18
FLICKER

"LOST HER," FLICKER SAID FROM HALF A BLOCK AWAY, the nearest to the CCPD that her phone would work at all.

"She'll be fine," Glorious Leader said. "Just tell me what you see."

Flicker took a moment before responding. *Chaos* was the simple answer.

The lights had failed completely, leaving the inner offices lit only with a bobbing flurry of tiny screens. Flashlights were all the phones were good for, now that Crash had shredded the local repeater tower.

Everything was a blur of motion in Flicker's head. It was dizzying, being in people's viewpoints when they were running around in darkness, eyes twitching and jerking. Some of them were evacuating, filling the stairwells. Flicker could hear the shriek of smoke alarms from the front steps.

Finally she found a stable pair of eyeballs, the detective seated across from Scam. That gaze went from Scam to her partner, a big guy who was striding away, shouting into his useless phone.

"Scam's still being watched. But things are pretty messy in there."

"It's under control," Glorious Leader said. He said this a lot during missions. "Before the phones went out, Anonymous told me he had them in sight."

"Right, Anonymous." Flicker always remembered the code name, even when the rest of it slipped her grasp. "But . . . this isn't good. I'm seeing a bunch of cops with drawn guns. Why would they lock and load for a fire alarm?"

"Maybe they think it's an attack."

"Um, it kind of *is*." Flicker cast her vision into the group with the brandished weapons. They were headed downstairs, past the ground floor and deeper. "What's in the basement, Bellwether?"

"Of a police station?" The clatter of computer keys. "The generator? The parking lot? *Mierda*. The holding cells."

"Wait." She went deeper, flicking herself from head to head. She was well past her usual range, but it was crowded in the CCPD, and her power used human beings like repeater towers, leapfrogging from one pair of eyes to the next.

She found more people down there, a huddled group of them, their eyes full of darkness as hard as stone. Her view prickled with little stars of misfiring rods and cones, the fritz and glitter that sighted people saw when completely deprived of light.

Then, for a moment, the blackness was cut in two by a single flashlight. It searched among the looming shadows of a dozen men, found a door, then switched off again.

"Uh-oh," she said. "There's a bunch of people sneaking around down there. Not cops."

"Electronic cell doors," Nate said, his fingers still clicking on a keyboard. "They're designed to stay locked in a power outage. But you can't design for Crash."

"Okay. But where'd a bunch of prisoners get a flashlight?"

"From a cop," Nate said softly. "And probably not gently. Don't tell Crash. She'll lose it."

Flicker swore. Chizara was all about discipline. She lived by the credo of "Do no harm," always keeping away from hospitals and airports. She'd never been on a plane or a train in her life, afraid she'd let her guard down for one catastrophic moment.

"Focus on the mission, Flick."

At that tone in Glorious Leader's voice, her Zero discipline clicked back in. She pulled vision from the sparkling darkness of the basement and flitted back up to the window-lit office space on the second floor.

It was even more chaotic now. The glimmer of drawn guns, the lancing beams of big fat police flashlights. Some of the detectives were struggling into dark blue bulletproof vests.

"They know what's happening down in the basement."

"Good. That's a perfect distraction. Can you see Crash yet?"

Flicker was searching for Scam's eyeballs among the havoc, and finally she recognized his thin-fingered, freckled hands in the gloom. He was tearing up a notepad.

"They've left him alone," she said. "I think he's destroying evidence."

"So he's keeping his head. At least we didn't do this for nothing."

"I guess," Flicker said, unfolding her cane. "I'm going back. You might lose me."

"Stay outside. Be—" His voice crackled and spat as she walked toward the police station, and then her earbuds went silent.

Flicker snapped her vision closer, finding her orange dress among the milling, curious crowds watching the evacuation of the CCPD. The civilians who worked in the station were streaming down the front steps, blinking as they emerged from darkness into sunlight. A local news van was pulling up, the reporters inside no doubt thrilled about this banner day of bank robbery and police station chaos.

Flicker slipped among the crush, using her cane, her ears, and flickers of stolen vision to navigate, heading toward the front steps, which nobody had thought to block off yet.

She hoped that saving Rat Face was worth causing all this mayhem.

CHAPTER 19
MOB

MIKEY HADN'T CALLED BACK ABOUT GIVING HER a ride.

He was probably at work already. That was Mikey's deal: Dance all night, work all day and maybe dance the next night too. He said it kept him young. It also kept him busy.

So Kelsie didn't wait long. According to her phone, the police station was fifty-three minutes' walk.

As she checked the route, a thought went through her head: What kind of idiot robs a bank three miles from a police station? Of all the crazy stuff her dad had ever done, this made the least sense.

The day was heating up. She had to keep pushing the hair off her damp face. She was glad for the loose harem pants and crop top she'd worn clubbing, even if they were earning her more glances than she really needed right then. Her muscles weren't good sore anymore. They just hurt.

But maybe it was better that Mikey hadn't picked her up. She didn't like lying to him. He'd never been anything but a friend to her. Trouble was, she had no idea where to start with the truth.

The walk gave her time to think. When she was growing up, Dad had always said he could make anything better. He meant little things, like scrapes on her knee. And some big things, like the time in fifth grade when she'd freaked out at a playground fight—all those kids chanting *Kill him! Kill him!* in unison, and she'd almost wanted to join in. Or how every exam at school was like drowning in a room full of other people's fear, no matter how hard she studied.

Those were things Dad could deal with. But this was way bigger. Her dad had robbed a bank, and now he was going to prison.

As she drew closer to the police station, a sickly fear started crawling around in Kelsie's gut. How many years did you get for a bank robbery that got somebody killed? What if her father had pulled the trigger? What if he never came out?

The squawk of a police car echoed down the street, and her heart skidded two inches sideways in her chest.

The station was just ahead. A crowd was bubbling around it, onlookers and police officers. There were people streaming out of the station doors.

Kelsie stopped. Something was wrong.

She'd been feeling it for blocks now, the energy of the crowd making panicked zigzags low in her stomach. She'd thought it was her own anxiety. She hadn't realized it was *out there.* She sped up, taking the city blocks at a jog, heading toward the noise and panic.

Lights flashed in the police station windows, and alarms inside screamed and wailed. But the worst of it was the rush and wash of energies—broken connections, wild emotions. She felt like she was going down a waterfall.

Crowds were only good when they shared something. When they were united by a purpose or a beat. Then she could slip inside, be part of that something more.

But this was even more tangled than the bank robbery. Police, journalists, passersby were all pulling in different directions, a dozen crowds all braided and knotted up, refusing to be one thing.

As if they were tributaries cascading into a river, the spray thrown up by their collision blinded her, nearly wiped her off her feet. For a moment the world was awash with white.

She came to a halt a block away from the station, leaning against a wall to take deep breaths. Just like her dad had taught her. *In, count to three, then out.* Usually this helped when she had to tune out a crowd, when she had to be just a solitary girl in the middle of it all. To be Kelsie.

In, two, three . . . out.

But then a jolt came down the street, a fresh shock, and Kelsie lost herself again.

She was everywhere at once, stretched thin across the top of the bubbling energies. Fear flooded her eyes and blocked her ears. She had to pull herself out of the echoing tide, then drag everyone else with her because with this kind of panic, people might do something stupid. And her dad was still in there.

She had to make sure her dad was okay.

"Are you all right?" someone shouted in her ear.

She shook her head mutely. Whatever was going on in the police station, it was getting worse.

Someone was helping her, leading her by the elbow to a bench nearby. She leaned forward over her knees. She felt like she was made of drops of rain on a window, all the rivulets of herself blurring into something bigger. She gulped mouthfuls of air and tried not to pass out.

In, two, three . . . out.

When the nausea cleared, she realized the ringing wasn't in her ears. It was her phone. She ignored it. Probably Mikey asking if she still needed that ride. Whoever had helped her to the bench was gone.

Kelsie looked up at the station again. Maybe the police were evacuating people from the holding cells. They'd do that if there was a fire in the station. Right?

Her phone kept ringing. Finally she pulled it from her pocket. "Yeah?"

"Kels?" came a ragged voice. "It's Dad."

She pressed a finger to her other ear. "Dad? Are you okay? What's going on?"

"I did something."

"You robbed a *bank* is what you did!"

There was a pause. "You saw the news already?"

"I was across the street! That's what happens when you rob banks in broad daylight—*witnesses*." She stared at the station. Police were everywhere, scrambling and frantic. "They're letting you use a phone?"

"I got out."

It didn't make sense. None of this made sense. "What? How?"

"The security system must've failed somehow. The doors just opened up."

Two police ran past her in bulletproof vests. They were carrying rifles.

Her dad was still talking. "The lights went out all at once, Kels, and a bunch of alarms went off. We all just . . . walked out."

"Dad, are you crazy? It's like a war zone out here! The cops all have guns. You'll get shot!"

"I'm half a mile away already. Kelsie, you have to meet me."

She hunched over her phone, not believing any of this.

It felt like some new force was moving through her life, as powerful and strange as the ability she'd been born with. But at least she could see her father again.

"Okay, Dad. Where?"

CHAPTER 20

CRASH

CRASH CLUNG TO THE DESK, HER BONES SHAKING, throwing off the crushing pressure system by system, swimming up toward the surface through a glowing tangle of tentacles alive with stingers.

Someone put a hand on her shoulder. Muzzily she looked up at Scam. He was shouting, and shoving something at her that glittered in the dimness. A pink phone covered with fake diamonds—definitely not his.

Crash hauled herself up. Where were Scam's detectives? There, scrambling along the hallway toward the back, their guns pointed at the ceiling.

They must be thinking this was a terrorist attack. Messy.

"Let's get *outta* here!" Scam cried.

"Stairs this way." She would have run, but her legs had gone rubbery. Something big was building inside her, she could tell, something epic and out of control. "Uh-oh."

Crash grabbed for the desk again and missed, but Scam caught her. He was practically *hitting* her with the glittery phone, and he pulled out one of her earbuds, shouting over the smoke alarms, "Kill this phone, would you?"

She tried to push him away. What was gathering inside her was too big, too dangerous. Crashing something now would be like pouring kerosene on a burning fuse. She had to get out of this place.

Scam funneled his voice into her ear with a hand. "There's video on it! She was *videoing me*! At the *bank*! She's got me saying—"

"Yeah, yeah." Crash fended him off. He'd been incriminating himself, of course. Opening his big mouth and letting the bullshit fall out. She pushed him toward the central stairway.

"But there's video," he mewled.

She snatched the phone and smacked it into the metal corner of a desk. The screen blistered. She hit it again, harder. Glass fragments skittered across the desk and flew to the floor.

She shoved it back at him. "There, it's crashed."

He stared at the dead, shattered screen. His stunned expression started a laugh burbling up from deep inside her.

No, that wasn't a laugh. Not at all. It was something big and scary.

A walking massacre if ever there was one.

"Stairs." She pointed with a shaking hand.

Scam hoisted a green duffel bag up onto one shoulder, put the other under Crash's arm, and heaved her forward. Then they were at the stairway, a bigger space where the alarms didn't hammer quite as hard. Cops were running past, guns drawn—Crash wanted to laugh, they looked so earnest and alert. As if this were an alien invasion and not just a systems meltdown.

At the foot of the stairs, a guy was waving everyone through to the front of the building. "Get out! Move it!" They pushed on after the people crowding out into the lobby.

She'd let something bad happen, down in the basement. What was it again? She hadn't meant to go that far. . . .

Now all she could see were the phones, every single one in the CCPD. The local tower was down, but the phones were still struggling to connect, a flock of burning lights and fizzing pains. And the phones out on the *street*, too, and some in neighboring buildings. She could feel the call of the next tower on, and still farther away bulked the switching center with its unbearable complications and power.

The smoke alarms still shrieked; the fire control system pressed in on her. Everything was building into a wave, one she couldn't hold back much longer. She was slipping, losing control, her will no longer separate from the shattering networks around her. She was not going to be able to stick to the rules.

Do no harm? She didn't have a choice anymore.

She should never have come here.

Crash stumbled along, head down, only Scam and his duffel bag holding her upright. Shiny cop shoes scuffed and clumped on the tiled floor around her own. With her last ounce of willpower she turned away from Scam—she did *not* want him to see her face.

Because it was about to fall over.

All of it.

There was nothing she could do.

The pain, the strain of keeping those masses of tech functioning, surged out of Crash's body in a hot, sweet, glorious rush. If Scam hadn't been holding her weight, she would've slumped to the floor with the blissed-out shock of letting go. The entire building sighed to a halt around her, an airy, painless refuge in the middle of the downtown madness.

This was good. This was what she was *meant* to do.

She was Crash.

Some dim-faced cop was shouting in her face, "You okay, miss?"

She smiled at him, tried to nod, tried to speak, failed. Scam pulled her forward. She felt light in his arms, a creature made of fire and cotton candy.

Now they were in the reception area. The doorway to the street was bright with sunlight. They'd made it—

But someone stepped in and blocked the light, a big cop with a square head and shoulders like football armor.

"Hey!" he said to Scam. "Fuentes had you in for something, didn't he?"

Somehow, even in her rapture, Crash realized that this had all been a waste of time. They were going to haul Scam back inside, and probably arrest her, too.

It was all over. But worth it, just to taste *this*.

But then a kid—a tall, skinny boy, nicely dressed—came at the big cop from out of nowhere. He kicked the back of the cop's left knee, then pulled him backward by his shoulders. The cop's mouth opened, and he flailed and went down, and Scam was dragging her out the door.

She looked back—there'd been something about that boy. But he was gone. Maybe there hadn't been a boy at all.

It was so *bright* out here on the front steps. The summer sun amped up all the color in the world, and polished the palm-tree leaves to shining.

Crash stared at the sky. It was deep blue and empty and perfect.

Suddenly Flicker was on the other side of her, helping Scam support her. Even in her blissed-out state, Crash's training kicked in, her eyes going into seeing-eye-human mode, scanning the sidewalk in front of them, registering every seam and bump.

"You guys," she said. "That was *fun*."

"Are you okay?" Flick's voice sounded so real out here in the street air, instead of through earbuds.

"Totally. It's so good to see you!" And somehow Crash meant both of them, even if Scam was twitching and gawking back over his shoulder and sweating all over her.

Flicker shook her head. "That was insane, Chizara. I didn't know you could do that much!"

Crash laughed. It was *not* doing that much that was always so hard! And Chizara? For this wonderful moment there was nobody called Chizara, only crazy, reckless Crash, who could paint her name in darkness across the city.

Who could bring down the whole *world* if she wanted.

"They've still got that bank security footage of me," Scam muttered.

"Relax," Flicker said. "We'll take care of it."

Scam hoisted his duffel bag a little higher. "Where are we going?"

"To see our Glorious Leader!" said Flicker in a bad Russian accent.

Crash burst out laughing. Scam groaned.

"Come on," said Flicker. "This mess is going to take some debriefing."

They ran through the crowd of curious onlookers, Flicker fast and sure-footed thanks to Crash's eyes, the way the training missions had taught them, back when they'd all been friends and worked together, before Scam's voice had blown the Zeroes to pieces.

CHAPTER 21

BELLWETHER

"I NEED THE ROOM," NATE SAID.

His little sisters giggled, but they streamed obediently out, dragging their stuffed animals, wrestling masks, and capes made from bath towels behind them.

"Gabriela?" he called to the youngest before she disappeared. "Would you please mention to Mamá that my friends haven't had lunch?"

Gabby rolled her beautiful brown eyes at him and curtsied, then ran off behind the others, laughing. But the message would be delivered.

Nate stood there a moment, kicking a few toys his sisters had left—a plastic wombat, a cheetah made of felt—behind the riser under the movie screen. Why his sisters always wanted to play here in the home theater was beyond him. They ignored the playroom and backyard for days at a time, preferring these eight fat leather chairs and the purple carpeted floor.

But it was time for Nate to reclaim his sanctum.

He pulled a four-inch Blue Demon doll from a cup holder. It was new, beautifully hand-painted, and already chipped from too many combats. His sisters' *lucha libre* craze had lasted months now. Which was all very well, except for the occasional masked ambush when Nate emerged from his bedroom.

His phone buzzed. Anon.

Might be late. Following something up.

Nate put the doll down and keyed an *OK*. At least all four of them were coming.

It was annoying, having no agenda prepared for the first meeting of the Zeroes in almost a year. But this was like starting over, he supposed. If they left here feeling bonded into a group again, maybe Scam's little disaster had been worth it.

Nate needed to remind himself what Anonymous looked like. He reached into the riser's secret compartment, beneath the hidden wires and cables, and pulled out his stack of Zero files—he never kept anything about the Zeroes on his computer.

The Anonymous folder was mostly photos. Low angled and badly lit, most snapped in secret, the images were never clear enough to stick in his mind. The guy was a snappy dresser, though.

Which was funny, come to think of it. Why would a guy bother with fancy clothes when he was practically invisible? Well, more like forgettable. But still.

Nate pulled out his notepad, ready to add that to his list of questions. He reviewed the others: *Can Anon also see connections? Does his power follow the Curve? Invisibility as a function of memory? Does his own family recognize him?*

And there it was, written in Nate's own handwriting and dated a year ago:

Why does he bother dressing so well?

Nate sighed. It had been a while since he'd reviewed this file. Daily memorization was the only way to make the knowledge stick, and even then it only halfway did. It took all of Nate's focus just to sit here and read his own notes, to keep his thoughts from drifting. To remember that Thibault was real.

It was like trying to make friends with a puff of smoke.

It seemed only a few moments had passed when Gabby was back, announcing, "Your friends are here!" and fluttering away again.

Nate hid the files beneath his seat as the three of them came in. Crash looked wide-eyed and spacey, like she'd been pulled away from a nightclub at the peak of some expensive high. Flicker was using her cane, her power probably worn down from skipping across so many eyes. Scam's buzz cut was new, but otherwise he was his usual twitchy self. He was dragging a duffel bag behind him, and looked like a guy who'd lost a fight. With a bear.

"Take a seat, everyone," Nate said. They fell into the recliners as he took the stage.

Almost a year. That's how long it had been since the four of them had been in this room together. All that time they could have been training, building up their powers, learning to work together. Almost a year wasted.

And the whole blowup had been, in a way, Nate's fault. He'd struck the match.

But now the Zeroes were his again. He could see it in the lines of attention that lit up the air like sparklers, all gathering on him, like they always did. The others were skittish about being together again, still scarred from what had happened last summer. But they were too exhausted from the mission to fight his influence.

They needed reassurance. They needed to be led.

"You guys did great." Nate let his smile settle over them, flexing his power to tighten the connections. "Without any planning or prep work, we accomplished our mission. We rescued one of our own. By the way, Scam, welcome back."

He turned his gaze to Ethan, giving him the floor for a moment.

The little guy just cringed at first. He probably hadn't been called *Scam* in a while, and he didn't know what to say. But Nate gave him just the right look, guiding him toward gratitude.

"Um, right. Thanks, guys." It was Ethan's real voice, as clumsy and squeaky as always. "You, uh, really saved my ass."

There was an uncomfortable little pause here, because no

one was going to say "you're welcome," not to Scam. Speaking the words himself would only cost Nate respect, so he didn't bother.

Instead he drew the focus back to himself. "We'll always protect each other. Especially when our powers, when *what we are*, gets us into trouble."

That worked—the connections in the room grew a little brighter. The three of them were still full of adrenaline, still bonded by success.

That had always been the point of the training missions. Nate had gotten the idea from watching his cousins play baseball. They could spend a whole morning fighting, but then drop all their rivalries in an instant once victory was at stake.

Now, to find out what the hell had happened in the bank.

"So, Ethan. Your voice got you into trouble?"

"Yeah. I guess."

Nate stepped off the stage and sat down, setting the sparkling strands of awareness wavering, looking for a new object. He swiveled his chair toward Ethan.

The guy didn't want to talk, but Nate's attention drew the others' along with it, focusing the pressure until it was too much to resist. Ethan stumbled into an explanation of what had happened in the bank, something about a girl who hadn't wanted to hand over her ring. To keep her from getting shot, the voice had spilled the robbers' secrets, setting them against each other, and the heist had ended in gunfire.

But the girl had taken video of Ethan using his voice, and she'd given it to the cops. It all sounded very heroic and self-sacrificing, which meant he was leaving something out.

Nate couldn't quite tell what yet. Here in front of his former friends, Ethan didn't dare use his voice. But without it helping, his wobbly storytelling was hard to piece together, even when he was *trying* to tell the truth.

"They're going to find me," he whined. "The cops, they know my face!"

Chizara giggled in a very un-Crash-like way. "Any video your girlfriend took is gone, Scam. Even if the cops made a copy, it's confetti in a hurricane, like the rest of their data."

She laughed again, slouching in her chair, her usual regal posture turned casual.

Nate glanced down at his notepad and wrote, *What's up with Chizara?*

"But a bunch of cops *saw* me," Ethan said. "It's not like you erased their memories, too. And there's security footage. You gonna crash the bank's computers?"

Chizara raised an eyebrow, like this sounded tempting.

"Blurry bank cameras don't matter," Nate said, giving them both a calming look. "You never told them your real name, right?"

"Course not. But my *mom* works down there. . . ."

Of course, his mother the deputy district attorney. The bank footage would be part of the robbery investigation, and then the trial. Sooner or later, Scam was busted.

But what had he actually *done*?

"You haven't broken any laws, Ethan," Nate said in his most soothing voice. "The fact that you talked to the robbers might make the cops suspicious, but it's not a crime."

That was what really mattered—that Scam never had to explain himself to the law. Because once he started talking about his own power, it wouldn't be long before his inner voice traded everyone else's secrets as well.

Nataniel Saldana had big plans for himself, goals that would be a lot trickier if the public had any idea what he could do.

Ethan was nodding along, wanting to believe that everything would be okay. That was the key to getting people on your side—showing them a path to what they already desired. Once you'd done that, it hardly mattered that it was also *your* path.

Human nature was so easy to figure out when you could see it shimmering in the air. Most of the time Nate didn't even have to use his power to get what he wanted.

"When you asked the detective to call me," he said carefully to Ethan, "did he write my phone number down on a piece of paper?"

"Yeah, but I ripped it up."

"And his phone's memory is gone. Right, Crash?"

Chizara was still smiling. "Like I said, it's all confetti down there. But if the cops want to find you, they can pull the phone company's logs."

Ethan shrank a little in his chair, and Nate had to control himself.

"That doesn't matter. If they come around, I'll deal with it." Nate gave them all a cool, serene expression—like he was the only one in danger but wasn't worried at all. For a moment the room settled around him, the glitter of their adrenaline finally starting to soften in the air.

Then Flicker said, "So, Ethan, why do you keep looking at your duffel bag?"

Ethan stared at her in terror for a moment, then tried to shrug it off. "It's just my bag. Clothes and . . . stuff."

Nate wrote on his notepad, *Clever girl.* Then he stood and crossed the little theater, knelt, and unzipped the duffel bag.

Money. Countless rolls of it, wrapped tight with rubber bands. He heard Flicker whistle.

Nate looked up at Ethan. "Are you *serious*? You skimmed money from a bank robbery?"

"No! I was in the bank to put it someplace safe. It's *mine*."

Chizara flat-out laughed at this. "Okay. But whose was it before that?"

Ethan swallowed, like his skinny little throat was gulping down a golf ball. But his next words came out too smoothly. "Me and a friend drove to Los Alamitos on Tuesday, went to the track. Put our paychecks on Amarillo Rose in the fifth race. Forty-six to one. You can look it up."

"No doubt we could," Nate said mildly. Scam's inner

voice never got details wrong. Where it failed was the big picture.

"Since when did you get friends?" Flicker said. "And why does that money smell like stale beer?"

Ethan glared at her a moment, then deflated, like a puffer fish giving up.

"From this guy, Craig something. He works at some club. It was the night's take, from whatever extra they sell there."

"You mean this is *drug* money?" Nate took a step back from the duffel bag. "And you brought it into my house?"

"I didn't *want* to bring it here!" Scam cried. "I wasn't even trying to steal it! I just wanted a ride home."

Nate swore. He wiped the metal zipper pull with his shirt tail to erase any fingerprints. A criminal record did *not* go with his long-term plans.

The focus had gone out of the room now, the sense of connection, of team. Scam was an expert at disconnecting people, even when he wasn't trying to be an ass. Maybe because his power was so different from the others'. It was focused on individuals, not groups. It was narrow and selfish, a broken version of what the rest of them had.

"People are going to be looking for this bag," Nate said, sinking back into his chair. "Bad people."

"Maybe" came an unfamiliar voice. "But the money's not our biggest problem."

Nate looked up—sitting in the back row was a dark-haired

boy. It took a long moment to recognize him, and then real effort for Nate to keep his gaze from sliding away. He wondered how long the boy had been sitting up there.

Then he remembered the trick: Nate had to keep everyone else looking at the boy, so he could use the glittering strands of attention in the room to keep himself focused.

"Ah, you made it," he said. "Everyone, perhaps you remember Anonymous?"

CHAPTER 22
FLICKER

NOW THAT ANONYMOUS WAS SITTING RIGHT IN front of them, Flicker did remember.

She remembered his eyes, blue and intense. The dark hair in bangs that almost covered them. The long pale fingers, steepling together as he leaned back in the leather chair. His lean face, with that expression of intelligence and reserve, like someone content with watching everything from a corner of the room.

It was always startling, how handsome Anonymous was. Even *pretty*, if that was the right word for someone who looked so haunted.

Or maybe he was just shy, not used to anyone staring at him the way Glorious Leader was now, intent and purposeful, as if trying to catalog everything about . . .

"Thibault," she said. *That* was his name. It was French, as tricky to spell as the boy himself was to remember.

His blue eyes shied away from Nate, looking at the others.

Was he looking at *her*? Flicker tried to cast her vision into his, then remembered the other thing that she always forgot . . .

She couldn't put herself in his eyes. She'd never been able to. He was a blank spot in the room.

Now that was *really* weird.

She went to Chizara's vision, trying to triangulate. Yes, the pretty boy was definitely looking at Flicker. Suddenly self-conscious, she ran her fingers through her frazzled hair. She'd been running around downtown all morning, and probably looked like she'd ridden a bike here.

"What do you mean, Thibault?" Nate asked. "What problem?"

"There was a breakout," the boy said. His voice sounded a little husky, like he was getting a cold. Or maybe he didn't get much practice talking to people. "During the crash, some of the prisoners in the CCPD managed to get away."

Flicker was still in Chizara's eyes as they swung to Nate, widening a little. Of course. Nate had forgotten to warn Anon not to mention the escape to Chizara.

"Oh my God." Chizara's hands grasped at each other. "I saw those cell locks. I was *trying* to keep them online!"

Nate looked straight at her. "We don't know what happened, not really."

"We know *exactly* what happened, Nate. I broke the *whole damn building*!"

Everyone's eyes were on Chizara, and Flicker wanted to say something reassuring. But she could also feel her awareness of Anonymous slipping away, now that she couldn't see him.

An unwelcome but familiar wish overtook her: that she had her own eyes to control, to focus where *she* wanted.

"Thibault," she said, his name coming back to her just in time. "Did anyone get hurt?"

It worked. They all looked at him again.

He cleared his throat—he *was* shy. "Not sure what happened in the station, but I tracked a gang of them for a minute or two. They weren't on a rampage or anything, just trying to get away. They split up after a few blocks, melted into the crowd."

"Doesn't sound too bad," Nate said. "So what's the problem?"

"One of them had a limp," Anon said. "He was the bank robber, the one they showed on the news. He's free."

"Jerry," Ethan said softly, and all eyes went to him. "The voice talked to him in the bank. Made his robbery go sideways! So now I got the Craig and his drug buddies, *and* the cops, *and* a crazy-ass bank robber after me!"

Flicker put herself in Nate's eyes—he was scanning the room. Chizara's post-crash euphoria had vanished, now that she knew she'd let loose a bunch of prisoners. She was sitting up straight, staring at her own fidgeting hands. Scam looked even more like a cornered rat than usual, and for some reason he was clutching a blue-headed wrestler doll. Thibault pushed a hand nervously through his dark hair, and the pale half-moon of an ear peeked out. He'd realized that he shouldn't have mentioned the breakout in front of Chizara, but too late.

"We'll all deal with this *together*," Nate said, his voice taking on its most sonorous Glorious Leader tones. "We Zeroes can protect our own."

"Easy for you to say," Ethan muttered. "You don't have the whole damn city looking for you. I should just skip town. Take that money and *go*."

For a moment Flicker let herself think how much easier that would make all their lives. No more Scam creating mayhem every time he opened his mouth.

But then Nate said, "We can help." And Flicker knew those words were true, because the Zeroes stuck together. Always and forever.

Yes, this was Glorious Leader wielding his power, making them all feel connected, because he'd never let any of them leave Cambria. But it was still wonderful, this feeling that she belonged here with the other Zeroes. That she had allies who shared her deepest secrets.

Nate's power really was glorious, if you just let it work on you.

Of course, having Scam here made sinking into it a little weird.

"We'll use that bag of money to fix this," Nate was saying. "Get it back where it belongs and smooth this over."

Ethan was fighting him, squirming in his chair. "Yeah, but

money won't fix things with the cops. Or with my mom! And I totally earned this money. I'm not going to just give it to you!"

Nate was scribbling on his notepad: *Say something, Flick. He trusts you.*

"That money will just get you into trouble again," she said. "I'll keep it safe. So it's there when you need it."

Ethan was staring at her, the hopeful look on his face almost heartbreaking. Then Nate's eyes dropped to his pad again.

Thibault can hide him?

The name looked strange for a moment, until Nate glanced up into the back row.

Of course. That beautiful boy. Had she forgotten him *already*?

"Anon," she said. "You can take care of Ethan, right? Hide him somewhere until all this blows over?"

"Good thinking," Nate chimed in, as if it hadn't been his idea. "Just until we can fix things. He'll be safe with you."

Nate's gaze stayed on Anonymous, who let out a slow sigh.

"I guess I've got a place to park him. But it's not like I can keep him under control. Most of the time he won't even remember I'm there."

Flicker went into Scam's eyes, wondering how he felt about all this. He wasn't looking up at Anon. He was studying the wrestler doll with the blue head, its eyes and mouth outlined in silver.

"As long as Ethan's safe," Nate said, "while we figure out how to fix things."

"Yeah. Because we're so *awesome* at fixing things," Chizara murmured. She was staring at her own hands, her fingers rubbing at the lines on her palms, as if to wipe them away.

"Nataniel!" came a clear, bell-like voice from the doorway.

The others all looked up to see Nate's little sister Gabby standing there, a blue bath towel draped over her shoulders like a cape.

"Mamá says lunch is ready!" she said, then pirouetted once completely around and scampered off.

Everyone's eyes went to Nate, who smiled benevolently and said, "I'm sure you're all starving. This has been a challenging morning."

No one argued with that. Now that the dregs of her adrenaline had faded, Flicker realized how hungry it had left her, looking through a thousand eyeballs.

Sometimes it was these little gestures that made Nate glorious, even if his mother had made the food.

The others started to file out of the room, but Nate stayed. Flicker went into his vision again. He was writing notes to himself, things Thibault had said, the details of his clothes, even the way he sat. And now that she looked closer, she saw that Nate's notepad was balanced on a sheaf of papers. She saw more handwritten notes sticking out from the edges, and printed photographs.

Of course—this was how Nate always managed to remember Thibault better than the rest of them did. He might forget the person, but he remembered his own notes, the stories he told himself about Anonymous.

Which gave Flicker an idea.

She let the others leave, watching as Nate finished up.

Finally he slid the file beneath his chair and stood. "Shall we?"

She nodded and took his arm, let him guide her halfway down the hall.

But then she said, "Wait a second. The money's back there."

Nate shrugged. "It's fine."

Of course. Glorious Leader was the golden child of the house. No one touched his stuff without permission.

"But I want Ethan to see that I'm taking care of it."

"Right. Clever girl," Nate said. "I'll go get it."

Flicker drew him to a halt. "Don't get all helper monkey on me, Nate. Go say grace, before the rest of them scandalize your mother by eating unblessed food."

She unfolded her cane, staying in his eyes until he nodded.

"Okay," he said. "Sorry to make you hold the money, Flick. But the cops have my phone number. They might visit."

"Of course." She smiled at him. "Wouldn't want your political career ending before it starts."

"Yeah, but sorry it has to be you. It's just that Chizara's too fragile right now, and Ethan is Ethan. And Thibault . . . we don't even know where he lives."

Flicker smiled. That was the point in being Anonymous, she supposed.

She gave Nate a quick hug, though without the little kiss she'd used to place on his cheek. She couldn't do that anymore without imagining what Scam had said last year, even though she and Nate had never kissed in any other way.

Nate turned and headed down the hall, and Flicker made her way back into the theater. The duffel bag was easy to find. It smelled like beer and Ethan's nervous sweat.

She felt her way across the room, listening for any footsteps from the hall. Was this the chair that Nate had been sitting in? She reached beneath it and found the sheaf of papers.

She slipped the folder into the duffel bag, zipped it closed again, and hoisted it onto her shoulder. She wondered if Nate would be annoyed when he realized his notes were missing, or if he'd forget them completely. In any case, she was only borrowing them for a little while.

Long enough for her sister to read them aloud to her, to describe the photos, to make Anonymous real in the way that Lily made every story real.

Maybe her voice could finally stick that beautiful boy in Flicker's memory for good.

CHAPTER 23
MOB

DAD TOLD HER TO MEET HIM AT THE STADIUM.

He liked ball games, and Kelsie always went with him because she liked crowds. But there was no game today, no one around except a guy on a riding mower, making slow arcs in the stadium grass.

She spotted a lonely figure in the nosebleed section, two rows from the back. He wore a cap and sat hunched among the colorful plastic seats, invisible if you weren't looking for him.

Kelsie climbed the concrete stairs, so hot and dazzling in the afternoon sun. She really needed some sleep, and the emptiness dragged her down. Even the crowded streets outside, full of cops and anxious people, were better than the vast *nothing* of the stadium.

When she got to the top, her father looked the way she

felt—a thousand years older than yesterday. His stubble was gray on his sagging cheeks, and there were sweat stains on his shirt, which was black and long-sleeved, too heavy for the heat.

Kelsie's first words were, "Seriously, Dad."

He got to his feet and wrapped his arms around her.

"What were you thinking?" she said into his shoulder.

"I'm sorry, Kels."

She pulled away, her anger trying to spark. But exhaustion and relief won out.

"That's not an answer," she managed.

Her father shrugged, not meeting her gaze. "I needed the money."

"So you robbed a bank? What did you need *that* much money for?"

Dad shuffled along the row and sat down. He waited until she was sitting beside him. "I owe somebody."

"What?" Her mind was rolling, trying to take it all in. "Dad, you just broke out of a police station!"

"We didn't break out. I told you."

"The doors just opened, right." She shook her head. "That's nuts."

Her father spread his hands. "You think I shoulda stayed? With everybody running around in the dark? There was a cop near the cells, in an office full of TV screens. He got beat down. I couldn't stick around. Whoever came looking for us was going to be *pissed*."

"You think they'll be less pissed if they find you now?"

Dad gave her the look he used whenever she brought home her school grades. Kind of hurt and disappointed all at once. "It was my only chance. You think I'm better off in prison, only seeing my little girl through a plastic screen?"

That froze her. Dad had never really understood how crowds affected her. He just thought she was *sensitive*. But imagining a whole building full of desperate, violent men crammed between high walls of stone and razor wire, their rage held in check by clubs and guns and pepper spray, that was terrifying.

She could never set foot inside a place like that. She'd never see her dad again.

"Whose idea was this robbery, Dad? Yours?"

"It was this guy I owe, Nic Gargarin."

Kelsie frowned. She knew most of Dad's friends, at least by name. But no one called Nic.

"Came to Cambria early this year," Dad said. "With his uncle, a guy called Alexei Bagrov. They were looking to set up a base. They gave me a job."

"Then how come you owe *them* money?"

"It was that kind of job. They fronted me a few grand to start my own business."

"Doing what?"

He was quiet.

"Dad?" She waited. "You're selling drugs again. Don't even try to deny it."

He'd dealt before. Coke at the clubs, recreational amounts. But he'd always been scared of the people who sold in quantity. Her father was wired for day-to-day survival, not grand ambitions.

"How much money do you owe?" she asked.

"Thirteen grand."

"Oh my God." Her gaze fell, down to the playing field where the guy with the lawn mower was kneeling on the grass, tinkering with the engine.

"The stuff didn't sell. I was stuck owing the money."

Kelsie shook her head. This wasn't about money. "They carried a body bag out of the bank, Dad. What the hell happened in there?"

Her father didn't reply for a long time. He kept his gaze straight ahead, on the skyline beyond the home-run fence. "Hank got killed."

Kelsie felt exhaustion wash through her like a sudden summer downpour. She remembered Hank. A good guy. "Did you kill him?"

"Of course not." There were tears in Dad's eyes. "But it was my fault. He had my back."

Kelsie tried to keep her breathing steady. "What went wrong?"

"Nic told us the safe would be open, but we got locked out. We went to the backup plan—empty the tills and rob the customers. But there was this kid . . ."

His voice trailed off.

"A kid?" she asked softly.

"About your age. He started saying stuff. Weird stuff."

Her father looked scared. Not just old and defeated, but genuinely terrified. She wished she could take his fear away, the way she could ease the worry out of a crowd. But she was never good with anything one-on-one. "Like what, Dad?"

"He knew our names, and about Nic's arrest. He knew *everything.*"

Kelsie sat there, her hands gripped in her lap, waiting for it all to make sense.

Then something clicked.

"Did he have short hair? Like an army cut?"

Her dad's eyes widened. "Yeah."

"I saw him in the diner across the street. And after it was all over, two cops brought him out of the bank like he was someone special."

"So you know him."

"What?" She stared at her father. "How would *I* know him?"

"Because he knew you, Kelsie. He said your name."

CHAPTER 24
MOB

"NO WAY!" KELSIE FELL BACK INTO THE SMOOTH PLAS-tic of the stadium seat. "What does this have to do with *me*?"

Her father nodded slowly, like he was trying to work it out himself. "Only me, Hank, and Nic knew about the job, and we were wearing masks. But this kid lays there on the floor with my gun in his face, talking like he knows everything. Have you told any of your friends about me?"

"Nothing they hadn't figured out for themselves. And I didn't know anything about a bank job!"

"Right." He rubbed at his face. "And you'd never rat on your old man."

For a moment he seemed to be drifting off.

"Dad," Kelsie said with the sharp tone she used when he was high. "What else did this kid say?"

"He said you still miss your mom."

She just stared at him. The words seemed to echo in the emptiness of the stadium. The two of them didn't talk about her mother. Ever.

And right now, right after, seemed like a bad time to start.

"What else?" Kelsie managed after a while.

"He was talking like Nic had set us up, to get out of this drug charge a few months back. The cops let him go and nobody could figure why. And Nic only came to town this year. Nobody trusts him or his crew yet."

"And yet you were *robbing a bank with him*?"

"I owed them money." Her father sounded hollowed out, defeated. "But while the kid was talking, it all clicked into place. How I didn't really trust Nic, and how everything had gone wrong with the job. And then there were flashing lights outside, and I *knew* we'd been set up."

Kelsie shook her head. This wasn't her father talking. He was so easygoing; he wasn't paranoid even when there *were* people out to get him.

"So you *shot* him?"

"No! But I was yelling at Nic, and I used his name in front of all those people. That's when he pointed his gun at me. But Hank had my back."

It took Kelsie a moment to understand, but then a grim shiver of relief traveled down her spine. "They shot each other."

Her dad turned to stare at her. "Of course. You didn't think I'd hurt someone, did you? Geez, Kels."

She felt a faint smile on her lips. "I also never thought you'd rob a damn bank."

"Me neither," he sighed. "And it doesn't make sense anymore, what the kid said. I mean, cops setting up a bank robbery? Just to get *me*?"

Kelsie nodded. If the Cambria police were aware of her father at all, he was probably in last place on their most-wanted list.

"So Nic was the guy you owed money to?"

"His uncle, Alexei Bagrov." Her father's gaze traveled the empty stadium. "He's going to kill me. He's going to find me and kill me."

"Not if we get you out of town," Kelsie said, but it came out flat. Her father barely kept it together here in Cambria, where he knew everyone and most people liked him. He'd never survive in a strange city, pursued by both cops and gangsters.

She glanced around the stadium. It was completely empty now, apart from the two of them. The lawn mower sat alone in the middle of the field, its engine open to the elements.

She wondered if this was the last time she'd be with her dad like this. She pushed her hand into his, linking fingers and squeezing. Dad squeezed back.

"You gotta do me a favor, Kels. Go see Fig. He owes me a couple grand."

"Of course. That's enough to leave town, right?"

He looked away. "Just find Fig."

She nodded mutely, looking at her hands. Love and anger fought inside her with no outlet, no crowd to soak up what she felt.

"Okay," she said. "How do I get in touch with you?"

"I'll call." He put his arm around her shoulders, trying to smile. "You should stay with friends for a while. The police will be looking for me at home. And so will Bagrov."

Kelsie went cold despite the summer heat swelling up from the concrete stands.

Of course. If gangsters were after her dad, then they'd be after her, too. She felt sick and dizzy just thinking about it.

"But where will you stay, Dad?"

"I've got a few holes I can disappear into." He gave her that smile again. It was less convincing every time. "Promise me you won't go home until I got a way to fix this, okay?"

Hope twisted in her stomach. Maybe for once he had a plan. "Okay, I promise. But be careful."

"I'll be fine." Dad gave her a light punch to her shoulder, the way he always did when he had to leave home. Like he was heading out to some poker game.

When he got to his feet, Kelsie realized that she didn't want him to leave yet. She wanted to sit in the empty stadium and pretend a baseball game was going on below.

"That kid," he said, gazing into the middle distance. "Someone must have told him exactly what to say. *Someone* was out to get me, Kels."

She didn't disagree. Even Dad's friends spent most of the time angry at him.

Which meant there was even more to worry about than the cops and the gangsters Dad owed money to. Somebody else was after them. Some kid playing games with their lives.

"I'll talk to Fig tonight," she said. "See if anyone knows anything."

Her father smiled, his hand heavy on her shoulder. "Thanks, Kels. Sorry your old man's such a screwup."

She managed a smile. She didn't have the strength to argue.

CHAPTER 25

SCAM

ETHAN HAD THE DISTINCT IMPRESSION HIS LIFE WAS getting worse.

Not only did he have pissed-off drug dealers after him for stealing their bag of cash (and their car, come to think of it), he also had a homicidal bank robber (who was on the loose now, thanks to Chizara) hating him for messing up a heist. And then there were the cops wanting to grill Ethan about being buddies with said bank robber. On top of which he hadn't slept for thirty-something hours.

But worst of all, he had Glorious Leader giving him orders again, and taking his bag full of cash. *Hey, Scam, welcome back to the Zeroes. Say, have you heard about our new fee structure?*

What gave Nate the right to take the money anyhow? *He* hadn't been driven to a creepy cottage by a guy with no neck, or forced to listen to weird ramblings about "*doof-doof* music." Glorious Dickhead hadn't liberated the duffel bag from Taylor and the Craig, and from bank robbers, *and* from a police station, had he?

But here was Ethan, lying across the backseat of Nate's beamer, knees up, feet against the door, with no bag of cash to make up for the horror show of the last twelve hours. He wasn't even allowed to sit up like a normal person—Nate hadn't let them leave until Ethan was lying on the backseat, staring up at the car's ceiling and cursing the voice for ever calling his former friends for help.

Nate had acted like he was doing Ethan a favor, shipping him off to a hiding place. But he only cared about their powers staying secret. So why hadn't he come up with a rescue plan that didn't involve mass destruction of police property?

Chizara was overkill on two legs. Ethan's mother had a saying for the petty criminals she prosecuted: All they had were hammers, so everything looked like a nail. Chizara's problem was worse. She was a chain saw who thought she was a scalpel.

No doubt the police would *love* to hear how Crash had nuked the CCPD, and how it was all Glorious Leader's idea. The voice would give that story a *righteous* telling, if Ethan ever let it.

He rubbed at his face, which hurt from his jaw all the way up to his ears. Too much talking and too little sleep. Too much letting the voice yank his throat and his tongue. What he needed was a week in his bedroom with a stack of movies and a ton of easy-to-chew junk food.

All Ethan had wanted last night was to get home. If only he'd chosen some raver to bum a ride from, he would've been in his own bed before dawn. He'd probably still be asleep now, instead of hiding in the back of a car from a truly epic assortment of pursuers. A really comfortable car, sure, but not when you were lying across the backseat, heading for . . .

Wait, where *was* he heading?

Wait. Who was *driving*?

Ethan lurched up, scrambling for a grip on the front passenger seat. He hauled himself into a sitting position. Who the hell *was* that in the driver's seat?

Ethan's exhausted brain refused to click.

"Uh . . . ," he started.

The guy turned and gave him an annoyed look. "Keep your head down, will you? There's cops everywhere."

Ethan flopped back onto the car seat. Of course. The guy had given him the same *I hate you, Scam* look that Nate's crew all practiced daily. So it had to be him, the guy who was hard to remember.

Ethan lay there, trying to keep that fact in his mind: Anonymous was driving the car. There was something freaky about it, like being taken to another dimension. Ethan had no idea where they were going, or how long they'd been driving. Were they even still in Cambria?

What if the guy just dumped him by the side of the road a thousand miles away? Would Nate and the others even realize Ethan was gone? Or would he drop down the same memory hole as what's-his-name?

He had to focus, to get this guy on his side and find out where they were going. Even if his jaw already hurt like crazy.

Come on, tell this guy something he wants to hear.

"Sorry, Thibault," the voice said. "I must have dozed off."

At the sound of his own name, the guy jerked around to look at Ethan. The car swerved a little, shoving Ethan headfirst into the door. His head made a *thwack* against the handle, the impact reverberating all the way through to his sore teeth.

"Whoa," said the guy, turning back to the road. "Sorry. I don't drive a lot."

The car straightened out. Ethan reached up to rub the top of his bruised head.

"Yeah, I can tell, Thi—" Ethan began, but he couldn't work out how to say the guy's name. It had sounded French or something when the voice had said it.

He tried to visualize it in his head, as letters. Nope. Couldn't do it.

The guy chuckled. "What? Can't talk without help?"

"I can talk fine. Do you always swerve off the road when someone says your name?"

A shrug. "I was surprised you remembered, is all. But that wasn't you, was it?"

"Just trying to be polite." It was hard talking to the guy, especially without eye contact. Ethan's brain kept drifting away to the buildings slipping past the car windows.

"If you want to be polite, don't do that thing with me. No voice. Okay?"

"Happy not to." As Ethan reached up to rub his jaw again, he realized there was blue ink smudged into his palm. Right. Nate had made him write something there before they'd left.

It was the guy's name—*Thibault.* He tried to remember his one semester of French. The voice had been great at the oral exams. The written tests, not so much.

"Teebo?"

Thibault grunted. "Close enough."

The car slowed, rounding a corner, and then accelerated again.

Ethan squirmed around behind the passenger's seat, where he could keep his gaze on Thibault's profile. Even so, his eyes kept trying to slide away, like the guy was visual oil.

Ethan had to keep talking, or he'd forget who the guy was again and have another jolt of realizing he didn't know who was driving. Maybe he'd already had a whole series of mini freak-outs on this ride and had forgotten them all. As if the beamer's backseat was his own private hell.

He racked his brain for what the voice would say in this situation. Something charming.

"I like your shirt," he said.

The guy—*Thibault*, damn it—just glanced back at Ethan and rolled his eyes.

Crap. How did normal people keep up this conversation thing? Listening to the voice, it always seemed to Ethan like small talk was a bunch of horseshit. Why did everyone waste so much time on it?

He needed to say something *real*.

"Listen," Ethan said, then paused to check his hand. "Teebo, about last summer—"

"Are you using your voice?"

"No!" Seriously. This was like a conversation with his mother. "Can't you tell by now?"

"I can tell, Scam. But . . ." Thibault shrugged. "I just figure your voice could sound like you, if it wanted."

Ethan thought about this for a moment. "It's not that smart. It just knows what I want, and what people need to hear for me to get it."

"Well, what I want is for you to *not* use it," Thibault said. "See the problem? It could try to trick me."

"Yeah. Maybe." Ethan pressed a fist to his jaw, trying to push out some of the ache. He'd never thought about the voice pretending to be him, the *real* him. The thought was pretty scary, actually. "I won't let it do that, okay? I promise I won't use it on you."

"Are you sure? You seem to lose control sometimes."

"Well, kind of." Ethan frowned. "Wait. How do you know so much about it anyway?"

Thibault glanced back, smiling. "I know a lot about you guys. Especially you, Scam."

"Holy crap. Do you, like, *spy* on us?"

Thibault paused a moment, then said, "So what about last summer?"

Ethan's brain sputtered for a moment, wanting to hold on to what the guy had said just a second ago. It seemed important to remember. But the change of subject had knocked it out of his head, and he had to keep talking or completely forget what was going on.

"Yeah, last summer, when I dissed everyone. I'm sorry about that. I don't even know what I said, but Nate was being a pain, and I got really angry."

"You were a jerk, is what you were."

"Yeah, the voice . . ." Ethan shook his head. "*I* was a jerk. And I'm sorry."

The car eased to a stop at a traffic light. Thibault turned again to look at him. Ethan tried to give him a smile.

"Say that again," Thibault said.

"I'm sorry about what I said last summer. Whatever it was."

Thibault was quiet a moment, still watching.

"You're not using your voice," he said at last, like it was a fact.

"Nope. This is me talking."

"And you really don't remember what you said to me?"

"I don't remember half the stuff I say! It's like listening to the conversation at the next table, right? You can *hear* what they're saying, but most of it doesn't make enough sense to stick in your mind."

After a moment of silence, the traffic around them began to move again, and Thibault turned away.

"Sucks to be you," he said.

He was right about that.

CHAPTER 26

ANONYMOUS

IN THE ELEVATOR UP FROM THE PARKING LOT, Thibault felt Ethan's attention finally settle on him, sharp and focused. Elevators were good that way. Only a few square yards, nothing to look at but each other.

The lobby would be the tricky part.

"This place is pretty fancy," Thibault said. "And you look like a hobo."

Ethan glanced down at his shirt. A decent shirt, which was unusual for him, but sweaty and crumpled.

"I've never been inside a nice hotel."

"Just walk straight across the lobby," Thibault said. "Anyone looks at you funny, just remember: You *belong* here."

"Remember?" Ethan asked. "But isn't your superpower making people forget?"

Thibault sighed. "It's more complicated than that."

The doors slid open onto the Hotel Magnifique's spacious lobby, its marble floor a shiny lake with a thick, scroll-patterned carpet on the far bank.

They stepped out. The uniformed staff stood in the soft glow of their screens behind reception. Thibault knew them all by name, and he was glad to see that Janessa wasn't on this shift. She was a stickler about trespassers.

A couple of guests were getting checked in, and a few people lounged in the armchairs. A small group waited by the main door while the bellman, Tom Creasy, called for a cab out on the turnaround.

No cops, or anybody who looked like a drug dealer, so Ethan was safe from arrest or a beat-down. Which meant that he was really coming up to Thibault's room, invading his home.

Where was a revenge-crazed drug dealer when you needed one?

A few yards from the elevator, Thibault felt himself fading from Ethan's awareness. Shimmers of attention crisscrossed the open space like spiderweb threads, linking the crowd. Each group felt the flash of the others' conversations, reveled in the spark of shared laughter. But of all those simple human connections, none touched Thibault at all.

It was a seriously dick move on the part of the universe: Of everyone in this room, only he could see all those glimmers of awareness, feel them in his gut and as electricity on his skin.

But the glimmers never found him in return, not in any group bigger than a half dozen people.

That was what made him Anonymous.

Ethan, on the other hand, was lit up like a disco ball. He'd become the center of his own little web, throwing out a thousand strands of nervous awareness. Feeling out of place was a great way to get noticed.

The desk staff were looking now, the tendrils of their attention reaching across the lobby. They spared Thibault a glimmer of notice, which he chopped away with a flat hand. He'd learned as a little kid how hard it was to keep people's attention, but disappearing was always easy.

He grabbed a notepad and pen from the concierge's desk, scrawled his room number—*PH2*—and the words *Bellwether says go here.*

Ethan had drifted to a halt and was staring at the lobby's giant flower-and-twig arrangement. Five seconds' separation in the crowd, on top of all this unfamiliar luxury to gawk at, had erased any memory of Thibault.

"Scam!"

Ethan jerked back at the sound of his code name, then managed a puzzled look.

"Oh. You're that guy, right?"

"Read this," said Thibault.

Ethan took the note, saw Nate's code name. "Wait. This is a training exercise?" He had the sense to keep his voice low.

"You got it." Thibault pushed Ethan toward the main elevator bank. The guy was still walking too slowly, staring at everything with his mouth open, radiating a strong signal of not belonging. Useless.

To be fair, Thibault had lived in the Magnifique for three years now. He barely saw the place anymore, but back in the early days everything had screamed money and privilege and *What are you doing here, young man?* Even the cool, soft light felt expensive, falling through the draped windows onto the fat leather armchairs. The giant mirrors made it hard to tell exactly how big the lobby was, as if the luxury went cascading out into infinity around you.

It *was* pretty cool strolling into a place like this, living here, knowing how to navigate it all. But he could see how it could be intimidating. Especially if you looked like you'd slept in your clothes.

Just like Glorious Leader to think of every detail except lending Ethan a clean shirt.

It was almost a relief when Gerard left the concierge desk and glided across the marble toward them.

Thibault's first reflex was to appear out of nowhere and stage a collision. It had worked in the police station. But here it would only draw more attention, and Ethan had the voice, after all.

Thibault took a step backward into anonymity.

"Can I help you with anything, sir?" Gerard's tone was carefully neutral, but there was no mistaking it. He was ready to quietly muscle Ethan out of the place.

It wasn't Ethan who answered. All at once the nervousness slid off his face. He stood straighter, and his connection with Gerard thickened and brightened like a plasma lamp sparking toward a fingertip.

"My mother's here with the CADCOMP conference," the voice said, confident and crack-free. "I'm supposed to meet her outside the Lafayette Room."

The Lafayette Room. Thibault had heard the voice a hundred times, but there was something extra creepy about it knowing the details of this hotel, a place he'd kept secret from the other Zeroes. The place where he *lived.*

Gerard's expression relaxed into a smile, and his arms moved in practiced gestures. "Certainly. The Lafayette's on level four. Turn right out of the elevator."

"Thank you," said Ethan.

A curious flicker of Gerard's attention snagged on Thibault, who chopped it away and crossed the lobby after Ethan. The guy was tensing up again, turning back into—what had Flicker called him that time?—*that little rat-weasel.*

What a pain to be visible all the time, especially when you looked like Ethan, small and twitchy and crafty.

Thibault had once strolled through this lobby stark naked, just to see if he could. It had been way too easy. Turned out people didn't *want* to see the unexpected. Escaping anonymity wasn't as simple as stripping off his clothes.

Which was why keeping Ethan from wandering off was

going to be tricky. Even getting him to pay attention was exhausting.

As the two neared the elevators, laughter sprayed from the gilt-and-velvet couches in the hotel bar, a group having a few drinks before going out to hit Ivy Street. It was Friday afternoon, only a block from the nightclubs, the very place where Scam had stolen that money.

Thibault was going to have to keep him on a very short leash.

Why had he agreed to this nightmare?

Probably because at lunch, an hour ago, Glorious Leader had locked onto him with that anchor rope of charm, a hundred times stronger than the wavering strands Thibault managed with anyone else.

Nate could also see the shimmers of human interaction in the air. But his power was the reverse of Thibault's—he could amp those connections *stronger*, especially at a crowded table. He took the joy of a big group eating good food after a successful mission and *focused* it, until it felt like he was the only other person in the world, shining his glorious light on you.

And Thibault had fallen for the attention, like he always did.

That was the problem with wanting to be seen, the problem with *wanting* at all: Someone always used your desires to control you. You just had to look at Ethan: The voice's true power was that it knew what Ethan wanted. So as long as he kept wanting, he was its slave.

Thibault took a deep breath. It was all a reminder of the Middle Way—to face the world without desires. No good came from needing Nate's attention, or from fighting anonymity.

Wisdom says I am nothing. He repeated the Zen proverb under his breath.

The elevator came, and the two stepped in together.

Ethan stared at the handwritten note, then pressed the button for the penthouse floor. The light flickered on, off. He pressed it again. "What the hell?"

"Allow me." Thibault waved his key card.

Ethan backed off, startled. He watched Thibault slot the card and press the button. It stayed lit.

"Hey, thanks," Ethan said, as if to a helpful stranger. But as the doors closed, his flicker of eye contact settled into something real.

"Oh, right. It's *you*. Um . . ." He checked the name scrawled on his hand. "Teebo!"

Thibault took a slow breath, pushing his hair behind his ears. He was really taking another person into his hideaway, his fortress, his home. And out of everyone in the entire world, it had to be *this* person.

It was going to be a long weekend.

CHAPTER 27

FLICKER

"THE HERO OF OUR TALE HAS DARK HAIR, FALLING just above his collar. His eyes are sharp and blue, as if he's watching something carefully. Or perhaps some*one*."

Flicker smiled, not peeking, letting her sister's voice flow over her. When Lily read from graphic novels or picture books, she always began by describing the characters. Of course, this tale had only one character, and hardly any story at all.

"His parents are still together, it is believed. And he has two younger brothers, names unknown. But he seems to have left home three years ago, our Thibault, about the time his grandmother came to stay."

They were in the attic, surrounded by the musty smell of old boxes and dust. The air was hot with late afternoon. Muffled sounds of cooking came from below.

"He probably lives downtown, um, 'judging from response times.' In a hotel, some say. What *is* this, Riley?"

The threads of story fluttered away. "I told you, it's a file on someone."

"Is Nate stalking this guy? I mean, your boyfriend *is* kind of weird sometimes."

Flicker ignored this accusation. Lily had always been jealous of Glorious Leader—who wouldn't be?—and steadfastly refused to believe that Flicker had never even really kissed him.

"Anon's this guy we know," Flicker said. "Like, a friend. Nate keeps a file because we can't remember him."

"A friend you can't remember? Why the hell not?"

"Same reason I know you borrowed my striped socks today. Because superpowers. Now keep reading."

"I thought you were done with those guys after last summer."

"We're working it out," Flicker said. Lily was jealous of the others, as well. She didn't like sharing the secret of Flicker's power.

As her sister grumbled, Flicker let herself go blind again. Papers slid and shuffled on the wooden floor.

"Okay," Lily finally said. "No one knows where the hero of our tale lives. But he likes to take artsy photos of brick walls, and has good taste in clothes. I'm going to agree with Nate on that last one, but I wish he'd tuck his shirts in."

"What kind of shirts?"

"Why don't you just look, lazybones? I'm staring right at the photos."

Flicker shook her head. "Your voice will stick in my head better. If he's a character in a story, I won't forget. That's how his superpower works, I think."

"Does that mean I'm going to *forget* seeing these photos?"

"Of course not. But if you run into Thibault tomorrow, your brain won't make any connection between him and the pictures. Or something like that. If you're interested, there's a section called 'Theories' near the end."

Lily shuffled the papers again. Flicker hoped she wasn't getting the file out of order, but still didn't look. From being in the others' vision, she figured that part of Thibault's power had to do with how their eyeballs slid off him. It was as much about attention as memory.

Maybe if she didn't get caught up in *seeing* Thibault, his invisibility wouldn't matter so much. She would get to *know* him instead.

Her sister started reading again. The "Theories" section was mostly random questions and strategies for recording details. That was the key, Nate believed. If you made a habit of writing down things about Thibault, your brain would develop the reflex of coughing up whatever scraps it had stored.

But even Glorious Leader was always wondering how much he'd forgotten.

Flicker sighed. All these theories were telling her more about Nate than . . . damn. The name was gone again, and all she had was Anonymous.

"Wait," she interrupted. "This isn't sticking. Tell me a story. Any story, as long as it has elements of him. Details from the photos, or his family. Whatever might jog my brain the next time he's around."

"Um, okay." The sound of Lily's fingers drumming on the floor came through the heavy air. "Does it have to be realistic?"

Flicker smiled. "Of course not. You telling me fairy tales is pretty much the first thing I can remember. All memories are stories, kind of."

A soft "huh" came from Lily, as if this was a theory she could get behind. She'd had more fictional boyfriends than most.

"Can I make it a love story?" Lily said. "Like, make him hot, so he sticks in your *brain*?"

"I guess." Flicker managed to keep her voice even.

"Don't worry, Riley, I'll keep it PG. For now."

A hush fell over the attic, the sounds of cooking from downstairs fading, the tree branches settling around them.

"Once there was a girl named Riley," the story began. "Her heart was a secret garden, its stone walls cracked and weathered. And it was hungry."

Lily went on, telling a story borrowed from a dozen books and TV shows and movies. And slowly her voice began to change. Her lips began to form the words in that old familiar way, with the soft burr of their shared native tongue.

When the twins had been little, even before Riley's power had revealed itself, they'd spoken a language no one else could understand. It had been lost along the way, but sometimes the old patterns came back, their *r*'s softening in their mouths. At times it was strong enough that people would ask if they'd overcome a speech impediment. But what they had was an *accent*, long buried and shared by only two people in the world. . . .

"And one day she met a boy called Nothing, who lived in a secret castle, and she began to learn his ways."

CHAPTER 28
ANONYMOUS

"DUDE. THIS ROOM *KILLS*."

Thibault watched from the doorway, smiling at the wide-eyed look on Ethan's face as he took in the padded leather club chairs, the wall sconces fanning light up onto the textured wallpaper, and the picture window full of ocean and late-afternoon sun.

"I know," Thibault said, a little ashamed. "It's kind of too much."

"Too much? It's insane! I didn't know people this rich ever *came* to Cambria!"

"They don't, usually. These penthouse rooms mostly stay empty. That's why I live up here. So the hotel doesn't lose any money."

Ethan nodded slowly at the view out the picture window.

For a moment his attention seemed gone for good. But then he turned, one eyebrow lifted. "Doesn't lose money? You mean you're not paying for this place? You're *scamming* it?"

Thibault blinked. Ethan had the gall to throw that word at someone else?

"No one else is using it," Thibault said carefully. "I'm not stealing anything, just borrowing."

Ethan laughed. "Nice work, dude. It's so huge! The only hotel I ever stayed in, the beds took up the whole room. Where *are* the beds, anyway? Oh, I guess in here, right?"

As Ethan walked into one of the suite's bedrooms, Thibault felt himself disappear, snipped from existence by the wall between them. Ethan's voice faded into muttering, as if he'd only been talking to himself all along.

Thibault sighed. His ego always felt the burn, even if it was just Scam forgetting him.

Maybe they should switch to a smaller room. But the hotel was filling up as the big Fourth of July celebrations got closer, and anywhere bigger than an elevator would make him just as hard to see.

"You hungry?" Thibault called.

That got the guy's attention. He stuck his head out, looking puzzled for a moment. But then a big grin crossed his face, his memory of Thibault flickering back to life.

"Dude." He glanced at his palm. "Teebo, I mean. I could totally *slay* a hamburger."

* * *

It had been a long time since Thibault had ordered room service. There was no way to call it "borrowing." It was out-and-out theft.

He usually lifted unsold sandwiches and salads from the deli down the street, or overages from the farmers' market. But Thibault couldn't leave this room until Glorious Leader figured out the next step. Looking after Ethan was a full-time job, like having a kid. A kid with attention deficit disorder and half the city's gangsters and cops hunting him.

So they'd have to make do with what was on hand. Luckily, that was a fully staffed kitchen, anxious to satisfy the guests' every whim.

As they waited for the food to arrive, Ethan played with the bank of light switches by the door, the TV remote, and the electric window blinds.

Then he found the minibar.

"Teebo! What the hell! Why didn't you tell me about this?"

"Um, it's kind of tricky, replacing stuff from—"

But Ethan was already tearing open a Toblerone bar.

Thibault closed his eyes and took a slow breath, practicing stillness for a moment.

"You didn't forget about that burger on its way, did you?" He'd made Ethan watch as he logged into the hotel's network to place the order, so the fact that food was coming would stick in his mind.

"You said it would take half an hour, man," Ethan said with his mouth full. He strolled to the window. The ocean was glittering with the afternoon sun, just visible beyond the skyline of Cambria. "You must feel like you're the boss of everything, sitting up here."

"Not exactly," Thibault said. Was there any point explaining the Middle Way to this guy? If anyone needed some Zen in his life, it was Ethan. But whatever Thibault told him would slip out of his head.

Maybe if it was simple enough. "This room isn't mine, Ethan. Neither is that view. No one owns the sunset."

Ethan eyed the view, then laughed. "Dude. Anyone rich enough to shell out for this room *totally* owns the sunset. So how does your scam work? Do you just, like, turn invisible when real guests show up?"

Thibault stifled a sigh. No luck with Zen. But maybe superpowers would stay in Ethan's head. "I'm not invisible. People just have trouble focusing on me, and they forget me when they look away. Like a person walking behind you on a crowded street. You know someone's there, but you don't *think* about it."

"No kidding. Hanging out with you is like having a ninja around. You're always sneaking up on me!"

"That wouldn't happen if you *focused*." The last word came out sharply enough that Ethan's attention sizzled in the air. But shouting wasn't the answer. "I have a system here. I keep track of the hotel bookings, and move out if anyone reserves this room."

"So you hack their computers? Like when you ordered the food?"

"I just watch and learn. When it's busy enough at the front desk, people don't notice me, even if I'm looking over their shoulders."

"Pretty cool." Ethan took another bite of chocolate. "So you've really got this place worked out, huh?"

Thibault shrugged and turned away, letting their connection waver. He hadn't brought Ethan up here to show off his power. The point of teaching wasn't to feed your own ego.

But it *was* pretty cool, all his quiet observation of the staff, the protocols, the schedules. And at least his explanations were keeping Ethan focused, which made the guy less likely to wander out into the arms of hotel security.

"Getting a room is easy," Thibault said. "The tricky part is making sure I don't cost the hotel too much. Or add any work for the staff."

"You mean you clean your own room?" Ethan pulled back the chocolate bar wrapper, laughing.

"Chop the wood, carry the water," Thibault said. A little more Zen for Ethan to forget.

"Seriously? You scrub the toilet just so you can pretend you aren't stealing anything?"

Was that the voice, winding up for an attack? Thibault felt

a trickle of panic, but their connection was only the scratchy grabbing of an argument, not the talon grip of the beast. This was Ethan talking. He was keeping the promise he'd made in the car.

But he was still being a dick.

Thibault said evenly, "I don't pretend."

"All you guys pretend. You call me Scam, but Glorious Leader controls people's minds, and Flicker hijacks people's eyes—even the *government* doesn't do that. And look at this." He flung out an arm at the magnificent sunset. "You live rent-free in the sky! Crash might be a walking disaster zone, but at least she *admits* it when she's breaking the law."

"I know this is illegal." Thibault still kept his voice steady. "But it's not like I can get a job. And I control the effect I have on the people who work here."

"Well, aren't you lucky?" Ethan's sarcastic look was spoiled a little by the smear of chocolate at one corner of his mouth. "All in control of your power! Me, I've had this thing talking through me my whole life, and I *never* know what's going to happen next. Crash, too. We've got these frickin' fire hoses, and we're just hanging on to the handles. You and Flicker and Nate have got it *easy*!"

White-hot anger flashed through Thibault. This little rat-weasel thought being anonymous was *easy*? After what his voice had said last summer, in front of the whole group?

Of course, Ethan didn't remember that. If he listened to

his voice, then he'd have to take some responsibility for what it said.

Thibault managed to stay calm, but his throat felt tight. "I don't control my power. I can't *turn it off*."

"Sure you can! We're sitting here talking, aren't we?"

"That's because we're alone. If there were a few more people in this room, there'd be too many competing signals, too many other people to focus on." The sneer was dying out on Ethan's face. "Remember down in the lobby? I could barely get you to listen to me."

Ethan was listening now. All the scratchiness had gone out of their connection. "So you're like Nate and Chizara—stronger in a crowd?"

"Flicker, too. With more eyes around, she sees more. Yours is the only power that works best one-on-one." Thibault bit back the words "you freak." Compassion was the Way. "Even up here, when you wander into another room, you forget me."

"So you can't control it at all?"

"If I need to disappear, I can snip whatever connection there is." He made the chopping gesture across his face, holding eye contact so Ethan would feel the break but not lose him altogether. "But I can't turn my power off. People always forget me in the end. Do you have *any idea* what that means?"

Ethan looked blank. He really didn't remember what he'd said last summer.

Fine. Let him sit there and think about what anonymity

meant. It had taken Thibault thirteen years to figure out. Thirteen years to realize that he had to leave home, because trying to get his family to remember him only made it all hurt worse.

Of course, even if Ethan did understand, half an hour from now he'd lose it again. Thibault could explain ten times over how completely alone he was, but it wouldn't stick.

The only other creature in the world that would ever know Thibault was the voice, that beast inside Ethan. And it didn't really *know* anything, except as a means to further Ethan's desires.

Thibault flashed back to last summer at Nate's, to the same room they'd met in this afternoon. Nate had said something to piss Ethan off, and then Ethan had started venting on the others. There in the back row, Thibault had foolishly thought he was safe. There were five people in the room, usually enough to make him Anonymous.

But then Ethan's angry gaze crawled up and caught on him, like two hooks through Thibault's face into the person behind, the one that nobody ever truly saw. Without missing a beat, the voice tore straight into that *kid* inside him, like a hyena wrenching out chunks of flesh.

It hurt, but at the same time something inside Thibault—his younger self, always hungry for a solid connection—took a weird delight in the attack. Another person was looking into his eyes, knowing him, speaking his most private memories. It was everything Thibault had ever wanted: to be seen, to have his *insides* seen, to be understood.

But then the hyena's teeth had gone too deep, opening a vein of secrets Thibault didn't want to think about: those days in the hospital when he was thirteen years old—feverish, alone, thirsty, forgotten by the nurses. By his own mother.

That terrified, trapped kid had *hated* humanity for shutting him out. That kid was still inside this other, older Thibault who had found his own anonymous way within the Way.

And it could happen again, if Ethan lost his temper and lashed out. Sharing this penthouse with him was like living with an unexploded bomb.

A knock came on the door, and Thibault flinched, imagining police on the other side. Or angry drug dealers. Or Nate with a *finally found you* smile on his face.

Ethan had jumped as well, but now he laughed. "Dude. It's just the burgers."

"I know." Thibault pointed at the extra bedroom. "But you should hide."

"Why? Nobody in this hotel knows the cops are looking for me."

"Yeah, but if anyone sees you, they'll remember someone was in the penthouse. Me, they'll forget once I close the door. You got any cash?"

Ethan frowned. "Doesn't it go on the room?"

"Not really. Once I get back on the hotel network, this meal never happened. We have to tip cash or the staff gets nothing."

"Oh, right. Mr. Morality." Ethan laughed, handing over

a twenty. "Whatever. Lucky I kept a big wad of the Craig's money. 'Bellwether' isn't as smart as he thinks." He disappeared into the bedroom, a swagger in his walk.

It was Chuck at the door, a big guy with a smile as broad as his shoulders.

"Just leave it here inside the door," Thibault said, handing over the twenty. Today he didn't have time to hear for the fifteenth time how Chuck had played college football, blowing out his knee senior year.

Thibault pocketed the check, got Chuck outside, and snipped the connection just in time. As the door swung shut, Ethan came wandering out of the bedroom, looking dazed and uncertain.

"Who the hell are *you*?" he said.

Thibault took a slow breath. *No one and everyone, buddy. Just like you.*

"My name's written on your hand," he said. "Hope you're still hungry."

CHAPTER 29

MOB

"YOU LOOK FUNNY," LING YELLED OVER THE MUSIC. "Never seen you jumpy in a club before."

Kelsie tried to smile. She didn't know how to explain that her dad had robbed a bank and she was hiding from mobsters. And Ling didn't watch the news.

"Just tired. Didn't make it home today, so I had to sleep at Remmy's."

Ling laughed. "If you can call that sleeping."

"Hey," Remmy yelled from across the table. "My dorm room is five-star!"

Kelsie had to smile at that. When she'd showed up at Remmy's that afternoon, saying she needed to crash, he hadn't asked any questions. He'd just said, "Stay as long as you want.

There's no food and the TV's busted." Then he'd headed out to a math study group.

His bed was comfortable enough, but sleep wasn't easy. Her dad was facing life in prison, and she'd been made homeless by the threat of mobsters. At least final exams were over, and the dorm's mellow summer-term buzz had watered down Kelsie's anxiety.

That was why she'd dragged Remmy and Ling to the Boom Room tonight. Even with her life turned upside down, Kelsie always found safety in numbers.

The Boom was an old-fashioned place with live music and a young crowd. It played roots, blues, soul and funk, and maybe some Tejano rock or bluegrass. It had a canopied doorway and a wide, guitar-shaped sign on the roof. No self-respecting gangster would be caught dead here in a million years.

Kelsie didn't always like the music at the Boom, but she trusted the crowd. Maybe it was the live music, full of feedback loops between band and audience. Or maybe the folks here just knew how to have a good time. It was where Kelsie went when she needed to feel safe.

It was also a good place to find Fig, who owed her dad three thousand dollars. The Boom was the first place Fig had taken Kelsie when he found out she loved dancing in a crowd. Fig was about halfway between Dad's age and hers, and had somehow managed the trick of being friends with both of them.

Fig was always good at steering Dad away from anything too dangerous or stupid. Kelsie was pretty sure her father hadn't asked for Fig's thoughts on the whole bank-robbery idea.

Fig wasn't at the Boom, but at eleven he'd be bartending at Fuse next door.

Until then, there was nothing to do but dance.

"Come on, fess up," Ling said a few songs later. "You got a stalker or something?"

Kelsie shook her head. But she kept scanning the crowd, looking for that guy from the diner. The guy with the duffel bag who'd gotten inside her dad's head and made the robbery go wrong. How had he known her name?

It had to be from the clubs.

"A stalker?" Remmy yelled over the music, and turned to Kelsie. "There somebody you need beaten up?"

He flexed a bicep, and Kelsie just laughed and shoved him toward the mosh pit at the front of the throwback hard-core band onstage. Three chords and three minutes per song, about a billion beats a second.

She couldn't drag anyone else into this business of her dad's. They were all her friends, Remmy and Mikey and Ling and a dozen others. But she'd never opened up to any of them, not one-on-one. She wasn't wired that way.

Her dad had always warned her against too much trust. Trust was tricky when your life was one con after another.

And she'd started helping him when she was ten years old.

He'd never realized what his little girl was doing—she wasn't sure herself, at first. But she knew it was real. She could nudge a poker table into a cheerful carelessness that made them bet high. She could defuse a group's anger when they realized they'd been scammed. Dad called her his lucky charm.

But that same power also tanked her school grades, because every exam was like drowning in a room full of other people's fear, no matter how hard she studied. And her power was the reason she'd never had a boyfriend or a girlfriend. Not even a best friend.

Because crowds were always *better*.

This close to the stage Kelsie was bumped and jostled, knocked and pushed. But it felt good. Every time she spun around, people were smiling, mouthing the words *sorry* or *my bad*. She was only sorry there weren't more people banging into her.

That guy in the diner had known her name. And he'd mentioned her mom.

That wasn't just stalking. That was reading her mind. Getting inside her head, where no one was allowed.

What if he was in this room, watching her?

Kelsie took the energy of the crowd and ramped it up. She unleashed all her anger and fear and channeled it out of herself. She bounced it off the people in the room, turned it into pure heat and power.

The energy on the dance floor ballooned, pulling her away

from everything Dad had told her, everything he'd done to ruin their lives.

The music pulsed faster than any heartbeat, as fast as nervous twitches or neurons firing. Kelsie slipped into the center, becoming one with it and all the bodies around her.

She shut her eyes and danced it out, teased and bumped and shook to the beat and the power of the mob. She hadn't felt safe all day, ever since she'd seen Dad in that blue car by the bank. But she was safe here, in the heart of this storm.

A roar went up and she opened her eyes. A reedy guy in jeans and no shirt teetered at the edge of the stage. A hundred hands reached up and he jumped, then drifted across the room on a surface of sweaty palms. There was a sudden focus in the crowd, all their energies surging up through that one body held aloft like a sacrifice.

Kelsie sent her anxiety into that buoyant hub of sweat and muscle and *pushed* . . .

The guy soared now, carried by the crowd and Kelsie's will. She shut her eyes, sensing his passage through the fingertips of the crowd. She pulled him in a circle, a rock in a sling, faster and faster as the music built toward the climax of another three-minute song.

"Jesus," she heard Ling say, and opened her eyes.

The guy slid frictionlessly, as if those sweaty palms beneath him were ice. His face was pale, his mouth open in a scream lost in the music.

"Oh, God," Kelsie said, and her grip on the crowd sputtered. The guy slipped among the outstretched arms, crashing to the floor at speed.

The song came to a sudden end, one of those hard-core stops like someone had stabbed the mute button. The guy stumbled out of the crowd, bleeding and astonished.

Kelsie ran after him. Detached from the surrounding buzz, she felt all her anxiety tumbling back down on her.

"I'm sorry. I'm so sorry," she kept saying.

By the time they reached him, he was throwing up in the corner. The people around him were in retreat, laughing or horrified, no longer united by the strange power of Kelsie's magic.

Ling was right beside him, her hand on his gleaming back. "Dude. You okay?"

The guy wiped his mouth with the back of his hand. As he turned to look up at Ling, Kelsie spotted the exact moment when he saw how beautiful she was.

"I'm good," he managed. "How's it going?"

That was boys for you, whenever they saw Ling.

It looked like all he had was a nosebleed. Kelsie felt her relief echo in the crowd around her. A barback had already started mopping up the vomit.

Ling said, "I'll get him some water. Want a drink?"

Kelsie shook her head. Drinking only made her sleepy, and she didn't need to sleep; she needed to be up. Just maybe not as up as she'd been a minute ago.

"Sorry about that," she said to the guy. "Glad you're okay."

He looked at her blankly. That was the thing about not trusting anyone—nobody knew this was all her fault.

And that moment of focus while he'd surfed the crowd . . . that had been amazing. She'd forgotten everything that scared her.

Kelsie needed strength tonight, and this was definitely the place to get it. She just had to be more careful.

The guy was climbing back to his feet, already twitching to get on the dance floor again. So as the first note of the next song struck, Kelsie took a deep breath and threw herself back into the crowd. She took its energy and pushed higher, keeping the dancers banging. Her anger and fear was slowly turning into something clear and hard, like ashes crushed into a diamond.

Sometimes the effort gave Kelsie head spins and she stumbled and fell. But somebody caught her; somebody always caught her.

Maybe she could get through this. She just needed to find her crowd.

CHAPTER 30
SCAM

"PREPARE TO DIE!" ETHAN CRIED, LEANING FORWARD on the couch, his thumbs flying across the controller. He was back in the Gold Palace at last, one boss fight away from the Transmog Apple.

The Grand Vizier began his endless entrance speech. Ethan skipped past it, then launched a fusillade of missiles and spells.

The battle was fast and furious, the Vizier's lightning versus Ethan's fire, blue magic versus red. But Ethan was *supreme* at this game.

Not the greatest boss fight ever, pure thumb twitch, but satisfying. Ethan still couldn't believe his luck that this hotel room had *Red Scepter III*.

But then something weird happened.

That little elf—the annoying one from a few scenes back—

showed up in the throne room and started pinging away with his bow. Before Ethan could react, two vampire arrows were sunk in his back, each of them leaching a life point every second.

"What? Wait!" He tried to spin and return fire, but the Vizier was still spitting out lightning. . . .

And suddenly Ethan was dead.

The next arrow whistled through his fading form and struck the weakened Grand Vizier, who crapped it on the spot. And the little elf went dancing past their corpses to grab the Transmog Apple.

"No way!" What was *wrong* with this hotel game system? Nonplayer characters weren't supposed to *win*. Had it reset itself to expert mode again?

Ethan went to the startup menu. But it wasn't set to expert.

It was in two-player mode.

"What the . . ."

"Owned again!" came a voice from beside him. "Exact same spot!"

Ethan jumped halfway off the couch, astonished to find someone sitting right next to him. Adrenaline shot through his system, all his game-world anxiety exploding into reality.

It was . . . that guy. *Again.* There was something Ethan was supposed to do now—a joystick fighting move baked into his reflexes.

He glanced at his hand. A name was written there.

"Thibault." It came rushing back. "You cheated, man!"

"Not hardly!" Thibault laughed. He was pale, with dark hair and intense blue eyes. He looked more familiar every second.

"But I thought you were some random elf!" As he said the words, Ethan realized that this had all happened before. Every time he sank too far into the game, his awareness of the world around him faded, along with his awareness of his opponent.

"Them's the rules." Thibault held out a piece of hotel stationery. Written on it was an agreement in Ethan's own handwriting. Thibault scored a point every time his wussy elf got the Transmogrification Apple, even if Ethan forgot what was going on.

At the bottom was the score: seven to zero.

"This game sucks," Ethan said.

Then he remembered the rest of it—he was being pursued by the cops, the Craig, and a deranged bank robber. On top of which he was staying in this luxury hotel room illegally.

He looked nervously at the door. "Crap. Was I too loud?"

"No one's staying on this floor but us." Thibault shrugged, put down his controller. "But yeah, maybe we should hit the sack. It's almost eleven."

"Eleven?" Ethan looked up at the clock on the kitchenette wall. "At *night*?"

The last thing he remembered was eating a burger that afternoon.

What if living with Thibault was giving him brain damage? All those slices of time being snipped out . . .

And then it hit him.

"Damn. It's been over twenty-four hours since I talked to my mom! She's going to kill me if I don't call her. Lend me your phone? Chizara nuked mine."

"Mine too," Thibault said tiredly, like they'd already had this conversation. "I was there, remember?"

"Right. Then I'll use the . . ." Ethan turned to the table next to the couch. The big plastic handset of the hotel phone was there, covered with buttons for room service and laundry, and also with a note:

Don't use the phone. —Bellwether

"What?" Ethan asked. "Why the hell not?"

Thibault sighed again. "Have you forgotten that bad people are looking for you?"

"No, but my mom must be too! It's been a whole day. She's going to panic and call the cops!"

"She *is* the cops, Ethan. She can get a call traced, and you're wanted as a material witness. So no calls from here!"

"Okay, okay." Ethan stood up and headed for the door. "I'll go down to the street and borrow someone's—"

On the door was another note:

Stay in this room until further notice! —Bellwether

Ethan rubbed at his scalp. "Why are there notes from Nate everywhere?"

"Because you keep forgetting *that I exist*!" Thibault came around in front of him, staying in his view, keeping between him and the door. "You have to stay out of sight. The cops want you, and so does that dealer you stole the money from. We're only a block from Ivy Street, where this all started!"

"Yeah, but I'm wearing different clothes." Ethan wondered if this was true, and looked down. Yep. Some part of him had remembered Thibault lending him a shirt. A really nice one. "I may not be as invisible as you, but my face doesn't exactly stick in people's minds, you know?"

"Still not a good idea, Ethan. If you want, *I* can go down and borrow a phone to call her. But you stay here."

"Right. My mom's gonna *love* that, some stranger phoning her, saying, 'I've got your kid, lady. Trust me, he's okay, but he can't talk to you.'"

Thibault frowned. "Maybe not my best plan. But you can't leave this room. The last time the cops picked you up, we had to vaporize every computer in the CCPD to get you out!"

Ethan swore. The whole insane rescue plan hadn't been *his* idea.

"Just let me leave a message for her. With everything that happened at the police station today, she won't even be home."

"Tomorrow morning," Thibault said. "When angry drug dealers are all in bed."

Ethan groaned. Tomorrow was too late. It was too late *already*. If his sister, Jess, found out he'd disappeared for a whole day, she'd kick his ass all the way from Afghanistan.

There was an itch in his throat—the voice ready with some

devastating insult to paralyze Thibault where he stood. The guy might think he was Mr. Zen, but the voice always knew how to crumple anyone with even a sliver of self-doubt. . . .

"Don't you *dare*," Thibault said.

Ethan swallowed hard, forcing the voice all the way back down his throat. "Relax. I promised you I wouldn't. I can call her tomorrow."

Thibault didn't move. "Are you sure?"

"Yeah. I just need some sleep."

Thibault nodded. "I guess we both do."

Ethan managed a tired smile. His throat felt like he'd swallowed a paperweight, but at least he'd kept his promise to Thibault. The voice had done enough damage today.

Plus, Ethan had a better idea.

He said good night and headed toward the door to the suite's smaller bedroom, repeating his plan to himself again and again. He broke it down to a series of actions, nothing to do with . . . that guy. Or anyone, really.

It was just a list of things he had to do.

Ethan went into his bathroom and drank one glass of water after another, until he was certain that his bladder would wake him up in a couple of hours. And before crawling into bed, he took a pen from his bedside table and wrote on the notepad . . .

Go down to the street and call Mom.

Be as quiet as you can.

Ignore the fucking notes.

CHAPTER 31
MOB

FIG WAS ALWAYS EASY TO SPOT. HE WAS BARELY five feet tall and wore a white T-shirt that glowed blue in Fuse's lights. He ate only protein and worked out two hours every day.

Kelsie gave him a brief wave as she approached the bar. She still sizzled from the Boom, like she could fly across the crowd herself. The music here was sharper, a fierce stab of electronica with a thudding undertow of drum. Kelsie felt it in the soles of her feet and in the hollow cavity of her chest.

But the sight of Fig's expression brought her back to reality.

Her dad was in trouble. And so was she.

"Kelsie." Fig shook his head, lips pursed. "How you doing, kid?"

She climbed onto an empty bar stool and pushed up from the bottom rung. "Not so good."

Fig picked up a glass and started polishing. His deep voice cut through the music. "What a train wreck. Cops everywhere, looking for the guys who escaped. Your dad okay?"

Kelsie settled back onto the bar stool and nodded, not wanting to shout.

I saw him, she mouthed.

Fig's expression stilled. Years of working in Fuse had made him an expert lip-reader. He scanned the room. Then he put the glass down and gestured her toward a door at the end of the bar.

Kelsie followed him into a cramped, badly lit hallway. The flimsy walls shivered with the music.

"Saw the news at the gym," Fig said. "Your dad's photo came up, I almost face-planted on the treadmill. You know he was planning this?"

"Of course not."

"Ain't that some crazy shit?" Fig shook her shoulder. "I would've broke his arm to stop him."

Kelsie nodded, unable to talk. Here in this empty hallway, away from the safety of the crowd, her dread was an icicle in her chest.

"And that computer thing at the police station," Fig said. "So much *weird* today."

"Yeah." Kelsie glanced at the closed doors in the hallway, hoping no one was listening. His bar jobs might've made Fig good at lip-reading, but his hearing was terrible. His voice boomed even when he was whispering. "Is there somewhere . . ."

Fig led her into a crowded storeroom, packed with beer kegs and shelves of stacked glasses, piles of ledgers and receipts. At the far end of the room was a desk. A big guy sat there with his back to them, counting money into a bag.

"Don't mind him," Fig whispered loudly. "There's nothing he hasn't heard before."

"Okay." Kelsie let out a breath. "My dad needs that money you owe him."

"I'll bet. I was sorta holding it for him. Until he got out from under with the Bagrovs."

The guy at the desk stiffened, still with his back to them. "Those *shitheads*!"

Fig didn't seem to notice. "Your dad hasn't told you any of this, I guess."

Kelsie shook her head. "Not till today."

"New in town. Into drugs, gambling, the whole deal. *Really* ticked off the local establishment."

He glanced toward the guy at the desk, who Kelsie figured was part of the local establishment.

She'd always known that side of the dance scene. She could tell when a new drug came to town. It changed the flavor of the crowd, made it light and airy or hard and mean. Chemicals had never been her thing.

It must have shown on her face, because Fig gave her a half smile and said, "Not all of us are naturals like you. Some of us need that extra *oomph*."

"I'm not judging." She held up both hands. "Can we stay on topic?"

"Sorry. Your dad always talked about moving up." Fig looked disgusted. "But the stuff the Bagrovs got him selling? Worst drugs on the street."

Kelsie felt the last strand connecting her to the feel-good dance crowd snapping. "Heroin?"

"I wish. Stuff's called krokodil. Dissolves your body."

"Wait. What?" Kelsie glanced at the guy at the desk. He was still counting cash as if they weren't there, totally focused.

"It's made from acid," Fig said. "Like, literally. Your skin rots away where you inject it. You're walking around and people can see your *bones*. Then your liver gives up."

"That sounds crazy, Fig. Like something they'd make up to scare kids."

"I seen it happen."

Kelsie felt herself breathing harder. "My dad would never sell anything *that* bad."

Fig shrugged. "Probably didn't know what he was getting into. The Bagrovs aren't exactly known for long-term relationships, you know? Can't settle too long with a product that kills people. That's why they came to Cambria. They needed new customers."

And new employees, like her dad, Kelsie realized. Disposable people to do their dirty work.

"I can't believe he'd do something that stupid," she said.

"Yeah," Fig said sadly. "But didn't he rob a bank today?"

Kelsie stared at the floor. Sure, her dad had been running cons as long as she could remember, but she could've sworn blind that he would never rob a bank or kill anyone, with a shotgun or a needle.

"Listen, Kelsie. I can get you that three grand tomorrow. If you need a place to stay, you're welcome at mine."

"I'm staying with friends," she said, and Fig frowned protectively. She gave him a grateful smile. "But maybe. Depends how long before I can go home, I guess."

"Things'll get back to normal. In the meantime, if you need anything . . ."

"There's one other weird thing," Kelsie said, "that maybe you know about. My dad said there was a kid in the bank, my age. He knew all their names, like he was waiting for them there."

"No way." Fig shook his head. "That job was *tight*. Everybody was shocked when the news hit."

But at the desk, the other guy in the room had frozen. A fifty-dollar bill was in his hand, clutched so tight his fingers had turned white.

Slowly he swiveled in his chair and fixed Kelsie with a piercing blue stare.

"Did you say a kid?" the man asked. "At the bank?"

"Yeah?"

The guy became perfectly still. It was uncanny, because

she could've sworn he hadn't been moving anyhow. But then he must've stopped moving some more. Maybe he'd stopped breathing.

Then he rose to his feet. Slowly, like it took a huge effort to lift his body. He squeezed through the storeroom toward them, turning sideways so he could fit his shoulders between the shelves and the kegs.

Kelsie backed as far as the narrow space would allow her. It was like watching a truck coming right at her on the emptiest street in the world.

Even with Fig next to her, Kelsie felt her fear building, flowing out and into the crowd down the hallway. She felt it swirling into the people listening to the synthesized rattle and hum that shook the shelves to either side of the advancing wall of flesh.

"Craig," Fig said, "this is my good friend Kelsie."

Craig ignored him. "You know that kid? The one from the video?"

"The video?" Kelsie turned blankly toward Fig and then back to Craig. No one spoke.

It had been a really confusing day already, so she took it slow. She made sure to speak very carefully, because she didn't want to miss any details about this guy who'd screwed up her dad's life.

"Um, Craig?"

"That's me," he replied. "And I'm asking, *do you know the kid in the bank video?*"

Kelsie took a breath. "What video?"

CHAPTER 32
ANONYMOUS

THIBAULT WAS GOING TO DIE IN THIS HOSPITAL.

He'd known it as soon as they'd put him in this crowded children's ward. His connection with Mom was fading fast.

"Don't leave me!" he wept from his bed. "Don't go away!"

"I've got your brothers to get off to school tomorrow," she said, already looking at the door. "It's their first day back."

"There are too many people here!" He knew he'd disappear. He'd explained it to her so many times, but she never remembered.

"The nurses will take care of you, honey." His mother bent and kissed him, and tried to pull away.

He grabbed her arm and hung on for dear life. "You'll forget me!"

"That's just the fever talking. You'll be home again in a day or two, Thibault. We'll visit you tomorrow."

"You won't."

A passing nurse paused, stared at them both. "You're a big boy to be acting like this, aren't you?"

Embarrassed, Thibault had let go of his mother's arm. She'd left the ward without looking back.

And of course she hadn't come back.

The fever got worse. Three days later his mouth felt like it was made of parched flannel. Midmorning had been the last time he'd had a drink, when the doctor had made his rounds and kicked up a fuss about how dehydrated Thibault was. Three patients had just been discharged, so for a while the ward had been empty enough for Thibault to be noticed.

But then, after that wonderful blue plastic cup of water, after that sad little hospital meal, which he could have eaten three of, after that nurse patting him and telling him not to cry and going to find him a treat and never coming back, those beds had filled up, and he'd been forgotten again.

He was going to die here.

He had a little alarm button, but every time he called a nurse with it, she'd walk straight past him. Or hear him beg for water and walk away nodding, but never bring it.

Five minutes later he'd be calling out, "You forgot me!" as she whisked past, carrying someone else's bag of saline, or pain pills for that whiny kid near the window. His voice was fading as thirst cracked his lips. Soon no one would hear him at all.

Thirteen years old, and he was going to die. Maybe then his power would fade, and the staff would notice his corpse at last.

Now, four years later, he stared at the ceiling of the penthouse suite of the Hotel Magnifique, recalling the moment when he'd realized, through the muddle of fever, that he was on his own. Not just there in that children's ward, fighting to crawl to the bathroom for a long drink from the tap, but everywhere and forever.

He knew then that he had to have a plan. A plan for getting well without help from the nurses and doctors. A plan for getting home. And a plan, eventually, for leaving home, to cope with what he was.

He needed control, over his own space and his own mind.

And when he got it, Thibault had told himself, his teeth chattering in a chill between flushes of fever, he would always *see* what was going on around him. He would never be blind, like those nurses and doctors walking past.

A small sound shook him from his thoughts. A rustle from the next room.

Thibault sat up, groggy and dry-throated, grabbing for the bedside table. He still couldn't sleep without a glass of water within reach.

Another sound, a familiar click—*the penthouse door closing.*

Thibault bolted out of bed and into the main room. The note on the door had been unstuck and dropped onto the floor. He wasted precious seconds checking the other bedroom. By the time he looked into the hall, the elevator doors were closing.

"Rat-weasel," he said softly, his voice still dry.

Five minutes later Thibault was out on the street in a Hotel Magnifique bathrobe. He would've lost too much time putting on pants, or even shoes.

It was Friday night, only a few blocks from Ivy, and even this late the street was full of people, electric with their *wanting*. They wanted to get drunk, to get laid, to be seen—they wanted to be wanted.

Needles of curiosity flicked across him, people's eyes caught for a moment by the barefoot guy in the plush white bathrobe. But Thibault kept his mantra going in a steady murmur—*Form is void and void is form; nothing to see here, folks*—cutting away people's notice as quickly as it formed.

Down the street, at the intersection with Ivy, a pair of cops scanned the crowd. Awareness crackled out of them. The police were still on alert, of course, looking for the prisoners who'd escaped.

Thibault quickened his pace.

It took an endless, awful minute to find Ethan. He was in among the Ivy Street crowds, walking up to a group of women in sparkly dresses and five-inch heels.

Thibault didn't intervene. He might as well let Ethan get

this done. The guy had the voice, so it wouldn't take long to wangle a phone and reassure his mom. As soon as he did, Thibault would yank him back to the Magnifique.

"Um, you guys?" Ethan was sputtering. "I mean, girls. Could I, like . . ."

The girls just laughed, gliding around him in that practiced way women avoided drunk and obnoxious men.

"Seriously?" Thibault muttered. Why hadn't Ethan used the voice? Had he decided to grow a conscience *now*, of all times?

But then one of the girls turned back. She snapped a picture of Ethan with her phone and whispered something to her friends. Thibault sidled a little closer to them.

"Was that *him*?" one said.

Which was weird. But Thibault couldn't leave Ethan to follow it up. The guy was already approaching a straight couple walking arm in arm.

Use the voice, you idiot, Thibault thought as hard as he could.

Ethan did. His whole posture changed.

"Hey, if you let me borrow your phone for two seconds, you can take a selfie with me!"

The couple stopped, stared at him.

He gave them a cool, radiant smile. "Yeah, it's me all right, the guy in the bank video! Seriously. Give me one minute with your phone and we can do a selfie."

"Oh man, it *is* you! Sure, I guess," the guy said with a laugh, and handed over his phone.

What the hell was going on?

The couple whispered to each other as Ethan turned back into Ethan, dialing and sputtering into the phone.

"Hey, I'm staying with a friend, this guy Tee. Lives real close to the center of town, so I'm . . . you know, gonna crash here. But I busted my phone, so you won't be able to reach me . . ."

Spit it out. Thibault scanned the street. Was that skinny guy staring at Ethan? Did he look like a vengeful drug dealer?

"Okay, let's do this!" Ethan had turned back to the couple, full of the voice again, beaming like a celebrity greeting his fans. He stood between the two while they snapped half a dozen photos from arm's length.

The moment they lowered the phone, Thibault stepped up and grabbed Ethan. "Come on, man. You know you shouldn't be out here."

"What the hell?" said the woman, all three of them staring at the madman in a bathrobe who'd come out of nowhere.

But a gleam of guilty recognition soon dawned in Ethan's eyes. "Oh, yeah. Sorry, er, Teebo. I forgot."

Thibault didn't answer, just dragged Ethan back toward the Magnifique.

Whatever had happened, whatever this video was about, he was pretty sure the whole situation had just gotten much, much worse.

CHAPTER 33

CRASH

WHEN SHE WOKE UP THE NEXT MORNING, IT TOOK A moment for Chizara to remember. At first all she knew was bliss.

She'd slept hard and deep, untroubled by her parents' feeble wifi network. The yards were big out here in suburban Cambria, and the nettlesome fingertips of the neighbors' devices hardly reached her room at all. For once, all those itches were well and truly *scratched*.

She stretched like a cat, feeling lazy strength in every limb.

And then, midstretch, she remembered—that humongous power that had reared up and taken hold of her yesterday, it had opened the cell doors. Those criminals were back on the streets because of her. And what other systems had it messed up? Calls to 911? Officers needing backup?

She could only imagine.

All that data gone to confetti. Who knew how many investigations she'd ruined? How many more criminals would go free because of her? Sure, the systems at CCPD had been garbage, kludged together from a dozen different generations of tech. That mess had *deserved* to be torn down—but it should've been backed up first.

And Chizara had destroyed it all without warning.

She had released the thing inside her, instead of keeping it caged. Lying there, she wondered if this was how Scam felt every morning.

The thought made her need a shower. She jumped out of bed, snatched up her robe, and swept along the hall to the bathroom.

One of her brothers was in there, humming and dressing.

She knocked. "People gotta work!"

"People gotta play ball, too." Ikem's voice came through the door.

"Ikemefuna!"

"Za-raaa!"

She rattled the handle. It gave, and she opened the door a slit.

"Go away! Or I might tell Mom what you got up to yesterday."

Another jolt of guilt went through her. "Working all morning, lunch with my friends."

Ikem laughed. "Oh yeah? All that badness at the police station sure looked like it had your *superpower* stink all over it."

"Nothing to do with me." This was what she would say if the police came here asking. Not that they'd have any *reason* to think a sixteen-year-old schoolgirl had erased an entire building's worth of data. But even if they *did*, how could anyone prove it?

You couldn't go to jail for witchcraft here in America. They didn't even believe in juju.

Ikem was smiling. "Can you say that to Mom's face, when she's giving you the Look?"

"Sure I can. Now shoo!" Chizara sang, bustling inside, reaching into the shower stall, and turning on the tap. "I have my robe off. Nightgown's next!"

"Nooo!" Ikem darted out, slamming the door behind him. "It burns, it buuuuurns!" he cried as he ran away down the hall.

Chizara stood with the hot water streaming down her back, her head kinked forward to keep her hair dry, trying to recapture that enormous peace she'd felt yesterday at the station, that glorious quiet while everyone panicked and shouted around her.

It had been even better than out in the wilderness, where the emptiness was so huge and complete it was scary, one murmurless mountain, one silent tract of forest after another, empty of technology. Buildings full of babbling tech pained her, but complete silence in her mind also freaked her out a little.

She got out of the shower and wiped the mist off the mirror. She looked untroubled, almost smiling. The shower had washed away all her guilty thoughts, and her bones were purring. She hid her blissed-out expression in a towel, scrubbing her face dry.

She had to make amends. But her only income was from repairing toasters. How could she fix everything she'd broken yesterday?

"Morning, Mom."

"Good morning, Chizara." Mom's glance above the *Cambria Herald* was distinctly suspicious.

Her other brother, Obinna, straightened from closing the dishwasher. Chizara quickly hugged him in passing, just to annoy him, and he cried out as if her arms were branding irons, dodged around her, and fled upstairs. Ikem threw Chizara a smug look and followed.

"All this craziness down at the police station yesterday!" Mom said.

"What happened, exactly?" Not daring to glance at the headlines and photos, Chizara focused on getting her cereal down off the shelf. She and her brothers liked a normal American breakfast, not pap and fried plantain like her parents ate.

"Escaped prisoners, terrorists, everything breaking down. All those *computer systems* . . ."

Chizara turned from the fridge and met her mom's unwavering gaze.

"What are you saying, Mom?"

"What do you *think* I'm saying, Chizara Adaora Okeke?

Where were you yesterday when this . . . 'complete network failure' happened?"

"At the shop, putting CD players back together." She turned away to sprinkle cereal into her bowl. "And then I was at Nate's for lunch. With Flick—um, Riley and everyone."

"So you're all friends again? What a coincidence."

"Why would we want to mess with the police station? What good would that do anyone?" Though it sure felt like it had done Chizara some good.

"Enough talk, girl. Show me that phone of yours."

"My phone?" Chizara felt sick. The phone was in her back pocket, to take to Bob and ask if he could help her fix it. "What for?"

"I'm not a fool. Every time you misbehave, you buy a new phone." She reached across the table, snapping her fingers.

Chizara stalled, making a show of pouring milk into her bowl. She could feel the insides of the dead, cold device, where the tidal wave of power had melted silicon, warped metal, and scrambled memory. It was like a bomb site in there, all that intricate electronic filigree torn and tangled.

"*Now*, Chizara."

Reaching into her back pocket, Chizara wondered if dropping the phone would convincingly shatter it.

But then the happy purring in her bones heightened to a sharp thrill. In the second it took her mother to find the power button, a little *zott!* went through Chizara's guts, quite unlike the letting-go feeling of crashing something. It was more like puzzle pieces snapping together.

The phone gave itself a shake and came to its senses. She could feel everything inside it smoothed and straightened as good as new, all the connections knitted together the way they should be. As the screen lit up, the skin on her arms, face, and chest started to itch. The phone sang its startup song and reached out its eager wifi for a signal. Like it was sharing a joke with her, stepping in to save her.

But she'd done this herself. She'd *uncrashed* it.

Mom's face relaxed with surprise, and she handed the phone back. The factory settings' boot-up screen appeared; Chizara's wallpaper had been erased, along with the rest of her data. But Mom wouldn't notice that.

Chizara held her expression steady as the phone squealed and throbbed against her consciousness.

"If it wasn't you, maybe your friends?" Mom was giving her the Look, shaking the newspaper at her. She hardly trusted Chizara to restrain her power; a gaggle of spoiled white American teenagers had no chance of self-control.

Obinna had once described Mom's Look: *She just, like, injects some kinda truth drug in through your eyes.*

But Chizara held strong. "They had nothing to do with this," she said, not too fast, but without any guilty delay, either, and with a solemn, honest face born of awe at this jolt of new power.

"Are you sure this wasn't Nate's doing? Or that girl, Riley? If you know anything, we should go straight to the authorities."

The thought of her mother talking to the police forced Chizara to sit down. Would someone in the station remember an unfamiliar cleaner wandering the halls that day?

"They have *different* powers," Chizara mumbled, and started to crunch on her cereal. "Nothing to do with computers."

After an endless pause, her mother went from looking straight into Chizara's soul to frowning back at the newspaper.

You have to fix it. Since Chizara was five years old, Mom had been saying that, once she'd admitted to herself what her daughter could do. *You've got to be responsible about what's inside you. If you hurt anyone—whether you mean to or not, Chizara—you've got to find some way to make it right. Settle with your conscience.*

Little Chizara had nodded sulkily.

Square things with the people whose stuff you break. Every time, girl, do you hear me?

Now maybe she *could* square things. Could she uncrash everything she'd broken yesterday? It was worth a try.

She got up and rinsed her bowl and spoon, put them in the dishwasher. She kissed her mom on the top of her head as she passed. Her bones were humming again, wanting to *fix* something.

"You're my good girl?" Mom called out as she left the kitchen.

"I'm your good girl." Chizara was better than ever this morning. She couldn't wait to see how damn good she was.

CHAPTER 34
CRASH

CHIZARA PLUGGED HER PHONE INTO HER LAPTOP to restore her blasted data. Over the tech squeal she listened as Obinna and Ikem's friends arrived and her brothers shouted good-bye to Mom.

Then she stole into their room. In the bottom of their wardrobe were boxes full of outgrown toys, out-of-season sports equipment. Chizara rummaged right to the bottom of one box, then another.

Finally from the third she dug out the old handheld gaming console. She found the right kind of batteries in the charger on top of Obinna's dresser, took everything back to her room, and closed her door.

Staring at the lifeless console, Chizara flashed back to the endless *bloop*ing, *gleep*ing *rat-tat-tat* that had spilled from its speakers. But worse had been the chatter of its antennae, the pulsing search and grab of wifi and Bluetooth as it interacted with other consoles. Day and night, it had sandpapered the ends of Chizara's nerves.

She'd struck while Ikem wasn't actually playing it, so no one would suspect her. It was her subtlest bit of work up to that point, just frazzling that one chip. And oh, the relief!

Guy at the shop says it's toast, Ikem had said the next day. By that time she'd started to feel guilty, watching him drag the little plastic corpse out of his backpack, actual tears creeping down his cheeks.

That time she'd failed the confrontation with Mom's Look. *Guess you'd better find someone to fix it,* Mom had said.

And that's when she'd walked into Bob's restful, low-tech shop for the first time. He'd opened up the console and explained its workings to her, pointing out why it couldn't be rescued. And she'd seen the way forward. She could learn a bunch of stuff she needed to know from this guy, and at the same time make it up to Ikem.

Once Bob saw that she was serious and started paying her, her first two paychecks bought Ikem that bike he'd had his eye on.

So much healthier than a new game, Mom! she'd said.

Mom had given her the side-eye, but had to admit she was right.

Now, here in her room, Chizara sat down and took a deep breath. Had the phone thing at breakfast been a fluke?

She turned on the game console. For an instant its insides flashed, but the light died as soon as the juice hit that tangled mess of circuitry.

Wow. Chizara had *thought* she'd hit only the processor chip—but that was a year ago. She'd been a lot clumsier then.

The strange feeling came again, that pulse in her guts. Just like with fixing the phone, her mind smoothed and combed everything straight. It worked at a microscopic level, calculating which particles to move and where—how did it know that? A month ago she'd needed Bob to remind her whether a positive terminal was red or black.

But she could see it now, the circuits the way they should be. The map was there in her head already, as if all those pin-pricks and itches and pains from e-things and i-things had been *teaching* her something all along. . . .

A moment after she saw it, the circuit was whole again, the startup fanfare playing. That tinny music had once made her cringe and weep, but now she glowed along with the microchip. The screen flickered and the silver logo popped up and started to spin.

She'd really uncrashed it. The game's home screen arrived, with its awful little zombies. Ikem had been crazy about those zombies. He would imitate their chilling screams as they attacked. Dazedly Chizara watched the tutorial unfold—sitting back and covering one eye as the itching wifi fingers clawed the air.

But she was Crash; it was her job to *break* things. The only fixing she ever did was the manual kind that anyone could do, the rewiring, soldering, replacing, screwing-back-together kind.

She turned the game off, took it back to the boys' room, and left it on Ikem's desk. She got her backpack together for work, went down to the kitchen, and put some plantain and some leftover jollof rice into a microwave container for lunch—enough for Bob, too, to make up for abandoning him yesterday. Mom was upstairs getting ready for her work up at the Igbo community center. Dad was in the laundry, humming as he clanked through his toolbox.

Chizara still felt wonderful, even if the newspapers were calling her a terrorist. Her mind kept throwing accusations at her, about the criminals at large, about all the other damage she'd done yesterday, but her body felt light and agile and strong, rested and ready for anything. This uncrashing business seemed *right* somehow—it balanced out yesterday's big destructive storm. She hoped Bob would have something complicated for her to repair today.

But how would she explain it to him if she willed a laptop back to life? Luck? The weather? The general flakiness of modern technology? Maybe she could just say it out loud: *It's my superpower, Bob.* And then she'd shrug, and he'd laugh, not believing her for a second.

"Good-bye, Mom—good-bye, Dad!" Chizara called, and her parents' farewells floated out the front door after her, into the fresh summer morning.

CHAPTER 35
ANONYMOUS

ETHAN SAT HUNCHED OVER HIS ROOM SERVICE breakfast, watching the video again.

Had the poor guy slept at all? Thibault wondered. Or just sat there all night, clicking play again and again?

One viewing had been enough for Thibault.

When they'd gotten back to the penthouse last night, a search on "guy in the bank video" had gone straight to a pink, jewel-encrusted blog called SoniaSonic. Ethan's face was right at the top, blurry, cheek to the floor, eyes rolling up into a blink, mouth open. He looked like a zombie. A really easy-to-recognize zombie.

And when you clicked play, it got much worse.

"But the cops took her phone!" Ethan said for about the hundredth time. "And Chizara crashed it!"

"She sent herself the video, or it backed up to the cloud," Thibault said, also for the hundredth time. Was Ethan forgetting everything again, or was the guy in shock?

"A quarter million hits now," Ethan said in a pinched voice, like he was having trouble breathing.

Every time he refreshed the screen, the video's view count jumped. It wasn't every day the internet got to see an amateur video of a bank robbery in progress. Especially one showing a random customer messing with the robbers' heads.

"Listen, Jerry. I like you." Ethan's voice came from the laptop's speakers, as cocky as a three-card-monte artist turning over a wrong choice. "You just want what's best for Kelsie, after all."

"No wonder bullets started flying." Thibault carved out a spoonful of honeydew melon but didn't eat it. His stomach was too jumpy. "Must've freaked poor Jerry out, hearing his daughter's name."

"Poor Jerry?" Ethan cried. "What about poor *me*? The guy with the gun in his face!"

"If you were so scared, why start talking at all?"

Ethan tore his eyes from the screen. "To save that girl, Sonia. She had some stupid ring, and she wasn't going to give it to the robbers. He was going to shoot her, Tee!"

Thibault stared at him. "That's what you're going with? You were saving a damsel in distress?"

"Well, there was also . . ." Ethan mumbled the rest into a forkful of home fries.

"Sorry. Missed that."

"Jerry asked me about my duffel bag."

Thibault sighed. It figured. For something as meaningless as money, Ethan had managed to get his face in front of a quarter million people, all of whom could help track him down. By now every cop in Cambria must have seen that video, not to mention Ethan's drug-dealing buddies. And what about Jerry and his gang? They'd be busting heads to find out how some kid knew their names.

"Guess your mom is now officially the least of your worries."

"Don't remind me. That message I left last night isn't going to keep her calm, not after she sees this."

Ethan stood up and started pacing, feet crunching over spilled corn chips.

It occurred to Thibault that they should clean the room soon, maybe even vacate. Someone had booked the penthouse for the Fourth of July, less than a week away. The Magnifique had a great view of the fireworks, and of the doomed Parker-Hamilton Hotel down the street. He and Ethan might have to move to another hotel.

And by the time they hit the street, another million people would know what Ethan looked like.

Thibault was tempted to use the manager's password and lose that reservation. But that would not only screw the hotel, but also some poor—well, rich—traveler.

He'd also gotten an e-mail while he was online. From

Flicker, which was a first. No text, just the subject line: *How's it going with the weasel wrangling?*

Thibault grinned to himself as he tidied up, wondering exactly how to reply. Something short and witty? Or should he tell her about all the crazy on the street the night before? Or ask if she'd seen the bank video?

Of course, she'd probably already forgotten she'd written him.

It was weird with Flicker. Her awareness wasn't like anyone else's. The visual connection didn't come from her; it bounced through other people's eyes. And Thibault could always feel the tickle of her listening to his footsteps, or her questing awareness of his scent. He could never quite bring himself to snip off her attention.

"About to deposit the biggest bag of money I've ever seen, and I start talking to some girl!" Ethan muttered, kicking at chip fragments on the floor. "Just because she had that cute haircut. Like I *care* about Patty Low? I should get my mouth sewn shut!"

Thibault piled the plates on the room service tray. "Too late for that."

A bright spike of attention hit him from Ethan's narrowed eyes. One way to heat up a connection was to bug the hell out of someone—Thibault had always teased his little brothers to keep them focused.

"Thanks for your positive feedback, Tee."

"I'm serious." Thibault wiped his fingers on a napkin and

added it to the pile. "Well, not about needle and thread. But sooner or later, you'll have to control your voice."

Ethan stopped pacing. "Easy for you to say. You and Nate and Flicker all have powers you can—"

Thibault held his hand up.

"We already had this conversation?" said Ethan.

Thibault pointed to the hand, the agreed signal. For some reason, gestures stuck with Ethan better than words.

"None of our powers is easy to deal with," Thibault said. "Especially growing up. I mean, how young were you when the voice hit?"

Ethan shrugged. "It started talking before I did."

"Before *you* did?"

"Yeah. If I wanted something, I just opened my mouth and noises came out. I thought everyone did that. I thought that's what talking *was*."

Ethan's gaze drifted to the window. Thibault waited for their connection to fade, but it held, a bright thin beam between them, almost *too* intense.

"It took a long time to understand words, even the ones coming out of my own mouth. Maybe I'm kind of stupid—but hey, why did I *need* to understand them? The voice took care of everything. I just watched."

Thibault stopped cleaning up and sat down. He'd known that the hooks of the voice went deep into Ethan, but not this deep. Deeper than language.

"So how did you learn how to talk for yourself?"

"Took a while to figure out that I even *had* my own voice." Ethan wore a wry smile on his lips, as if learning to speak was a scam he'd pulled. "But the voice doesn't work when I'm alone. And you know how little kids babble to themselves? I had to figure out why it felt different when the voice wasn't handing words to me."

Ethan looked up, and the connection between them was so strong and bright and steady, Thibault knew Ethan had never told this to anyone else.

"So the voice taught you to talk, but it got in the way, too."

"Yeah, it made it too easy. Still does. At school they think I'm dyslexic or whatever—I'm great at oral exams but I bomb all the written tests." Ethan laughed, like this was a big joke on the teachers. "For a while I thought I could make myself as smart as the voice was. I'd listen real hard when it talked, and then look up words in this big dictionary they had in the library, on a wooden stand. But then . . ."

Ethan squirmed and the connection sputtered.

"Then what?" said Thibault.

"There was this teacher. He was always picking on me. And one day he told me I was lazy one too many times. So I let the voice loose on him. It said he was only mean and bitter because his mom was schizophrenic. The whole room went quiet, everyone shit-scared. But he went on with the class, real serious, and he never bugged me again. So I thought that word, 'schizophrenic,' must be awesome. I looked it up—once I worked out how to spell it."

"Oh. Wow."

"Yeah. It turned out schizophrenics were people like *me*. With voices in their heads. If that's not me, nothing is." Ethan stared out the window again. "So I stopped looking up words. And a week later they got rid of that big dictionary, because the internet was better. But I was like, great, that stupid book's gone that told me I'm crazy. Maybe no one else has to know."

"Man. That sucks." Thibault's fateful book had been a tattered paperback, *Zen for Beginners*, picked up at random from a secondhand bookstore. In it he'd found the Way all laid out for him. Fifteen hundred years of wisdom that stared straight into the void, that made nothingness okay.

Which made Thibault okay, because he was definitely nothing. The Buddhist *śūnyatā*, emptiness personified.

But when Ethan had found himself in a book, it hadn't been among the koans of the Way. Instead he'd stumbled on "schizophrenic" and mistaken it for satori. And he'd been scared of himself ever since.

"Ethan. I don't think you're schizophrenic."

"Really?" Ethan turned to face Thibault, hopeful, scared.

"Really. These things we have, they aren't mental issues; they're *powers*. Like superheroes have." Thibault almost laughed—he'd never said the word out loud before.

"You think?"

"Sure. We just suck at them right now."

"Zeroes, not heroes," Ethan muttered, his attention scattering. People lost focus like this when they were in pain, as if they were trying to melt out of sight. Like everyone had a little slice of Thibault's power in them.

And hell, maybe the kindest thing would be to make that happen. All Thibault had to do was swipe his hand across his face and leave the room, and Ethan's memory of this conversation would fade.

But this was the first time they'd said anything really meaningful to each other. Thibault couldn't just throw it away.

"I should e-mail Nate about that video."

Ethan nodded. "Yeah, you should. Because you might have a nice place to stay, but I gotta live with my mom. And she's going to tear me a new one if I don't get home soon."

Thibault met his gaze. Their connection was still there, but it was built of fear and exhaustion. First thing in the morning and he already felt tired.

He reached for his laptop. "Sure thing. Maybe if we get Glorious Leader's ass in gear, he'll come up with a plan to get you out of here."

CHAPTER 36

CRASH

CHIZARA TRIED NOT TO SEEM TOO CHEERFUL AT work that morning. She was supposed to be recovering from a migraine, not reveling in newfound powers.

But she worked hard, all focus and attention. And it almost surprised her when her new talents didn't flare up and fix these blenders and radios, when she could see so clearly what had to be done. But no, she had to go hunting for tiny replacement lightbulbs in Bob's collection out back, or clean out a toaster's workings with an old toothbrush. Maybe these burned-out filaments and bread crumbs were too *big* for her power to wrestle into shape. Too gargantuan compared to microscopic circuits.

There was no stress working with clunky machines like this, but yesterday's glories had raised a possibility: Maybe toaster repair wasn't why she'd been put on this earth. Maybe her true work was waiting for her someplace else, someplace not so safe and pleasant, which offered the challenges of dealing with Nate and the others.

It was a thrilling but scary thought, and Chizara was glad to have this job, this shop, these simple responsibilities to shelter in.

After their lunch of Mom's leftovers, Bob asked her to replace the power cord on an old TV. The customer's terrier, left alone in her apartment one day, had chewed through the cord.

"Tell me the dog didn't electrocute itself."

"Oh, he was smart," Bob said. "He pulled it out of the wall first."

It was a long cord, so it was easy to cut around the bite marks, strip the wires, screw them into the plug, then screw the plug back together.

At the first flicker of light on the screen, Chizara braced herself for the trickle of wifi. So many televisions were networked, as if everyone was dying to read their e-mail on a TV screen. But this one was charmingly old and dumb. It emitted nothing but a brassy flourish of breaking news from Cambria Local and the earnest face of Molly Roswell.

". . . has been placed into an induced coma after being assaulted in yesterday's prisoner escape at the North Bride Street headquarters. Police are still unsure what caused the computer malfunction and security breach."

Molly kept talking, but for a moment Chizara couldn't parse the words.

"That was some weird stuff," said Bob, looking up from a circuit board. "You hear about it?"

Chizara nodded slowly. The purring had gone from her bones.

"Some." Her voice came out flat. "I saw the newspaper this morning."

A picture hovered over Molly Roswell's right shoulder—a policeman in full dress uniform. He was smiling, and his name was Reggie Bright.

Chizara tried to listen, but the words kept not making sense: *medically induced coma, family man, beaten while trying to prevent prisoners . . .*

And then, with cruel suddenness, Molly Roswell moved on to a story about homeowners insurance. Bob kept looking up from his soldering iron, as if statistics about grease fires were just as dramatic, just as meaningful.

Chizara was scared to open her mouth in case a huge, anguished howl came out. A man, a *family man*, someone's father, was in a coma because she'd lost control. Because of that glitch with the holding cells they'd all shrugged off at Nate's yesterday, unaware that a man had been beaten half to death.

Or had the rest of them known?

She pulled the television's plug from the wall, and the screen winked into darkness.

"Stretch break," she managed, and walked to where her bag rested on the bench. Her phone was in there, the one she'd been so pleased about fixing. Well, fix *this*, girl. What good was repairing phones and game consoles if you screwed up so bad that someone wound up in a coma?

A walking massacre.

Chizara made it down the hall and out the back, shut the rusty door behind her, and crouched against the outside wall. She switched her phone on and waited with a hand over her eyes while it woke itself up and made its connections, stabbing at her brain. All that "porn-face" stuff of Scam's, that meant nothing next to this new horror.

She called Nate.

"Chizara? Are you okay?" He sounded dead serious.

"So . . . you *knew*?"

There was a silence on the other end—he was *thinking* about his answer, considering how best to say it. Disgust and plantain welled up in Chizara's gut, and she thumbed end call. She was almost sick, right there in the alley. The Zeroes had ruined a man's life, just to save Scam from his own big mouth.

Her mom's voice rang in her head. *Any kind of gift, you can use it wisely or stupidly. Whether it's strength or a good brain, or some strange thing like you've got, Chizara. Just ask yourself every time you use it: Is this going to hurt anyone? Is this going to do any harm?*

And Chizara *had* asked herself those questions, she really

had. But then the thing had gotten so big, with the police station so crowded, and all those networks tangling in her mind. How was she supposed to stop her power when it got that big?

Of course, there had been a moment when she'd had a choice, to hold back or let it roll through her. Kneeling by the detective's desk, realizing that smoke alarms and card key readers wouldn't be enough. Thinking, with a whiff of exhilaration, *Time to do some damage.*

It was moments like those that killed people, removed husbands, fathers, from the world. Permanently, unforgivably. Doing some damage. Having some fun.

The Zeroes protecting their own. Nate had made it sound so noble.

Well, it wasn't noble. It was just playing with too much power, like child soldiers with AK-47s in their hands. It wasn't glorious, or beautiful, or any of those things she felt when her power had hold of her.

She was a demon, just like Scam had said.

The phone went off, blaring pain into her hand. *Glorious Leader.*

She almost threw it at the wall. But her need to yell at him was as strong as her anger.

"What?" she spat, holding the phone as close to her ear as she could bear.

"I'm coming to see you. We're going to talk this through."

"Talk it through? You can't *talk* something like this

through—a man's in a coma, and we're responsible! How much less *conversational* can something get?"

"I'll be on my way in five minutes, Chizara. Where are you?"

"I'm at work, Nate. I've got another hour to go, and I'm going to work that hour, not lie to my boss and sneak out for some stupid mission that puts someone in a coma. This is the end of missions for me, Nate. The end of your 'training.' The Zeroes just got evil!"

"We didn't know this would happen."

"But you knew yesterday, right? And you didn't tell me."

"I knew he was in a coma. But it's medically induced, to help him stabilize."

"He's so bad off, it's *better* to be unconscious? And instead of mentioning it, you fed me *lunch*? Why? In case you needed me to crash something else before I heard?"

"I was hoping for a better outcome."

The coldness of that! Her breath, snatched away, came back with a little laugh of disbelief. Who was the demon here?

"Oh, Nate, you're going to make a *great* politician."

"Can we just talk? Can I come and meet you after work?"

"Do what you want. Just make sure you walk, or ride a bicycle or something. Get some beat-up cab. You show up in this neighborhood in one of your fancy cars, people'll think you're a dealer moving in. And I won't tell them otherwise."

She slapped the phone off, biting her lip hard to keep herself mad. Righteous anger was so much better than that about-to-cry feeling. She got up and paced the alley, sucking in deep breaths, huffing them out, preparing to go back inside and be normal, get her job done, learn something new about old tech. Something mechanical, made out of dumb materials that did what they were told.

This was what she was going to stick to from now on, unless she could read *all* the consequences, *right* to the end, and see that nobody got hurt in any way.

She dragged open the door and went back inside.

CHAPTER 37
BELLWETHER

THE CALL ENDED WITH A LOUD CLICK, AS IF CHIZARA had thrown her phone against a wall. Or maybe her anger had crashed it.

Nate frowned. Hadn't she destroyed her phone *yesterday*?

Maybe she'd bought a new one already, which was too bad. He'd planned to buy her a replacement on his way over, a little reminder that being part of the team had its benefits. That the Zeroes took care of their own.

Not that any gift would repair the damage done yesterday.

Nate texted his father's secretary, canceling lunch. Papi would be annoyed, but not as annoyed as if Chizara had a crisis of conscience and confessed to the police. On the radio they were calling yesterday's events *terrorism*. Which was ridiculous, but it made all the relevant jail terms about ten times longer.

The irony of this disaster was that the training exercises had helped Chizara most of all. Nate had watched her abilities sharpen, evolving from a blunt object into an instrument of specificity and finesse. And her confidence had grown, her sense that she was *entitled* to wield such power.

Until now.

So what if she'd slipped a little? Nate doubted that the Cambria Police Department had any earthshaking investigations under way. As he'd always told Chizara, every crash she conjured was simply a reminder to *back up that data.* Anyone who didn't deserved what they got.

If only Chizara hadn't opened those cell doors. Or if the escapees had managed not to put anyone in a coma on the way out. Was *that* so much to ask? Now Chizara was in danger of losing all the focus she'd gained yesterday, of throwing it all away to wallow in guilt and shame.

And after all that effort, Ethan's video had still made it out into the world. Sonia Stoller, a.k.a. "Sonia Sonic," must have sent it to herself before handing her phone to the cops. Maybe next time Chizara should just crash the whole internet.

Nate filed that thought away.

He found his sisters in the front room, playing with his old set of Formula One cars. They had made a track with strips of cloth from Mamá's sewing scraps and built a grandstand from shoe boxes, full of dolls.

Gabby, always the instigator, was lofting a bright green

Lotus Renault through the air. "I've lost control! Run!"

She took it spinning into the grandstand, neatly decapitating a Misterioso, Jr., doll. The other sisters managed the fleeing of dolls from the stand.

"I'm on fire!"

"Me too!"

"We're all *doomed*!"

He cleared his throat, and they looked up guiltily from the carnage.

"I'm going out." Nate took the keys to the Audi from the bowl beside the door. It was one of their best cars, and had just been washed. If anyone in the Heights took offense at shiny chrome, Nate knew how to deal with that. "Tell Mamá I'll be back for dinner."

"Okay," Gabby said, then made a rumbling explosion sound as the Renault crashed against a couch leg.

When Nate opened the front door, he found himself face-to-face with three adults. The man wore a cheap suit and fedora, and the two women were both in gray business wear.

Cops, and much sooner than he'd expected. Nate wasn't ready for this. They looked a little surprised themselves at the door having opened without a knock.

Nate gathered himself. "May I help you?"

"I'm Detective King," one of the women said. "This is Detective Fuentes and Deputy District Attorney Cooper."

Cooper. Ethan's last name. This had to be the dreaded mother.

Detective King smiled warmly. Apparently it wasn't too suspicious, being a bit nonplussed when a pair of detectives and a DDA showed up at your door.

"We're looking for a Mr. Nataniel Saldana." She said his name with a decent accent.

Nate managed to smile back, trying not to think of terrorism charges erasing his future.

"That's me. Please come in. After I see your badges, of course."

He kept the visitors in the front room. Mamá was working in the back garden this afternoon and wouldn't be inside anytime soon. A citizen for twenty years, she still got nervous in the presence of authorities, which was the last thing Nate needed.

More important, his sisters were here. He pulled them from their game and arranged them along the couch, forcing the two detectives to stand. He and DDA Cooper had the two chairs, so the real conversation would be between them. More important, the presence of his sisters gave him an audience to work with.

Nate's training missions had shown that it took six people to form the beginnings of the Curve. It was in crowds of six or more where Crash could really wreck things, where Flicker could throw her vision half a mile, and where Anonymous truly vanished.

But of all their powers, Nate's was most affected by the Curve. Being a leader was pointless without a crowd to follow you.

Nate had seven in this room. The cops didn't stand a chance.

"This is about a phone call you received yesterday, about eleven in the morning." King had a printout in her hand—phone company records, not a memorized number. There was no point in pretending the call hadn't happened.

Besides, King would've recognized his voice by now.

Nate gave her a momentary puzzled look, then nodded. "Right. That crank call."

"You thought it was a joke?" She raised an eyebrow.

"Of course. They said it was for someone called Scam."

"Scamiglia," King read from her notepad. She took a step closer. "And it was me you were talking to."

"I'm so sorry, Detective. All I heard was 'Scam.'" Nate shrugged. "I thought it was an old friend of mine. This guy was always playing jokes. Always lying about everything, you know?"

At these words Ethan's mother sat a little straighter.

Detective King was looming over him now, so Nate let his perfect smile drop into a frown. The room cooled a little.

His sisters felt it too, the promise of conflict, the play of dominance and focus that lit up the air like sparklers. This was a game for them, one that Nate had raised them to play. Their attention settled over him like a mantle, his to use, and cold little glares stabbed up from their dark and beautiful eyes.

Detective King took a step back.

"What was this friend's name?" DDA Cooper said.

"Ethan. But everyone called him Scam."

The muscles of her jaw tightened just a little. Yes, definitely his mother.

Using Ethan's code name was a risk. But the name made the lies of yesterday *his* fault—and, by extension, his mother's.

"Scam," Nate said again, respecting the power of repetition. "Because he was always lying."

Following his lead, his sisters turned their baleful glares on the deputy district attorney.

Detective Fuentes asked something, but Nate ignored him, shut him out of the conversation entirely. He sharpened his connection with Ethan's mother, but softened his disapproval into an invitation for her to speak again.

"Got any idea where he is?" she asked.

"None." Nate liked to think he was an excellent liar, but his words always tasted a little bit crisper when they were true. Ethan had gone off somewhere to hide, but where or with whom wouldn't come to mind. "We hung out a lot, last year. But it's been a while."

"So you haven't seen his video?" Fuentes asked.

Nate stared at him, as if the question made no sense, then turned back to DDA Cooper. "Is Ethan okay?"

He drew his sisters along, and their little faces opened with concern.

She didn't answer at first, and the detectives looked uncomfortable. It was probably tricky having a DDA along when she was the mother of a suspect, or a material witness—or whatever Scam was.

Fuentes cleared his throat. "Why did you claim to be a lawyer? When I get a crank call, I hang up."

Nate spoke directly to DDA Cooper. "We always used to joke with Scam—with Ethan, I mean—that he would wind up in jail one day. I thought he'd gotten a friend to pretend to be a cop, like it had finally happened. So I played along."

"You know," Fuentes said, "misrepresenting yourself to a police officer, that's a felony."

"I didn't know who you were." Nate looked up at the two detectives, lowering the full weight of his disdain, and his sisters', on them. "Really, Detective King. You were asking for some lawyer called Scam, who didn't exist. And you kept talking about 'Terrence,' who also doesn't exist. The whole thing *was* a joke, wasn't it? On you."

The two of them took another shuffle backward. They'd lost track of a kid who was both a material witness to a homicide and the missing son of a prosecutor. On top of which their department had lost a whole station's worth of suspects, with one of their own put into a coma in the process.

Their confidence was shaken. He could see it in the unfocused glimmers of their awareness.

They asked more questions, but Nate held his nerve. He and his sisters nodded and smiled when DDA Cooper spoke, shook their heads when the others did. Not so much that the detectives would notice, just enough to worry their hindbrains, to urge them gently backward and out of the conversation.

Soon they were clear across the room. Ethan's mother had been stripped of their protection, left alone on the armchair, which had a broken spring and was never very comfortable.

For a moment Nate felt sorry for her. Raising Ethan couldn't be easy—you'd always wonder if the way he'd turned out was your fault.

"I haven't seen him since last summer," Nate said to her. "He lost all his friends on the same day. Spouted a bunch of stuff he couldn't take back." He saw that she believed every word of that.

Maybe it was better to be caught off guard like this. If he'd had time to prepare, he would have come up with stories, lies. But the perfect weapon against Scam's mother was the truth, the one thing she'd never heard from her son's mouth.

"There was a group of you?" Fuentes was still trying to sound tough, though by now he was backed up against a potted fern. "Maybe one of the others might know where he is."

"Maybe so. But I lost touch with them all, after what Ethan said to us. He busted up the group." It was practically *cheating*, sticking so close to the facts, so he added a lie: "I don't know how to find them."

"Just give us names," Detective King said, pulling out a notepad.

Nate smiled and made up three names. Most teenagers

didn't have listed phone numbers, and people moved away from Cambria all the time. If the detectives felt like they'd gotten something from the visit, they could leave without losing face.

This had been instructive, but he was late for his meeting with Chizara.

"Thank you," said DDA Cooper before she departed, extending her hand. And for a moment Nate worried that he'd connected too well. The last thing he wanted was for her to look him up again, hoping to learn more about her son.

But he took her hand and deployed his warmest look of concern. "We didn't part on the best of terms, but wherever Ethan is, I really hope he's okay."

CHAPTER 38
SCAM

"RIP OUT YOUR SPINE AND MAKE YOU EAT IT!" ETHAN sent a spray of potato chips across the coffee table.

He hadn't meant the spray as a distraction, but that was the moment when Thibault made his fatal mistake. His tree sprite dangled a moment too long from the embezzler vine and took a fireball right in his face.

"Die! Die! *Die!*" Ethan cried. This rage high felt good, like the fireballs were destroying the fact that he was being hunted. Turned out *Red Scepter III* was the only thing that stopped him thinking about everyone who wanted him dead or in custody.

The sprite made one last leap for the tree branch overhead, but a fireball connected halfway up.

"Finally!" Ethan fell backward on the couch. "I killed you *good*, Tee!"

He turned, ready to gloat some more, but Thibault was staring at him, wide-eyed.

"Oh," Ethan said, surveying the coffee table. "Sorry about the chips."

"No." Thibault still looked astonished. "I mean, yes, that was disgusting. But you remembered me!"

"Oh, right." Ethan had been fully into the game, all the way down in that animal level where every twitch of the wizard was an extension of his own body. But not once had he forgotten Thibault next to him. And not once had he thought about angry bank robbers or angry cops or his inevitably disappointed mom.

Thibault was grinning hard, like a troop of Girl Scouts had just handed him all their cookies.

Ethan looked back at the screen, where he'd left his wizard motionless. Poor guy was getting pecked to death. Ethan chuckled. All that mattered was his revenge on Thibault for seventeen straight losses.

Ethan even remembered the score: seventeen kills *to one* now!

"I guess we, like, bonded or something."

Thibault laughed. "Maybe you're like those bacteria that get resistant to antibiotics."

"Gee, thanks. This is a big deal!" It felt even bigger than killing the tree sprite. "I mean, has this ever happened to you before?"

"With Nate, once or twice."

"Oh, right, of course. Glorious Leader."

"He'd set up meetings." Thibault dropped the controller to his lap. "Just me and him in the middle of an empty field. And the next day he'd e-mail and tell me what we talked about. Like he'd taken *notes*."

"Impressive," Ethan said, despite feeling a stab of jealousy. Trust Glorious Leader to make it an experiment.

"Once we went camping in the Redwoods," Thibault said. "We got as remote as we could, and he didn't lose me for three straight days. He'd record stuff with his phone, or take notes while we sat around the campfire. It was almost like I was a normal person."

Ethan squirmed. "You mean, except for being recorded."

"Yeah. Nate's not normal himself, exactly."

"It always feels like we're part of a game for him. Like, those training missions? I mean, seriously? Training for *what*? Does he really have some big plan for the Zeroes? Or is he winging it like everybody else?"

Thibault was staring at the screen, watching the restart button pulse. "You know what's weird? It kind of sucked, not being able to disappear. Not being able to do what I wanted, because this other person was around, expecting things. Like conversation, all that stuff."

"Oh, man. Small talk. I hate that."

Thibault shrugged. "It was too much, being normal for that long. I don't know how you guys can stand to be *seen* all day."

"Normal doesn't work for me, either," Ethan said. "Talking for myself? I suck at that. The voice just *knows*, man. I'm trying to use it less, but never at all? I'd be toast."

Thibault turned to face him. "But what about all the damage it does? A guy got shot in that bank robbery."

"Not by me." Ethan held up both hands in surrender. He'd just managed to forget about the bank robbery again, but Thibault had to go and remind him. "Those guys loaded their own guns. That's the kind of people they were. Seriously, Tee, is there anything I could say to you that would make you *kill* someone?"

"Don't make me answer that," Thibault said, and went silent. There was an intensity about him that kept Ethan quiet too.

When Thibault finally spoke again, the words came slowly, like something bubbling up from deep in the ground.

"You think you've got it made, up in your fancy hotel room. All your fancy shirts. But none of it makes up for crawling home from the hospital and walking into your own house, sick as a dog, and finding Grandma set up in your bedroom. Your stuff given away to your brothers. Mom and Dad looking past you the way everyone does, talking to the person behind you. Like they never had an oldest son."

Ethan stared. It was like Thibault was reciting some weird passage from a play. Almost like he was talking with another voice.

Thibault kept going. "And the funniest part is, you think

that calm place is Zen inside you. Bullshit. That's cold rage, pushed right down where you can't see it anymore. But you can feel it, right?"

The room fell silent, and Ethan understood. "That's what I said to you last summer, right? How'd you memorize it?"

"It kept playing in my head, over and over." Thibault flicked a potato chip across the floor. "And yeah, what you said that day almost made me kill someone. Words can do that, Ethan."

For a moment he wore a look of unguarded rage. At Ethan.

"I'm sorry, Tee. I don't even know what I was talking about. I was just so mad at Nate. . . ."

But it made sense now why Thibault lived in a hotel. His *family* had forgotten about him. That was pretty messed up.

"They really gave your room away?" Ethan asked.

"I was at the hospital, and my grandma needed a place to stay. Once she moved in, there were six people in the house. Too many for them to remember me. The Curve, like Nate always says."

"That sucks," Ethan said, suddenly glad that his power was strictly one-on-one. No crazy crowd effects like the rest of them.

Thibault sighed. "The worst part of last summer wasn't what you said. It was that I felt *grateful* for someone saying it. Like finally someone saw me. Sometimes I almost want to piss you off again, just to prove that the voice would never forget my secrets. I guess people want to be known, even when it hurts. Like dogs that crawl back to the masters who beat them."

"Crap." Ethan had never felt so awful. Thibault wanted the voice to remember him, because he didn't think Ethan could. "I'm going to remember what you just told me, Tee. Not to diss you with it! But, like, as a friend."

"Oh, yeah? Prove it."

"Okay," Ethan said at once. "Um, how?"

Thibault thought for a moment. "I got a bad case of *Scepter* breath. I need a shower and some serious toothbrush time. I'll shut both doors, so you can't even hear the water. And when I come out again, we'll see what you remember."

Ethan swallowed. A shower was maybe ten minutes. And if he failed, if Thibault walked back in and Ethan just stared at him, then every honest thing they'd shared would evaporate.

Worst of all, it would mean *the voice* was a better friend than Ethan.

"No problem," Ethan said casually. "Take your time."

Thibault gave him a look, like he expected to be disappointed. But Ethan shooed him away.

"Fine. I will," Thibault said. He got to his feet and headed for his room, shutting the door firmly behind him.

"Okay," Ethan muttered. "Just waiting for my buddy Tee."

He almost reached for the dropped controller, but slipping away into the game would be lethal. He stood and started pacing, keeping the blood flowing to his brain.

"Teebo is my buddy." Ethan pictured the guy's intense blue eyes, his long hair, the disappointed expression he would have if Ethan forgot him. "He's just taking a shower, brushing his teeth."

He stared out the window. It still gave him a buzz, seeing all of Cambria spread out below. He could see Ivy Street from up here, where the Craig was no doubt lurking, ready to crush Ethan if he saw him.

"Not if I see you first," Ethan muttered.

He wondered if a penny thrown from up here would kill someone. That had always sounded like bullshit. Maybe a shoe, though.

And for a no-neck like the Craig? A couch.

Crap. He was supposed to be thinking about someone else, not the Craig.

He glanced at his palm. The ink had long since been rubbed off by a sheen of *Scepter* sweat, but the gesture made it click in his brain.

"Teebo!" he said aloud. "He's gone, but he'll be back. He had *Scepter* breath."

Ha. *Scepter* breath. Ethan breathed into his own hand. He had a little *Scepter* breath himself. But brushing his teeth would probably make him zone out.

No problem. Just keep walking and thinking about Teebo.

He made a tight circle around the padded armchairs in the middle of the room. Each time his attention started to slip, he'd check his hand again. The gesture kept reminding him of Teebo and everything he'd said. Tee had just told him why he'd left home. His parents forgetting him, something about his grandma. And how the voice had tortured him with it last summer.

Ethan couldn't forget any of this, ever, or he was a bad friend.

Where had Tee gone? To the store?

Ethan came to a halt, feeling sweat trickling down the inside of his arm. *What* store?

It didn't matter. The point was that his name was Teebo, however the hell you spelled it, and he was Ethan's best . . .

There was a sound outside the door. Tee was back.

Ethan crossed the living area and pulled it open.

"Teebo!" he cried.

But it was a young guy rolling past with a laundry cart. The guy came to a halt, looked at him, then at a clipboard hanging from the cart.

Ethan's heart sank. He was hiding from the law and his mom and evil bank robbers. And now he'd opened the door to a stranger.

"Housekeeping." The guy scratched his shaved head. "Uh, I didn't know this room was occupied. Do you need service, sir?"

"Um . . . ," Ethan began, then let the voice take over. "We're staying here by special arrangement. Mr. Penka told us we wouldn't be disturbed."

"Sorry, sir." The guy waved the clipboard. "You're not on the list, so nobody's going to bother you."

Ethan returned to his real voice. “Thank you. Um, bye.”

He shut the door and leaned his back against it, swearing in a whisper.

That had been a close one. But the guy had believed him. The voice wasn’t all bad, no matter what Teebo said.

Ethan smiled. That name, it was still with him.

A moment later Teebo appeared in his bathrobe, rubbing a towel through his hair and trying to look nonchalant.

Right. He’d been taking a shower.

Ethan tried to pretend he wasn’t freaked out and soaked in sweat. That he hadn’t forgotten where Tee was and stupidly opened the door to potential danger. Because remembering your best friend’s name was no big deal.

He flopped onto the couch and said, “Hey, *Scepter* Breath. Want me to kick your ass some more?”

CHAPTER 39

FLICKER

"THE HERO OF OUR TALE SEEMS TO HAVE A THING for cracks in walls," Lily said, a smirk in her voice.

Flicker ignored the words, focusing on the photographs in Lily's hands. They were close-ups of faded graffiti, cracks in asphalt, and brick walls textured with age. All of which supported Nate's theory that Anon lived in a hotel here in downtown Cambria.

According to Nate's notes, the style was something called wabi-sabi, which was about appreciating imperfect and transient things. An interesting choice for someone who slipped out of memory so easily.

Flicker wondered if Nate had stolen the camera, or if Anon had given him the images. Did the boy called Nothing *want* to be found?

"Quit shuffling them," Flicker said. "Just focus on one."

They had to be systematic. Everybody in town had seen that stupid video of Ethan by now. The two would need help soon, whether Anon wanted it or not. And these photos were the only way to find him.

Lily grumbled, but chose a photo and settled herself against the cool stone of the Cambria Library main branch. The sounds of traffic were all around, and a soft breeze made the printout shiver in her hands.

The photo showed a chipped cement wall with a jagged crack running through it. Clinging to the wall was a tiny green plant that had taken root in the gap. More cracks stretched away from the leaves, as if the plant were pushing outward, a small force, persistent and irresistible.

Flicker placed a steadying hand on Lily's shoulder. "Story, please."

"Okay," her sister began, eyes locked on the photo. "The boy called Nothing stared at the walls of his secret castle. They were thick and strong, built to last a thousand years. But no wall is without cracks and fissures, and he knew that one day he would walk free, past the castle walls and out into the sunlight."

As Lily spoke, Flicker left her sister's vision behind and flung herself outward into the crowd. She moved fast, fluttering from head to head, needing little more than glimpses.

Nobody was staring at the walls, of course. Or at cracks in the pavement or the places where old paint had chipped away from brick walls. People stared at their phones, or watched traffic lights or the heels of the people in front of them. They glanced at newspaper headlines, ads, and signs in shopwindows.

But in the periphery of those glances were the things that a boy called Nothing took photos of—fractures and crevices, broken pavement, bleached stone. In those edges of vision Flicker was looking for a match.

She hopped farther, across the streets and down alleyways, to the farthest reaches of her range, which was a long way here in the downtown crowds. But she found nothing that resembled the tiny green plant clinging to a gray cement wall.

Then it struck her, and she sighed. "Of course. It's a *plant*."

Her sister's rambling story came to a halt. "What?"

"It's probably dead by now. Or flowered or whatever. That picture could be from a year ago."

Lily made another grumbly noise. She wasn't fully on board with the whole finding-the-fictional-boyfriend project. When presented with the plan that morning at breakfast, she'd said, "Sounds really mature, Riley. Like being one of those fans who forget that TV actors aren't really the characters they play."

But a few minutes of cajoling in their private accent had convinced Lily to come along. She liked being included when superpowers were involved.

"Can you find one without a plant?" Flicker asked.

"Whatever." Lily shuffled through the printouts until she reached a photo of a wall painted a brilliant sky blue. The paint was gone in two big patches, leaving exposed stone bearing flecks of half a dozen other colors.

Flicker squeezed her sister's shoulder. "Perfect. That blue should be easy to spot."

"If you say so." Lily stared at the picture for a moment, as if collecting threads of narrative from the fissures and flecks, and began her story again.

By the time late afternoon had covered the streets of downtown in shadow, they'd found three matches: the blue wall, a rusted red door in an alleyway, a bus-stop bench with splintered wooden slats. All three photographs had been taken in the same one-block area.

"What's around here?" Flicker asked. She had retreated into blindness, dizzy from scattering her vision like leaves in a storm. Darkness felt steadying and solid.

"A couple of bars," Lily said. "Not like the clubs on Ivy. Scuzzier."

"Anywhere he could live?"

"No apartment buildings, just offices. And the Magnifique, I guess."

"Of course," Flicker murmured. Her borrowed eyes had been glancing up to admire it all day—towering, terraced, wrapped in glass. The tallest and most expensive hotel in Cambria. The boy called Nothing really did live in a castle.

She'd found him.

"Seriously?" Lily asked. "That place is like a thousand a night. How rich *is* this guy?"

"Not rich. Magic. Haven't you been listening to your story?"

"Yeah, but it's a *story*. And what you guys have isn't really magic. It's just a mutation or something, right?"

"Or something," Flicker said with a shrug. Glorious Leader had a lot of theories. Mutations, radiation, eating genetically engineered foods or expired Twinkies. The fact that they'd all been born in 2000, a year with a lot of zeroes in it. So to speak.

"You know these are just stories, right?" Lily sounded worn out. "I'm just making stuff up."

"But that's what everyone does. Before we really know someone, we're looking at the surface and guessing, embroidering."

"Um, Riley, this is more like *stalking* than embroidering."

"This is me helping a friend."

"Well, I'm done here," Lily said. "You coming home?"

Flicker shook her head. She was going to sit in the lobby of the Magnifique until she found Anonymous.

He'd been alone long enough.

CHAPTER 40
BELLWETHER

THIS SIDE OF TOWN WAS FULL OF EYES.

The Heights was a poor part of Cambria, watchful and tight-knit, wary of newcomers. As Nate drove onto the street where Chizara worked, he felt the weight of all that vision.

Not that he was worried about the attention his mother's Audi attracted. Nate knew exactly what to do with attention.

There were plenty of shady spots available, but he parked in the sun, where the car's chrome would sparkle. As he stepped onto the curb, he felt the focus of the street settle over him. The girls playing handball against the convenience-store wall, little kids swapping stories on a stoop, old men playing dominoes—all of them paused a moment, and Nate smiled.

He didn't try to deflect their admiration of the car, his dress shirt and hundred-dollar sunglasses, or the gold rings shining on his finger. Instead he gathered every twitch of envy and smoothed it into respect. Nate felt it register with the crowd that he belonged here. Otherwise how could he look so serene?

He moved gently away from the parking spot, careful not to draw the web of attention with him. It settled where he had first smiled at them, the whole street suddenly wary and protective of that glittering car.

Don't touch that. Someone important owns it.

"Took you long enough," Chizara said.

She was hunched over what appeared to be the guts of an electric toaster. Heating elements, springs, a dozen screws lined up neatly on the wooden table. Only the deco chrome shell with its two bread slots revealed what those parts had been.

What a waste, using her talents this way. Like a brain surgeon clubbing seals for a living.

"I had unexpected visitors," Nate said, putting a little tightness in his voice.

Chizara's eyes widened, her annoyance derailed by a pulse of fear. Her mind had gone straight to the police. Nate nodded gravely.

She carefully set down her screwdriver. "My ride's here, Bob. Gotta go."

An older man, hunched at his own desk over another scattering of parts, glimmered with interest. Nate settled him with a smile.

As Chizara straightened her tools, Nate scanned the shelves lining the walls of the workroom. They were full of junky appliances and rusty parts. What would it be like to be too poor to buy a new toaster when yours broke?

Nate liked money. It was a sleek and clever invention, beautiful in the way it lubricated power and focused people's attention. But it had a clumsy, brutal side too. Money bludgeoned people without it into silence, shut them away in neighborhoods like this.

Nate knew that anyone who rose to power had to take one side or another in that contest of meanings. But he hadn't decided which one suited him yet.

"You ready?" Chizara said, brushing past him. "I split my lunch with Bob. I'm hungry."

Nate gave her his most radiant smile. "I'm buying."

"There were two detectives. And Ethan's mother."

Chizara let out a slow breath between pursed lips. "She's a detective, right?"

"A district attorney." Nate looked for the waitress, needing more water, but she'd disappeared again. The place was almost empty. He'd planned to take Chizara to a crowded restaurant downtown, somewhere with a crowd, an audience. But she'd insisted on this tiny Korean place near her home. Even full, it would barely contain enough people to get the Curve going.

Chizara wasn't giving him an inch.

"Did they say anything about Officer Bright?" she asked.

Nate took a moment to look somber. "Of course not. Their visit had nothing to do with those criminals escaping. They just wanted to ask why Ethan called me."

"What did you tell them?"

"The truth. That we used to be friends. And now we're not."

Chizara settled back into the squeaky plastic of the booth, looking thoughtful. "Not friends anymore? You seemed happy to have him back yesterday."

"Whether he's my friend or not, Scam needs us," Nate said. "We all need each other."

"Yeah, we do *such* great things together."

Nate sighed to himself. He'd come up with that line in the car, and it had been a good one. But he'd used it without laying any groundwork, and the restaurant was too empty for his power to help.

On top of that, his throat was dry, which made his voice sound weak and desperate. *Where* was the waitress?

Chizara wore a grim smile. She knew he hated bad service.

Nate gazed at the menu, which was coated in plastic and frayed at the corners. "This is quaint. What do you recommend?"

"I recommend that you delete my number from your phone," Chizara said. "And that you and your friends stop playing with these powers."

"We're not playing. We're learning how they work."

"And what did you *learn* yesterday? How to get someone killed?"

"Officer Bright isn't . . . ," Nate began, but arguing the definition of "dead" was exactly the wrong way to win her trust. "It's terrible what happened. And it's my fault for pushing you too hard. But if you ignore what you are, and let that itch build up, what do you think will happen?"

Chizara drew back in her seat, but she was still listening.

Suddenly he saw how to convince her. Not loyalty to the group, not self-improvement. An appeal to her morality.

"Let's say you keep yourself under control, Chizara. Maybe for a year, maybe ten. But Crash is still inside you, growing stronger. In the end, what happens? You take out a hospital? An airplane overhead? A whole *city*?"

She held his gaze, but a nervous swallow moved her throat.

"We found out yesterday how powerful you are. You might be the strongest of us." The words gave him a shiver—of jealousy? No, the irritation of seeing power wasted on the unwilling.

"So how do I stop myself?" she asked softly.

"Not by repressing what you are—by *mastering* it. You have to practice like an athlete, every day."

"Like Scam does?" Chizara shook her head. "Every time he lets that thing inside him talk, he winds up with less control, not more."

"Ethan's different. Another species." Nate shuddered a little as he spoke. The last time he'd put it that harshly was last summer, about ten seconds before Scam tore the group to pieces. But keeping Chizara was worth playing every card. "He doesn't get stronger in a crowd like the rest of us. His power's connected to his own ego, not to the people around him. He's the opposite of us."

She was silent, staring out the window, and the waitress finally appeared.

"You order for us both, Chizara." Let her be in control.

She ordered everything extra hot, another way to keep him off balance. But nothing in this place would match his mother's love of habaneros.

When they were alone again, he took a drink of water and said, "It's not only the difference in your power, Chizara. It's who you *are*. You have discipline. You have ethics."

"Maybe for now," she said. "But yesterday felt so *good*. What if I love crashing things too much to stop?"

Nate nodded, hiding his surprise. Anyone could see that Chizara enjoyed being Crash, but he'd never heard her admit it aloud.

"Yesterday changed me." Her eyes glazed over, like they had after the crash yesterday. Her focus left him, drifting into memories and doubt.

"Changed you how? What happened?"

"A man's in the hospital because of us."

"What changed, Chizara?"

She looked frightened, ready to draw herself back and tell

him nothing. He had to act now, with no crowd to help him.

All he had left was the twist in his power, the one he'd discovered two years ago when he'd been in love with Flicker. When he'd needed to show how much he trusted her, to reveal how vulnerable he was behind his charm.

It hadn't worked out the way he'd hoped—they were still just friends. But showing himself to Flick had been worth it even so.

The problem was, he didn't trust Chizara that way. But the Zeroes couldn't lose her. They were all in danger if they didn't stick together.

Nataniel closed his eyes, weighing the full measure of the power inside him. And then he let it drop. His guts rose up in him, like he was in an elevator with a snapped cable. The channels of dominance that extended in all directions, hungry for attention and obedience, fluttered powerless.

Now he sat exposed before Chizara, unprotected, feeling a wretched and unfamiliar sense of *neediness.*

"Please," he said. "Tell me what happened."

She stared at him a moment. She'd felt the absence right away.

"You four are what matters to me," he said. "I can't lose any of you, not even Ethan, or I'm nothing. Zilch. Nada."

His throat was dry again, and his voice sounded pathetic. He felt an awful certainty that if she rejected him now, his heart would break.

"I'm pointless without you, so if you're changing—"

"I can fix things now," Chizara said.

Nate sputtered to a halt, trying to understand. He was so thankful for any answer that it was hard to breathe.

"Fix things?" he managed.

"My phone. And my brother's video game. I reached inside and fixed them." Her voice sank to a whisper. "Since what I did to the police station, I can uncrash things."

It took a long time for the words to sink in, but when they did, they kicked Nate's power to spinning again. All his tendrils of dominance and attention twisted to life, hungrier now than ever.

A moment later the waitress was at his side, obediently filling his water. Nate drank it all in a gulp, then pointed at the glass again. She poured, lingering at the task, drawn by his greedy power. In the awkward silence he searched for words to make Chizara understand.

She was the only one of them whose power went beyond other human beings, reaching into the guts of objects and changing reality.

If she could learn to transform as well as destroy, anything was possible.

But telling her that wouldn't be enough. Chizara needed to see that she was not only powerful, but *worthy*. She had to atone for the life that yesterday's mission had destroyed. To know that her power was worth embracing, Chizara had to save someone.

It was up to Nate to make that happen.

CHAPTER 41
MOB

IN A BACK ROOM OF FUSE, KELSIE WATCHED FIG count out three grand.

It was all ones and fives, beer-stained bills from the tip jar and register. It was taking a long, *long* time. Fig smoothed each note with the side of his hand and built clumsy piles of cash.

When he was done, she stuffed the bundle into her bag. The scent of beer rose up from it.

"You couldn't take this to a bank and swap it for twenties?" she asked. "Would've been lighter. Smelled better, too."

"Nah," Fig said. "Too many bank robbers."

Kelsie glanced up at him. Fig was managing not to break into a smile.

"We are so not laughing about this yet," she said. "My dad's in deep."

Fig's expression grew sober. "I know."

Her dad's trouble was way bigger than anything Kelsie knew how to fix. Whenever she tried to come up with a way to help him, her thoughts circled along the same path. If only he hadn't taken that job with the Bagrovs, or tried to rob a bank. Or if that creepy kid hadn't spooked him.

Who *was* that guy, anyhow?

Craig said his name was Axel, and that he knew stuff he shouldn't. Seemed like Axel knew a *lot* of stuff. If that bank video was anything to go by, he knew more about her own dad than Kelsie did.

She'd watched it twenty times by now. He'd really said Kelsie's name, and mentioned her mom, too. Which totally creeped her out. Maybe the Bagrovs had sent him to mess up the robbery. Maybe Axel had been following her dad, spying on him, waiting for an opportunity to screw him over.

Well, it'd worked. And sent Kelsie's whole life into free fall, too.

She hadn't been home since Thursday night. She was tired and scared and homeless, and her thoughts kept coming back to Axel.

The bank video was all over the internet, but the guy himself was missing in action. So where was he now?

Fig said, "You taking the cash to your old man tonight?"

"I have to wait until he calls."

"Where you staying?" Fig asked.

"At Ling's." And tomorrow night probably Remmy's again. Then maybe Mikey's. She couldn't think that far ahead.

"It'll be okay, Kelsie. You'll see." Fig gave her a reassuring smile. "You look nice."

Kelsie shrugged. Trying to cheer her up, Ling had lent her the sparkliest silver dress she owned. She'd paired it with silver high-tops, saying they were going to have fun tonight. Kelsie was grateful for the clothes, but she didn't feel sparkly. She just felt scared.

She hefted the messenger bag. The cash was like a brick in there.

"You gonna be okay with that?" Fig asked.

"Anyone messes with me, I can always thump them with it. Thanks for coming through, Fig."

He shrugged. "I always pay my debts."

They headed back out to the club.

The music tonight was down-tempo, chill-out tracks with a subliminal tribal beat. The crowd was smiling and loose, ready to be soothed into a kind of syncopated mellowness. They danced and shook it out like a big, cheerful animal.

Kelsie let herself drift into their simple, cruisy optimism. Something she hadn't felt all day.

"There's the smile I've been looking for." Fig grinned at her.

She linked an arm through his and leaned on his shoulder. Maybe it really would all be okay. Maybe her dad had a plan for the cash that would get him off the hook with everyone.

But then something like a bucket of cold water hit Kelsie.

She scanned the room for the source. Through the gentle rocking of the dancers came a different movement, something more determined. A group of six men pierced the dance floor like an arrowhead, a crowd within the crowd. She pulled the bag of money close. Was it the Bagrovs, here in the club?

But the men weren't headed her way. They were moving toward the door. And it was Craig marching at the front of the group, a fierce expression on his face.

"Where's he going?" Kelsie asked.

Fig followed her gaze. "To do some damage. Someone spotted that kid from the bank video."

She spun toward Fig. "Axel? Where?"

Fig shrugged. "Somebody who works at the Magnifique. Saw the guy in the penthouse."

"The *penthouse*?" Living it up while Kelsie couch-surfed her way into orphanhood.

Craig's gang was almost at the door, their angry intent like a swarm of bees rolling across the room.

Axel was in for the biggest beating of his life.

Which was fine with Kelsie, except that she had to find out what he knew about her dad and the bank robbery and the Bagrovs. She needed to know why he'd sent her life into this spiral.

"Gotta go, Fig." She gave his arm a squeeze and made a dash for the door, the heavy bag banging awkwardly on her hip.

CHAPTER 42

MOB

SHE MADE IT TO THE MAGNIFIQUE IN RECORD TIME.

It helped that she knew all the alleyways in downtown Cambria. Plus she was sprinting, and Craig's gang moved more like an army tank on legs.

When she reached the Magnifique's lobby, the size of it made her pause. She'd been to underground dance parties before, in abandoned factories and warehouses. This lobby was as vast and echoey as those, but gleaming with expense. She felt small and exposed in her little sparkly dress.

She headed for the elevators, feeling the buzz from the crowd around her. They were mostly guests, travelers looking for fun in a new town. She felt her own anticipation ramp theirs up a notch and loop back on her. She had to get to Axel before Craig and his goons did.

In the elevator, she hit the button marked PH.

It only blinked. The elevator doors didn't budge.

"Come *on*," she said.

A man in a suit stepped into the elevator. He pulled out a plastic card with the swirly Magnifique logo on it and slotted it into the elevator controls. Then he pressed the fifth-floor button, which stayed lit.

Of course. A hotel this fancy had real security.

Gratefully, Kelsie pressed PH again, but again the button only flickered.

"Gotta use your own card," the guy said. "They're programmed for each floor."

The door was already sliding shut, and Kelsie shot her arm out to catch it. The rubber bumpers bounced off her wrist.

"Oh, right. My boyfriend has it." She stepped out.

As the door slid closed behind her, Kelsie scanned the lobby entrance. At least Craig and his gang weren't here yet.

It had been a while since she'd picked anyone's pocket, not since she was twelve years old, but the old instincts clicked back in as she cased the lobby. A group was best, or someone in a hurry.

And they had to be rich. Somebody who looked like they belonged on the penthouse floor.

There was a large group at the concierge desk, arguing loudly with the guy behind it. As she closed in, Kelsie felt the undertow of their annoyance join forces with her own panic, redoubling both.

"Where are we supposed to eat!" one of them shouted.

The concierge stayed calm. "The whole city's booked up with Fourth of July tourists. But we'll find you something."

Kelsie bumped into the shouting man, got his wallet. She hit another of the group on the way past, fanning his coat pockets. Nothing.

Behind a giant flower arrangement, she opened the wallet. There, slipped in among the credit cards, was the Magnifique logo. The guy was still yelling at the concierge, so she dropped his wallet into the flowers. Dickhead.

But what were the chances he was staying on the top floor? She needed more keys.

She scanned the crowd again, making a map in her head of pockets and bags, then twisted her connection with the tour group, sending her anxiety toward them. Their noise ramped, until everyone in the lobby was looking at them, distracted.

She bumped a man in a linen jacket, fanned his pants pockets, and felt plastic. Lifted it while he apologized to her.

Kelsie kept moving, weaving in and out, skimming close.

She brushed against a young woman and emptied her jacket pockets with two fingers. Some cash, a credit card, a key card. Kelsie slipped the rest of it back into the woman's other pocket on another pass. The woman never noticed a thing.

Kelsie took the three stolen cards back to the elevator and swiped one across the reader, then another.

PH only blinked.

"Come *on*," Kelsie muttered.

She was down to her last card.

Craig and his gang entered the lobby. Their black T-shirts seemed to swallow the light as they marched across the glossy marble floor.

She swiped the last card across the reader and stabbed the PH button.

It stayed stubbornly dark.

CHAPTER 43

FLICKER

FLICKER WAS IN THE CONCIERGE'S EYES.

His long fingers were scrolling a touch-pad screen, his gaze flitting across requests from customers arriving in the next few days. The hotel was filling up, thanks to the big Fourth of July display. Everyone wanted a room with a view of the old Parker-Hamilton Hotel, which was scheduled for demolition during the show.

Every minute or so the concierge looked up, scanning the lobby in a discreet and professional way. Perfect for keeping watch, which Flicker had been doing for a few hours now. It was making her weird and spacey, spreading her awareness through the lobby for this long.

Flicker saw herself in her wingback chair, her bright red dress easy to spot. But as she gave herself a smile, the concierge's gaze slipped past her and came to a rest on a huge man strolling across the lobby floor.

The concierge stared. It was hard not to. The guy was as wide as a door, all shoulders and thighs. He wore a shiny black T-shirt made from enough silk for a parachute. Five other big guys cruised across the lobby floor with him, a formation of battleships.

A man in a Magnifique staff uniform came up and started talking to them, and the concierge's eyes dropped back to his computer screen.

Flicker sent her vision into the big guy's eyes. She couldn't hear anything from across the lobby, but it didn't seem like a confrontation. The two were huddled close, the big guy's eyes moving warily from side to side.

The hotel staffer, a short man with a shaved head, held out his empty palm, and the big guy pushed a stack of twenties into it. In return, the staffer produced a hotel key card and slipped it into the breast pocket of the big guy's shirt.

This was getting interesting. Flicker unfolded her cane and stood.

The big guy and his friends were headed straight for the elevators.

But before he reached them, a woman—a girl, really, no older than Flicker—in a very sparkly dress appeared and blocked his path. She stood about five feet tall and had as much chance as a rabbit trying to stop a bulldozer, but the guy came to a halt. The girl started talking to him, a fierce expression on her face.

Flicker was already closing in, and she caught their voices.

". . . cares about your stupid money?" the girl was saying. "My dad's in *jail* because of him! I want to be there when you—"

"Trust me, Kelsie," he interrupted. "You don't want to see what I'm about to . . ."

Their voices faded as Flicker passed. She couldn't stand there and eavesdrop, but this was way too interesting to ignore.

And *Kelsie*? She'd heard that name recently.

Right—Ethan's little rant at the bank. The voice had said *Kelsie* to the robbers.

Crap. This was about the bank video, and these people were here at the Magnifique, where Anon lived. It was all too much of a coincidence.

Flicker reached for her new phone. She had to get Nate here.

Not Nate—Glorious Leader. This was a mission: saving Anon's and Scam's lives.

Flicker skipped her eyes around the room. The argument was attracting attention from all directions.

The girl in the sparkly dress was in the big guy's face, practically yelling at him. The other five looked embarrassed that their leader was taking shit from this pipsqueak. But she kept going, talking with her hands, thumping the guy's chest, grabbing at his shirt. Something flashed in her hand as she pounded him—a hotel card key.

Was she a guest here?

"Dial Nate," Flicker said to her phone.

The big guy didn't get mad, just stared at the girl until he finally brushed her aside.

For a second Flicker thought the girl would go apeshit. But her anger seemed to switch off all at once. She watched them go, clutching her messenger bag, the hotel key still in her hand.

Why the hell wasn't Glorious Leader picking up?

Flicker pushed her vision back into the big guy's eyes. He led his men into an empty elevator, pulled the card key from his breast pocket, and slotted it into the reader. Then his gigantic thumb pushed the very top button on the controls, the one marked PH.

"Shit," Flicker said. The penthouse. Where else in the palace would the boy called Nothing live? "Come *on*. Answer!"

The button lit for a moment, then went dark again. The big guy's thumb pressed it once more.

The phone went to voice mail, and Flicker's words came out in a rush. "I'm downtown at the Hotel Magnifique. Anon lives here. And there's this gang of . . . goons, or whatever, here to kick Scam's ass. We need to warn them!"

It wasn't just Ethan in danger, she realized with a pulse of real fear. Anyone they found with him would be dead meat too.

She turned and headed toward the reception desk, navigating by sound. Forget keeping Anon's secrets—maybe she could convince hotel security to stop these guys, or to let her call the penthouse.

She cast her vision back into the elevator. The big guy was still pressing the PH button. The number wouldn't light, and the door didn't close. He swiped the card again, but nothing seemed to work.

Flicker slowed to a halt.

Suddenly the big guy was storming out, his eyes searching the lobby, coming to rest on the hotel staffer who'd sold him the key. He headed that way.

Flicker stood where she was, frozen for a moment. None of this made sense.

She flashed her vision across a hundred eyeballs, searching for the girl in the sparkly dress. There she was, disappearing into another elevator. Flicker tried to find her eyeballs, but a moment later the girl was out of range, the elevator climbing away from the lobby crowd.

Flicker's ringtone for Glorious Leader—"Hail to the Chief"—echoed across the marble lobby.

His voice was frantic. "Flick, I'm in my car! What's happening?"

"I'm not quite sure," she said. "But it's definitely happening *now*."

CHAPTER 44
SCAM

"I NEVER THOUGHT I'D SAY THIS," ETHAN MUTTERED. "But I'm totally over *Red Scepter III*."

"You're over *losing*, is what you mean."

Ethan opened his mouth for a witty comeback, but then he clamped it shut. The voice was in charge of comebacks, and it had been only a little over twenty-four hours since his promise to Thibault not to use the voice.

"You suck" was the best he could think up on his own.

A knock shook the door, and both of them jumped.

"You order anything from room service?" Thibault asked.

Ethan had tried once, but he'd forgotten the passwords. The knocking came again, hard and insistent, before he could admit this.

"Does that *sound* like room service?" Ethan hissed. He was

already on his feet and headed to his bedroom.

This was probably because of that cleaning guy who'd seen him earlier. The one he hadn't told Tee about. Crap. Hotel security must have figured out the room was occupied.

But it was okay. Thibault would work his forgetting magic and the whole thing would blow over. No need to panic.

Ethan stopped just inside the bedroom, out of view of the doorway. But he stayed where he could still see Thibault. The last thing he needed was to forget what was going on and wander back in.

When Tee opened the door, his expression changed. "Um, hello?"

"Where is he?" A girl's voice, angry.

She took a step forward, straight up into Thibault's face. Ethan caught a glimpse of her before backing away. She wore a shiny silver dress with matching high-tops. A white messenger bag was strapped across her shoulder.

Definitely not Magnifique staff.

Tee was too freaked out to answer. The girl pushed past him and marched into the room. She looked really pissed.

Ethan drew back another step, out of sight now. There were a lot of pissed-off girls in his past. Still, it was weird how he couldn't place this one. Even weirder that she'd tracked him down in Anon's secret lair.

More like impossible.

"It's just me here," Thibault was saying.

"Just you, huh?" the girl said. "So why are there two sodas on the table? And two game controllers? Axel was here, wasn't he?"

"Axel?" came Thibault's voice.

"Axel," Ethan whispered to himself. His knees went weak.

The only time he'd ever heard that name was out of his own mouth, two nights ago on an ill-fated trip with a paranoid drug dealer in a beat-up Ford sedan.

Which meant this girl was a friend of the Craig's.

"We don't have time to screw around," the girl said. "They're right behind me."

They? Ethan wondered if hiding was such a good idea. If this girl had found him, who else was on the way?

"Listen, I don't know what you're . . ." Thibault began. His words faded as Ethan stepped out of the bedroom.

"*Who's* right behind you?" Ethan said.

Now that he had a better look at the girl, she looked familiar. She had high cheekbones and soft, blond hair that curled to her shoulders. Her green eyes lit as she stared back at him.

"It's you," she said. "From the video."

"It's you," he said. "From the diner."

She was still looking at him. Suddenly all he wanted was for her to *keep* looking at him. He let the words bubble into his throat. "I'm the one you want. I can help fix this."

Whatever that meant. But at least the voice had stunned the girl for a moment. Her arms wrapped around her shoulders. "You can?"

"I can help your father," the voice said. "I know how to make amends with the Bagrovs."

The girl's gaze softened, filling with a hope that went straight through Ethan's skin. At the moment he didn't care who the Bagrovs were. He just wanted to help her.

"Okay. But we have to go," she said. "Craig's right behind me."

"Don't worry—" the voice began, but a surge of panic sent Ethan's own words crashing into his mouth. "Wait. *The Craig's* behind you?"

"Cambria's angriest dude," she confirmed. The voice's spell was broken. She marched over to where he stood. "We have to get out of here. Right *now*."

She grabbed hold of his elbow and began dragging him toward the door. Ethan went along with it. It wasn't every day a really hot girl in a sparkly dress showed up to rescue you. And if the Craig really *was* coming, it was time to move.

But then Thibault stepped in front of them, and the girl came to a startled halt.

"Who are *you*?" She'd already forgotten him.

Ethan would've killed for a power like Thibault's right then. Anything so the Craig would forget he'd ever existed.

"How did you find us?" Thibault asked. "How did you get up here?"

"No time for that, Tee," Ethan said. "Grab your stuff!"

Thibault didn't move. "My stuff?"

Ethan ran to the couch and pulled on his sneakers. "Craig is the guy I stole that money from. We need to get out of here before he redecorates this room with our insides."

"Not just Craig," said the girl. "He's got friends with him."

Okay. This girl in the sparkly dress was cute, but every time she talked, the situation got worse.

Ethan pulled a pillowcase free of the pillow he'd been propping himself on to play *Scepter*. He crouched by the minibar and started sweeping little bottles and candy bars into the case.

"Seriously?" Thibault said. "You're taking the minibar?"

"I *like* the minibar! If there's anything you want to keep, grab it." Ethan got to his feet. "Your place is about to be visited by a guy with a tree trunk where his neck should be!"

"And five of his meanest friends," the girl reminded them. She stood in the open doorway. "If they find me here, I'm probably as dead as you guys. So *move* already."

Ethan pulled Thibault through the door and into the hallway. "Seriously, Tee. The guy is scary."

"Okay. But how do you know we can trust her?"

Ethan hesitated. He wasn't sure why he trusted her. Because she was pretty? Because she'd busted in and said the one name guaranteed to make him jump out of his skin?

For all he knew, the girl might be working *with* the Craig. No way was he leading Thibault, his one friend, into a trap.

She was holding open a door marked FIRE STAIRS, her eyes on the elevators.

"They're almost here," she whispered.

"Look at her, Tee, she's as scared as I am."

"We don't even know who she is! Use your voice, Ethan."

"You want me to . . . ," Ethan began. But it made sense. He desperately wanted to know who the girl really was. Surely the voice could say something that would make her tell him.

The words came out in a rush. "Your dad made it out of the police station, right, Kelsie? So where is he now?"

She stared at him a moment, then suddenly the messenger bag was off her shoulder and swinging through the air. It struck Ethan like a sack of books, sending him staggering. She had a great swing.

"You think I'd tell *you*?" she cried. "After you ruined his life? After all that stuff you said in the bank?"

"Ow!" Ethan had to grab hold of the wall to keep from falling. His mind spun back to those awful moments on the cold marble floor of the bank. "Wait. You're Kelsie. The bank robber's daughter?"

"Oh, great," Thibault was muttering to himself. "This is *perfect*."

Kelsie readied the bag for another swing. "You know exactly who I am, Axel! You know *way* too much about everything!"

"I'm *Ethan*, okay?" And he didn't know much of anything.

Except that now his choice was between the neckless majesty of the Craig and this pissed-off daughter of a violent criminal. The voice would never tell Ethan himself what to do with a choice like that. But it might tell someone else.

Ethan opened his mouth, wanting very much to give Tee the best advice ever.

Right then the elevator doors chimed, and the voice only had three words:

"Run like hell."

CHAPTER 45
ANONYMOUS

DAMN IT, NO SHOES? AGAIN?

But "run like hell" didn't leave room for argument. Especially when Ethan's beast voice said it. So Thibault had run.

At least this time he wasn't in a bathrobe.

He took the stairs two at a time, the concrete cold under his bare feet. The others were already halfway down the first flight. The pillowcase bounced like a Santa sack on Ethan's shoulder, the minibar bottles clinking.

The girl's high-tops echoed in the stairwell. Swinging Ethan around the turns, she was making their descent into a kind of dance. She'd forgotten Thibault was following, the bright lines of her awareness focused on the stairs and Ethan.

But Thibault wasn't letting her out of his sight. He didn't trust her. She'd already whacked Ethan with her messenger bag—what would she do when she really got to know him? And where was she taking them, anyway?

Thibault caught up on the next landing and grabbed her sparkly shoulder. "Kelsie—"

She cried out and spun from his grip. She started to swing her bag, but then her memory registered him.

"I can get us out of the building," Thibault said while he had her. "But where then?"

"Ivy Street." She pulled Ethan onward.

Thibault stayed close, grabbing a few wisps of her focus. "*Ivy* Street?"

She slingshotted Ethan around the next landing, "We can disappear in the crowds. I know places to hide there."

"Crowds are a bad idea. Everyone in town knows Ethan's face—and half of them want to punch it!"

But she'd gone from him already, her connection as fleeting as the cold shimmers the stairwell lights sent over her dress.

Ethan looked up at him, still bonded by their time together.

"Ivy Street, Ethan?" Thibault shouted. "Cops? More of Craig's buddies?"

Ethan tried to slow, but Kelsie wouldn't let him.

And Ethan didn't want to resist her. Thibault had felt it the second Kelsie stepped through the door: Ethan's sharp, crackling interest. Man, look at that attention he was throwing after her—a big fat cable of electric iridescence. An instant crush.

Figured. Even after almost two days together, Thibault was nothing compared to a cute girl in a sparkly dress.

He sped up, grabbed hold of the stair rail, and swung around another landing. Gaining on Kelsie, he caught her bag strap.

"Kelsie, *listen*. Your dad robbed a bank! Why the hell should we trust you?"

She flung him an exasperated look and pulled away. "I want to keep Axel alive. Or whatever his name is—"

"Ethan." Ethan spoke up, like this was a school dance.

Thibault kept hold, scrabbling for the threads of her attention. "Why do you care?"

"We've got things to discuss. Like why he set my dad up with a bunch of Russian mobsters."

Russian mobsters? What the—

Kelsie jumped four steps to the next landing. Ethan happily followed suit.

"Just shut up and run, okay?" she called back at them both.

Thibault started sliding down the handrails now, from landing to landing. Only the finest filament of awareness floated back over Ethan's shoulder. He was too busy following Little Miss Sparkly into whatever trap was waiting. So much for all their heartfelt confessions.

On about the fifth floor it hit him—what would the Craig's guys *do* when they got into the penthouse and found no Ethan, no duffel bag full of money?

Thibault groaned as he slid down the next railing. It had been bad enough letting Ethan into his lair. But now a band of drug-dealing heavies was going to tear the place apart, getting madder as they went.

His clothes, his books . . .

He reached the ground level just as the others darted off into a service corridor. Thibault followed at a run along the wide concrete hallway, past the Magnifique's kitchens and storerooms, past a couple of kitchen guys—Basir and some new hire—who shrank aside to let them pass.

It was just *stuff,* Thibault told himself. It could all be replaced. He shouldn't have gotten so attached in the first place. This was a good lesson, a reminder that he was nothing, unattached to the world.

He should be grateful he and Ethan weren't being punched into paste up there.

Kelsie paused at a door, panting.

"What's on the other side of this?" she asked Ethan.

"The lobby," Thibault said, pushing past Ethan to reach for the handle.

Kelsie stared at him with confused half recognition. "Wait. Craig might have someone down here, in case Ethan got past them."

"What do his guys look like? They don't know me."

"Like bouncers, only bigger. Black tees, black pants. Tattoos." Kelsie was staying focused on him. Adrenaline helped.

"Got it." Thibault poked his head out the door and scanned the lobby. A hundred lines of awareness crisscrossed the vast room, the usual web of Saturday night buzz.

But then a sudden strand of attention smacked into his forehead.

Near the entrance, a muscly guy in black was looking straight back at him. He'd noticed the service door opening.

Thibault chopped the sticky strand clean off and shut the door. "The lobby's no good. We'll go out the employees' entrance. This way."

He led them back down the service corridor. He would have run, but a bald-headed manager, one he didn't recognize, was standing at the intersection ahead, staring at his phone.

Thibault moved softly in bare feet, hoping the guy wouldn't look up. The others followed—Ethan knew and trusted him, and Kelsie was locked onto Ethan.

Thibault would get them out of here, then call Nate and set up a meeting. Then Scam wouldn't be his problem anymore, and he could get back to check on his clothes and books, along with . . .

The thought gut-punched him.

His laptop.

He almost cried out right there, but the manager ahead of them was looking up from his phone now, surprised to see guests wandering around back here. He looked down at Thibault's bare feet.

When Thibault clipped the guy's attention, his gaze shifted to Ethan and Kelsie. But any misgivings were disguised with a bow and a tilt of the head like a good member of Team Magnifique.

Thibault hurried on toward the staff door. Everything on the laptop—journal, photo library, music—was password-protected and backed up online. That stuff was okay.

But he'd left the browser open. He'd been hunting for an alternate room for the Fourth of July, to get around those penthouse reservations.

The first thing anyone would see was the hotel's system. They'd see that he'd used the manager's login, and know someone had hacked the Magnifique. The game would be up, all his work unraveled, and he'd be homeless again.

Suddenly he hoped that Craig's henchmen would break every damn thing in the room. Anything to get rid of the laptop.

Thibault pushed open the metal staff door and held it wide for Kelsie and Ethan. On his way out he glanced up at the Magnifique with a stab of pain. He'd finagled his way so completely into this place; he knew it inside out, its rooms, its staff.

It was a weird kind of home, but it was *his*. The only home he'd had for three years.

Had he just lost all of it?

CHAPTER 46

FLICKER

"GETTING KIND OF DIZZY," FLICKER SAID.

"Pace yourself." Glorious Leader's voice was in her earbud, along with the sound of car honks. He was still miles outside of town, caught in traffic. With the Fourth coming up and the college students on vacation, downtown was hopping.

Flicker took a deep breath, letting herself linger in the remaining big guy's eyes. He was watching the lobby, but nobody had come in or out except tourists and the usual party crowd. The other five guys in black had acquired a working card key and headed up to the penthouse a few minutes ago. Surely they were there by now.

But where were Scam, Anonymous, and the girl in the sparkly dress?

Careful not to make herself dizzy again, Flicker let her

vision stray a little farther, out onto the streets around the Magnifique. She scanned the eyes of drivers edging their way across town, of stray revelers wandering over from Ivy, of window-shoppers and a policeman on patrol . . . "I can't find them outside."

Glorious Leader swore. "Can you call them somehow? Warn them?"

"I told the guy at the desk I had a friend in one of the penthouses, but he said they were unoccupied. He wouldn't even try!"

"And one of those goons is watching the lobby?" Glorious Leader asked.

"Yep." Flicker threw her vision back into the remaining thug's eyes. And there he was, the beautiful boy called Nothing.

Flicker's heart stuttered for just one beat. His dark hair, his haunted eyes. And he was okay.

But the boy made a chopping motion with his hand, and the guy's gaze drifted away.

"No." Flicker swept her vision around the lobby, seeking another vantage, but all she caught was a glimpse of a closing door.

"What's happening?" Glorious Leader said.

"One second." She cast her eyes past that door, into the hotel spaces behind the scenes, wide corridors with gray concrete floors and painted yellow stripes on the walls.

She found herself in a moving viewpoint, someone rolling

a room service cart covered with the remains of a steak dinner, the white tablecloth spattered with red wine and french fries. Flicker realized she hadn't eaten since lunch.

Then her borrowed eyes looked up, and at the intersection of two dark passageways, Flicker saw a bald man in a manager's uniform. It was the same man who had sold the big guy his hotel card key.

Flicker jumped into the man's eyes. He was staring down at his phone, but the screen was dark, and every few seconds his eyes swept up and down the gray corridors of the hotel.

Watching. Waiting.

"Got something," she murmured to Glorious Leader.

"My onboard says I'll be there in fifteen minutes. Saturday night traffic."

The bald man straightened. Down at the end of the hall, a sparkly dress had caught his eye, shimmering with the harsh fluorescents. Getting closer. There was Anon, his bare feet pale against the gray concrete.

They must have left the penthouse in a hurry.

The bald man barely looked up as the three went past. But his phone screen lit, his thumb swiftly typing: *Got em. Headed toward back exit.*

"They're almost out," Flicker said. "But they were spotted."

"By who?" Glorious Leader demanded. "You sure these aren't cops?"

"The opposite," she said.

"Mierda!" The sounds of fists pounding a steering wheel filled her earbuds. "Twelve minutes out."

She was in Scam's head now, his eyes tracking the sparkly girl's fluid motion in front of him. Flicker could hardly blame Ethan for looking—the girl moved like a dancer. She jumped into the girl's vision for a moment, just as the three of them burst out a big metal door and onto the street.

The girl glanced back once to make sure Scam was still following. Her eyes hardly registered Anonymous.

And then she was running again, in the lead, her gaze steady on their goal—the crowds a few blocks away. The perfect place to disappear.

Then they were out of range, and Flicker was blind, her head throbbing from the workout.

She pulled her cane out, heading toward the lobby exit.

"Change course for Ivy Street," she said. "Party of three, one in a short sparkly dress."

"Good work, Flick. Nine minutes and counting."

"Is Crash coming?"

"She didn't answer her phone. But what do you think?"

"Could be she's taking a tech break." Flicker sighed. "Could be she's saved Scam enough for one weekend."

"Maybe both." Nate gave a dry laugh. "We'll just have to do this on our own."

CHAPTER 47
MOB

THEY WERE ON IVY STREET AT LAST. KELSIE'S home turf.

The Saturday night crowd was cheerful and easy, enjoying the night air between clubs. Kelsie tried to hook into their feel-good vibe, but she couldn't reach it.

She was still holding on to the guy from the bank like a lifeline. He was going to fill in all the gaps about her dad until the world made sense again.

He dragged her to a stop. "I can't be out here like this."

She rolled her eyes. Maybe she should've waited for Craig. He might've let her ask a few questions before he pummeled the guy to death.

"What's the matter? Past your bedtime?"

"Seriously, there are *a lot* of people looking for me." He nodded toward Fuse. "Including the cops."

She followed his gaze. Half a dozen uniformed police were trailing into the club's front door. Of course. They were still looking for escaped criminals like her dad, and they probably wouldn't mind a chat with the kid in the bank video.

No way was she letting anyone else question him before she did.

"I'll get us off the street," Kelsie said. "But you've got some explaining to do . . . Ethan, right?"

"Yeah." He looked happy she'd remembered. "Listen, I don't know what it is you—"

"Why were you in that bank on Friday?" she cut in. "How did you know my dad was going to rob the place?"

Ethan blinked. "I didn't. Why would I walk into a bank robbery *on purpose*?"

"Good question." She pulled him forward, weaving through the crowd. "You said my father's name, even though he had a mask on. Then you said *my* name. You were screwing with his head. *Why?*"

"Ow!" Ethan replied.

She loosened her grasp on his wrist. A little. "And just now in your hotel room, you mentioned the Bagrovs. How do you know them?"

"I don't," he said.

Kelsie tightened her grip again.

"It's hard to explain," Ethan whined. "But . . . I have this *thing*."

She waited for him to say more. Ethan's expression was full of panic, but she could see the wheels spinning in his head. He was deciding what to tell her.

But Kelsie needed the truth. She let everything that had happened to her in the last two days—her fear, her confusion, the loss of her home and her dad, her *grief*—rise up and reach for an outlet in the crowd. She felt the energy on the street shift up a gear.

"Ethan? Please. Tell me what's going on."

It was working. Ethan looked devastated. Which was exactly how she felt.

He spoke in a rush. "Okay, I have this power—"

He jerked suddenly away to one side. Somebody had bumped into him, a guy out of nowhere. He was dark and tall, familiar somehow.

"Oh, right," Kelsie murmured. There had been someone else upstairs, living with Ethan at the Magnifique. But he'd disappeared on the way here.

"Seriously?" he was saying to Ethan. "Was that *you* talking? You were just going to *tell* her?"

"Sorry, man," Ethan said, staring at the ground. "But she saved us."

What were they talking about? Ethan had been about to say something, but this new guy was seriously distracting. . . .

She dragged Ethan closer, her mind focusing again. She'd

let herself get distracted by the crowd around them. She had to get him someplace quiet.

"I need a pen," Ethan said nonsensically.

"What?"

"To write his name with." Ethan was staring at the palm of his free hand. "It rubbed off. I'm going to forget his name!"

Great. Turned out the guy was high, or a psycho of some kind. Maybe he'd just been babbling random words in the bank and gotten lucky with their names.

But that didn't make sense. Jerry was a common name, but Kelsie? And both of them *together*?

No. Somewhere down in his wasted brain he knew something.

"Teebo!" Ethan said, pulling on the front of his shirt. "I remember, because Teebo lent me this shirt. Do you have a pen? He was just here, but he disappears in crowds. . . ."

Ethan wasn't what she'd been expecting. He was a lot weirder.

"Look, Ethan," she said. "When Craig finds your room empty, he'll head back to Ivy. We have to get off the street."

The mention of Craig made Ethan quiet and obedient again. He let her guide him down the street, mumbling the nonsense word "teebo" over and over.

"Are you faking this?" she finally said. "You didn't seem this crazy upstairs. And in that bank video, you were totally smooth."

He drew her to a halt and leaned in closer to whisper, as if anyone could hear him over the blare of nightclub music and crowd babble. "You deserve to know. But I need someplace quiet. It works better one-on-one."

Kelsie nodded as if that made sense. Whatever it took to get this guy someplace where she could interrogate him. She knew a bunch of hiding spots around here. She just had to pick one where none of Craig's friends would stumble on them.

Then she saw the Boom Room ahead, its guitar-shaped roof signboard lit up by a string of dancing lights.

"I know just the place." She tried to drag him forward, but Ethan anchored her to the spot. "*Now* what?"

She spun. A short guy in a crumpled white jacket had his hand on Ethan's shoulder. He was rocking gently like he was happily stoned.

"You're that kid," the stranger said.

"Nah. I'm really not," Ethan said, trying to move around the stranger.

"From the internet!" The stranger turned to his friends in the crowd. All of them looked just as stoned. "Hey, bro, don't we know this kid from the internet?"

"Totally, bro," said one them. "He's the kid in that bank video."

Kelsie felt a bubble of curiosity surrounding Ethan. She tried to grab hold of the energy and tamp it back down—the last thing they needed was attention—but gossip was slippery and small, like minnows bursting out.

One of the guys was shouting, *"Hey! We got a celebrity!"*

Kelsie felt her ears pop. The focus of the crowd was gathering like nasty weather.

She dragged Ethan a few more steps toward the Boom Room. Usually a crowd was good cover. Safety in numbers. But a feedback loop had already formed. People were staring at Ethan, then other people noticed and turned to see what everyone was staring at. . . .

A camera flash went off. Ethan put a hand up like he was warding off a blow.

"Coming through!" Kelsie tried to break the growing focus of the crowd. "Excuse me."

Then someone was right in front of her. A tall dark figure.

Her brain searched and spun—the guy from upstairs again.

"Not this way," he said, hooking a thumb over his shoulder. "Police."

There were two cops near the door of the Boom Room, their eyes drawn by the rumblings of the crowd around Ethan.

She scanned for an opening in the throng, but the tall guy placed a firm hand on her shoulder.

"Your bigger problem is back there," he said. "There's not much I can do against those guys."

Even as he said the words, Kelsie felt the heavy, unswerving approach. The mini crowd of giant men closing in, full of purpose. No point even looking.

Craig was on Ivy Street.

"Thanks," she said, but to no one in particular.

Great. Ethan's craziness was contagious. Now she was talking to herself. Beside her, Ethan let out a strangled whimper.

The two police officers were closing in from the direction of the Boom Room, drawn by the activity around Ethan. She felt their professional curiosity merge with the crowd's more primitive, rampant interest. She felt Craig's intensity ramp up as he caught sight of Ethan.

"Get him out of here!" someone whispered in her ear.

"I'm trying!" Kelsie turned, but there were only strangers around her.

She pulled her messenger bag in close. The crowd was starting to crackle with her uneasiness. That was good. It gave her something to work with. She took hold of their anxiety and *pushed.* Enough to get them swirling, moving in a wheel around her.

She glanced at Ethan. He was trapped in the same loop as the rest of the crowd, his panic arcing higher.

She pinched and twisted his wrist. Hard.

"Ow! What was that for?"

"You have to stay separate from the mob," she said. "Trust me, okay? It's about to get crazy."

Ethan didn't seem convinced. He still looked like he was going to make a bolt for it. Fair enough. Craig was still powering through the crowd behind them. The cops were closing in on her left.

They needed cover. She had to unleash the full power of a crowd storm *right now.*

She reached into her bag.

CHAPTER 48
BELLWETHER

AT LAST THE LIGHTS OF IVY APPEARED THROUGH the windshield, gaudy and chaotic.

Nate parked the Audi on a side street, got out, and took a long look at the crowd.

"A short sparkly dress?" he muttered. Seemed like half the women in the street glittered, and every dress was the same length—about as short as it could be.

He slipped one earbud back in as he walked. "You still there, Flick?"

"I'm on Ivy," she said. "I think they're in trouble. But it's hard to track. Too many eyeballs."

"Try to get into Scam's head and stay there."

Flicker didn't answer. Her breath was short and sharp in Nate's ears.

Nate kept his voice calm. "Tell me what you see, Flick."

"Can't tell whose vision is Scam's. Shit, I've never been down here at night before. Drunk eyeballs are the *worst*."

Nate was at the edge of the crowd now. The flashing sign of the Boom Room threw trembling shadows on the sidewalk, and shoulders jostled him.

No wonder Flicker was overloaded. It was a perfect summer evening, less than a week till July Fourth, and everyone was here on Ivy.

He'd have to use his own eyes.

A bike rack next to the curb bristled with handlebars and wheels. A NO PARKING sign stood next to it. Nate placed a foot on top of the rack, grabbed the sign pole, and pulled himself up. He wobbled for a moment but managed to steady himself. For a moment he felt like a kid watching a parade.

Once he opened up his sight, looking across the top of the crowd was dazzling. The glittering lines of their attention were scattered and spinning, pulled in all directions by flashing signs, thumping music, bare skin.

No focus. Nothing to work with.

He swallowed a bitter taste. There was nothing more repellent than a shapeless, leaderless horde.

Then he saw something—a channel of laserlike attention slicing through the crowd. It came from a cluster of men in dark clothes. They were big, and their black T-shirts sucked up the nightclub lights.

"Flicker," Nate said. "Those guys who were after Scam. Were they wearing black tees?"

"Yep. Just got in their heads. They're looking straight at Scam."

Nate followed the lances of their focus down the crowded street, and finally saw her—the girl in the sparkly dress. Beside her was Scam. They looked paralyzed, staring back at the approaching group of men. The girl's hand was locked around Scam's wrist, like he was a little boy she didn't want to lose in the crowd.

Too far away for Nate to reach them in time. And he doubted he could distract those big men from their purpose. They looked too determined for charm to sway.

But the crowd . . .

A crowd would always listen to Bellwether.

He just needed their attention.

He jumped down from his wobbly vantage on the bike rack and ran for the nearest car. A Porsche sedan, late model and freshly waxed—there was no way it didn't have an alarm.

He jumped up onto the hood, his heels landing with a metal *crunch*.

A second's pause, and then an earsplitting shriek erupted beneath him, pulsing in his feet, his ears, his bones. The crowd's attention whirled upon him, gathering into a web of focus.

It was Bellwether who stepped onto the Porsche's roof as the energy built, raising his hands into the air, feeling the flow of focus streaming through his fingers. He was best with words and smiles, but sometimes one had to make do with gestures. He made two fists, readying to set the crowd in motion . . .

But then something odd happened.

A fluttering plume erupted into the air above Scam and the girl with the sparkly dress. The burst of paper billowed up and outward, carried in a roiling cloud by the ocean breeze.

It was money, dozens of bills. The web of attention Bellwether had gathered shivered—a second later it was unraveling, disintegrating in his hands.

An explosion of money trumped a car alarm any day.

But the organism he had forged from the crowd didn't fall apart. The focus he'd given it scattered as people lunged for flitters of cash in the air, but something new took shape. The mass began to swirl, a hurricane forming, with Scam and the girl at its center.

Nate stared at his own hands, empty of glittering light. Who was doing this? Who had stolen *his* crowd?

"Holy shit. What's happening?" came Flicker's voice in his ears, barely audible above the shriek of the car alarm.

"No lo sé," Nate murmured.

"Everyone just went apeshit. Is that *money*?"

"Yeah. And something else." A force was moving through the mass of people, shaping the shimmering lines of their attention. But it didn't point to anyone; it was like a thing let loose by the crowd itself. A whirlpool sustained by its own power.

Was this some kind of natural phenomenon, like the greed storms Nate had seen at holiday sales?

The girl in the sparkly dress was in motion again, dragging Scam through the swirling mass of people. Scam stumbled behind her, but she moved like an athlete, slipping gracefully into the current of the crowd. She seemed to know its contours perfectly.

The cloud of money had broken the web of attention that Nate had made, changing it into something completely different. His own crowds always had a focus—himself. But this one had no leader, no center. It was nothing but a shape, an energy, as if all of them moved to the same unheard music.

And that girl was the DJ.

"It's her," he said.

"What's her?" Flicker's voice was wan in his earbuds. "Shit, I'm going to be sick."

"Switch your vision off, Flick. I've got this."

"Go blind, here? I'll get knocked down!"

"Then get clear!" Nate tore his eyes away from the sparkling girl for a moment, scanning the throng for his best friend. "This crowd could go loco."

"Have to help the boy . . ."

Nate had lost sight of Flicker, but he saw the big men in black trapped, like trucks trying to thread their way through a flock of sheep. Their muscles and glares were no good to them here in this dancing, bouncing crowd.

Where were Scam and the girl? Lost in the maelstrom.

"Mierda."

He should go after them, find out who she was. But Flicker was stuck in this riot somewhere, her vision overloaded . . .

Beneath him the car alarm chirped one last time and went silent.

Nate looked down. A red-faced man in a blue shirt stood staring up at him, holding a key fob.

"What the *hell* are you doing on my car?"

Nate gave the man a soothing smile.

"Is this *your* car? If you'll just give me a moment to explain."

Judging from the guy's face, it might take longer than that.

CHAPTER 49
FLICKER

THE CROWD WENT WILD WHEN IT SAW THE SPARKLY girl's money.

Too many eyes were in Flicker's head. Not like switching channels, the way it usually worked. More like staring at a bank of a thousand TVs, every one showing the shakiest vomit-cam movie she'd ever seen. The sound was up way too high, the shouting of the greedy crowd pressing on her ears. The bump and crash of shoulders kept her off balance. So many feet stepping on hers.

She shouldn't have gone so deep into the crowd, but Flicker had seen him, the beautiful boy, lost in the middle of it all.

Which was worse in a riot: to be blind or invisible?

It hurt, having all these TVs colliding in her brain. But she couldn't turn her vision off, not yet. She needed another glimpse, to make sure Nothing was okay. Those guys in black were coming for Scam, and the brave, beautiful boy might try to get in the way.

Or the crowd itself might crush him.

Flicker had never seen anything like it. The money flying into the air, the sudden change in intensity. All those points of vision in her mind, changing from eyeballs into a thousand floating cameras set loose in a hurricane.

It had no pattern at first, just the random madness of everyone grasping after fluttering bills. But then suddenly, impossibly, a shape had started to form, as if the crowd had an intelligence.

Back when they were both twelve, Nate had taken her on a bike ride one night, Flicker perched on his handlebars. To amuse himself, he'd bellwethered the other cyclists they'd met along the way, forming an armada of bikes—fixed gears and stocky off-road BMXs, carbon-fiber wonders with solid disks instead of spokes. A flotilla of spinning chrome, flowing around obstacles like a shiny blob of mercury let loose in the dark.

Then he'd told Flicker to ride, to pedal and steer herself with her vision scattered through the peloton behind them. In the grip of Nate's power, those dozens of eyes merged into a single viewpoint. And she'd kept upright for mile after mile, wobbly but imperious, secure in the god's-eye view of herself from all directions at once.

It was happening again, all these drunken eyeballs somehow

coalescing. But tonight they weren't all staring in the same direction. Instead of focusing on one glorious leader, they formed a pattern, a spinning shape, a vortex made of people.

Whatever was doing this wasn't *leading* the crowd, but forming it into some kind of . . . creature. Something with its own personality, its own logic.

No, not logic. More like emotion.

"It's a new power," Flicker said to no one. Her earbuds had been yanked out in the tumult.

Whatever was controlling the crowd grew stronger, the shape clearer in Flicker's mind. Her vision clicked a little farther into place, and she saw everything . . .

. . . the men in black tees, brought to a puzzled halt.

. . . Glorious Leader at the edge of the storm, working his charm on an angry man.

. . . the sparkly girl pulling Scam through the crowd, like she knew every step of their wild dance. *Like she was in charge.*

But Flicker didn't care about all that, because the boy called Nothing was lost among all those eyes that couldn't track him. What if the crowd storm battered him to pieces?

She spotted her own red dress, tried to guide herself toward where she'd first glimpsed him. The crowd shape was starting to fade already, or her brain was overloaded from juggling all those eyeballs. Flicker was buffeted, and stumbled, and fell.

And someone caught her.

Someone whose eyes she couldn't see through, whose hand

fit into hers perfectly. They ran through the crowd together, and she caught only glancing images of his bare feet pale in the darkness as he danced across the glitter of broken beer bottles. It was him, it was that boy, Anonymous.

Then they were out of the crowd, in an alley between a nightclub and a closed tire-changing shop. They stopped, safe at last, and Flicker gratefully cast away her vision.

Darkness crashed down around her, full of fireworks and shooting stars from her overloaded brain. Her head was pounding, her dizziness tipping the whole earth sideways underfoot.

"Anon," she said, just to ground herself.

"Whoa," his voice came. "How'd you know it was me, Riley?"

She smiled, half motion-sick, half giddy from her god's-eye view.

"I just do."

CHAPTER 50
SCAM

ETHAN COULD FEEL THE THUD OF DANCE MUSIC through his shoes.

He was standing behind the biggest guitar he'd ever seen. Sure, it wasn't real. Just a sign adorning the rooftop of the club Kelsie had dragged him into. Past the bouncer and into a back room, up the stairs like she owned the place.

"I can't believe you did that," he said. "The thing with the money? That was pretty badass."

It had been *seriously* cool: Kelsie standing there on Ivy Street with her chin high, her arms flung up above her. And a rain of greenbacks falling past her shiny dress. The stuff music videos were made of.

"It wasn't badass," Kelsie said glumly. "It was expensive."

"Right. Sorry." Ethan realized that he didn't want to say

the wrong thing here. He wanted Kelsie to think he was at least halfway as cool as her. Without really meaning to, he let the voice trickle into his throat. "You probably needed your money for something more important."

"It was my dad's." Kelsie stared at the bag, her voice breaking. "He needed it to save his life, thanks to this fix you put him in. And instead I wasted it saving *you*."

The voice had nothing. It was one of those situations where the best thing was not to talk. But putting the blame on him didn't seem fair.

Ethan tried it on his own. "Technically your dad was already . . ."

Nope. The voice had been right. Kelsie's expression suggested that she didn't want to hear that, technically, her dad had already been robbing a bank when Ethan met him.

"Anyway"—he switched gears—"thanks for getting us out of the Magnifique, before the Craig made me into ground meat. And for saving me again on the street down there."

"I didn't do it to save you," Kelsie said. "Well, maybe I did, *technically*. But if you don't give me some answers I'm going to start yelling until 'the Craig' hears me. He'd probably be happy to parkour his way up the side of the Boom right now."

Ethan held up his hands in defeat. The thought of someone as huge as Craig precision jumping his way up the side of a two-story building was actually pretty frightening.

"Okay," he said softly. "Whatever you need to know."

Ethan glanced down at the canopied walkway in front of the club. No sign of the Craig, and the crowd was beginning to ease up. Just a few cops milling around, probably wondering what had happened. All the bills Kelsie had thrown into the air were gone.

And no sign of the other guy, Ethan's friend. He'd been helping them escape, but they must have been separated in the crowd. Ethan held up his hand, but whatever he'd written there two days ago was gone.

"We played *Red Scepter*," he said out loud. "*T-H-I-B* . . . crap."

"What are you babbling about?" Kelsie asked. "Do you need some kind of medication?"

"You sure you don't have a pen?" he asked. "I need a pen before I forget his name."

But he'd already forgotten. Ethan glanced down at the shirt he was wearing. The shirt was his friend's, and his friend's name was . . . *Anon!*

That wasn't quite it, but close.

Kelsie glared at him, her green eyes shining. The sea breeze caught her hair and sent it out in a spray of pale curls above her shoulders. Her dress rippled and shone in the neon of the Boom Room's sign. She was maybe the most awesome girl who'd ever hated him.

He felt the voice lurch up, tickling his throat. He really

wanted Kelsie to like him. The odds were pretty much against it, of course. She blamed him for a bunch of things already, and he couldn't trust the voice for this. It only cared about the short term. It said stuff that would make someone like you for the next five minutes, which usually meant lying And when people found out about his lies, they never trusted him again.

Ethan didn't want Kelsie to like him for only five minutes. Plus, one slipup with Kelsie and she'd probably throw him off the roof and into the waiting arms of the Craig.

He gritted his teeth against the voice.

Kelsie gathered herself. She looked like she had a lot to talk about.

"So what do you know about the new drug dealers in Cambria? The ones selling krokodil?"

Ethan frowned. "Is that a reptile?"

"It's a drug," Kelsie explained. She looked really upset about it. "Okay, let me start simpler. Why were you in the bank Friday?"

"I was . . . banking?"

"This isn't a joke, Ethan."

He felt the voice itching to get out, but clamped it down. "Honest. I was in the bank to put away some money. Money I'd come into . . . unexpectedly."

"You stole it from Craig." Kelsie watched him coolly.

"Pretty much."

"So why'd you decide to screw with my dad?"

"I don't know anything about your dad! Except that he is one scary guy."

Which was the wrong thing to say. Again.

"He isn't!" Kelsie cried, looking like she was about to swing the bag at him. At least it would be lighter now. But this was not going well.

Ethan gave in to the voice. "He is when he's carrying a gun that big, Kels. And wearing a mask. But maybe that's not his usual outfit?"

The words seemed to make a difference. She looked at him, her eyes bright and green and sad. "I guess you were scared. You were all pretty scared in there."

"Well, *I* was, anyway."

"I still can't believe he did it. He's not like that. He's never hurt anyone." Kelsie leaned on the wall beside the guitar billboard. The pulsing neon light was making a halo of her hair. "Now the Bagrovs are looking for my dad and me. I can't even go home."

"I can't go home either," Ethan said, and that made her turn and look at him again. *Really* look at him, like they shared something.

The weird thing was, he'd said it with his real voice. And it had *worked.* Maybe if he stuck to honesty for once . . .

"All I wanted was a ride home. That's how this whole thing started. The Craig gave me a ride."

"Seriously? That guy did you a favor?"

"He thought I was someone else. One of his boss's, um, henchmen."

Kelsie nodded. "I can see how you convinced him, what with your knowledge of criminal lingo. Seriously? 'Henchmen'?"

She was making fun of him, but he didn't mind. There was nothing mean in it. Just the fact that she was talking to him made anything she said okay.

But then her eyes fell. "My dad's always been a criminal, as long as I can remember. But he doesn't rob banks. He owed money."

Ethan wondered what kind of cash-flow problem would drive a guy to rob a bank. For a moment he was glad for his voice. He could always weasel his way into money when he needed it, or get a free ride somehow. And usually with less danger than the average bank robbery.

As long as he didn't get any more rides from paranoid drug dealers.

"How'd you know all that stuff about us?" Kelsie asked. "You said our names. You mentioned . . . my mom."

Ethan sighed. She was never going to let this go.

And Ethan found he really wanted her to be okay. She'd saved him twice already that night. Plus she was cute and sad and lonely, and Ethan got that. He was lonely too. He wanted her to like him for more than just the next five minutes.

Whatever helps Kelsie the most, he thought. *Whatever makes us closer.*

He hoped those two things went together. Then he let the voice take over.

"That wasn't me talking," Ethan heard himself say. "That was this thing inside me. My other voice."

CHAPTER 51
ANONYMOUS

THIBAULT KEPT A FIRM, STEADY GRIP ON RILEY'S arm. She sat on the pavement, swaying, head in hands.

"Anon," she murmured again.

"Still here."

Riley's connections were always hard to read. Other people's were mostly single-strand visual threads, but all of Riley's senses played a part in hers. Right now her attention was all around him, a shimmer in the dark alley, like oil rainbows in the air.

She lifted her face, pale behind dark glasses. "Ugh, wow. Too many people. Too much everything."

"There's a bench over there." He pointed, then realized the gesture was useless. "Back near Ivy."

"The ground is fine for now," Riley said, pulling her arm free and taking his hand.

"Whenever you're ready."

At the mouth of the alley the crowd milled past, as if they hadn't been rioting a minute ago—or brawling, or dancing, whatever the hell that had been.

Who'd have thought a handful of money would drive people so crazy?

Kelsie had, apparently. And now she and Ethan had disappeared. Into one of the clubs, probably. It would take him all night to search every place on the strip.

But he couldn't even start, with Riley sick like this.

She leaned against him. "This is so weird. It's like I've stepped into one of Lily's stories."

Lily. Her twin sister. But what stories?

"Um, maybe you hit your head. You sound a little concussed." But her connection didn't *feel* concussed. It coiled and gleamed around him very intently.

"No, I just got spread out too far."

It took Thibault a moment to process this. "Your sight, you mean?"

"It was such a big crowd, and so frenzied, diving after that money. All those eyeballs got jumbled up and . . ." Her head dropped forward into one hand, and she took a few deep breaths.

"Maybe think about something else, Riley."

"Call me Flicker."

"Sure, okay. I guess this *is* kind of a mission."

"No, I just like Flicker." She turned her head and managed a smile. "It fits me better."

He'd never really talked to Riley, alone. And he hadn't spied on her as much as he had the other Zeroes. Using his anonymity to spy on any girl felt like stalking. But spying on a blind girl seemed way over the line.

And of all of them she seemed least likely to do something dangerous with her power. She was too levelheaded.

"Flicker it is. You can call me Thibault, if you want."

"Thibault, right. But I kind of like Anon. I always thought it was funny, how no one can see you, but they can say, *See you, Anon.*"

"Yeah, Nate's little joke on me."

"He's not that subtle," she said. "But he does like Shakespeare. *Macbeth*, mostly."

Thibault laughed, surprised. Usually Riley—Flicker—had nothing but praise for Nate. Glorious Leader's little sister, Ethan used to call her. Which made what the voice had said to them last summer that much squickier.

"Okay, Anon." Riley stood, letting go of his hand to brace herself against the alley wall. Thibault rose beside her. She wavered and took his arm. "Where did you say that bench was?"

"This way."

Even with the riot finished, a lot of people were going by on Ivy, forming a glittering web of attention. Thibault waited for their signals to fray the bond between Flicker and him.

But Flicker's awareness of him stayed bright, shifting on the air. It was so different from someone using their eyes. She was taking in messages with her whole body. Her hand shimmered in the crook of his arm, picking up the pressure of his elbow. When he nudged an empty beer can out of her path with his bare foot, filaments of her attention reached down toward the sound.

He could feel it on his skin, the way she was listening to him breathe.

When her knee brushed the bench, she let go of Thibault and sat down with a swirl of her long red skirt. She patted the seat beside her.

"Sit close, Anon, so I don't lose you."

"I'm used to people losing me," he said, obeying.

"Not me." She smiled past him toward Ivy Street. "I found you in that stampede, after all."

"That was crazy, wasn't it? This girl who was with us started it. On purpose. She threw a bunch of cash into the air."

"I saw her," Flicker said. "In the shiny dress. Who the hell was she?"

"Kelsie, the daughter of one of the bank robbers. Scam's voice mentioned her—you know about the bank video, right? So now she wants answers from Ethan." He shrugged. "That's why she saved us, I guess. Just showed up and warned us about these goons who were coming for Ethan. The guys he stole money from."

"I saw them, too," Flicker said

Of course, she wasn't really blind. Thankfully, she wasn't using her sight now. He hated to think what he looked like. Sweaty and disheveled, with dirty bare feet.

"She threw money in the air to get Ethan away from them," he said. "She knows how to make an exit, all right. I've never seen a crowd go nuts like that, even over free cash."

"It wasn't just the money," Flicker said quietly. "I saw something else at work. Nate saw it too."

"Nate was here?" Something went off in Thibault's head, and he pulled away from her. "Wait a minute. What were *you* doing here?"

She turned to face him. "I was kind of . . . spying on you."

Thibault swallowed. "Spying?"

"I was in the lobby of the Hotel Magnifique when all this started. I saw those guys come in, the ones all in black. I tried to warn you they were headed up to the penthouse."

She knew about the penthouse? A hollowness opened up in his stomach.

"But then you got away," said Flicker, "with that girl, out the back. And when I saw where you were headed, I told Nate."

Thibault stood up and took a few steps back from her. Flicker's senses reached after him, soft bright tendrils. Her interest churned like liquid opal in the air. Broken glass glinted around his bare feet, but right now he hardly cared.

"So Nate knows about the Magnifique?"

Flicker shook her head. "It's not in his file."

"You've read his file on me? And he sent you to keep watch on us?"

"That's not the way it was, Anon."

Her attention wisped at his mouth every time he spoke. He wanted to chop it away and vanish. "He's known since that camping trip, hasn't he? Gets me a little drunk, makes me drop hints. *Bastard.*"

"No." Flicker slipped her glasses back on. "I figured it out myself."

Thibault hesitated, hanging on to his anger.

She reached out a hand. "Before I lose you, Anon. Let me explain."

Their connection was dimming. It had only taken a few steps' distance, a jolt of anger, and the filaments connecting them had faded. He could just stand here and disappear.

But what did she mean, she'd *figured it out*?

He sat down again. Not as close this time.

"How?" he demanded.

"In Nate's file. The photos you took. Cracks in the wall, faded paint. They were beautiful."

Despite his anger, Thibault felt a blush creeping up his face. His wabi-sabi photography phase had ended a year ago. The thought of anyone else seeing his artsy photos, those earnest images of transient imperfections, was like someone leafing through his middle-school poetry.

"But how did you find me with those?"

"I matched them to where they were taken." She was smiling now, proud of herself. "All it took was a little help from Lily, and borrowing a few thousand eyeballs. After a while I noticed that all the locations were clustered around the Magnifique."

"Whoa" was all he could say.

"I know, it was sneaky. But with everyone looking for Scam, I was worried. Plus, I was curious about you."

She sat very still, her senses looped around him to assess how he was taking this.

How *was* he taking it? His gut was a tangle of feelings.

But something didn't quite add up. "Wait. How did you keep me in your mind long enough to hunt me down?"

"With help from my sister, Lily. She told me stories about you."

Thibault shook his head. "But how does *she* know anything?"

She's not even a Zero. It made his skin crawl that someone outside the group was involved. Bad enough having Glorious Leader prying into your life, but a stranger?

"She starts with something real, from the file, then adds to it. She weaves it into the kind of story she knows I like."

"So she's just making stuff up?"

"Pretty much. But her stories have enough reality in them that fictional you connects up with real you. At least, that's what I think's happening."

Thibault couldn't speak for astonishment.

"So are you mad at me?" said Flicker.

He didn't answer. Part of him felt furious, violated, betrayed. But another part was still that kid who craved someone seeing him. And the way she'd tracked him down was amazing—beautiful, even.

And in a way, none of it mattered anymore.

"Well, I guess it's no big deal, you knowing where I live. As of half an hour ago I don't live there anymore."

She nodded. "Right. Because those guys who were chasing Scam know about it now."

"Worse. The hotel might." He told her about the laptop, the manager's login. She listened, and winced in sympathy a few times, and not once did her attention drift off him. *Yes, this is what it's like when normal people talk to each other.*

"What next?" she said when he finished. "Do you have a place to stay?"

"I have a backup hotel." Of course, *those* passwords had been in his laptop too. He could download them from the cloud, but with what? Thanks to Chizara, he didn't even have a working phone. "I'll manage something. But let me drive you home. Nate's car is still in the Magnifique garage."

"Thanks, Anon. I'm not really up to the bus. And hey, my mom keeps spare toothbrushes in our bathroom drawer." She smiled. "I mean, assuming you don't have one on you."

"Um, no." It was starting to dawn on Thibault that he had nothing. It didn't get much more Zen than this. "I don't even have shoes."

"Yeah, I saw." Flicker shook her head. She was getting her color back, breathing easier. "I doubt my mom has any spare shoes that fit you."

"Still, a toothbrush," he said. "Every little bit helps."

She lifted her face, as if she were staring at him through the dark glasses. It was weird, feeling such a strong connection to someone who couldn't even meet his eyes. Weird, but he liked it.

"Good, then," she said. "A ride home would be lovely, Anon."

CHAPTER 52
SCAM

ETHAN STOOD ON THE ROOF OF THE BOOM ROOM, gaping dumbly at Kelsie.

He couldn't believe what had just happened. In all his years living with it, the voice had never outed itself.

"Your other *what*?" Kelsie said.

Ethan opened his mouth, waiting for the voice to jump into action again.

Nothing.

Great. Kelsie was expecting him to say something revealing, something honest, something that made *sense*, and the voice had left the building.

What the hell was it up to? Was the voice pulling some crazy mind judo because it thought *this* was the way for Ethan to get close to Kelsie? By talking for himself?

No way. The voice was just dicking with him. Again.

Ethan wanted so bad to connect with Kelsie. Sputtering in his usual half-assed way was not going to get that done. He thought once more:

Whatever makes us closer.

He opened his mouth again. Not even a tickle in his throat.

Screw it, then. If the voice wanted to be outed, that's what it was going to get.

"It just talks," he finally managed. "Whatever I want, the voice gets it. But it's kind of out of control, too."

Kelsie shook her head. "Maybe we should go back to *technically*."

Ethan had been leaning against the edge of the roof. But now he straightened.

"Look, I can tell you exactly what happened in the bank. But you'll probably think I'm crazy."

"I already think that," she said quietly.

"Check." In a weird way, her admission made his next words easier. He didn't have anything to lose. "I have this power. Like a superpower."

Kelsie raised her eyebrows. "A superpower?"

"More or less. It's not always super."

"But it lets you know stuff you couldn't possibly know?"

Ethan was impressed. She was halfway to figuring it out. "Almost. Except I don't really *know* anything. I just talk like I do."

This was the part where he expected her to laugh, or hit him again with the depleted bag of money, or whip out her phone and call the Craig to schedule a beatdown.

But for some reason she actually seemed to be considering his words.

"How long have you had this . . . power?"

"Ever since I can remember. When I was little, it would just pop up and say things. I didn't even know that was weird, at first. I just figured that was how talking worked for everyone. You opened your mouth and words happened."

"Since you were little," Kelsie murmured, as if that part had scored a point in his favor. "So are you rich? I mean, if you can take money off a psycho like Craig that easy, you could get it off anyone."

"It wasn't *easy*," Ethan cried. "He drove me out to this creepy house in the forest. I thought I was going to get shot! Getting out of there was mostly luck."

She was staring at him, still suspicious, but at least she wasn't hitting him with the messenger bag. And she was still paying attention to him. Ethan wasn't used to this. Usually when he told the truth, no one believed him.

"I just wanted a ride home," he went on. "I didn't *plan* to steal anything—I only drove off to get away from the Craig and his boss. And that money was in the car."

"So you don't use your powers for evil?" She was mocking him again.

"I try not to make it hard on other people. Like in that hotel room, I made sure not to mess it up too much." Ethan wasn't sure where those words had come from. They weren't quite his, but they weren't the voice, either. Stray memories of something someone else had told him. "Chop the wood, or whatever. It's a Zen thing."

"You're weird," Kelsie said, a look of deep concentration on her face. "You're, like, seriously strange and weird."

Ethan nodded once, slowly. "I can see how you might think that."

"So let's get this straight." Kelsie shook her head, like she was wiping away a dream. "In the bank, you used this so-called power on my dad, right?"

"I wanted him to leave my bag of money alone," Ethan said. "So the voice started talking to him, saying whatever would make him focus on something else."

"The voice?"

"That's what I call it. I have no idea where the voice gets its intel from. I don't understand half the stuff it says. It doesn't even work all the time, because sometimes there's just nothing you can say."

Like right now, when you were trying to explain a superpower to someone who thought you were crazy. There was no way he was going to bring up all the other Zeroes and make his story even *more* confusing. One thing at a time.

The weirdest thing of all was that Ethan's own words still

seemed to be working. Kelsie's glare had softened. She looked suddenly small and sad.

"So it was just an accident," she said. "You saying my name."

"Kind of."

"And you don't know anything that can help me with the mobsters who are after my dad?"

Ethan shook his head. "I don't know anything about that."

She seemed to take that in, but it didn't make her happy. "I was just intel to you? Something to use to get your way? Nothing more than a . . ."

"Scam?" Ethan said quietly.

Kelsie stared. Her eyes had gone cold. "Just a noise you made so you could score a free ticket out of the bank."

"Yeah, well." Ethan swallowed. "I did have this huge gun pointed at me."

"Hank got killed because of what you said. He was a good guy."

"I'm really sorry." He meant it too. Out of all the apologies he'd had to give in the last two days, this one felt the most real.

Kelsie shivered, and Ethan realized it was getting cool. He reached for the pillowcase at his feet and dumped the minibar contents on the rooftop. He offered the pillowcase like a jacket, but she ignored it.

She picked up one of the tiny bottles of vodka on the ground. "Prove it. Say something right now with your superpower voice. Something about me that no one else could possibly know."

She twisted off the bottle cap and took a swig.

"Um, it's tricky. The last couple of days, every time I use the voice, bad things happen."

Kelsie snorted. "Like spending the night in the penthouse of the fanciest hotel in town? Sounds traumatic. *Prove you're not lying, Ethan.*"

Ethan closed his eyes. All he could think was that he really wanted this girl with the green eyes and windswept hair to believe him.

And with that, the voice tap-tapped on his throat. All he had to do was open his mouth and let it out. So he did.

"Your dad taught you to pick pockets when you were nine, and how to cheat at poker. One time he won four thousand bucks on one hand—aces over jacks—and all you got was braces. When you were six, you walked out of your house alone and made it all the way to a football game. The home team won and it was the best feeling you'd ever had. When a tooth falls into a metal sink, it goes *tink*."

"Whoa," Kelsie said. Then she finished the rest of the tiny bottle in one gulp.

Ethan found himself smiling, feeling back in control, until the voice added, "What, did you think you were the only superpower in town?"

Kelsie's eyes went wide. But she didn't argue.

Ethan closed his mouth carefully. He had to replay the words in his mind a few times before they made any sense.

Then he looked into Kelsie's unblinking gaze. She believed him now, really believed him, and Ethan suddenly knew why.

In his own voice he said, "Holy shit, *you* have a power too?"

CHAPTER 53

FLICKER

IT WAS ONE OF THOSE DREAMS THAT KEPT GOING after she woke up.

Too many eyeballs. Too much motion. Her bed in a vortex, that vortex jammed inside *another* vortex—both of them spinning way too fast.

Flicker searched for her sister's vision in the next room; sometimes a dose of sight steadied bed spins. But Lily was still asleep. Same with the parents downstairs, and out here in empty suburbia there were no other eyeballs in range.

Flicker felt for her water glass. Her throat was dry, like she'd talked all night. But with who? Lily had been out when she'd gotten home from Ivy Street, and Nate hadn't come in after dropping her off. . . .

Wait. She hadn't seen Nate last night. Someone else had given her a ride.

But she'd been in Glorious Leader's BMW. Flicker remembered that expensive smell.

She hadn't drunk any alcohol. There was no explanation for this slice of missing time.

Maybe coffee would help.

Pulling on her pajamas, Flicker rewound her memories of the day before. She and Lily had spent the afternoon downtown, looking for the beautiful boy called Nothing. And they'd found his castle, hadn't they?

She remembered staking out the lobby of the Magnifique, the thugs in black tees who'd been outwitted by the quick-fingered girl in the shiny dress. Then the chase across to Ivy Street, and that maelstrom of money, bodies, eyeballs. And a new power at work—the sparkly girl.

But then it all got fuzzy.

She must have found him, the beautiful boy. That was why she couldn't remember. Only Anonymous was the right shape to fill her missing time.

Flicker smiled, because now that she knew what she was looking for, she glimpsed him among the whirling leftovers of her dream: dark-haired and handsome. She'd spotted him in the crowd, gone after him, and after that . . . she couldn't remember.

Buttoning her pajama top, Flicker padded to her bedroom

door and out into the hallway. But at the top of the stairs, her hand on the rail, she hesitated.

If Nothing had brought her home, where was he now? Back in his castle, probably. No, wait—headed off to some new hiding place, because the thugs in black T-shirts had found his old one.

But another answer tugged at her brain, and Flicker didn't go down to the kitchen. As if drawn by a scent, she crept past Lily's room to the end of the hall. There she reached out into the air before her and found the dangling cord.

She pulled it softly, slowly. The creaks of rusty springs and unpainted wood clamored in the Sunday morning calm. When the attic ladder was down, Flicker checked the eyeballs in the house again—nothing but the pink of closed lids limned with slanted sunlight.

She found the first step with a bare foot, ascended the ladder carefully. She was still dizzy from her dream, and there was no point rushing. There was probably nothing up here anyway.

The smells of the attic drifted down to meet her: the mustiness of old books, of boxes and papers and the old leather chair Dad refused to throw away. Scents salted with memories of playing up here with Lily. Or listening to her stories.

That's why Flicker had come here. Something to do with stories.

But at the top of the ladder she found herself a little confused. Why exactly hadn't she gone downstairs for coffee first? It had slipped her mind again.

So Flicker did what she always did when things weren't making sense: She listened.

It took a while, even in the silence. But eventually her ears found the sound—someone breathing, soft and even. Someone she couldn't throw her vision into, not even to find the sparkling rods and cones of darkness. And there was only one person like that in the world.

"Anon," she said quietly.

The breathing stuttered, resumed. He was fast asleep.

Flicker climbed out and knelt on the attic floor, focusing on the sound of his breath. She kept all her attention on it, careful not to let herself slip back into forgetfulness.

Anonymous was here, in her home. The beautiful boy, the mysterious Nothing whose eyes she couldn't see through.

Finally Flicker pulled the ladder up behind her. It closed with a bump, and the rhythm of his breathing broke again, and then came a soft sigh.

"Anon?" she whispered again.

A sudden rustle of movement. "Oh, Flicker. Hey."

His voice was hoarse, like hers, because of course it was the two of them who'd talked half the night, up here in the attic.

"It's me, Anonymous," he said. "Like on a mission . . . Um, wait. Did you just say my name?"

"I did." She felt a proud smile steal onto her face.

"Huh." A pause. "Sorry. I was going to leave early so I wouldn't scare you. But I didn't have a phone to wake me up."

"You didn't scare me. I'm glad you didn't leave."

The sound of him sitting up. "But you must have . . . stumbled on me, right?"

Flicker shook her head. "I came up on purpose. I had a notion you might be here."

His breathing changed at those words. Then a soft "Whoa."

"Yeah, it's weird. But it makes sense, too. This attic is where Lily told me about you first. Her stories are why I can remember you."

"You told me last night. We talked for a long time." Something about those last words made her lips tingle. "She made me a fictional character, so you'd remember me."

Flicker nodded. "That's why I knew you were up here. It's like you were *born* up here in the attic—I mean, the image of you in my head. *Actual* you was clearly born somewhere else."

"Clearly." A smile in his voice, and the little bone creaks of stretching. Then the rustle of putting on a shirt.

Right. He wouldn't have slept in his clothes up here in the hot, musty attic. And yes, there was the sound of him slipping on pants.

She didn't want him to think she was peeking. "Last night, when we were talking. Did I mention that my power doesn't work on you?"

"You've told me before. You can't find my eyes, like I'm not here." The rustle of his shrug. "Which figures."

"What do you mean?"

"I'm not part of all that—attention, seeing, remembering. It's all a web of connections, and I don't belong." The resignation in his voice made Flicker want to reach out to him. "Your power is a part of all that, but I'm not. I'm nothing."

"Nothing. That's what my sister called you in her stories," Flicker said, then added, "I guess that sounds mean, doesn't it?"

"It sounds accurate."

She tried to smile. "Well, at least I can't spy on you. So you get some privacy."

Flicker ran fingers through her hair, feeling how snarled it was. It was odd, not being able to see herself while talking to someone.

"I get plenty of privacy. Privacy's overrated." The floor creaked as Anon stood. "But I should probably go. Your parents would freak to find some guy up here, right?"

Flicker was fairly sure they would. Not for long, though. Just a little flutter of consternation, then they'd forget all about the boy upstairs.

But the mood of this morning had been so mysterious and sweet. She didn't want it descending into farce.

"Where are you going?" she asked. "I mean, if you don't mind telling me."

"I haven't figured that out yet. But I should go back to my hotel first, just in case my laptop's still around."

"The Magnifique," Flicker said. "That's where you live, right?"

"Lived."

The anguish in his voice made a memory fall into her head, like a piece of sky. "You were mad at me last night. Because I tracked you down."

A pause, long enough to make her nervous. "You remember that?"

She nodded.

"Right, I was," Anon said. "But only at first, then I was flattered. And then I was *impressed.* Even Glorious Leader never managed to find me, and he's been trying for years."

Flicker felt a blush starting, and half turned toward the attic door. "I'll go with you. In case you need some extra eyes at the hotel."

"I'd like that." He sounded like he meant it. "Um, do you have any shoes I can borrow?"

Another flash of memory: bare feet and broken glass. "My dad keeps a pair of flip-flops by the pool. I'll get dressed and meet you downstairs."

She went to the attic door and started down the steps, paused, and turned back to him. "See you anon." The words felt familiar—she must have used that joke last night, once or twice. Was Anon rolling his eyes, embarrassed for her?

But his voice sounded steady and relaxed. "See you, Flicker." He might even be smiling.

CHAPTER 54

MOB

KELSIE AWOKE WITH HER PHONE BUZZING ON THE BED beside her. It took a moment to recognize the slatted blinds and tasteful writing desk—she was in the spare room at Ling's place.

A sputtering came from the floor. It was Ethan, snoring away in a borrowed pink sleeping bag that was too small for him. Confirmation that last night hadn't been a crazy dream. Or nightmare.

They'd sat on the roof of the Boom Room half the night, talking about their powers. She'd always believed her power was real, but meeting Ethan had turned it into a different thing entirely. Not just a weird fluke, maybe part of a bigger plan. Like the two of them were *meant* to find each other.

She couldn't ignore that it had happened now, when she really needed help.

Kelsie checked her phone. A message from Dad, finally—an address.

She leaned over the end of the bed and gave Ethan a shove. "We have to go."

He squinted up at her, his eyes thick with sleep. His clothes were crumpled, but his army haircut gave him a look of combat readiness. "Go where?"

"I'll tell you on the way," she said. "Come on, before Ling's folks find you up here. They think all boys are after her."

The night before, Kelsie had dreaded introducing Ethan to Ling. But instead of the usual preening guys did when they met her way-more-beautiful friend, Ethan had only given Ling a weary salute.

He was sliding out of the sleeping bag. "Um, you saw what happened last time I went outside, right? I'm, like, a celebrity now."

"We'll get you a disguise, then. And if we get into trouble, you can always use your voice, right?"

Ethan grunted. "One-on-one, yeah. But it's not much good in a crowd."

"Weird," she said. "My thing *only* works in a crowd."

He was on his feet and searching for his shoes. "Maybe we're two halves of a whole. Like we were meant to find each other."

Kelsie stared at him. It was like an echo of what she'd been thinking a minute ago. But the words had sounded a little too smooth.

"Was that your voice talking?"

"Kind of." Ethan looked away. "I mean, yeah."

She grinned at him. Finding someone with another power was a relief, even if it was the power of bullshitting. Two superheroes helping her dad was better than one.

"We could be a superpowered duo," she said shyly.

"Totally. That."

Kelsie was still wearing the T-shirt and shorts Ling had given her to sleep in. Clean enough. She slipped into last night's high-tops and grabbed the messenger bag, which had maybe a thousand bucks left in it.

She led him out of the house without a word, careful not to wake Ling or her folks.

They didn't talk much as they walked the dozen blocks to the bus stop. Kelsie kept looking over her shoulder, in case the Bagrovs had sent someone to follow her and find her dad. Having an internet celebrity in tow didn't help the feeling of being watched.

At a convenience store Ethan pulled out a fat roll of twenties and bought a bottle of water, a baseball cap, and the biggest pair of sunglasses on the rack. Kelsie held the cold, sweating water bottle while he tried on the glasses. He grabbed a couple of chocolate bars and tried to offer one to her, but she waved it away.

"Not sure about that disguise," she said. "You look like you're *trying* to be incognito."

"Anything so my mom doesn't find me. I should call her

again, but not from your phone. She can track phones." He looked kind of proud as he finished the chocolate bar and started on the second. "Where're we headed?"

"To see my dad."

Ethan balked. "Great. Another person who wants to kill me."

"He doesn't!" Kelsie said.

Ethan stared at her.

"I mean, your voice freaked him out," she said. "But he's never been a killer."

"He wasn't a bank robber till Friday."

Kelsie let the comment slide. There were lines her dad wouldn't cross. She had to keep believing that. And anyway, she'd tossed away most of her money saving Ethan. He owed her.

On the bus Ethan hunkered down with his head against the window. But Kelsie still had too many questions to let him sleep.

"Here's what I don't understand. Why us two? Out of all the people in the world, why do *we* get powers?"

Ethan slid his sunglasses down and gave her a careful look, like someone studying a poker hand. "Were you born in the year two thousand?"

"Yeah. September."

"Me too. June. Could mean something.

Kelsie shook her head. "Two thousand's just a number."

"Yeah, but everybody made a big deal out of the new millennium. They thought all the computers would crash at midnight!"

"But they didn't. And weren't millions of people born that year?" Then it hit her. "Wait—there could be others. I mean, if there's two of us in a little city like Cambria, there'd be tons of people in the whole world!"

"Maybe." Ethan shrugged. "But maybe it's just us, Kels. And we were put here to help each other, no matter what."

The words made something click inside Kelsie. The thought of an ally, born to help her, who would never fail her like her father always did, sent something rushing into her. Like a crowd spilling onto a dance floor when the perfect song played. That was what she'd always been missing—someone special among the crowd.

Then she realized that Ethan had called her *Kels*, which only her father did.

"Wait. Was that your voice again?"

Ethan just shrugged, like he wanted to skip the whole subject. Like he didn't want to talk about superpowers. Even though he'd just met the only person who shared this with him.

Which made no sense.

Ethan pulled his cap down low and Kelsie let the subject drop. For now.

They changed buses twice before they reached the tenements on the outskirts of town. The neighborhood had been mostly abandoned years ago when Cambria had exploded in some other direction, ignoring the city planners.

Kelsie didn't like empty places. The broken windows and wide, still streets felt lifeless around her. Once the bus pulled away, it was like stepping into a painting. No car horns, no ringing phones or overheard conversations. No crowds, no energy, no pulse.

"This place sucks," she said.

Ethan pulled off his hat. "At least nobody's going to recognize me."

Kelsie had the address in her phone, but the reception was shaky and the map trailed off at the edge of the tenements, like no one had bothered to tell the internet about this place. She felt a moment of panic. Dad's message had said he was keeping his phone off to save battery, so she couldn't even call him.

But then she felt it.

One point of energy in that whole empty space, pulling her forward. Like an oasis in a desert. There was a crowd here someplace. Ragged and dispersed, but definitely a crowd. Or maybe several little crowds, chasing each other around a chemical high that arced steep, sweet and spiky.

She felt herself—her *power*—reach out for it. Reach it and scale it until she was balanced on top of a bright pinnacle, too sudden and too steep. Like when cheap ecstasy swept through the clubs on summer weekend nights.

She let her power pull her forward, letting the synthetic elation fill her, becoming something genuine. This was something she could do that nobody else could. She could find people lost in this empty place. This was *her* power.

"Stay close," she told Ethan.

But too soon the energy began to empty out from beneath her.

Kelsie felt herself spinning down, dragged under. The quick, cheap high was wearing off. Soon the crowd wouldn't be a crowd anymore. They'd go back to their individual needs, and Kelsie would be lost again in the eerie quiet.

She started to run, not caring whether Ethan kept up with her. She had to find her dad before the crowd's high gave out.

Five blocks later, with the feeling almost faded, Kelsie had found the place. A building like all the others, a gray two-story apartment block with boarded-up windows and doors. Broken beer bottles littered the long grass in front of it.

"How do we get in?" Ethan said.

Kelsie shook her head. Dad's text hadn't included instructions.

Around the side of the building they found a window where the boards flapped loose against the frame. It was too high for Kelsie to reach, so Ethan knelt and laced his fingers.

She hesitated. The climax of a few moments ago was building again. It burst upward in a narrow geyser, like an icy-cold bottle held against the space between Kelsie's eyebrows. It was strange, crisp, distorting.

She steadied herself, placed a foot on Ethan's hands, and pushed. Scrambling under the loose plywood, she tumbled into blackness.

Kelsie liked dark clubs just fine, but this place was different—

cave dark. The darkest dance floor was lit by a thousand stars compared to this. The air smelled sickly sour, like fruit gone bad.

She waited for her eyes to adjust, and dimly the room took shape. There was trash piled against every wall. A thick layer of dust rose from the floor with every step she took.

Ethan came scrambling through, landing awkwardly beneath the window. Dust billowed out from him, like he'd set off a softly thudding bomb.

He coughed and peered into the dimness. "Where to now?"

Kelsie pointed at the floor. A path through the dust led from the window to an empty doorway, the floorboards gleaming dully in one narrow line. Beyond was a hallway, even blacker than the room.

"Yeesh." Ethan stood up, dusted his knees. "Your dad sure knows how to hide."

"Always has." Kelsie was almost proud.

She pulled out her phone and shone it at the doorway. The darkness of the hallway seemed to drain away the feeble illumination.

She took a careful step through, shining light down at the path in the dust. The floorboards creaked, a soft and hollow sound beneath her feet. Ethan came shuffling behind her, his breathing audible in the silence.

Kelsie took slow steps, her skin tingling at every groan of the wood. In the building around her swirled sharp, discordant highs and crashes, all out of rhythm. She'd been right. It wasn't one group, but many, each huddled in its own room chasing spiky rainbows.

She let herself drift among the spires of ecstasy, looking for any familiar note . . .

Until a cold hand took her shoulder, clutching hard.

CHAPTER 55
MOB

KELSIE JERKED BACK, SPUN HER PHONE AROUND.

It was a man—maybe. In the pale light his face looked like jelly. His eyes were lost in puffiness, and his jaw was covered by angry red welts. Kelsie bit back a scream.

"What're you doing here?" the man said. The words slurred out through the few teeth left in his slack mouth.

Cratered sores traveled along his outstretched arm, like burns. And on the inside of his elbow Kelsie could see through to tendons and the dull glint of bone.

"Oh my God!" Her fear echoed out, sending a tremor through the building, through all those junkies already wary of discovery. She tried to control it, to grasp some of the icy certainty of their addiction. But she could smell the man too clearly, the rot and the putrid stink of flesh gone bad. She gagged.

When the man took a step forward, reaching for her again, Kelsie froze.

"Leave her be, Tony," Ethan said with sudden authority.

The man grunted, a rolling, liquid sound. He dropped his arms to his sides, like a wind-up doll running out of juice. "You know me, kid?"

"Your mother sent me," Ethan said.

It was the voice talking, Kelsie was certain, with none of Ethan's usual hemming and hawing. He sounded so smooth and confident that her paralysis broke. She took a step back.

"My mom's dead," Tony slurred, his squinty eyes fixed on Ethan. *Not* looking at Kelsie, thank God.

"I'm in touch with her," Ethan said.

There was a strangled gasp from Tony. "No way. Screw you."

"She's with your aunt Bertha," Ethan's voice said. "They both say they're sorry. None of it was your fault."

Ethan glanced at Kelsie, and somewhere way past his smooth expression she saw terror in his eyes. It was so weird to watch his power on display.

But it was working. In the glow of Kelsie's phone, Tony's melting face somehow showed amazement.

"They said that?"

Ethan nodded. "You were too little to know better. They shouldn't have left you alone with your little sister. You didn't know what a seizure was."

A single tear oozed across pale flesh, sparkling. "That's what I always . . . I didn't understand."

"They know that now, and you're forgiven," Ethan said, and then his voice shifted. "So, like, do you know a guy called Jerry?"

Tony hesitated, and his pale face turned to Kelsie. "You're Kelsie, huh. Why didn't you say so? Your dad said you might show up."

"Oh," she said. "Nice to meet you, Tony."

"Sorry to spook you." The man turned and shuffled into the darkness.

As they followed, Kelsie looked at Ethan. "Thanks."

"Don't thank me until we're out of here," he muttered.

Astonishment pulsed in Kelsie as they followed the man through darkness. The voice inside Ethan had reached into that man's mind and found something old and broken buried there—and fixed it, just a little.

His superpower was some serious shit.

Her father had changed.

His face was ashen. The skin on his neck hung loose like turkey jowls. He still wore the shirt he'd had on two days ago, and he smelled worse than ever.

Tony had led them up a flight of stairs to a room lit by a slant of light from a loose board over a window. A small group of people slouched on the floor, their eyes glassy. The chemical high still simmered around them, dissipating slowly, tugging Kelsie down with it. She had to focus on her father's face to keep from being swept under.

"I'm sorry to make you come here, sweetheart." Dad glanced over her head at Ethan, and his expression froze.

"This is my friend Ethan," Kelsie said carefully.

"The kid from the bank." Dad stood, his hands in fists.

"Uh, hi, Mr. Laszlo," Ethan said.

"You brought *him* here?"

"We can trust him," Kelsie said, standing between them. "He's not with the Bagrovs. He's just a guy who was in the wrong place."

"A guy who knows an awful lot about us, Kels," Dad said.

"He was just . . ." Kelsie sighed.

She'd only tried to talk to her dad about her power once, when she was ten. He'd laughed it off, saying little kids always thought they were the most important person in the room. But she hadn't meant that. Working a crowd never made her feel important. It just made her feel part of something bigger and stronger than herself.

Right now was definitely not a good time to try reopening the superpower conversation. But she had to get him to back off from Ethan somehow.

"All that stuff he said, he was just messing with you."

Her father turned to Ethan. "Messing with us, when we had guns in our hands?"

"I'm real sorry, Mr. Laszlo," Ethan said.

It sounded exactly like the kind of thing her dad would say. *Real sorry.*

"You should be!" Her father took a step toward him. "You got Hank killed!"

Kelsie placed a hand on her father. Somewhere upstairs, a small group had found another source of euphoric high. She felt it skyrocket through her like an elevator rising too fast. She latched onto it and drew it down into this room.

"It's all going to be okay, Dad."

Then Ethan's smooth voice came from behind her. "I'm here to make amends, Mr. Laszlo. I'm going get you off the hook with the Bagrovs."

Kelsie felt her power working, and a murmur went through the other junkies in the room. Her father's expression finally eased—he wanted to believe. He wanted what Ethan said to be the truth. And with Kelsie's power pulling him up and into the borrowed euphoria, he almost *did* believe it.

"You can help us? Really?" he said, eager as a little kid.

"I can fix this for you and Kelsie," Ethan said, simply and firmly. Definitely the voice.

Kelsie let out a breath. She ratcheted up the ecstasy another inch, until her father was almost grinning.

He turned to her. "And you trust him?"

"I do." She asked softly, "Dad, how do you know about this place? Who are these people?"

"They're my customers."

The people sitting in the dark were all like Tony, with puffy faces and melting skin. Bones that showed through.

"*You* did this to them? Dad, these people are sick."

Her father's expression changed again. But the image was loose and crumbling, like a retina burn from staring at the sun too long, the edges all falling away. Kelsie realized her phone had dimmed to save battery.

She let it go dark.

"They're people with no place to go," Dad said.

"Like me," Kelsie said, trying not to feel bitter.

Dad squeezed her shoulder, and for a moment she thought he would make this better somehow. But instead he said, "Fig gave you the cash?"

"He did, but . . ." She hesitated, a hand on the messenger bag. "I had to use some of it. There's a thousand left, maybe less."

"A thousand?" His voice had gone dry. "I need more than that, sweetie. Maybe you can get it for me?"

Kelsie stared. Didn't he see what she'd been through already? "What are you planning to do with it? You're not going to buy more krokodil, are you?"

Dad's eyes narrowed. "What do you know about krok?"

"Fig told me you were selling it for the Bagrovs. And that it kills people."

"I take care of my customers," Dad said stubbornly. "I'm not Alexei Bagrov."

"Oh my God, Dad." Her eyes went to Tony. There was no way she was going to help her dad sell anything that melted people like plastic dolls.

She felt the crash of a nearby crowd as another high wore off. It reached out, swiped her, and rebounded, soured by her own anguish. They would be scrabbling for more drugs right away, trying to fill the void she was reflecting at them. She tried to pull herself back inside her own skin.

"Kels, I'm in a lot of trouble here. I need enough money to make my own product; then I can get right with the Bagrovs." Dad adjusted the collar of his shirt.

That was his tell. It meant he was about to grift her, to bluff. And she'd seen the dark smear beneath his collar.

"That's a scab on your neck. Tell me you're not taking this shit yourself!"

"Once or twice. To show the customers it's harmless."

"Harmless? *Look* at them!"

Her father took a step back, surprised at how her cry of pain had rippled through the building.

He looked so hurt, but for the first time in her life Kelsie was too angry to feel sorry for him. She'd been raised in the family of Dad's mismatched con-artist friends, where drugs and jail time were no big deal. The longest her father had ever disappeared was eight months for possession. He'd laughed about it, making jokes about eating three meals a day for the first time in his life. Back then it hadn't seemed scary at all.

But now, standing in this stinking, terrible place, she knew the truth. This was death. He was going to kill himself and all these other people. And he was going to drag her down too.

"Kels—"

"Forget it, Dad! You can't throw away your life just because you don't want to face up to what you've done. You can't have the money."

He was silent. The whole world seemed silent right then.

She handed him the water bottle she was still carrying, the one Ethan had bought at the convenience store. Then she pulled out a fistful of bills from her bag and thrust it at him. Probably only fifty dollars, not enough for him to do any real damage.

"I'm sorry, Dad. I'll come back with food, okay? For everyone. And we'll work out what to do next."

He looked at her, not angry anymore. Just sad. "You're a good girl, Kels. I'm sorry to put you in this."

She reached out and gave him a quick hug, smelling the sweat and dirt and that sickly-sour scent that came from hopelessness and hiding in a building without running water. "Be careful, Dad, okay? I mean it."

Dad hugged her in his wiry arms. "Okay, Kels."

He sounded defeated. She'd never heard that in his voice before.

She pulled free and moved back along the hallway, Ethan falling into step beside her. As they moved away, Kelsie's pulse skidded with the scattered unease of the mob.

CHAPTER 56
SCAM

OUTSIDE, THE DAYLIGHT SEEMED MORE INTENSE THAN Ethan remembered.

All the colors were brighter, like the muted world inside the house had sent his eyes into overdrive. The dying grass in front of the abandoned houses was a more vivid yellow, the graffiti more discordantly vibrant.

He put his sunglasses back on.

But it wasn't the light that was weirding him out. It was the whole uncanny vibe of that drug den with its scabby, decaying inhabitants. Every minute he'd been inside, inexplicable emotions had passed through him.

"Kelsie, did you feel sort of . . . happy in there? Like, a contact high?"

"That was me, trying to keep my dad from punching you."

"Oh. Um, thanks." Ethan hadn't quite gotten his head around Kelsie's power yet. The night before, on the roof of the Boom Room, she'd explained she could control the energy of a crowd. But it could also control her. It was pretty complicated, but Ethan was old friends with complicated. Complicated lived in his mouth.

"A lot of blissed-out junkies in there," she said. "I borrowed what they were feeling, to keep things calm. People are like herd animals—they share emotions. I just lend a hand."

"It reminded me of . . ." He remembered feeling fuzzy and calm on the bank's marble floor, like liquid valium was pumping into him, along with three helpings of Thanksgiving turkey. "During the robbery, all us customers zoned out. Was that *you*?"

Kelsie gave him a sad look. "For all the good it did."

"All my fault," he said, half hoping Kelsie would argue. But she didn't.

She slouched with her head down, scuffing her high-tops on the pavement as they walked. She looked tiny and defeated. He couldn't imagine what it was like to see someone you loved in a place like that, taking an awful drug like krokodil. Kelsie wanted to get her father some food, but Ethan thought the guy would be better off with a hospital. He looked half dead. They all did.

Ethan missed his home in the nice part of Cambria. He missed his mom and he missed Jess. Being born into a family of straight shooters might be a pain, but nothing compared to a con-artist druggie father. He vowed to call Mom the minute he found an untraceable phone.

"I'm sorry," he said.

"For what?"

"For . . ." For being anywhere near that bank on Friday. For needing a ride home. For stealing a bag full of money that put him right in the way of a desperate Jerry Laszlo.

But without that crazy roller coaster of events, he never would've met Kelsie. He liked Kelsie. A lot. Probably more than she liked him, and that still didn't stop him liking her in a big way.

She'd saved him from the Craig, she'd thrown thousands of bucks into the air, and she'd hidden him from various interested parties overnight.

Which made not telling her about the other Zeroes totally selfish. But she'd been so *fascinated* when he'd told her about the voice, like his power was something amazing and cool instead of this awful hijacker in his body.

In all that glory, Ethan had missed the opportunity to mention he wasn't the only other person with a power. And leaving out the truth was like any scam—if you rode it long enough, you couldn't get off.

"I'm just sorry I can't help you more."

"Hey," she said. "It was pretty handy what you said to that guy Tony. About his mom and his aunt. I think you really helped him."

Ethan smiled. The voice had done him proud in there. First with scary Tony and then with Kelsie's dad.

Maybe his stupid voice was getting better. Maybe it was developing beyond its usual short-term thinking. The weird thing was, it had felt good to use the voice again. Like shaking hands with an old friend.

"You think I was right, not giving my dad the money?" Kelsie asked. "I feel like I let him down."

"Your dad let *you* down, not the other way around."

Kelsie gave him a lopsided smile. "Is that your voice talking?"

"I don't need the voice for this. Trust me, I'm a world-class expert in letting people down."

She smiled at him gratefully. Ethan beamed in return. Every time Kelsie looked at him, it was like a light turned on.

A black sedan went by, out of place in this part of town. It reminded Ethan of the Craig's advice about never driving anything fancy. Though maybe this guy wasn't trying to lie low.

The driver was a man in a suit with pale skin and thick black hair. Beside him was another guy in a suit.

"Dad has nothing," Kelsie was saying to herself. "No food, no clothes. I had all his money, and I threw it away last night."

"That was my fault," Ethan said.

Then he realized something. When it came to money, he could help Kelsie out. Money was something he could manage. But it would mean telling her about the other Zeroes. . . .

"I should just tell the police where he is," Kelsie said. "I mean, what's worse? Being in prison or winding up dead?"

Ethan reached out clumsily to rest a hand on her shoulder. "I think I can help. There's something I haven't—"

Kelsie froze. "You see that car?"

Ethan glanced up. "Yeah, it went past before."

"Last time I saw a car circling the block, it was really bad news."

"It's probably just . . ."

Ethan's words faded as the car drifted to a halt beside them. The two men got out. The driver came right over toward them, a tall hook of a man with a bend to his spine. The other guy stayed by the car, like he was ready to take off. Like this was a robbery.

Ethan was all set to offer them the roll of twenties in his pocket, but he didn't get the chance.

"Kelsie Laszlo?" The driver said with some crazy kind of accent.

"Nope," Ethan said right away.

The guy's eyes flicked once toward Ethan and then back to Kelsie. "We're looking for your father. There's a price on his head. Any idea where I can find him?"

Ethan looked at Kelsie, who gave him a beseeching look. Ethan realized with something like pride that she wanted him to use the voice.

Ethan willed it to take over his throat, anything to make these guys believe he and Kelsie had nothing to do with Jerry Laszlo. Anything to help Kelsie. But the voice had nothing to say.

Which probably meant they already knew exactly who Kelsie was, and that her father was hiding nearby.

"Like, we don't know what you mean," Ethan tried in his own voice. It cracked on the last word.

The guy finally gave him a solid look. "Huh. The boy from the bank video."

"Um, what video?"

The guy laughed. "And here with Jerry Laszlo's little girl. I believe this is called a two-for-one. How lucky can a guy be?"

Okay, these guys knew everything. The voice couldn't unwind that. So Ethan had to want something simpler.

This guy needs to leave us alone. Ethan sent the thought spiraling out. And there it was at last, the wonderful feeling of the voice pulling upward toward his throat and jaw, full of certainty. *Come on, voice. Just like in the tenements. Win this thing!*

The voice said, "My friend. What did you say your name was?"

"I didn't." The man's smile was coldly polite.

"I'm going to call you . . ." The voice seemed to hesitate, but of course the voice knew exactly what to say next. "I'm going to call you Misha."

Misha started, which filled Ethan with happiness.

"Yeah, I know who you are, Misha," the voice went on. "You'd be surprised what I know. Like how Alexei doesn't think much of you."

Misha shook his head. "You don't know Mr. Bagrov. You don't know shit."

"What I know is, he told everyone important not to mess with Kelsie," the voice continued breezily. "Because Miss Laszlo here is doing business with him. So how come Mr. Bagrov didn't bother to tell you that?"

Misha gave a dry laugh. "He's doing business with kids like you?"

Kelsie nodded once, her jaw set in defiance. "That's right. Picking up where my dad left off."

Misha stared at Kelsie's sparkly high-tops and Ethan's crumpled shirt. "Don't make me laugh. You kids don't even have a car."

"Only a dipshit brings their ride into a neighborhood like this," Ethan heard himself say.

Misha's eyes flicked to his shiny black sedan and then up at the broken windows of the building behind them. The voice had played him perfectly.

But then the other guy spoke up. "Let's check this with Mr. Bagrov."

He pulled open his jacket to reach for his phone, and Ethan saw a gun strapped to his side.

The voice died in his throat, and Ethan felt a sudden resentment for all the other Zeroes. Why was his power so crap at lying to more than one person at a time?

"Wait!" Ethan said in his own useless, shaky voice.

Both the mobsters stared at him, expecting more.

Ethan really wanted these guys to leave them alone. He wanted to get out of this creepy dead-end part of town. He wanted to live another day, maybe go back to the Moonstruck Diner and drink bad coffee for hours. He wanted to call his *mom*, for Pete's sake. He put that all into one articulate thought and prayed the voice had a plan.

"Okay," he heard himself say. "Go right ahead, Boris. Call him. And when you do, tell him you got a present for him."

Misha smiled. "You mean you two kids?"

"Nope." Ethan grinned, but inside he was chanting *please, please, please*, focusing every bit of his will into his power. "Jerry's three blocks that way, in the tenement with the broken bottles on the lawn, second floor. But move fast. He won't be there long."

Beside him, Kelsie gasped. "You . . ."

Ethan felt his stomach leap into his throat, pushing the voice out of the way. "Oh, crap."

Misha's expression changed to one of pure greed. Both of the men slipped back into the car. "Thank you, my friend!"

And just like that the voice had done it again.

CHAPTER 57
MOB

KELSIE RAN, HEADING AFTER THE FANCY CAR. BUT half a block later Ethan was grabbing her, dragging her to a halt.

"Kelsie, wait!"

She pushed him off, swung a fist at him. "Oh my God, Ethan! Why did you do that?"

Ethan looked stunned, like he couldn't believe what was happening either.

"It's too late," he said. "I screwed up. But we can't beat them there."

She spun away from him. The car was three blocks away, already in front of the building full of junkies. The Bagrov men were out front, banging on the boarded-up door.

She started running again, outpacing Ethan, shouting as she got closer. In the empty suburb, her voice rolled and rolled. At last she felt an answering spark of anxiety from inside the tenement. People had heard her.

But Ethan grabbed her again, bringing her to a skidding stop.

"We can't, Kelsie! Those guys have *guns*!"

The crack of wood came from down the street, and both of them spun to face it. A board came tumbling down the tenement's front steps, and the two men disappeared through the doorway.

"Dad!" Kelsie couldn't escape Ethan's grasp, so she dragged his weight behind her, his sneakers skidding on asphalt.

She could feel the people inside the tenement bonded in fear. But the mob only lasted seconds. They thought it was the cops coming in and scattered in all directions.

"Run!" she cried.

Ethan was in front of her now. He looked scared, his freckles standing out on his pale skin.

"Why did you *do* that?" she screamed at him.

"I'm sorry," Ethan said.

The world was spinning, smears of color dancing across her eyes. First she hadn't given her dad the money, and now *this*.

Kelsie tried to pull away, but she was weak with exhaustion. She couldn't remember the last meal she'd eaten, the last decent night's sleep she'd had. "You could've told him another building. Any building! You sent him right to my dad!"

"I wanted us to be safe," Ethan said numbly. "I forgot about keeping your father safe too. My voice didn't understand."

"You kept saying you wanted to help!"

"I do!" Ethan cried. "But I don't know what the voice is going to say! It's out of my control."

"Then you shouldn't use it at all!" she yelled, turning to the building again. "Help me fight them."

"What are we going to do against mobsters with guns? They'll just take us, too. We have to get out of here."

She flinched as the fear inside the building shifted to hard panic. Misha and his pal must have stumbled into a roomful of junkies, guns waving.

"My dad's gonna think I led them right here."

"Listen. Jerry owes them money, you said. That's what this is all about. I can get money!"

She stared at him. He had scammed a free room at the Magnifique and stolen a bag of cash from Craig. But what if the Bagrovs wanted blood?

"Can't you talk them out of taking him at all?"

Ethan shook his head. "Once they get on the phone with Bagrov, we're dead meat. Please."

He reached out toward her but Kelsie knocked his hand away. Her head was throbbing like an overamped speaker from the panic down the street.

She tried to latch onto the energy coming from inside the building, to organize it into some kind of resistance. But it scattered like birds. Like panicked junkies, pretty much.

"Listen," Ethan said. "Can we please have this conversation

someplace far way? What if Misha calls for backup?"

"Not till I hear your plan for saving my dad!" Kelsie braced herself. "And don't even *think* about using your voice on me."

"Okay." Ethan was panting, and took a moment to speak again. "There's something I haven't told you yet. I have this bag of money."

"Craig's money. I know."

"Right, but there's another thing." Ethan nodded. "The part where I *don't* have it."

Kelsie groaned. His other voice might be a bullshitter, but at least it usually made sense. "Do you have it or not, Ethan?"

"My friends are holding it for me." He hesitated. "Friends who are like us . . . with powers."

"Powers." Kelsey stared at him. *"Superpowers?"*

He nodded.

Of course. Where there were two, there had to be more. Maybe lots more, just like she'd said on the bus. And Ethan had pretended to be too sleepy to talk about it.

"Why didn't you *tell* me?"

"I was getting to it." Ethan looked terrified. "It's just that we're, like, a secret group, and I had to make sure you were—"

"You let me think we were the only ones!"

Ethan opened his mouth, but Kelsie waved his response away.

"Save it." She took one last look at the tenement. "Okay. Let's go meet your superfriends. *Anyone* who's not you."

CHAPTER 58

CRASH

CHIZARA WALKED DOWN THE BASEMENT STAIRS OF the Central Cambria Police Department, a little wobbly in her heels. Up ahead, beyond the jail cells, the IT guys were showing a group of managerial types into the server room. She hurried to join the back of the crowd, frowning down at the fake paperwork on her clipboard.

Stuffy air flowed out of the room, and the hallway smelled strongly of cleanser and bleach. Chizara tried not to think why, pushing the beaten cop out of her head. This was her chance to make up a little for what she'd done, for the bad things she'd let happen.

The room was full of metal shelves with rows of black and beige boxes, none of them showing a wink of life. But she could still sense the patterns around her. Like walking into the burned-out shell of a house—maybe a whole burned-out town—one that she herself had torched. Slowly Chizara began to match these empty shells to the pulsing systems she'd seen in her head before she crashed them on Friday.

That giant gray box there, next to the boss guy with the lightning-bolt logo on his shirt, she recognized the innards of that. She'd frazzled them during the big crash, right before she'd started to lose it.

"So when that power spike hit," the boss guy was saying, "this UPS should've cut in and kept the power steady. We'll put in a new one for you, no problem, but the weird thing is why the mains relay is stuck. So first we're gonna run some tests—"

A woman in a gray suit spoke up: "You been keeping up the quarterly maintenance?"

"Right on schedule," said the guy. "Every check we've ever run, she failed over just like she should."

"Of course it did," murmured a young guy just in front of Chizara to his buddy. "Guy knows how to cover his ass, doesn't he?"

His buddy nodded, then glanced over his shoulder, registered Chizara as a stranger, looked her up and down. She was every inch the serious young assistant with her clipboard, in the navy-blue skirt suit she'd begged Mom to buy her so she could look like an American girl at church on Sundays.

It had been easy, sneaking into the CCPD. There were so many groups here—tech people, insurance adjusters, police brass—a big enough crowd to lose track of whose assistant was whose. Chizara smiled back at the guy, her mind reaching through into the server room, trying to see exactly what she'd done.

The UPS was the least of it, just a giant switch that she'd stopped from doing its automated rescue. Littered around it were caramelized circuit boards, burned-out fibers, and blasted switches. It should be a beehive in there, hundreds of buzzing insects stinging her brain. She should be curled up in a corner from the pain.

But everything that could hurt her had been annihilated. A nanotornado had ripped through these intricate, delicate machines, leaving every connection broken. She was ashamed of herself—she'd lost control in a big way.

But whoa, it had been sweet.

Chizara's mental fingers extended to cover the multiple failures she'd caused, every single bee she'd killed. It shouldn't be too hard to fix, right? It was just a matter of opening her mind to all those tiny, thwarted connections, feeling around the shadowy map of the dead network for its arteries, its nerves, the filaments that poured the power through. If she could just reset that pulse, and push it smoothly back into the tangled microthreads of metal—

There. With a lurch inside her, the UPS came to life.

The people at the door jerked back all at once, like a field of grain socked by a gust of wind.

"What the hell—"

"Did you do that, Roger?" The boss woman had to speak up to be heard over the winding-up buzz of the UPS.

"Didn't touch a thing!"

A stumpy pain tree lit up inside Chizara, pulsing as it sucked up power from the unharmed backup batteries to push it through the sleeping servers. She could see everything better now, could feel how the tornado had thundered through the room, tearing out so many tiny pieces as it went. As she followed the spreading network of paths, each busted connection she passed unmelted and retethered itself, lighting up another fine channel of pain in her.

Her skin began to burn and twitch, her temples to throb.

But Chizara stood still, accepting the punishment, blindly staring down at the clipboard in her unsteady hands. Her teeth sang and her bones shuddered, and a grunt of discomfort sat in her throat. She reached for the next dead server, and the next, and there was another over there. . . .

"Hell *no*!" Roger shouted. "Shut it down! Shut it down! Chris! Arnie!"

Chizara leaned against the wall, her mind flitting through the workings in the servers, lighting tiny torches all the way. No one looked at her; they were all transfixed by the scrambling emergency inside the room.

"Is it working again?" said one of the suits.

"Yes! But it's gotta be done in sequence! We need the network up first, and then the SAN, and only *then* do you bring up the—shit! *How is this happening?*"

The clipboard fell from Chizara's trembling hands. She bent to grab for it, and it felt so much better down here near the floor that she stayed crouched, reaching out, feeling the connections divide and multiply, the pain tree extend, a finer, denser net riddling her skin. The guys in the server room crashed around like trapped rats, diving to shut off each new piece of tech as it tried to revive.

"Thank you," she breathed to them. It was like they were working with her, helping her manage the clamor, manually controlling her pain.

And then she reached the end. Not the end of the tree, not the full rebuild. But the place past which she couldn't push any further. She could see where she needed to go—the next layer of crash points arrayed there all tinily twisted and gummed up. But she didn't have it in her.

She tried once more—gritted her teeth as hard as she could and pushed.

And . . . nothing.

Chizara stood up again, hugging her clipboard to her. The little crowd was abuzz, shaking heads, shrugging shoulders. But the buzz inside Chizara had died back to the single fat beehive of the UPS. The energy that had flooded into her with the big crash, that had stored itself inside her—was it all *gone*?

"Damn it!" she whispered, and turned away from the server

room. She walked toward the stairs, trying to look confident, like she belonged. But her spine felt like a wilted stalk of celery, and a trickle of sweat crept down her back.

She trudged the stairs back up to the first floor. What had happened?

She'd reached out just like in all her practice runs, and she'd *seen* what she had to do. But the fixing power had deserted her. She could feel the space where it should be, dry and empty.

All she had left was the nagging of the other revived systems—*crash us, crash us!*—like always.

It was so tempting to recharge herself. She had to get out of the building.

Crossing the reception lobby, Chizara kept her head high and her posture professional. An officer coming in held the door open for her with a smile, and she smiled back, stepped out, and took a deep breath of the fresh summer air.

Okay, at least she'd fixed *something* before her juice ran out. Demons never fixed things, did they?

She took long strides on the sidewalk, her heels clicking. Her new power might have abandoned her, but working it had left a nice buzz behind.

Then her phone rattled in her jacket pocket, sending a charge of hard, itchy pain into her side. She smothered a gasp, snatched it out, and glared at it.

Glorious Leader. "What is it, Nate?"

"You hungry?"

"Why do you care?"

He laughed, and she winced at the noisy buzz of it. "I just thought you might need a bite after your morning's work. You're at the police station, right?"

She made herself keep walking. Nate was always trying to psych her out with his guesses.

"I'm busy," she said. Maybe after a long, rejuvenating walk, the fixing power would come back.

"But you gotta eat, right? Getting a whole police station up and running, that has to take it out of you. I'm over in the park. Scored a bench in the Sundial Garden. It's a beautiful day and I got you a sandwich at the Kosher Deli."

Chizara narrowed her eyes at the people lolling on the grass across the street, all smiling, laughing, clapping each other's shoulders. She examined the lift in her own heart, and saw it for the fake it was. This was all Nate-generated euphoria—he was sitting in the park, spreading out a cloud of goodwill to pull her in.

But she *was* hungry. Ravenous, in fact. Fixing that server room had hollowed her out like a gourd.

"Okay," she said weakly. "I'm on my way."

She switched Glorious Leader off and put him in her pocket. Hadn't she already told him to leave her alone?

Sure, it was impressive how he'd read her so right, worked out where she was and what she was doing—all that attention focused on *her*. But it was also kind of creepy. With anyone other than Nate it'd be downright stalkerish.

But Nate wasn't a creep, just a guy with an Ultimate Goal that he wanted everyone to fall in line with. *Which you're not going to do, Chizara,* she reminded herself as she crossed the street toward the park—at the same time as some childish, easily charmed part of her was thinking, *He bought me a sandwich!*

CHAPTER 59
CRASH

THE SUNDIAL GARDEN WAS BRIGHT AND BUSY WITH Nate-cheered people. He was at the center, arms spread along the back of the bench, grinning his champagne grin. Two soda cans sat in the shade of a Kosher Deli sack next to him.

Chizara felt her heart try to lift, her mouth try to smile. But she looked straight into Nate's eyes, poker-faced.

He beamed back at her. "Did it work?"

"Did what work?" She sat down on the edge of the bench, trying to tear her gaze from the sack.

Nate opened it and passed her a wrapped sandwich. "Your new power. Did you fix everything you broke?"

Chizara pulled open the paper and took a big, beefy bite, too big to talk around. She covered her mouth, watching him as she chewed and swallowed. He was hoping she'd fixed it all, as if that meant everything was okay and she could come back to the group. As if she didn't have Officer Bright on her conscience, whom no amount of uncrashing would fix.

"Maybe ten percent of what I destroyed," she finally said. "But then it ran out and I couldn't fix any more. I guess I'm back to breaking things now."

"Ran out?" Nate looked more intrigued than sympathetic. "You had a new power and then you lost it?"

She lowered the sandwich half to her knees. Her first swallow was going down slowly—she hadn't chewed it well enough. Too hungry.

"I think I need to crash something else before I'll get it back. Like it was an afterglow of wrecking the police station. But it faded."

She was glad she wasn't saying this to Ethan. His voice would find her use of "afterglow" hilarious. But Nate would get it. He understood how much she wanted her power to be different. Better.

"You don't have to guess," he said, his eyes locked steady on hers. "We can help you figure it out."

Around them the picnicking people grew silent, almost serious.

"I can see what you're doing, Nate," she said. "I can tell the difference between my own feelings and the ones you want me to feel."

He shrugged and laughed, and the pressure eased.

"A guy can try, can't he?"

"Not if the guy wants me to trust him. You want me back in the Zeroes? It'll take more than a sandwich and a few Bellwether tricks."

Nate waved her accusation away, unwrapped his own sandwich. "I have some good news for you—I found another Zero."

"Are you serious?" Chizara kept her voice neutral, waiting to see what she really felt about this, in her deepest, most Nate-proof heart. And she took a second bite. She could forgive Nate a lot if he would just let her eat.

What if all it took to get her fixing power back was a few hundred calories?

"Last night," he said, "during the mission I called you about. Something weird happened."

Chizara stared at him, remembering that panicked call. *Someone wants to beat up Ethan!* Like *that* was news.

"So those goons didn't catch Scam? Otherwise you would have started with that."

"Yeah, he just called me." Another wave of his hand. "But that's getting ahead of ourselves. It all went down on Ivy Street last night. Ethan was running from the guys he stole that duffel bag from, and there was this girl helping him. The bad guys were closing in, and this girl *did* something with the crowd. She pushed it into a frenzy to help Ethan get away." Nate's eyes were wide, his sandwich forgotten. "You should've seen it."

A pulse of horror went through Chizara. "You mean she's like you?"

Two Glorious Leaders? Just. No.

But Nate was shaking his head. "It was different. She didn't focus them on herself. She didn't lead them; she brought them together and made some kind of *organism*. Something that had its own agenda."

Chizara didn't know what to make of this. Creating a crowd organism and setting it loose didn't sound responsible, exactly. "And what did this thing want to do?"

"Just pick up money, at first. And then it pretty much decided . . . to dance." Nate smiled, like he wanted to jump up and show his own moves on the grass right now.

Chizara glowered at him, fighting the mood that flooded into her like the sunshine, amplified by the picnicking Sunday crowds.

"Well, it's good you found someone," she said carefully. "You've got a replacement for me already."

"No, don't you see? There are six of us now!"

"Uh, five. Oh right, but there's that other guy." She snapped her fingers, trying to remember his name.

"Anonymous. And with six of us, we're a crowd all on our own. A self-contained Curve! We won't need anyone else around to get stuff done."

Slowly she raised her eyes. Nate was aglow with excitement and certainty. Beyond him a dozen people's faces floated out of focus, smiling too, each a sunflower following the sun. She felt the pressure of his warmth, his pleasure; it would be so easy to cave in. *Great! So what'll we do, now that we're a complete team?*

Except that was the problem. Once they were a crowd on their own, the Zeroes would fall in line behind Glorious Leader. Nate's spell would be just that crucial little bit stronger—who'd be able to resist him?

Chizara worked a strand of beef free of her teeth with her tongue. Part of her wanted to do the wise thing and run away right now. But she also wondered, who was this new girl?

Was she another Nate, all big dreams and personal magnetism? Would she lock horns with him over who should be the most glorious Glorious Leader?

Or would this girl fall for his charm as the others all had, and follow him on crazy missions, no matter who wound up getting hurt?

Now that her hunger was less acute, exhaustion was crashing down on Chizara. Using her power had sucked everything from her body, not just the crash buzz left over from two days ago. She folded the wax paper over the bitten end of her sandwich, placed it neatly in the sack between them.

"You can meet her tonight," Nate said. "When Ethan called, he said she wants to meet us. Zeroes meeting at six o'clock, then dinner."

Chizara wanted to turn away, but she managed to summon

the strength to meet Nate's gaze again, resisting the full force of his charm on her psyche.

"Just come and meet her," he said.

"There are five of you, Nate," Chizara said softly. "With this new person, there are five. If you want to be a six-pack, you still have to find one more."

She had time to see his face fall before she stood up and walked away. For a few seconds it was like wading through oncoming water, all the attention, all the woeful looks on everyone's faces.

But then Nate relaxed his hold on the crowd, and they became themselves again, their separate groups, their own unhindered, unexaggerated personalities. They didn't care who she was anymore as she stalked across the Sundial Garden to the gate.

Nate had let her go without a fight. He knew, as she knew, that she'd be too curious about this new power to sit at home while the rest of them got together.

And more important than mere curiosity, Chizara needed to warn this new girl that no power came without a cost.

CHAPTER 60
ANONYMOUS

WHEN THIBAULT AND FLICKER ROUNDED THE CORNER, the Hotel Magnifique towered ahead. For the first time ever, the sight made Thibault's heart sink. He'd been an idiot for risking his home to help that little weasel Scam.

Best friends, right. The guy had probably forgotten all about him by now.

He was glad for Flicker's arm hooked through his, her sight lines pinging from strangers on the street to keep him in view. Otherwise he couldn't face this.

At the main doors of the hotel Tom Creasy greeted them with a professional smile. Thibault might be in yesterday's crumpled shirt, but at least he had shoes on, lifted from Sack's Shoe Barn next door.

Inside, staff were coming and going behind the reservation

desk. Thibault had timed this perfectly for the shift change. He slipped in, taking a blank key card from the drawer and waking up a computer.

"You know how all this works?" Flicker asked, leaning against the desk in front of him like a guest.

"Three years of practice," Thibault said glumly. He typed in Katie Chirico's ID and password, hit enter, and gave a little grunt of surprise.

"What's up?" Flicker asked.

"Changed her password. I'll try someone else's."

Flicker looked thoughtful, then drifted away down the long desk, the tendrils of her listening settling over the assembled staff.

Thibault decided to go straight to the top, trying the hotel manager's login.

This account has been suspended. Please consult the Personnel Manager.

Suspended? Charlie Penka's account? That made no sense. He retyped the crazy Czech password.

This account has been suspended.

"What the hell?"

"Are you hearing this?" Flicker was back, nodding at a gathering of staff at the other end of the desk. "Everyone's supposed to change their passwords."

Thibault looked. The staff were tautly wired together with bright connections; something big was up. The news about changing passwords had just reached the afternoon shift.

But maybe the graveyard shift didn't know yet? If he used one of their logins . . .

There, he was in. He rattled in the details and dipped the card.

"Also," Flicker said quietly, "does 'penthouse two' ring any bells?"

Thibault groaned. "Yep."

"Some guys are working up there," she said. "From Vaneddi's?"

"Fanetti's. They're industrial cleaners. Not a good sign." Thibault logged off and walked out from behind the desk.

He led Flicker across the lobby so fast that a few barbs of notice stuck to them, which Thibault swiped away. The elevator took forever to come, then stopped for no apparent reason at the seventh-floor café while he quietly seethed.

Finally they reached the penthouse level. A cleaning cart was parked outside his old suite, full of mops and steam vacuums and bottles of bleach. The door was propped open, and Thibault leaned forward and looked in.

The coffee table was in splinters, the TV cracked. Shards of glass littered the floor.

After three years of chopping the wood and carrying the water, of his trying so hard to keep this room looking vacant, the dismal sight was a punch in the gut. It was almost impressive, how much damage Craig's thugs had done in the minutes before they'd followed him and Scam and Kelsie out into the night.

And he had to admit, Kelsie had really saved them from a serious beatdown. If he ever saw her again, he'd apologize for doubting her.

One of the guys in coveralls looked up from scrubbing the carpet. His gaze slipped from Thibault to Flicker.

"Did something happen last night?" she asked. "We're in the other penthouse, and we heard some noise."

He took in her dark glasses and cane, decided she was harmless. "Bunch of kids got in. Been living here awhile, by the look of it. Clothes and video games and stuff."

Thibault walked in past her, chopping away any interest from the Fanetti's guys. His clothes were in a pile, torn and glittering with broken glass. His books ripped in half, with the tattered copy of *Zen for Beginners* in a dozen pieces, as if the goons had given it special attention.

But far worse, his laptop was gone from its place on the desk. No shards of plastic anywhere, so either the hotel or Craig's gang had taken it intact.

"Don't envy you guys your job today," Flicker said. Her sight lines were hopping around the room, taking it all in. It filled Thibault with shame for her to see his home looking like a disaster zone.

"Sorry, ma'am." The work-crew boss was approaching the door, ready to close it and enforce Fanetti's famous discretion. "We've got work to do."

Thibault slipped past just in time. The door closed with a

firm click, shutting him out of his home. And he had no idea where to go next.

"You okay?" Flicker asked, a hand on his shoulder.

"I'm fine." His voice was hoarse again. "Those were just things."

"Yeah, but they were *your* things." Flicker moved closer, leaned against him. "It seemed like a really nice room."

He nodded. "It was."

"I mean, that *view*," she said. "Those workmen couldn't keep their eyes off it."

He should have taken a last look, instead of mourning his broken junk. But yes, the view was gone as well.

"No one owns the sunset," he said, and walked toward the elevator.

As they rode down, Thibault asked without much hope, "Did you see a laptop anywhere?"

"No." Flicker still stood close. "You can't go back later? And live there, I mean, after they clean it all up?"

He shook his head. "Not if Charlie Penka's account is suspended. The hotel knows someone was hacking the system. They'll redo their security. Start over from scratch."

Just like he was going to have to do.

Flicker's attention filled the elevator like a cloud of scent. "Did you say Charlie Penka? Down at the desk, someone was saying he got fired."

Thibault closed his eyes. "Oh, man. I used his account for room service—food for that weasel Scam—and for maintenance supplies. Years of stealing, all of it on Charlie, along with what those thugs did last night."

Flicker's hand on his was soft, careful. "But it was just gossip, Anon. Downstairs, nobody could believe it. They all said no *way* was he fired."

"I know, I know," groaned Thibault. "Because he's the greatest boss in the world, and his kids are so cute in that picture on his desk. Everyone loves him."

The elevator came to a halt, and the doors slid open. But Thibault didn't even open his eyes. He should just stay in here, a guilty ghost riding up and down forever. No one would notice.

All his years of *chop the wood, carry the water* had been nonsense, hadn't they? The whole idea that he could take what he wanted without affecting anyone was bullshit. Like Chizara had said a million times, there were always costs.

The door closed them in again, the elevator waiting on the ground floor.

"You think the hotel has your laptop?" Flicker asked. "We could try to get it back."

"Doesn't matter. My data's all backed up and encrypted. But the moment they opened it, they would've seen the reservations screen and Charlie's login."

"Yeah, but won't you need it at whatever hotel you go to next?"

He barely had strength to shake his head. "And get some other manager fired? I can't risk that."

Flicker leaned closer, and Thibault finally opened his eyes. The smoky tendrils of her attention were all around him. She was working so hard not to lose him, when all he wanted was to disappear. If only she'd tracked him down a week ago, when he'd lived in that magnificent suite, instead of now with all his strategies revealed as vanity and bullshit.

"I was fooling myself," he said. "Thinking I could take what I wanted and not hurt anybody. I'm about as Zen as Scam and his voice. Someone else always pays the price."

"Maybe you're being a little hard on yourself."

"Hard? Hell, it's easy for me. I can walk away. But Charlie Penka must be wondering what just hit him." He shook his head in disgust. "Your sister was right to call me Nothing."

"I told you about that?"

"This morning." He swallowed his disappointment that Flicker had forgotten. She could hold on to a lot, but not everything. "It's okay. I call myself the same thing."

"But you *aren't* nothing." Flicker's hand pressed against his chest, like she was trying to make herself believe in him. "I mean, you're right here."

Thibault shrugged. "It's from a Zen saying: 'Wisdom tells me I am nothing.' It reminds me that it's better not to fight what I am. Fighting it only makes it hurt worse."

Like now, the way he was starting to like Flicker. *Really*

like her. Apart from the mind-blowing fact that she was mostly remembering him, she was just so Zen about everything. Without him asking, she'd understood last night that he needed a place to stay, and she'd been totally cool about finding him in her attic this morning.

And the way she'd tracked his hotel down with those old wabi-sabi photos, that must have taken monklike patience.

Maybe Flicker's power made her think differently than most people. She saw the world from so many perspectives, and seeing was half of enlightenment.

But standing here with her was making him ache for something he couldn't have. Something that didn't even make sense, given what he was. He would always disappear in the end, forgotten, no matter how hard she tried.

As if to mock him, a jaunty tune filled the elevator.

He turned to Flicker, who'd pulled out her phone.

"Your ringtone is 'Hail to the Chief'?"

"Only for Nate," she said with a smile.

The conversation only lasted a moment. Then she pressed the open-door button and pulled Thibault out into the lobby.

"He's called a meeting. The sparkly girl is coming in."

CHAPTER 61

CRASH

"SO YOU GUYS REALLY HAVE POWERS?" THE NEW girl asked. She was a skinny little thing with blond curls, short shorts, and a shiny top. Despite her party clothes she looked tired, thoughtful, and a little suspicious.

Suspicious was good, Chizara decided.

The question was, could this girl withstand Nate's charisma for more than five minutes? Chizara herself was in the back row of the home theater, arms folded, legs crossed, trying to keep the Curve at bay. Another person in the group did make a difference.

Maybe six really was a crowd.

Wait, *six*? Ethan, Nate, Riley, the new girl, and Chizara herself were five . . .

Right. That guy sitting next to Riley. Forgettable Handsome

Guy. He and Riley were hand in hand, sharing glowing smiles.

Chizara smiled a little herself. Well, hooking up with the guy was *one* way to remember him.

"Yes, all of us have powers," Nate said. "And they're all different. But you probably want proof." He smiled, like he had a presentation all prepared.

"What I want is help," said the new girl—Kelsie was her name. "I need to get my dad away from these bad guys."

"*Really* bad guys," Ethan added. "Russian mobsters."

Chizara raised an eyebrow. According to the bank video, Kelsie's father was the robber who'd held a gun in Ethan's face. And now Ethan wanted to rescue him?

That was like very un-Scam-like behavior.

"What they mostly want is money," Kelsie said. "A lot."

"Money isn't a problem," Nate said, and Kelsie's curious green eyes widened, like she'd never even dreamed those words before.

When Nate had passed out new phones to replace the ones Chizara had crashed, and given one to Kelsie, too, just to bring her up to the Zeroes' minimum standards, she'd made the same face. Girl wasn't used to presents like that.

But presents were never free. The daughter of a criminal had to know that, right?

"Of course, paying off kidnappers can be dangerous," Nate said. "That's where our powers come in handy."

Kelsie sized them all up and still didn't look impressed.

"Any of you have a power that can stop a bullet?"

Chizara smiled again. She was starting to like this girl.

"Not quite," Riley spoke up. "But we can stop it from coming to that. Take a picture of me."

Kelsie shook her head. "Do what?"

"Pull out your new phone and take a picture." Riley looked smug behind her dark glasses.

Kelsie's hand went to her pocket, and she frowned.

"Looking for this?" came a voice from behind the girl. It was him, Anonymous, the phone in his hand.

Okay. Six people in the room made him a *lot* harder to notice.

"Now type something on it," Riley said.

Kelsie took the phone from Anon's hand, looked at it a little suspiciously, then started texting.

"'Full house,'" Riley said a few seconds later. "'Aces over jacks,' whatever that means."

"Whoa," the new girl breathed. She let her hand fall. "You read my mind?"

"Nope. I saw through your eyes."

Chizara wondered why Riley was running the meeting, and glanced at Nate, who was scribbling furiously on his notepad.

Which Flicker could read, of course. Was he telling her what to say?

Did he *always* do that?

Nate looked up at her, as if sensing her attention. "Would you like to go next, Chizara?"

"What do you want me to crash, Nate? Your fancy theater? Everyone's new phones?"

"Maybe this." He produced a mushroom-shaped object covered with LEDs. It was off, silent, but Chizara hated it on sight.

"I don't even know what that—"

Nate flipped a switch on the mushroom's side.

Its howling slapped Chizara back in her seat. It shredded the air and sawed against her skull, pushing to get through and boil the brain inside.

She fought back in a spasm of self-preservation. Her mind made a big clumsy swipe at the screaming thing.

All the house's systems sputtered around her, the smart thermostats and motion-sensitive lights under attack. The theater downlights flickered, and the air ducts moaned like a smoker's lungs.

But Chizara scraped together the last fibers of her own will and sent all those plates back into the air, got them spinning again. The lights brightened, the faltering air-con returned to a steady hum.

Only the hateful mushroom thing stayed dead, its internals blasted. Smoke puffed out its top, and its LEDs gave one last hopeful twinkle and died.

"Oh my God." The new girl turned to look at Chizara, her eyes wide.

Ethan was goggling at her too. "Are you okay?"

"Nate, that was *not cool*," said Riley.

Panting, Chizara sat forward. "Nate, do you *want* me to crash your whole house?"

He *winked* at her, the jerk. "I knew you'd keep control. It's a cell phone jammer." Nate sniffed at the last wisps of smoke. "Theaters use them to keep phones from ringing in the middle of a play."

Chizara shivered, the awful air-shredding screech still ringing in her ears. "Guess I'm not going to a play anytime soon."

"So that's your power?" Kelsie asked. "You zap electronic things?"

Looking into those wide green eyes, Chizara felt a trickle of sweat slide down her forehead. Good. Let the girl see how it hurt, how hard it was to control. "Noisy ones, yeah. Networked ones."

"And she's starting to be able to fix them too." Nate's pride radiated out into the room, a warm soothing wrap around Chizara's raw nerves.

She tried to ignore how good it felt. That was just human experimentation, what Nate had done.

"Cool," said Kelsie in an awed voice.

Nate set down the toasted jammer. "So when we pay your dad's ransom, Flicker can see what's going on from every angle. Anon can step in if he needs to, out of nowhere, and Crash shuts it all down if things go wrong. We'll keep those mobsters honest, I promise you."

Kelsie nodded, like she believed for the first time that the

Zeroes were up to this. "So you guys are a team—like *real* superheroes. How did you all meet up?"

"Flicker and I go back a long ways," Nate said. "I can see people's awareness in the air. Hers looks . . . different."

Riley shone her best little-sister smile straight at him, and Chizara wondered whose eyes she was using.

"But Thibault brought the rest of us together." Nate looked a little pained to admit it. "His power makes him a keen observer. He can tell when people don't fit in."

"Sure," Anon said. "Because leading a hundred bicyclists across town is totally subtle. Right, Nate?"

"It worked out exactly as I hoped." Nate focused his smile back on the new girl. "Of course, as Thibault's power also makes him the wrong choice as a leader, I stepped in."

Kelsie's eyes managed to hold on to Anon for a moment, then slid back to Nate. "I guess you guys weren't looking on my side of town."

"I don't like nightclubs," Anon said. "People tend to step on my feet in crowds."

"But at least we finally found you," Nate cut in. "Most of us were there on Ivy Street last night and saw what you did. But I have questions."

"Okay." Kelsie shrugged. "But it's not like I know how I got this way. I mean, it just *happens*."

"We're all just guessing, learning," Nate said, his smile leaking into Chizara's bones. "So let's say we're paying your dad's ransom and a bad guy pulls out his gun. How would *you* stop him?"

Kelsie shook her head. "One guy? I can't do anything. But I can keep a whole group from getting jumpy. If there's a crowd that's bound together somehow, with music or a sense of purpose, then I can give its emotions a nudge. But it can nudge me back, too. Crowds have a sort of personality. I get inside that, and it gets inside me."

Nate gave her a thousand-watt smile, maybe because he was learning so much, or maybe just to remind everyone that no crowd had ever nudged him for a second.

"So you're like the DJ at the party," he said. "Changing the mood. Maybe that should be your code name."

"DJ?" Chizara had to snort. "That's pretty bad, even by our standards."

"A code name?" Kelsie said.

"We use them on missions," Nate said. "To keep our identities hidden."

"On *missions*?"

Chizara liked Kelsie's incredulous tone. *Yes, we call them missions.*

"How about Emoticon?" Riley said.

"Sucks," Ethan said. "Magnify would be better."

"Crowd Control?" Nate said.

"That's your job, Nate," said Anonymous, back next to Riley. "Plus, it's two words. That goes against the rules."

Riley stared at him. "We have rules?"

"Frenzy!" Ethan cried.

Kelsie just looked at them like they were all crazy. "You guys can call me anything you want, as long as you get my dad away from the Russian mob!"

"Mob," Nate said softly. "A crowd that has a personality. That *wants* something. We'll call you Mob."

Kelsie groaned, like she was losing hope fast. Chizara felt sorry for her.

"Kelsie," she said in her best Mom voice. "Maybe instead of relying on a bunch of teenagers, you should call the police."

"But they'll put him in jail."

"He's a bank robber," Chizara reasoned. "Someone died in that robbery. Am I the only one here who remembers that?"

Tears began to well up in Kelsie's eyes, and Chizara felt something fill the room. A sadness that ached down in her muscles, worse than all the fancy tech in Nate's house.

For a moment she thought they all might see sense. Might give up this crazy ransom plan and let adults handle it.

But then Nate stood, spreading his hands out. "If that's what you want, Kelsie, we can always call the police. But first, let me show you *my* power."

And something else filled the room, pushing out the despair—a focus, a seriousness that Chizara had never felt among them all before. And a hopeful feeling, like they could get through anything together. Of course, Nate had five—*six*, with Anonymous—Zeroes to work with. He was really Glorious Leader now.

And Kelsie must have wanted what he was giving her, because as her face brightened, the sense of purpose in the room redoubled. Nate pulled them all in tight, until Chizara was practically leaning forward in her chair, ready to work, to concentrate, to give every scrap of her attention to the Ultimate Goal.

But she knew it was a lie. She had to fight this.

Nate stood happily at the center of it all. "Before you decide, Kelsie, let's just see if we can come up with a plan. Okay?"

"Not me," Chizara said, and it took every ounce of her willpower to stand up and walk to the door.

"Crash," Nate called softly. "Where are you going?"

She ignored him, but turned just outside the door and said, "Be careful, Kelsie. People get hurt when we use our powers. In the middle of a *police station*, people get hurt bad! Imagine how it'll go in a room full of gangsters."

They all looked at her, and for a brief moment she had them. But then Nate drew his hands through the air toward himself, like a puppeteer gathering all his strings. And their heads turned back to face him, eager to hear more good news.

Chizara turned and walked down the hallway, her legs wobbly from the struggle. She might have lost, but at least she could rob Glorious Leader of one last measure of the Curve.

CHAPTER 62
SCAM

THREE DAYS.

Three long days of drug dealers, bank robbers, angry cops, and creepy mobsters. And yet this gym was still scary.

Ethan figured this was the kind of gym where people worked out for the purposes of secret and highly illegal fight clubs. The woman at the front desk looked like she could pummel Ethan with her little toe. Even the voice was intimidated, lurking deep in his larynx like a mouse.

It didn't help that the sweat stink was so bad, like it was pumped into the place. Ethan dipped his nose into the collar of his shirt, which also hid his face from anyone who might recognize him as the bank-video guy.

"Creepy clientele," he muttered through his shirt.

"Your friends call you *Scam*," Kelsie said.

"Yeah, so?"

"So you're not free of creepiness yourself."

Ethan didn't argue. It was the first thing Kelsie had said to him since they'd left the staff meeting. And if she was talking to him again, then maybe one day she'd forgive him for getting her father kidnapped.

Also, Ethan was mostly trying to avoid the death-ray stare of some guy in a gray hoodie. The guy looked amped up on steroids, curling a loaded barbell like it was feathers.

"Is your contact here?" Ethan said.

"Fig's always here," Kelsie replied. "And don't use your voice on him, okay? He's my friend, and your voice just messes things up."

"Roger that."

"*Your* friends seem pretty cool, by the way."

"Yeah, I guess they are. Sorry I didn't mention them sooner."

He was really glad the Zeroes had promised to come through for Kelsie. Glorious Leader, of course, couldn't resist another addition to his superhuman zoo. But it had been pretty cool, seeing Kelsie's eye widen when she saw the home theater, like Ethan was part of a group with a secret lair or something.

It almost made Ethan sentimental for last summer. At least, the summer they'd been having *before* he'd blown it up—before Nate had *made* him blow it up. The summer of running around Cambria, training to be superheroes, thinking they were the most powerful people in the world.

Not that Ethan wanted all that back. He didn't need the Zeroes to be his friends again after this. He just needed them to help Kelsie.

He followed her through the gym. She didn't seem freaked out by the criminal vibe here. The music was playing loud and hard, and she even danced to it a little. Like the meeting with the Zeroes had given her hope.

Wherever she went, the whole place sparked up. Even Gray Hoodie Guy seemed more cheerful. He picked up the pace of his bicep curls like he'd just taken a shot of adrenaline.

Ethan felt kind of ecstatic himself. He always felt better around her, but this was maybe more than usual.

"This is you, right? You're making us all . . ."

"Upbeat?" Kelsie grinned. "You bet it's me. Now I know I'm not the only one in the world with a power—"

"Glad to help with that."

"You left out some stuff." Kelsie's scowl only lasted a second, and she was bopping again. "But it feels good now, like it's a normal thing to have."

"Helps to have people who understand you."

Ethan remembered the first time he met the Zeroes. Or rather, he didn't quite remember, because Anon had been the first one to say hi. But then Anon had introduced him to Bellwether and Flicker. And they'd all found Crash a few months later. And being a team with them, that was maybe the best two years of his life.

"They seem like regular people," Kelsie said. "I was expecting superheroes, I guess."

"Definitely not. But Nate wants to help you. Riley, too. And . . . Thibault."

"Who?" Kelsie frowned.

"The other guy. He'll take a while to sink in." Ethan was pretty proud that he still remembered Anon's name. The memories had faded while he'd been running around with Kelsie, because she was so sparkly and distracting. But seeing Tee at the meeting had recharged his memories of the penthouse.

"Chizara's not into the whole group thing, is she?" Kelsie said.

Ethan shook his head. "She thinks we're kind of careless."

"Gee. Wonder where she got that idea."

He shrugged. "We don't need her for Nate's plan."

They did a circuit of the weight room, Kelsie dancing ahead while Ethan followed. The sweat smell was even sharper in here. Most of the bodybuilders nodded or smiled as Kelsie passed, feeling that rush of energy that swirled around her.

When they reached a room with aerobic equipment lined up like machines of war, Kelsie made a beeline for the treadmills. A short guy in a tight shirt was in full sprint, sweat flying off his face.

"Hey, Fig," Kelsie said.

Fig heaved himself up with both hands to the rails of the treadmill, letting the mat spin beneath him.

"Hey, Kels," he gasped. "Who's your friend?"

"He's gonna help me get my dad out of trouble."

Fig gave Ethan a once-over. He looked unimpressed, but hit the treadmill stop button with his knee and leaped lightly from the machine. "Any friend of Kelsie's."

"Likewise." Ethan shook the guy's incredibly sweaty hand, then wondered if it was okay to wipe his palm on a trouser leg.

"Somewhere private?" Kelsie asked.

Fig grabbed a towel and led them through a doorway and out to a small, empty courtyard. Sunlight glinted on the circumference of glass windows. It felt like the inside of a fishbowl.

Fig mopped his face with the towel. "So is there a plan?"

Kelsie said, "I need to get in touch with the Bagrovs."

"They'll eat you alive."

"I want to pay back my dad's debt. We've got money."

"Thirty grand," Ethan said proudly.

Fig cast a dubious look at Ethan. "What's your interest?"

Ethan had seen that look before. It was paternal, like Fig was saying, *Make sure you have my little girl back by ten.*

Ethan stood a little straighter. He kind of liked that Fig thought he might be boyfriend material. Maybe even *dangerous* boyfriend material.

Kelsie had told him not to use the voice, so there was no point trying to lie.

"It's my fault Jerry's in trouble. I want to fix it."

Fig raised an eyebrow. "So you're that bank-video kid. Thought so."

"Yep," Ethan said.

Fig chewed his lip, as if this didn't make any sense. "Sounds like both you kids got good reason to stay clear of the Bagrovs. Do you know *anything* about these guys?"

"I know I can't give up on my dad," Kelsie said softly. "We take care of each other. We always have."

Fig sighed, like he was having a hard time working out how to explain something really complicated. Ethan hated that look. His mother used it on him all the time.

He'd left his mother another message that morning, saying that he was okay and would be home soon. Ethan knew he had to face the music, once Kelsie's dad was safe.

"If you've got money," Fig was saying, "the best thing you can do is take it and get out of Cambria. At least until summer's over. Maybe by then the Bagrovs will find a new town to pick on."

Ethan figured that wasn't a bad idea. He wished he'd done that when he'd stolen the Craig's car. He could've kept driving until he hit LA. Or Mexico.

But then he wouldn't have met Kelsie.

"These Bagrov guys," Fig said. "They'll take your money and still do what they want with Jerry. I mean, if they haven't already . . ."

He let the sentence trail away.

Kelsie took a step forward. "What?"

"Come on, Kelsie. You know." Fig pulled his towel off one

shoulder and flicked it onto the other one. "Your dad was in deep."

"Don't talk like that, Fig," she pleaded. "We've got money. That's all they want, right?"

"You have to understand." Fig dropped his volume from a booming baritone to something a little softer. "Jerry's not coming back from this one. And I'm not going to let you wind up in the same place."

Kelsie glanced over at Ethan in mute appeal. Without Fig's help, the money was useless. Ethan didn't have the first idea about how to get in touch with gangsters, and he was glad to see that Kelsie didn't either.

She gave him one small nod and Ethan let it happen. He focused on how much he wanted to put things right with Kelsie. He hadn't wanted anything this much in a long time. It practically *hurt* to want something this much.

Get it right, voice. Get Fig on our side.

"Jerry told you a week ago, Fig, that if anything happened to him, he wanted you to take care of his little girl."

Fig shook his head. "You knew Jerry?"

"I wasn't in that bank for my suntan," Ethan heard himself say. "I was there because *Jerry wanted me to be.*"

Fig was just staring at him now.

"Yeah, we set the whole thing up. It was supposed to go down different, with the Bagrov guy getting shot instead of Hank. More money for Jerry, so he could leave town. And a video to prove that Nic was a fink. That's right, Sonia Sonic was in on it too."

Ethan's mind reeled as he listened. Man, the voice was *outdoing* itself this time.

"I told Jerry it might not work. And he said, 'You fix it if it doesn't. Buy me out. Fig'll help you. Just tell him everything.'" The voice took a break for a second, barely long enough for Ethan to swallow. "So I'm telling you everything, Fig. You going to come through or not?"

Fig gave him an astonished look. "*Jerry* thought all that up?"

"Yep."

Fig blinked once, slow as a lizard, then nodded. "You wait right here."

Ethan watched him stride through the gym and straight to the guy in the gray hoodie, of all people. After a brief conversation, the guy pulled out his phone.

"Okay," Kelsie said. "That was impressive. But I can't help but remember how things worked out last time you used the voice."

Ethan had been thinking the same thing. What had Fig said the Bagrovs would do to him and Kelsie? Eat them alive?

Fig returned to the courtyard. "They want double what Jerry owed. Twenty-five grand."

"We've got it," Kelsie said.

"Head out to Hurricane Hauling and Demolition. Their office is out on Memorial Drive. Some guy called Misha will be there."

Ethan sighed. "Great. That guy."

"When?" Kelsie asked.

"In three days," Fig replied. "Fourth of July at seven p.m. Unmarked cash."

"Thanks, Fig," Kelsie said. She gave him a light punch on his overdeveloped upper arm. Her mood was infectious, spilling across the gym and making Ethan smile.

"Don't thank me, Kelsie." Somehow Fig wasn't included in Kelsie's ramped-up optimism. "Just promise me, anything goes wrong, you get the hell out of there. Let Jerry fix it himself."

"It'll be okay, Fig," she said. "I've got new friends. Friends who can help."

Fig turned his narrow glare upon Ethan.

"We'll look after her," Ethan confirmed.

Fig looked like he didn't believe it.

Ethan couldn't blame the guy.

CHAPTER 63

FLICKER

SOMETIMES, WHEN THEY WERE ALONE LIKE THIS, IT felt like the attic was breathing.

Maybe it was how close they were—legs entwined on the old couch, her hand resting on his knee, the rustle of his clothing in her ears. Or maybe it was the summer heat, which carried every tremor of motion through the still, almost-liquid attic air.

When Flicker had come to the attic, she'd curled up with him straightaway, as if her body knew that this was how they'd wound up last time. Whenever that was.

It was tricky, keeping track of everything. She repeated her jokes a lot, and he kidded her about it. Which seemed unfair.

But other memories were easy, always at her fingertips. She knew that Anon had arrived Saturday night, and that the family didn't realize he was staying up here, not even Lily. Flicker also knew that he had a name besides Anon, but it was annoyingly tricky to remember. She also recognized his scent, his touch, and the sound of his breathing, as if her senses had their own private stash of memory, immune to his power.

Or maybe, after all those stories, the attic was magic.

"Do you ever go see your family?" she asked that afternoon. "That's a new question, right?"

"Yeah, it is. And I go there once a year, to my youngest brother's birthday party."

Flicker asked carefully, "Do your parents recognize you?"

"Sort of. When my mom looks straight at me, she gets this smile, like I'm her kid off at college and she forgot I was coming. But she's glad to see me. Until she looks away." A pause, and then his voice was softer. "It's harder since my grandma moved in; the house is too crowded. But they've still got my picture up everywhere."

Flicker pulled him closer. "They must miss you, then."

"I guess." He shifted beside her, maybe a shrug. "But they must wonder where I am, when they look at those pictures. And I guess their friends ask. They probably have some story they tell. Something that sticks in their head, even if I don't. My mom takes a lot of pictures. I photo bomb them, so there's always new pictures of me around."

"Maybe that's why she takes so many," Flicker said. "But don't they talk to you?"

"My parents don't—well, hardly. And my middle brother doesn't remember me at all. But Emile, the littlest, knows who I am." Anon laughed. "He should. I get him the same damn present every year."

"Seriously? What?"

"A rock."

Flicker laughed. "Gee. I never get rocks for my birthday."

"Me neither. Last year I got him a red almandine garnet."

"Wait, you're serious. Like a gem?"

"It's a crystal, made of iron and aluminum. He had all the other species of garnets, so now he's got a full set."

Anon sounded proud of his work, and Flicker smiled.

"I didn't even know rocks had species," she said.

"Emile says they're alive. Just very slow."

The ache in his voice sent a flash of anger through Flicker. "Your mom and dad, they shouldn't have left you in that hospital. They should have *remembered.*"

The moment she said the words, she regretted them. Anon's breathing hitched, a tremor moving through his body next to hers.

"Sorry," she said. "Shouldn't bring that up. I'm an idiot."

"No." He took her hand—that perfect fit. "It's just . . . I told you about the hospital the first night I was here, three days ago. And you still remember."

Flicker shrugged. "Who could forget a little kid getting left alone in a hospital?"

"Well, you all forgot it the first time you heard it. When Scam's voice said it last summer."

"Oh." She shuddered. It was hard recalling that day, after what Scam had said to her and Nate. *You want to bang your little sister, don't you?* Flicker had already known Nate was in love with her, but hearing it out loud—*that* way, in front of all of them—had changed their friendship forever.

Nate's power was tangled up with his ego in messy ways. And Flicker knew she was a walking reminder for him that charm had its limits.

Anon felt the shudder and squeezed her tighter. "It's okay. I'm glad you forgot what Scam said to me. But I'm also glad you remember when *I* told you."

"I do. Perfectly." She even remembered Anon's voice as he'd told her the story. Hoarse and dry, like he was still in that hospital bed, sick and thirsty and alone. "When I told Lily about it, she added a whole chapter to the story of Nothing."

"Great," he said, like maybe it wasn't.

"Sorry to spill your secrets, Anon. But Lily's stories are how I remember you, just like your mom and her photos. Lily can't forget you, because you're just a fairy tale to her. She's my extra brain, sort of."

"So you keep telling me," he said, then laughed. "Secret twin powers, activate!"

"Okay, I can see how it's weird."

She felt him shrug, and he said, "I'm just worried you'll

get disappointed by the reality. Instead of a prince, I'm a guy whose parents forgot him. Instead of a castle, I have a stolen hotel room. *Had* one, anyway. Now I'm basically homeless." He deflated with a sigh. "Haven't slain any dragons lately either."

She laughed. "It's not like you slayed—slew?—any dragons in Lily's stories either. That's not really her kind of thing."

"No?" He sounded disappointed. "So I slew giants? Vampires, maybe? What *is* her thing, exactly?"

Flicker felt a squirm starting inside of her but didn't let it come to the surface. With Anon lying this close to her, he would feel it if she cringed.

"Lily thinks you're my fictional boyfriend."

"Your what?"

"Haven't you ever you read a book"—her voice dropped a little—"or you're watching a movie or whatever, and there's a hot girl in it, so you pretend she's your girlfriend? You know?"

"Sure," he said. But from the sound of it, he didn't know.

She tried again. "They weren't really stories per se, with bad guys and quests and plots and stuff. I mean, they'd start off that way. But they always wound up drifting into, um . . ."

"Boyfriend stuff?" His body trembled—he was either having a stroke or he was at the edge of laughing.

"Yeah. I know it sounds silly," Flicker said. "Especially compared to you and Ethan being really mature and killing tree sprites in *Red Specter* or whatever."

Whoa. That memory had come out of nowhere, just in time.

"It's *Red Scepter*, not *Specter*," Anon said. "And I killed no tree sprites. I *was* a tree sprite. Totally different."

"Yes, I can see the distinction. Being a fictional tree sprite is way less silly than having a fictional boyfriend."

"One key difference is, *there are no real tree sprites.* Fictional is the only kind of sprite there is. But there *are* real boys." His hand slid from her shoulder down to her waist, tracing every inch between.

It sent a shiver through her, and she turned to face him.

"Yeah, okay. That *is* different." Flicker was pretty sure they'd never had this particular conversation before. "Tell me more."

"There's not a lot to tell," he said. "Except that real is better."

"This sounds doubtful. I've had some awesome fictional boyfriends."

He drew her closer, spoke softer: "Yeah, but real is real."

Their lips met, and the shiver came again. It traveled deep inside her, reaching all the places where she was pressed against Anon. Her legs, her lips and tongue, her skin. Even her breath trembled in her mouth.

When they pulled apart, it took a moment to speak again.

"Whoa," she finally said. "Was that the first time? Our first kiss, I mean?"

"The first one like *that*," he said, sounding breathless and a little amazed.

She smiled. Close enough.

CHAPTER 64

BELLWETHER

THE ANONYMOUS FILE WAS MISSING. GONE.

Nate stared at the space where it should have been, the compartment in the home theater riser where all the wires and cable were stuffed out of sight. He couldn't remember putting it back here after the last meeting, or even taking it out in the first place.

There'd been a lot going on, with Mob joining the group and a mission to plan. And anything that had to do with Anonymous could slip your mind.

Nate looked underneath the seats. Nada.

What if he'd left it somewhere around the house? For his parents to find, or the housekeeper?

He pulled Chizara's folder from the compartment and headed for the kitchen, where his sisters were decorating a cake for their Wednesday youth group. Gabby had drawn a Sacred Heart in icing, which looked more like a strawberry wearing a crown of thorns.

"I need you three to look for something."

Gabby didn't look up. "We're making a cake, *hermano*."

"I can see that. But it's twenty bucks for whoever finds what I'm missing."

That got their attention, and he held up his file on Crash.

"Like this, but much thicker."

They looked down at the half-decorated cake, then back at him. He gave himself to greed—thoughts of candy, of dolls, of everything twenty dollars could buy—and that little nudge broke the stalemate. They were off in a flurry of shouts.

In the afterglow of using his power, Nate wondered if Kelsie could have managed a trick like that. Did she command the crowd, or did it command her? Or was she like a rider on a horse, guiding a more powerful creature with the cut of spurs?

It occurred to him that it was time to start another file.

On the way to his room he was distracted again—the doorbell. Nate checked through the living room windows and swore.

DDA Cooper was outside. Detectives King and Fuentes weren't with her, so she was here as Ethan's mother, not as a district attorney.

Letting her in was a bad idea. But she would only come back again later, and maybe next time his parents would be home.

Nate opened the door.

* * *

They settled in the living room, just the two of them. The girls were still searching the house, so gathering any sort of crowd was impossible.

One on one would have to do.

"How can I help you, DDA Cooper?"

"You know why I'm here," she said. "My detectives might not have enough to bring you in for questioning, but you know more than you're saying."

Nate hesitated. At the door she'd looked tired and distraught. But now she sat straight in her chair, as if administering a punishment.

"I don't know where your son is, ma'am."

She was silent a moment, measuring that statement.

"But you know *something*."

Nate looked up and found certainty in her eyes. She wasn't going away without some kind of information. But admitting he'd lied to investigators wasn't a possibility. That was a felony, and she was a prosecutor.

This called for a new direction altogether.

"After you left, I started looking for him," he said.

She pulled out a notepad. "Where exactly? Give me places."

"Well, not actually *looking* for him." Nate was paralyzed a moment, but then it came to him. "I found that bank video. I figured he must be loving that, you know?"

She just stared at him.

"The way he talked back to those bank robbers?" Nate continued, letting the words come to him. "Everyone in the world seeing how clever he was. How he always knows exactly what to say."

Her cool expression faltered a little. The video must have been baffling, her son knowing the name of a bank robber's daughter—but also weirdly familiar. Surely she'd heard Scam spout inexplicable knowledge before.

"You still haven't told me where you looked for him," she said.

"Online. There were thousands of comments on that video." Nate never read comments, which were pointless, leaderless babble, but he was certain there was no shortage of them under Sonia's video. "All those people saying, 'What cojones on that little—' Oh, sorry."

DDA Cooper gave a shake of her head. "What does this have to do with finding Ethan?"

"I figured he'd want to read all that. He always loved people seeing him mouth off. So I left a comment myself. Nothing big. Just, 'Hey, it's your old buddy Nate. Where the hell are you?'"

"And he responded?"

Nate nodded. "About an hour later."

"This was on Sonia Sonic's blog?" she asked, pulling out a notepad.

"No." That would be too easy to check. "One of the sites that linked to it."

DDA Cooper was uncertain whether to believe him, but she wanted to. "He left a message on my phone, saying he'd be home soon. Did he mention that, or say where he was?"

Nate sighed. "No. He said the whole bank thing was a joke of some kind. And how he was scared, because of those criminals escaping. He figured the bank robbers were looking for him. He didn't think it was smart to come home yet."

Nate realized he was practically telling the truth.

"What site was this? Maybe we can trace him."

"I really don't remember. And his comments disappeared the next day. He must have gotten scared and deleted them." He shrugged. "So I deleted mine, too. I didn't want to get him in trouble."

DDA Cooper was staring now, as if the proof of Nate's story had disappeared a bit too conveniently. Which was fine, as long as she had a glimmer of hope that it *might* be true.

As long as she spent the next few days scouring blogs, instead of showing up at Nate's house again.

"If you're lying about this—" she began.

"I think he wants to come home," he interrupted, letting the truth fill his words. The truth that Ethan would be home eventually, and that he, Nate, felt sorry for her.

"When?"

"Soon," Nate said. Then he made a decision—more truth. "This weekend, in fact. He said there was something he had to do first, to put all this video nonsense to rest."

"Put it to rest?" She shook her head. "What kind of joke was it, anyway? I mean, the way he was talking in that bank. Like he *knew* those men. He used their names. My detectives think he must have been in on it!"

Nate shook his head. "I've watched that video a hundred times, trying to figure it out. He must have heard the robbers talking to each other. And then he decided to be a smart aleck."

Something in those words clicked. An exhausted smile came over her face. "That sounds like Ethan. He's always pulling things out of thin air."

Nate stared at her, wondering what it was like to raise Scam. Did his parents think he was a genius? A psychopath? Possessed?

It couldn't have been much fun. Ethan always refused to talk about his power's first appearance.

"He would say weird stuff to us, too," Nate said. "Like he *knew* things about us that he couldn't have."

DDA Cooper's gaze was fixed on some distant point. She looked more exhausted every minute. "When he was little, we thought he was a genius. He spoke in complete sentences at two."

Nate nodded attentively. Two years old? Flicker had been almost eight when she'd started seeing through her sister's eyes, and Thibault had managed to live with his family until three years ago.

Nate wondered if DDA Cooper would mind him taking notes. Probably.

"But then it changed?" he asked, giving her the full wattage of his attention, wishing there were a crowd here to focus it.

"Right when he turned four, he started to have episodes. One moment he was his usual self—smart, articulate. But then he'd try to repeat the same words, and he would babble them, like a toddler again."

"Did he seem . . . different? I mean, when he was stumbling for words. Like he was a different person?"

She looked up at him, the spell broken by the oddness of the question. Or perhaps because the answer was *yes*.

"Sorry, someone's calling," Nate said, before she could ask what exactly he meant. He pulled out his phone, set it to record audio, and laid it facedown beside him. "No one important."

She leaned forward. "I need to find my son. He's been missing for days. If there's *anything* you can do . . ."

"I'll try to find that blog again, and leave more comments. This time I'll let you know the moment I hear from him. I promise."

She stared at him, mistrust warring with hope. But she pulled out a business card and handed it to him. "Call me right away."

Nate accepted the card, then gave her his most solemn expression. "Is it okay if I mention you? To remind him that he has a home to go to."

She sighed. "Things haven't always been perfect at home. His father left us when he was little."

Nate wondered if Scam's voice was responsible for that, spouting the wrong truth in the middle of some tantrum. A childhood version of last summer.

He knew he should send Ethan's mother on her way now. It would be too easy to slip up, to give himself away. To make her want too much from him.

But this was a golden opportunity to find out more about Ethan's upbringing, and how his power had manifested.

"Maybe if I mentioned his sister," Nate said. "Seems like he misses her a lot. Is she deployed right now?"

DDA Cooper nodded, still unsure about opening up. But Nate was a connection to her son, a lifeline for her hope, and she had nowhere else to turn.

"He worships Jessie," she said softly. "Since they were little, she's the only one that could ever make him tell the truth."

Nate glanced at his phone, hoping the battery would hold. Then he leaned forward and listened, a list of questions already forming in his mind.

CHAPTER 65

CRASH

"ARE YOU SURE ABOUT THIS?" IKEM ASKED.

Chizara and her little brother stared up at the main entrance to Cambria County General Hospital. Chizara's head was already aching from all the tech.

She hadn't been inside a hospital since she was born. All those years of being careful when she ran, of making sure not to so much as twist an ankle. She'd been lucky—*everyone* had been lucky—that she'd never broken a bone or come down with any serious illness. So much could go wrong inside this broad white building . . .

A massacre waiting to happen.

Ikem might not know how much this hurt, but he knew enough to look frightened. "Why do you have to do this, anyway?"

"I have to prove that I can train myself. That I don't need Nate and his crew to get stronger."

"But what if you can't control it, Zara? You could crash the whole place."

"I'll warn you before I get anywhere near that."

Ikem reached out and took her hand. "Let's get it over with, then."

Hand in hand they went slowly up to the glass automatic doors. As they passed through, the weight of the electronics bore down, until Chizara could barely see the vast white space, the staff striding about, that man in the wheelchair.

She bit her lip. This was what she'd come for, wasn't it? To test herself against a mass of tech like this.

"You okay?" Ikem asked. "You're, like, crushing my hand."

"I know," she said. "And I'm not going to let go. Couldn't do this without you."

"So, you're ready to go up those stairs?"

Chizara swallowed a rush of panic, then nodded.

Halfway up the first flight, the pressure closed down behind her and cut off her escape. She heard herself whimper, and sweat broke out all over her skin.

"Keep going," Ikem said. "He's only one floor up."

Chizara put out a shaky hand to the rail. "Uh-huh. I remember."

He helped her creep up to the landing, make the turn. A patient and an orderly on the way down stopped and stared.

"It's her therapy," Chizara heard Ikem say. "She's scared of people."

"You're doing great," the orderly said, peering over her spectacles.

Chizara managed a smile that practically creaked. It was like all the plates from all the restaurants in the whole world were stacked up, *really* badly, on top of her. And if she wobbled even the littlest bit . . .

When they were alone again, Ikem said, "You look terrible, Zara. Let's get out of here."

"No—I'm holding it all. There's just so much!" She probed the labyrinth around her, the sensors, the diagnostic machinery, the forests of surgical aids in the operating rooms downstairs, the miniature pumps shunting fluids into and out of people's bodies. "So many machines, all talking to each other . . ."

"You sound like a stoner!" Ikem hissed.

She straightened up, and he grabbed her hand again. He was a good brother, she thought sloppily, sentimentally, before her mind rushed back to coping with the onslaught of intricate pain, elaborate light, filigreed power. She was *so close* to buckling and letting the whole massive weight come crashing down around her.

But it wasn't going to happen. Yes, she was in the middle of a major hospital. Yes, she was about to break every bone in her brother's hand. Yes, she could hardly see straight. But she was still walking, could still read the signs: PEDIATRICS, PULMONARY, ENDOSCOPY—

"There it is," she muttered.

INTENSIVE CARE UNIT.

"So many flowers," Ikem whispered.

"Like a funeral," Chizara said.

A policeman stood outside the double doors, beside the mountain of flowers piled across two tables. Beyond him a hundred machines beat and blinked in the ICU. The pain felt like it would melt Chizara's bones.

Her voice came out soft but steady. "Are these all for Officer Bright?"

The officer took in her trembling hands, her sweaty skin, and nodded.

"Did they run out of room inside?" said Ikem in an awed voice.

"Can't put flowers in the ICU," the man said. "Germs breed in the water."

Chizara nodded, then led Ikem to the glass doors. Peering through, all she could see was a nurse passing, blinking equipment, a man with a tube running into the back of his hand.

Chizara reached her mind out to all the glowing machines clustered around each ICU bed—the monitors and drips, the pumps and ventilators and dialysis machines. All the equipment was running perfectly, but none of it could heal cells, could mend organs. The most she could do was not interfere, just sweat and tremble and not let a single chip blink out, a single power-carrying filament fail.

But she was tiring. She could feel it. She didn't have much longer.

In a little room off to one side, a woman sat dazed, tearless. A policewoman was holding her hand and talking to her.

Through everything else Chizara felt those needles of guilt. She took a deep breath, trying not to get distracted.

But then she saw them.

On a couch opposite their mother sat three children in a row.

A realization slipped into Chizara, the finest, sharpest blade skipping across the tendons of her will. Officer Bright's kids weren't out exploring the hospital corridors, entertaining themselves, getting up to mischief. They were sitting there staring at nothing, hoping their father would come back to them.

Through the blur of welling tears, the lights in the ICU flickered. Her bleak thoughts shook all those delicate systems, and two small, sharp alarms went off on the other side of the doors. Here in the corridor, the air-conditioning coughed and struggled.

"Zara!" hissed Ikem at her ear.

Chizara blinked hard. Her brain began to scramble. A tsunami built on the horizon.

A nurse ran past. Someone shouted. Officer Bright's wife woke from her daze, and the kids looked around frightened.

"No," Chizara whispered. Not this.

Stepping away from the door, she reached deep, deeper than she ever had before, groping for resources she wasn't sure she had.

She all but flattened herself, forcing her mind under the great teetering weight of the tech. She spread herself out in a million directions and lifted, everything straining nearly to snapping, from her core out to her fingertips. She pushed back the swelling wave of disaster, pushed herself up into the pain until she nearly howled with it.

But she didn't howl. *Just hold it up, Chizara. Hold it* all *up, for as long as it damn well takes.*

One of the alarms shut off . . . then, at last, the other. The air-conditioning recovered its rhythm and purred on.

Chizara took Ikem's elbow, spoke low: "Get me out of here."

"Should we run?"

"Slow and steady, so I don't lose my grip."

As they walked back into fresh air, the load lifted off Chizara, transforming from ravening demons to a massed choir behind her.

She let go of Ikem's hand and put her face up to the breeze.

"I am never, ever doing anything like that again." Ikem backed away ahead of her. "I thought you were going to die! Or break that whole building!"

She glanced over her shoulder at the hospital. It still pulsed with a thousand machines. But it didn't hurt anymore, at least not from out here.

"You think *you* were scared?" she asked, but Ikem had

already turned and bounded down the footpath toward the street.

She turned and followed him down the street toward the strip mall—she'd promised him ice cream after this.

The hospital visit had been painful, and dangerous. But now she knew.

The big crash at the CCPD had made her stronger. Maybe her fixing power had faded in the end, but her willpower had grown. A week ago she couldn't have set foot inside that hospital.

Sure, Nate's training had worked, had strengthened her bit by bit. But Chizara could train herself, create her own missions with her own Ultimate Goal, which was to do no harm. She didn't need the other Zeroes around, complicating things, distracting her. Using her for their own selfish ends, making her destroy property and put people's lives in danger.

And she didn't need to be part of some plan to pay ransom for a bank robber. If someone was kidnapped, you called the police, not a bunch of teenagers with powers they didn't understand.

Too bad Kelsie didn't see that. But that was her choice.

"Come on, Zara!" Ikem danced back to her. "Aren't you starving?"

She was, Chizara realized as she pushed open the door into the ice cream joint. She was hungry and exhausted from fighting against her power.

She couldn't stop Nate from playing with other peoples' lives, but she could walk away. She could nurture her power her own way.

And if he came around to charm her again—well, that was fine too. She would test her will against Glorious Leader's any day.

CHAPTER 66
ANONYMOUS

"SO THE FICTIONAL BOYFRIEND IS REAL," LILY SAID.

Thibault smiled, resisting the urge to snip her gaze and disappear into the shadows of the attic. He had promised Flicker to make this meeting work. Her theory was that the two of them would never be really connected until he got to know Lily, too. Because of magic twin stuff.

Besides, at seven o'clock tonight the Zeroes were paying Jerry's ransom to the Russian mobsters. If it went like most of Glorious Leader's plans, there would be a lot of stress and chaos, the sorts of distractions that made people forget Thibault existed. So this afternoon was probably a good time to cement his connection to Flicker.

Thibault stuck out a hand. But instead of shaking it, she

brushed past him and sat down on the attic couch beside her sister. Okay, Lily was feeling territorial.

Well, what did he expect? This stuffy little attic was the twins' sacred place. It was full of their old toys and clothes, and the walls were covered with the tactile maps from which Flicker had learned the shapes of the continents when she was little. His being here was like Scam invading the Magnifique.

"I thought you'd be taller," Lily said. "And I was expecting a nicer shirt, like in Nate's photos."

"I told you," Flicker said. "He lost everything."

"Oh, right," Lily said. The beam of her attention trembled, like a barbell over a weight lifter's head. She was trying really hard not to lose him. "Guess there's no time to pack when you get busted hiding in a hotel room."

Keeping eye contact, Thibault sat down on the musty leather chair with its squashed-flat cushion. "It's not like I can get a job and pay rent."

"Couldn't you be a spy or something?" Lily asked.

He smiled. "My spy boss would forget me. And do you really want the government using my power?"

"Dude. You're already in my *house*. Would working for the government make it any creepier?" Lily gave the wry mouth twist that passed for a smile with her. "But you get spied on yourself, don't you? All those photos. All those theories of Nate's. He's kind of obsessed with you."

Thibault pulled a *maybe* face. The way he felt about that

file was pretty much the way Lily felt about him.

"Don't worry. You're in good company." Lily put an arm around her sister. "He used to be obsessed with Riley, too."

"Don't be weird, Lily." Flicker pushed her sister's arm away. "Nate studies all of us Zeroes. That's just his Glorious Leader thing."

"Yeah, but he *loved* you." Lily turned to smile at Flicker, but her awareness of Thibault didn't fade. It was growing steadier, if anything. And it still contained a touch of acid.

Thibault could tell that he fascinated Lily, but she didn't trust him, or much like him.

Suddenly Thibault wished they'd done this in a bigger, airier room with more distractions. He wasn't used to someone focusing on him for this long. It was wearing him out.

Maybe if he lightened the mood. "I should thank you, Lily. For helping Riley remember me."

"Yeah, you owe me. I painted such a pretty picture." She smiled. "At least that's one thing you live up to."

Thibault met her gaze, trying not to blush. Lily wasn't bad-looking herself. It helped that she had Flicker's eyes, Flicker's wide, clear forehead and strong cheekbones. Though her face was sharper, and where Flicker's senses were smoky and soft, Lily's awareness was like daggers.

But their connection to each other was unwavering. Maybe twin bonds were something special. Like those long-married couples sitting side by side in the Magnifique lobby, never speaking, never looking at each other, but aware of each other right down to their bones.

"Give me time and maybe I can live up to your fairy tales," he said.

Lily gave a quiet guffaw. "You sound like you're asking for her hand in *marriage*. But it's okay, Anon." She patted Flicker's knee. "You have my blessing, you two."

"Oh, get *over* yourself, Lil-Pill," Flicker said. "You know where you can shove your blessing."

She rolled her eyes for Thibault. *This* was the version of the twin face he felt comfortable with: the rounder, more open one. A solid band of attention angled at him via Lily's eyes. Flicker was seeing him directly for a change, not in glimpses through a stranger's vision.

But it was better when he and Flicker were alone, when he was a voice, touches, smells, and tastes. He felt himself starting to blush at the memory of Flicker's fingertips, light and sensitive on his face, traveling down his body, her voice whispering in the stuffy darkness.

"OMG, look at you two." Lily laughed. "Is this true lurve I see before me?"

Thibault grinned. Maybe Flicker had been right, and meeting Lily really would make their connection stronger.

"Forgot to warn you." Flicker was grinning too. "Lily said we weren't allowed to be, and I quote, 'all over each other' in front of her."

"You guys have to break me in gently," said Lily. "I'm a fragile flower, you know." And she did the mouth-twist thing again, but it didn't seem as funny.

How many levels of sarcasm was Thibault dealing with here? Was this a conversational game, thick with in-jokes? Or a quietly brutal fight where the combatants knew all the buttons to push?

He dared some sarcasm himself: "A fragile flower. So I've noticed."

"I'm sure you notice a lot of things." Lily's voice lost its jokiness. "You found all those crazy friends of Riley's first, didn't you? And you still spy on them?"

"*Annnd* she goes for the guts," Flicker said wearily.

"Must be handy," Lily powered on, "finding out on the sly what'll impress a girl. Were you ever in this house before? Like, when Riley *didn't* know you were here?"

"No," he said with a clear conscience. "But yeah, I've spied on the others. To stop them doing too much damage."

"So you only use your power for good? Plus the occasional nice shirt or fancy hotel room?"

"Sorry, Anon," said Flicker. "She promised to be polite. But Lily's always been jealous of the Zeroes."

"Jealous?" Lily asked. "I'm just worried about you, Riley. Your power is a blessing. But as far as I can tell, the rest of these guys are pretty much *cursed*."

Thibault actually flinched—at the word, at the vicious

stab of attention that went with it. For an awful second it was like Lily knew him, *really* knew him, the way Scam's voice did.

Flicker turned to face her sister. "That's a shitty thing to say, Lily."

"It's true!" Lily's eyes were off him now, her focus flowing toward Flicker.

And in that moment of relief, of no longer being the focus of all this drama, Thibault instinctively reached out and snipped the rest of her connection, just to give himself a rest. Just for a moment.

He stood and walked softly to the other end of the attic. He realized he was sweating all over.

Lily was still talking. "He can't *live* here, Riley."

"He doesn't want to!" Flicker protested. "There's just this one thing we've got to do with the Zeroes this evening—"

"And what if there's *another* thing after that, and then another? And he just erases your memories of it? What if he's moved in before and you can't *remember*?"

"Lily!" Flicker's voice was soft and horrified. "That's not even how it works."

Thibault turned and cleared his throat. But he'd severed the connection too well.

"You don't even know him," Lily said. "And his family's so screwed up they abandoned him in a hospital! Shit like that turns people into psychopaths. *Serial killers!*"

"Lily, stop!"

I can hear you, Thibault tried to say, but his voice caught in his throat.

Lily turned at the strangled sound, and her eyes widened. "Oh. Shit. You're still here."

Silence thickened the air. Thibault reminded himself to breathe. When Flicker had remembered the hospital story, it had meant everything. But from Lily's mouth it was an ice pick in his stomach.

Her words had skated so close to what Scam had said last summer.

"I can't *believe* you, Lily," Flicker said.

"How was I supposed to know he was there?" Lily turned to Thibault again. "Honest, it's like you disappeared."

Her awareness left him again, folding in on itself in embarrassment and humiliation as she stood up from the couch.

"This is too weird, Riley," she muttered as she crossed the attic. "How am I supposed to know when he's watching us?"

"Lily," Flicker called. But her sister lifted the handle in the floor and hurried out of sight. The hatch slammed closed with a bang.

Flicker's eyes glistened. "I'm so sorry."

"It was my fault," Thibault said. "I cut the connection."

"But you promised."

"I just needed a break from . . . from all that focus. It was like . . ." Like Scam's voice, knowing Thibault well enough to hurt him. "I'm not used to that kind of drama. People aren't supposed to notice me."

He tried to compose himself. Without Lily's eyes to use, Flicker couldn't see him anymore, but he felt utterly revealed before her.

She stood up, the strands of her listening drawn to his ragged breath. She crossed to him and put her hands on his shoulders. "She'll forget what she said, right? We can try again."

"I guess." He looked down into her worried, unseeing eyes.

"So can *you* forget what she said, Anon?"

Thibault wasn't sure. But that didn't matter. "She's a part of you, Flicker. I'm not going to give up."

"And it's not like she really thinks you're a serial killer," Flicker said. "This is just weird, that's all. Finding out a stranger's in your house."

"I know. And it wasn't fair, disappearing like that. My bad."

"It wasn't anyone's fault." Flicker leaned warm against his chest, her fingers in his hair. "But next time, do us all a favor and stay."

CHAPTER 67
BELLWETHER

NATE KEPT HIS EYES ON HIS PARENTS' OLD CADILLAC a hundred yards in front of him. Mob and Scam were in it, headed to meet the Bagrovs. The exchange was fifteen minutes from now, at an industrial park at the edge of Cambria.

"Anybody following them?"

"All clear, Bellwether." Flicker sat next to him in the front, scanning the cars ahead for anyone showing too much interest in the Cadillac.

If the Bagrovs had someone watching Mob and Scam, then that someone might be trailing the two of them right now. So Nate was staying a hundred yards back, careful not to be spotted bringing in backup.

Which was just him and Flicker, because Crash had

remained obstinate about not coming along. Oh, and also . . .

Nate glanced up, and there, sitting in the middle of his rearview mirror, was Anonymous.

"Oh, hey," he said.

"Hello again," Anon said.

Nate sighed. "Could you guys, like, *talk* or something?" The two had been holding hands at the meeting at Nate's on Sunday, but now there was a heavy silence between them. "I need to focus on driving, not on remembering you exist."

"Okay, here's some small talk," Anon said. "After we get Mob's father out of danger, I'm finding a new place."

"Right," Nate said. So that was the reason for the silence—hiding in Flick's attic wasn't working out. He didn't feel any hostility in the car, but Nate knew better than anyone that loving someone left you vulnerable. A lot of things could go wrong with an anonymous boyfriend.

"You don't need to know where I live, Bellwether. If for some reason e-mail and phones aren't working, you can always ask Flicker."

"What he means is, don't try to find him." Flicker smiled at Nate, at if she were a reluctant bearer of this message.

Nate raised his hands from the wheel in surrender. He was just glad that Anon was connected to someone in the group. He'd always been worried by how isolated the guy was.

"Ten minutes," he said, eyes on the car's GPS. "It's all under control."

"Okay. This is weird," Flicker said. "The driver behind us just checked out your license plate."

Nate took a slow breath, easing off on the pedal a little. The Cadillac with Scam and Mob in it drifted a little farther ahead.

"Maybe he's looking for a letter," Anon said. "Like that game people play on road trips."

Flicker shook her head. "The passenger's watching us too."

Nate swore. "If it's the Russians, we're screwed. It's only supposed to be Scam and Mob at the meet-up!"

"They're not looking at the Cadillac." Flicker's finger drummed the armrest between them. "Just us."

Nate stared at his rearview mirror. The car was too far back to tell anything. "What do they look like, Flick?"

"I don't have eyeballs on them," she said.

"I got it" came a voice from the backseat.

Nate told himself to *focus*. Anonymous was here, of course, and he could turn around and stare straight at them without being noticed.

A moment later he said, "The passenger's a big guy, wearing a hat. The woman driving is almost as dark as Chizara. Not exactly Russians."

"Worse," Nate said. "Cops."

Anonymous leaned forward between the front seats, making his presence felt. "So you know them?"

"Detectives King and Fuentes," Nate sighed. He'd connected too well with Ethan's mother, so she'd put out an APB on his car in case he went to meet Scam. Some cop along the way had spotted him and alerted the detectives.

"They still haven't noticed Scam," Flicker said.

"That's because they're following *me*," Nate said, slowing a little more to let the Cadillac get still farther ahead. "Short version: I was stupid, and let my research get in the way of the Goal."

"We can't lead them to the industrial park," Anon said. "If the Bagrovs smell cops, everything goes to shit."

"And if those detectives see Scam, they'll pull him over," Nate said. "And he's in a car with the bank robber's daughter and thirty grand. Even the voice won't be able to explain that."

"Can you lose them?" Flicker asked.

"Eventually." Nate gripped the steering wheel. He could gather a posse of truckers around him, the way he used to do with bicycles, then slip away down an exit ramp. And if he couldn't find any truckers, there was the traffic coming into town for the big Fourth of July display tonight. "But it'll take a lot longer than ten minutes."

Anon pulled out his phone. "So we call it off, right?"

"No," Nate said. They needed to help Mob rescue her father, or she'd never trust them again. "You two go in, just like we planned. You keep watch, Flick, and, Anon, you slip in and do whatever needs to be done. You can do this without me, right?"

There was a moment of hesitation from them both, but

then Flicker reached her hand back and took Anon's. Nate could feel the pulse between them.

Whatever had gone wrong at home, Flickonymous was still happening.

"But how do we get there without bringing the cops along?" Flicker asked.

"It's me they're following. They don't even know who you guys are. I'll let you off as close as possible."

"I'll cut off their attention," Anon said. "And once Flicker whips out the cane, they won't think twice about her."

"Screw you," she said, and reached back to smack his knee. "Cops fear me."

Nate's eyes dropped to his GPS map. The sooner he veered away from Memorial Drive, the less chance the detectives would have of spotting Scam. He could let Flicker and Anon off on the far side of the industrial park, maybe ten minutes' run to the Hurricane Hauling and Demolition building.

The plan was sound, even without Nate there to guide them.

That was real leadership, after all. Making your people strong enough to stand without you.

But it had never quite worked that way with the Zeroes.

"Text Scam and Mob that you'll be a few minutes late. And that I probably won't get there at all."

CHAPTER 68
MOB

KELSIE LET ETHAN DRIVE. SHE WAS TOO NERVOUS to do anything but stare out the window, and the Cadillac they'd borrowed from Nate felt too fancy for her to be in charge of.

They were on Memorial, headed east toward Hurricane Hauling and Demolition. It was quiet out here. Not as quiet as the tenements had been, but empty enough that her crowd power felt hollow in her ribs.

Her phone buzzed. Kelsie pulled it from a pocket. "That's funny."

Ethan gave her an anxious look. "What's up?"

"The caller ID says 'Anonymous,'" she said. "It usually says 'Unknown.'"

"That's Thibault. You put him in your phone; you just

don't remember. Nobody ever remembers him the first couple of . . ." Ethan's face broke into a grin. "Hey, I remembered his name. *Finally!*"

"Right. At Nate's," Kelsie said quietly. There had been a guy there, tall and good-looking. He'd been kind of quiet, but how had she *forgotten* him?

"So what does Tee say?" Ethan asked.

Kelsie opened the text. "Damn. He and Flicker are going to be ten minutes late—and Nate might not even make it! Something about cops on their tail."

Ethan slowed the car. "We have to stall."

"No way," Kelsie said. "Fig said if we keep these guys waiting even one minute, it's all off!"

She gave Ethan a hard look until he accelerated again.

Great. She'd put her trust in these friends of Ethan's, and the plan was already falling apart.

They had these amazing powers, but they hadn't seemed like the most dependable bunch. Flicker had been enthusiastic, but she'd been distracted by something. Or someone? Right, that good-looking guy again. And then there was Nate, with his class-president smile. The sort of boy who always had to be in charge, and who never let a group think for itself. And Chizara had refused to take part at all, saying they should call the cops instead of pretending to be superheroes.

Which was almost starting to make sense.

"My dad's screwed, isn't he?"

Ethan shook his head. "Those guys will come through. They rescued me on Friday, and I don't even deserve it. They'll totally be there for you."

"I hope so," she said. Ethan was scared, she could tell. When he was nervous like this, his crew cut made him look less like a marine and more like a little kid.

She couldn't afford for his voice to screw this up. Her dad's life depended on it.

"Listen, Ethan? Thanks for having my back. I know you're going to stay focused."

Ethan looked embarrassed. "Least I could do. You know. After everything."

Kelsie didn't think walking into a warehouse full of mobsters was the least he could do. But she was glad he was doing it.

The Hurricane Hauling sign loomed at them on the right.

"I guess this is it," Ethan said. "You sure you don't want me to drive around the block, wait for our backup?"

Kelsie shook her head. "Too late. They've spotted us."

Three men were standing outside the open warehouse door. As Ethan slowed and turned into the driveway, they waved the car inside.

"Three of them," Ethan muttered. "I was hoping there'd be only one guy to talk to."

"No, it's better if there's a bunch," Kelsie said. A group was easier to nudge in the right direction. Maybe she could keep everybody calm and focused.

My power is strong, she reminded herself. *My power can do good. My power can right wrongs.*

"What I really want is backup," Ethan said. "The anonymous dude and the all-seeing girl would be pretty awesome right now. Even Glorious Leader might come in handy."

Driving into the warehouse was like being swallowed. A deep shadow engulfed them, cutting out any glimmer of the setting sun. There were huge construction machines everywhere, some on wheels, some on treads like tanks. Excavators with large, metal jaws or pincers and some kind of machine mounted with a giant steel needle to pierce the ground.

The machines were almost as intimidating as the men in bulging suits. Kelsie could make out two more in the shadows. That made five, plus her and Ethan. Not a bad number.

She could feel the group's energy forming in the space—a fledgling crowd.

She could keep them calm, at least. Though that wouldn't prevent anyone from *calmly* shooting her and Ethan in the face.

Ethan brought the car to a gradual halt. "There's Misha."

"Check out the guy with him," Kelsie whispered.

The stranger was tall and broad-shouldered. He wore an expensive suit and his gleaming, shaved skull was tattooed with several rows of tally marks, like he was keeping score.

"What's with those tats?" Ethan asked.

She swallowed. "I *so* don't want to know. Can we keep the engine running?"

"Won't do us any good." Ethan nodded toward the rearview mirror.

Kelsie looked over her shoulder. A couple of old Mercedes had pulled in behind, blocking their exit. She exchanged a queasy glance with Ethan.

"Ready?" he asked.

She nodded. "Let's get this thing over with, nice and easy."

She hoped that's what the Bagrovs wanted too.

CHAPTER 69

MOB

KELSIE GOT OUT OF THE CAR.

The gangsters' nervous energy filled the room, strong enough to set her nerve endings singing. And all that energy was focused on her and Ethan.

She took a long, slow breath, stifling the anxiety rising in her gut. Then she slipped into the skittish buzz of the warehouse and softened it, mellowed it out.

She felt their resistance, their desire to stay fixed in that raw, angry place. But they gave in eventually. She settled them, like little kids who didn't realize how tired they were.

Her power was strong. Her power could do this.

"Misha! My old friend," Ethan said, his other voice smooth and soothing. He stuck out a hand, like a slick young salesman here to close a deal.

Misha smiled leanly. "Bank boy. I'm so glad you came along."

"Wouldn't miss it. You going to help us out today, Misha?"

"I'm going to try, my friend."

"Is my dad okay?" Kelsie felt her interruption jangle the web of tension in the room. She reminded herself to play this cool.

Misha slid his gaze over to look at her. "He's hanging in there, little girl."

He sounded almost gentle.

"I want to see him."

"I understand completely." Misha nodded half a dozen times. Then he gestured to the man beside him. "But introductions first. This is my boss."

"Mr. Bagrov," said Ethan's other voice. "Been a long time."

"Do I know you?" Alexei Bagrov rumbled.

"Remember that thing back in Chicago? I was part of Zuyev's crew."

Kelsie swallowed, realizing the real problem with Ethan's voice. Beyond the fact that it had no morals and no wisdom, it had no fear.

"Little punk like you worked for Roman Zuyev?" Alexei looked like he might laugh. "You don't mind if I call him right now? I can confirm."

Alexei pulled out a phone.

Kelsie looked over at Ethan. For a moment, the terror in his eyes didn't match his smooth expression. But then he opened his mouth and that weird, creepy voice started talking again.

"You go right ahead. But I don't think he'll hear the phone ringing. He's been six feet under for the past two weeks."

Alexei frowned, then began to laugh in a low, coughing stutter. "Thought nobody outside Zuyev's team knew that yet."

"You got that right. Except you, of course," the voice said, and Ethan followed that up with a smile that looked kind of loose and surprised.

Kelsie felt the energy in the room ease out even more as Alexei laughed. The men started to visibly relax, their shoulders slumping. They grinned, like this was the best joke they'd ever heard.

She spoke into those shreds of goodwill. "Mr. Bagrov, when can I see my dad?"

Alexei turned to her, his laughter still in his eyes. There really was something wholly creepy about Alexei Bagrov, and she didn't need a superpower to spot it. Some people had a vibe, one that trickled out into whatever group they were part of. Alexei's energy was practically bouncing off the warehouse walls, as if he was eager for some kind of sick thrill.

On the other side of Alexei, Ethan looked unhappy. But his voice said, "You understand, the lady wants to check the quality of what she's paying for."

"Of course," Alexei replied. "But first I'll check the money. Make sure it's not traceable."

"It's definitely not that," Ethan assured him. He reached

into the driver's side to pop the trunk of the car, and Kelsie showed them the duffel bag. When Alexei gestured for her to open it, she unzipped the bag to reveal the thirty grand in cash.

"And now you take the bag out of the trunk, please." Alexei took a step back, as if he thought it might explode.

"Let me do that, Miss Laszlo," Ethan's voice said.

She stepped away automatically. It was hard not to obey those firm, confident commands. Ethan came around, pulled the duffel bag out, and dropped it at Misha's feet.

When a few bundles of money rolled out, Alexei nodded in satisfaction.

So far, so good. Kelsie let out a breath.

She prayed that Ethan's voice was going to stay on target. That Ethan wouldn't slip up and forget that they were here to save her dad as well as themselves.

"And show us, nothing else inside?" Misha continued.

Ethan squatted and rummaged through the open bag, stirring the wads of rolled-up cash.

"Nothing but dollars in here," the voice said. "We've got no reason to put a tracker in. We just want Jerry Laszlo back."

Ethan held up a wad of the stuff, but Alexei gestured it away like it was dirty. He indicated for one of his colleagues to step in. The man took the cash from Ethan, slipped off the rubber band, and started flicking through it.

"It's nonsequential, used," Ethan said, with that preternatural calm. "From a small-time operation on Ivy Street."

"Drug money?" Misha asked.

"Is that a problem?" the voice said, like it knew it wasn't.

"Not for us," Alexei confirmed.

Kelsie was glad Ethan was there. And his voice. She couldn't imagine trying to get through this on her own.

She worked to stay on top of her fear so it didn't bounce around the room. The men around them seemed content to watch and wait while the one guy counted.

"It's thirty thousand dollars and change," she said.

"Thirty?" Alexei looked pleased. "The price was twenty-five."

Ethan's voice said, "Consider that interest. An investment in a beautiful new business association."

Kelsie tried to smile. Every time it spoke, the voice ratcheted up the stakes just a little. Like a mark at a poker table, it couldn't resist pushing its luck.

"So here's my question," Alexei said. "Four days ago, you handed Jerry to my colleague Misha here. And now you're buying him back? Why?"

"It was all part of my plan. I wanted to meet you personally," Ethan's voice said. "Nothing makes for an introduction like a smooth transaction."

Alexei Bagrov beamed, and Kelsie stifled the temptation to tell him and the voice to get a room already.

Instead she said, "Mr. Bagrov, can you bring my dad out now?"

"Oh, he's not here," Alexei said casually. He spoke over his shoulder. "How's the money?"

"Good," said the other man, still counting.

"But we paid you," Kelsie said, trying to staunch the panic before it leaked out into the crowd. "You have to give me my dad back!"

It was the wrong thing to say. Apparently Alexei didn't like to be rushed. The stare he gave her made her pulse beat faster in her ears.

The guy nearest her reached for a gun at his hip and brought it around so it was in front of him, pointing at the floor. He kept his eyes on Kelsie, his knuckles white on the gun grip.

Ethan held out his hands. "So just tell us where he is, gentlemen. We'll go get him. Save you the effort."

"Not necessary," Alexei said. "We're happy to reunite you with your father. But if you want to see him, you'll have to come with us."

Kelsie was about to agree when Ethan's voice spoke up. "Now, wait a minute, gentlemen. You're changing the rules."

"What rules?" Alexei smiled. "Tie their hands."

Misha looked surprised, but hesitated only momentarily. Then he came toward them.

"Wait!" Ethan said in his real voice, the fear evident.

Kelsie watched Ethan open his mouth like he was about to say something else. But nothing came out.

"Ethan?" she said.

He was still silent. One of Alexei's men grabbed her wrists, pulling her arms behind her.

"Scam?" she cried.

He looked at her sadly and shook his head.

A bag came down over her head, blocking her view.

CHAPTER 70

ANONYMOUS

"HOLY SHIT," FLICKER SAID. "I JUST LOST MOB'S VISION!"

"Is she . . ." Thibault slowed. "Did they . . . ?"

He didn't have the breath to finish. They'd been running for five minutes, as fast as Flicker could go. The industrial park was huge, the warehouses growing bigger and the streets wider as they ran, like some kind of nightmare. And he had to call out every possible danger he could see coming up—gravel, potholes, curbs—cursing the fact that he was the one person whose vision she couldn't use.

Flicker's expression shivered, changing as she switched viewpoints.

"No. But they put a bag over her head. Scam's, too. The guy whose eyes I'm in, he just shoved them into a trunk. A Mercedes. Black."

Thibault stared at the warehouse across the parking lot. HURRICANE HAULING AND DEMOLITION was painted in giant letters on the side.

So near, but too late.

"Let's get closer," he said. "Maybe I can get in there before they drive away."

"I don't know," Flicker said. "Those guys look pretty scary. Like you could punch one in the face and he'd just laugh it off."

"How many?"

Her face did that thing again, shifting moment by moment as she cycled through every viewpoint in the warehouse. He could see why Nate had named her Flicker.

"Five or six?" she said. "Plus Mob and Scam."

"They won't notice me," Thibault said. "Let's go."

They ran again. Flicker was off in her own headspace, her eyes inside the warehouse, so he had to lead her along flat ground, avoiding curbs and concrete parking barriers.

As they neared the building, Thibault felt a glimmer of the people inside—all that focus leaked through the walls, like when Glorious Leader was working a room. Someone big was in charge in there.

There was a side door, but a chain-link fence stood between them and it. He laid Flicker's hand against the metal.

"Can you climb this?"

Riley hooked her fingers through the links, frowning at the sky. Thibault tried to sense more from the arcing signals in the building. But he only knew that the people in there were focusing *hard.*

"They're getting into cars," Riley said.

Thibault started to climb the fence, but then something buzzed up along the road beside the warehouse. He jumped down and spun around, ready to fight.

But it was just a delivery scooter. PIZZA2GO! was written on the insulated box behind the rider. It zipped past and into the driveway next door.

"The cars are moving," Riley said, clambering up the fence.

Thibault's mind went numb with panic. Taking on a half dozen gangsters was crazy enough, but there was no way for him to stop cars in motion.

In front of the next warehouse the pizza guy switched off the scooter and stuffed the key into his jacket pocket. He took a stack of pizzas out of the insulated box.

"Sunlight spilling in!" Flicker cried from the top of the fence. "The doors are opening up! They're leaving!"

Thibault reached up and took her arm.

"It's too late to get inside."

"So what are we supposed to do?"

Thibault had recovered and was back in mission mode, where you just had to grab the solution at hand. "I have to leave you here, Flicker. I'm going to follow them. Will you be okay?"

She jumped back to the ground, took his shoulder to steady herself.

"I'll be fine! Move it! They're turning a car around, but they'll be gone any second!"

"And you can make it back on your—"

She grabbed his other shoulder, pulled him close, and kissed him.

"I'll be fine. Now *go*!" She blew another kiss at him two-handed, as if she were throwing him away.

He stumbled backward, then spun around and sprinted across the next parking lot. Up ahead, the pizza guy was being waved in by a girl in coveralls. A tight little connection shone between them, either a mutual crush or a bad case of pizza hunger on her part.

He ran harder, wishing he was wearing broken-in sneakers instead of shiny new shoes.

By the time he burst through the doors, there were easily ten people in the reception area. More workers in brown uniforms were crowding in.

"Pepperoni, and lots of it!"

"Where's my Hawaiian?"

Thibault slipped through them, hacking away any glances they threw him, heading for the girl in coveralls. She was counting out money to the pizza delivery guy. His jacket pocket gaped open so wide, anyone could have taken the key.

A moment later Thibault was out the door and dashing for the scooter, key in hand. A black Mercedes sedan was already easing out of the driveway next door. Two big sunglasses-wearing guys were in the front seat, and a bald-headed man was in the back.

Flicker stood in the shadow of the warehouse, one hand in her hair, the other reaching out searchingly along the road. She was trying to read what she could from the receding car.

Thibault straddled the scooter, stuck in the key, and started the engine.

CHAPTER 71

ANONYMOUS

THE SCOOTER WAS A TWIST-AND-GO. AT LEAST HE wouldn't have to learn gears on top of everything else.

Thibault steered the little machine across the parking lot, getting the feel for the handling, the accelerator. The buzzy revving bounced off the warehouse fronts; then the echoes fell away as he got out onto the industrial park's entrance road.

The black Mercedes was up at Memorial, waiting to turn right. That was a relief—he didn't feel like tackling a left turn right away.

As he pulled in behind, a thin line of awareness touched him from the driver of the Mercedes, bouncing off the rearview mirror. He'd heard the buzzy engine behind him.

Thibault chopped the faint thread away, then checked out the controls between the handlebars. It was simpler than he'd expected, like riding a toy. And it had almost a full tank of gas, so he didn't have to worry about that.

The Mercedes pulled out, and Thibault turned after him.

And then they were on Memorial Drive, the scooter's weeny engine screaming up to top volume as he tried to keep up with the more powerful Mercedes. There was a lot of traffic, all of it moving fast.

Drivers' attentions lanced forward and darted across to other lanes to read the situation, the flickering lines crazy delicate among all the thundering machinery. It was hard work just controlling his fear as a pair of semis roared by. He felt like a rabbit in a herd of stampeding buffalo.

Thibault had stopped riding bicycles when he was ten. All those drivers almost running into him. *I didn't even see you! Where the hell did you come from?* He was okay in a car; people registered the machine, not the person inside. But on a bicycle, you mostly noticed the person, not the spindly frame and wheels below them.

He'd never tried a scooter or a motorcycle. Until now it hadn't been worth the risk. But here he was, flying along the highway, probably halfway invisible to every other driver, and with no helmet to save his braincase if someone swiped him off the road.

And all to save the druggie father of Scam's new friend.

Would the big insulated pizza box, painted with Pizza2Go!'s garish logo, be enough to attract other drivers' attention?

Probably not. Thibault swore and swerved into the next lane as an Escalade cut him off. Could the guy not see him, or was he just a dickhead?

At least the gangsters in the Mercedes wouldn't spot him. All he had to do was keep the damn thing in sight. . . .

They were headed back into town. That was good, right? They weren't going to throw Mob and Scam off a cliff, or take them out into the desert and shoot them. But wherever they were they going, what could Thibault do on his own?

He got ahead of the Escalade and changed lanes to get in right behind the Mercedes. He wished he could let Bellwether know what was happening. But the thought of pulling out a phone right now was laughable.

At last the Mercedes crossed into an exit lane and led him out of highway hell. Shivering from breeze-chilled nervous sweat, his body aching from holding rigid, Thibault followed the smooth black car through the lacework of streets and lanes up around the stadium.

Finally it slowed and pulled into an alley behind some office buildings. Thibault hesitated at the alley entrance. The Mercedes was drifting to a halt at the other end, in the shadows of the two tall buildings on either side.

Thibault switched off the scooter, kicked down the stand, swung his stiff body off. A shimmer of attention came at him from the alley, but he hacked it away, leaned back against the brick wall, and peered around the corner.

The Mercedes' trunk popped open, but Thibault could see nothing but blackness inside. The three guys were out of the car—wow, they were all muscle, their cheap suits straining to hold them in.

The bald one went to the trunk, flipped it wide open, reached in, and lifted out . . . a familiar duffel bag.

Thibault shut his eyes and beat the back of his head gently against the brick.

"You idiot!" he whispered. "You useless, impatient, stupid . . ."

He pulled out his phone. There were seven messages from Riley that he hadn't heard through the scooter's buzzing. He ignored them and dialed her.

"Anon! You okay?"

"You tried to tell me, didn't you? There were *two* black Mercedes."

"Yep. And you followed the money, right?"

"They just unloaded it. Did you see where they took Scam and Mob?"

"The other car was headed back toward town when I lost their vision. They were right behind you for a second—almost hit you! Then the pizza guy came out and started freaking out."

"Poor guy. Should I come pick you up?"

"I'm already in a cab. I updated Bellwether. We're meeting back in town to try to figure out what to do next."

"I guess I'll catch up with you there, then?"

"I guess. But you might want to, uh, *liberate* a certain duffel bag on your way here? Maybe we can get them to try this again from the top—and not screw us this time."

"Good idea."

"But Anon?" Riley's voice softened. "If you have to choose between getting the thirty grand and coming back in one piece . . ."

"I hear you. I'll be careful."

"Make sure you are," she said.

CHAPTER 72
SCAM

ETHAN HAD BEEN ROLLING AROUND IN THE TRUNK of a car for God only knew how long. Then he'd been hauled up countless flights of stairs by thugs who thought it was funny every time he tripped or staggered. His knee throbbed from where he'd fallen on it—the exact same spot twice. Then he'd been shoved against a rough concrete pole.

And all this with a bag over his head that smelled of diesel and grease. He hoped it was diesel and grease, anyhow, and not the panic-breathed saliva of the last guy the Bagrovs had kidnapped.

Right now they were tying his hands behind him with enough rope to harness two ships.

Ethan released his voice. It was easy. He wanted to be free. He'd never wanted anything so badly.

"Misha!" the voice said through the bag. "You don't want to do this."

The bag was pulled from his head. It was dark, wherever they were.

"I'm sorry, my friend." Misha sounded genuinely sad. "But Mr. Bagrov—"

"Alexei's never gonna take care of you, Misha. Look what he did with our deal!"

The voice went on talking, but Ethan was barely listening. He was looking around the large, empty room they'd been brought to. Like a hotel conference room, but dusty and abandoned-looking, missing furniture and light fixtures. Just four thugs with flashlights.

A bank of windows had a view onto the setting sun, and Ethan was sure he could hear something outside. A megaphone, maybe? He couldn't make out the words. The speech ended, and distant music started.

Across from Ethan was another man, also tied up. His head lifted and caught a beam of flashlight.

Whoa. It was Jerry Laszlo. Probably.

His face was bloodied and bruised. Blood had dried into the gray whiskers on his cheeks, and dripped all over his dark shirt. Blood caked his nose so hard he was breathing through his mouth.

"You're right, my friend, we had a deal," Misha was saying mournfully. "But Jerry here made us all very angry. And whatever you were pulling at that bank, Mr. Bagrov didn't find it amusing."

"Your deal was with *me*, not Laszlo!" the voice said. "Are you a man of honor?"

"I am, my friend. But I am also a loyal man, and orders are orders."

Ethan stopped listening to the conversation. Kelsie had come stumbling into the room, a greasy bag over her head too. Two of the gangsters sat her down and tied her to a pole a few yards away.

When the bag came off, she looked scared. Ethan felt his heart lurch as her fear pulsed through the room.

"Ethan?" she said, blinking. "Where are we?"

He shook his head.

"No" came a cracked, thin voice from across the room.

Kelsie turned. "Dad? Oh my God! What have they done to you?"

Jerry looked at them glassily, like he couldn't quite see that far through his blackened eyes. "Kelsie?"

Jerry tried to say more, but he was wheezing and coughing so hard he couldn't get it out. That was probably for the best, Ethan figured.

After everything they'd been through, Kelsie was finally reunited with her dad. But not in any kind of way she would've hoped.

Kelsie was talking softly to her father, pulling at the ropes that bound her to the concrete pole.

Ethan turned back to Misha. He couldn't remember the last time he'd been this scared. Not even a road trip with the Craig had scared him like being tied to a pole in an empty building by a bunch of treacherous gangsters.

Based on what they'd already done to Jerry, whatever happened next was going to be bad.

The voice felt his fear, his rank desire to escape from this place, and turned it into words. "Misha! You listen to me. Alexei is a psycho. You really going to let him abandon a couple of kids? *Here* of all places?"

Misha checked his watch with his flashlight. "We must go now. Sorry, kid. I liked you."

Ethan swallowed. Liked? *Liked?* That was past tense!

He took a deep breath and let his voice loose. His good old, faithful, reliable best friend, the voice.

"You can't leave us here to die!"

Oh, *crap*. The voice knew what they were planning. It always knew the score.

"Ethan?" Kelsie said. "What's happening?"

The voice didn't answer her. It was still working on Misha.

"Did your father raise you like this? Is this what he meant when he told you about honor? Doing something like this to a couple of teenagers?"

Misha looked sickened, which didn't make Ethan feel any better.

There was a sound from Jerry then, a kind of wet, gurgling cough. "Don't leave my little girl here. Please. What did she ever do to you?"

Ethan turned to Misha in one last, desperate attempt to understand what was going on. He tried to use his real voice, just to ask Misha how they were going to die.

But his real voice wouldn't work at all. He was too freaking scared.

"Dad," Kelsie said softly. "I'm sorry I failed you."

And then Ethan realized what he really wanted—for Kelsie to live. Even if he didn't make it himself. Which was totally unexpected and really kind of selfless. Man, what a stupid time to realize he felt this way about her.

He summoned every shred of the voice, the all-knowing, uncaring voice. The voice like a perverse genie always trying to please him. He wanted money, the voice got him money. He wanted girls to talk to him, it said the right thing to hold their interest. And now all he wanted was for Kelsie to be okay.

"Think of your little cousin. Think of Natalia! Kelsie's only a few months older than her! You can't do this."

Misha took a step back. It was working.

"Think of someone leaving Nata tied up in a place like this, with only a few hours left. Think of her crushed inside a mountain of concrete and steel, smeared out of existence, turned to pink jelly!"

As Ethan realized what it was saying, the voice sputtered out. It couldn't talk for one simple reason—Ethan was so afraid that he could no longer breathe.

Kelsie blinked. "What did you just say?"

"The Parker-Hamilton," Ethan squeaked. "The building we're in is that building—the one they're blowing up! The Parker-Hamilton!"

Misha nodded sadly.

Ethan tried to summon the voice to tell Misha whatever it would take to release them. He opened his mouth a couple times but nothing came out.

The voice knew nothing would change Misha's mind.

"Misha," Ethan said at last, in his own squeaking, pants-pissing, weasely tones. "Please?"

"I'm very sorry, my friend." Misha reached over and squeezed Ethan's shoulder.

Which was when Ethan got really, really mad. He hadn't been this angry since last summer, cornered by the Zeroes in Bellwether's show-off rich-guy home theater.

After everything he'd been through, the Craig and the bank robbery and the cops and the reunion with the Zeroes and the avoiding his mom and finally this. *This.* Dumped in a building that was set to explode. By a guy who wouldn't stop calling him *my friend*.

For a moment he didn't care whether he lived or died. All he felt was rage.

And that's when his voice, the voice of no consequence, really let loose.

CHAPTER 73

SCAM

"YOU'RE RIGHT ABOUT YOUR SONS, MISHA. THEY'RE gonna be bigger men than you." The voice sounded like a snarl now. It was done wheedling. Now it was rounding for the kill.

"What?" Misha paled.

"Alexei will promote them one day, and those two brats you helped bring into the world will topple you. They already *hate* you. You've known it since the moment Petya was born. He will *supplant* you one day!"

Ethan didn't know what "supplant" meant, but if the expression on Misha's face was any guide, it was a pretty gruesome thing.

"How do you know all this?" the man said.

The voice didn't answer, just kept on going. "Petya and Len are going to shoot you in the street and leave your body in a Dumpster. Just like you saw in that dream!"

Misha looked about ready to wet himself. "What *are* you, a demon?"

"Of course I am!" the voice cried out. "How else could I see into your soul? Glad you've finally realized, Misha."

The voice sputtered, and Ethan realized that for a moment he almost felt *sorry* for the guy. But he reminded himself that his life was at stake—hell, *Kelsie's* life was at stake—and his anger soared to new heights.

"You think a few hundred tons of rubble will stop me from haunting you into the grave, *my friend*? If you don't let all three of us leave right now, I'm going to save your sons the effort of killing you and drag you straight to *hell*."

Misha dropped his flashlight. It rolled at his feet, sending huge shadows lumbering across the walls. The other gangsters were also rooted to the spot, dumbfounded and incapacitated by the voice's demonic spewing.

Tears were streaming down Misha's face.

Okay, that wasn't normal. No way could the voice do that to a bunch of grown men. Plus, the voice was usually a one-on-one deal.

Then Ethan felt it, the fear moving through the room, echoing down the empty and abandoned corridors, across the dusty carpets. The entire empty hotel groaned with terror.

He glanced at Kelsie, who looked wide-eyed and horrified. Of course—she was *helping* him. Like with the crowd on Ivy

Street. Only instead of throwing money, she was letting her own terror redouble the voice's hellish ranting.

Kelsie nodded back, urging him on.

"Right!" Ethan turned toward the huddle of men by the door. "Who else wants to mess with *this demon*? And who wants to live?"

The men looked terrified. Ethan felt the voice bubbling away in his larynx, itching to get out. But a sharp, piercing shrilling stung through the room first.

One of the thugs pulled a phone from his jacket pocket. "It's Alexei. Wants us back there."

A little snap went through Misha. "Alexei would kill me if I let you go. And not just me. My whole family, little Natalia too."

"You think I can't come for Natalia?" the voice roared.

Misha thought for a moment, then said, "My cousin has never wronged you. And I think you are a demon of honor."

And he walked out the door. Misha was gone. The thugs were gone. And all the flashlights were gone. The only light that remained was the hard streaks of sunset from the windows.

"Crap," Ethan said. One badly timed phone call had ruined everything.

Kelsie's voice came from the gloom. "Did he just call your voice a demon of honor?"

"I know, right?"

The three of them were silent, except for Jerry's labored

breathing. Ethan listened to the sounds outside. The music stopped, and he heard a crowd laughing and cheering. They were waiting for the fireworks to start. For the big finale that would be the Parker-Hamilton blowing up.

The occasional rolling floodlight lit the side of the building

"Can you hear that crowd, Kelsie?"

"I can feel it. They're pretty excited."

Ethan straightened, the ropes around his wrists tightening. "So make them do something. Like storm the building!"

Kelsie shook her head. "They're too far away to feel me. And I doubt they'll be coming any closer. This place is wired with explosives."

She looked up above her head. On the pillar above her was a big orange package labeled C4.

Wow. They really were going to be pink jelly. Pink *mist*, more like.

They were quiet for a while, until Jerry spoke up. "Kid?"

"My name's Ethan," he said quietly. "Ethan who screwed up your robbery and blew thirty grand trying to ransom you. My friends were supposed to help us, but they didn't show. Maybe they got scared. Maybe they thought I deserved what I got. I guess I have zero friends left."

"Ethan?" Jerry said.

"Yeah, buddy?"

"Thank you for trying to save me. But you shouldn't have brought my little girl along."

"That wasn't *my* idea!" Ethan banged his head back against the concrete pole. It hurt.

"You're not helping, Dad," Kelsie said.

"This sucks," Ethan said, struggling against the ropes around his wrists. "I just wanted a ride home!"

"Ethan, you're not helping either."

"But that's all I wanted. Then the Craig's money fell into my lap, so I wound up in that stupid bank." Ethan was rambling; he knew it himself. "But I just wanted to get home before my mom grounded me. I can't believe I never talked to my mom!"

"At least you scared the crap out of Misha," Kelsie said.

Ethan stared at her, wondering how she could be so calm. Maybe channeling all that terror through the room had left her numb.

He wished it had done the same for him. He was feeling every moment of this. Plus his head still hurt from banging it on the column.

"Maybe your friends will save us," Kelsie said.

Ethan shook his aching head. "How would they even find us? Besides, they *bailed* on me, Kelsie. They hate me."

"I don't think they do," Kelsie said. "I was in that room with you all. And what they feel for you isn't hatred."

Ethan groaned. "I have this feeling you're going to tell me what they do feel, and it's going to be even worse. Like contempt, or pity, or some word I don't even know."

"Maybe *individually* they're still mad at you," she said, her voice softer as the last light of sunset faded in the room. "But groups are bigger than their members. Sometimes they're a little wiser. So yeah, together I think they feel . . ."

Ethan waited, trying not to listen to Jerry breathe. But Kelsie had stalled.

"For Pete's sake, what?" he asked. It turned out he really *wanted* to know what the Zeroes thought of him. "What do they feel about me?"

"Hopeful," she said. "They have hope for you."

Ethan closed his eyes, and a pain that had been burning inside him since last summer lifted just a little. He realized something that he'd hidden from himself since then. He wanted to be a Zero, damn it. Wanted to hang out with all those stupid freaks, enacting Glorious Leader's nutso plans, pretending to be superheroes instead of knuckleheads who should be locked away.

But it didn't matter now, because sometime after nine o'clock tonight he and Kelsie and Jerry were all going to be turned into pink mist and then buried forever where no one would ever find their shattered bones.

"Hope," he said. "Gee, now you tell me."

In the darkness he barely saw Kelsie shrug.

"I thought you should know," she said.

CHAPTER 74
FLICKER

"STILL NOTHING." FLICKER LEANED BACK INTO THE BMW's passenger seat, giving her vision a rest. "These buildings are all empty."

"Thank God it's the Fourth of July," Nate said. "We could never do this on a workday."

Flicker pressed her fingers into her temples. True, it was a lot faster reaching into an empty warehouse than going floor by floor, room by room. But it also took real brain effort to stretch her awareness across those parking lots, searching for eyeballs that weren't there.

"We should go downtown, Nate. Anon said that's where they took the money."

"Can you handle all those eyes? Those fireworks are less

than an hour from now, and the crowds have been building up since noon."

"More people is *better*. I'll have more range."

"Yeah, but Ivy Street on a Saturday night overloaded you. What will half a million people do?"

Flicker shrugged. "They were drunk, and going crazy thanks to Mob and her bag of cash. I'll be fine."

She heard his fingers drumming on the steering wheel.

"Look at it this way," she said. "I'm not lying in the trunk of a mobster's car with who-knows-what about to happen to me. Worst I can get is a headache!"

"We don't know that. I don't want you to break yourself."

The concern in his voice made her smile. If it were anybody else—Ethan, Anon, even Chizara—he'd be telling her to push her power to the limit. Damn the torpedoes and bring on the human test subjects.

"You're sweet, Glorious Leader. But we need to find Scam and Mob."

"Okay, I'll head into town. Just take one more look, Flick. I don't want to miss *anything* out here."

Flicker let her vision loose again, searching for eyes. The drivers were easy to ignore, whipping past much faster than Nate's crawl, their eyes on the road. She didn't find anyone in the darkness of a trunk, or with a hood over their head.

Out this far there were almost no pedestrians, and the

factories, warehouses, and auto-repair places were all closed for the Fourth. No one but security guards watching TV, and homeless people.

"Nada," she said. "Let's *move*, Bellwether."

The car's acceleration pressed Flicker back into her seat, and a tremor of excitement started to build in her stomach. Finally she was going to see what happened with a *real* crowd around her.

"You'll tell me if it gets too much?" Nate asked.

"I'll be okay. The day I found Anon's hotel, I was smack in the middle of downtown, flitting all over the place."

"Right, about that." Nate's voice shifted—he'd turned to face her. "You never told me how you found him."

"Nope. And I'm not giving you ideas about how to find his next place either. Just drive."

"I'm driving. Fast!" Nate said, and she felt a swerve as he changed lanes. "But I'm impressed that you found him when I never did. I assume your power had something to do with it?"

She laughed. "Not telling. Boyfriends beat Bellwethers."

"Boyfriend?" Nate's voice was steady, hard to read. "So this is serious."

"Yeah, it is. I mean . . ." A glimmer of vision flashed past on the roof of a nearby building, but it was just someone with a six-pack who'd found a distant view of the fireworks. "It's hard to tell *how* serious, exactly. Because I'm never quite sure how things are . . . progressing."

An awkward silence. That thing Ethan had always said, about Nate being like her big brother, was sometimes way too true. And the much worse thing, the one the voice had said last summer, was always lurking around the corner. If only because the voice had said it out loud.

For a distraction Flicker put herself in Nate's eyes.

Whoa. This was much faster than she'd ever seen him drive before. It was nice to know that Mob and Scam were more important than Glorious Leader's spotless record.

"Must be weird, forgetting," Nate said. "He'll always know more about you than you know about him."

"That's not his fault. He's not *trying* to keep things from me."

"Sure. But if he wanted to, he could tell you one thing one day, something completely different the next." Nate's voice grew softer. "Depends on whether he's a good guy."

Flicker reached out and took Nate's right arm.

"He's a good guy. I wouldn't feel this way otherwise."

"So you trust your heart." Nate's voice was raspy.

But his gaze was steady on the road, and the spires of downtown were rising up before them. This wasn't jealousy, Flicker was almost certain. This was concern.

"Not just my heart," she said. "I trust *him*."

The car was slowing. In Nate's vision, a river of brake lights streamed away, a titanic traffic jam of people headed in to see the show.

"Hold on to something," he said. "It's about to get bumpy."

"Wait, what—" she started to say, but the BMW was already leaving the highway.

The car slipped past the shoulder and went skidding down the highway embankment. Flicker found herself clinging to the dashboard, her teeth rattling in her head. Nate's vision was too shaky to hold, and she let herself go blind for a moment.

A smack went through the whole car.

"What the hell was that?" she cried.

"One of those barriers," he said, just as the beamer's tires hit pavement again. "Those things that discourage you from doing what I just did."

She went back into his eyes. They were down on the old service road, zooming along much faster than the cars above them on the highway.

"Whoa, Nate." She was seriously impressed. He was driving like a maniac, even though the cops were looking for his car.

"Get ready," Nate said. "Your head's going to be busy soon."

But Flicker had already felt it, the edges of the crowd. That host of vision, that ocean of eyes. It swept closer, and her mind began to sizzle.

She squeezed his arm tighter.

"Let me know if it's too much," he said.

"I'm good."

It was better than good—it was swimming in omniscience, in an all-seeing buzz of overloaded vision. Her mind was full of bright shimmers: people staring at the city lights, the sunset, the glowing screens of their phones. Kids waving sparklers and glow sticks in front of their eyes.

But even in these great numbers, the crowd didn't have the wild, convulsive intensity that had infected Ivy Street. Maybe this crowd was more sober, or maybe without Mob to turn them into a mad, pulsating gyre, it wasn't going to be so dizzying.

"Get as close as you want," she whispered, letting her vision flit and dart.

The mobsters wouldn't be holding prisoners in the street, so she shot up into the skyline. The windows were full of eyes—offices with views of the fireworks were throwing parties tonight, and of course the hotels were all full.

Flicker flashed through a thousand eyes a minute, searching for anyone in a small dark room, shoved into a closet, or staring down the barrel of a gun.

But they were all gazing at the horizon, where the fireworks would flash and tumble, and of course at the Parker-Hamilton Hotel. People were staring at the doomed building from every angle, and Flicker spun her vision in a circle around it, like walking around a dollhouse.

Okay, that was weird. The vast crowd should have been empty in the middle, a doughnut shape, with all those thousands of eyes staring in toward the hotel, but no one looking back out. And yet something niggled at Flicker's awareness from that hollow center.

Workmen putting the final touches to the demolition?

Wasn't it a little *late* for that?

Flicker stretched herself into the Parker-Hamilton and found three lonely pairs of eyeballs inside. It was dark in there, and for a moment she couldn't see a thing, as if she'd walked into a cinema from bright sunshine.

She made out naked wires hanging from the ceiling, dust in the air, and bare walls. Everything stripped away from the doomed hotel.

Then she caught a glimmer of a familiar silhouette.

"Scam," she breathed.

The car slowed a little. "You see them? Which way?"

"Straight ahead," Flicker said, her mouth suddenly dry. "Don't slow down. We haven't got much time."

CHAPTER 75

CRASH

"YOU'RE GONNA MISS A GREAT PAR-TEE!" SANG Ikem from the front door.

Chizara sang back, "I'm gonna miss a great big heeeaaad-ache!"

She'd already unplugged the home entertainment system. She was lounging on the sofa with a big bowl of popcorn and a book.

"Leave your sister alone," said her dad, passing through. "You know how it is with her. She doesn't like crowds."

"But it's going to be so great!" Ikem's eyes shone. "All those fireworks! The big ka-blam at the end! And then it'll all go dark for a second, and then they'll switch on the mega lights and press the button and down she comes, the whole hotel!" He waved his arms and made crashing noises.

"Sounds fantastic," Chizara said levelly. "But not worth

having my brain chewed on by sixty bazillion phones and cameras and pedometer watches and all those freaking—"

"Come on, Ikem! Obinna!" Dad called from the driveway. "We're getting in the car now. You ready, Mama?"

"I'm coming, I'm coming." Mom, dressed up American for this family outing, hurried into the living room, fastening an earring. She swooped on Chizara and kissed her. "Don't open the door to any crazy Fourth of July party people, all right?"

"Have a great time. Enjoy all the 'splodey things."

"Oh, I can hardly wait. Good night!"

The car started up with a painful tweak of electronics, then pulled out of the carport and drove away. Chizara breathed a sigh of relief and reached out into the house.

Damn, Ikem had left that game on upstairs. Should she just put up with that little itch, or should she go up and turn it off and make the house as perfect as possible?

She went back to her book. It was a good book—she kept getting lost in it and forgetting the popcorn was there. Half an hour later she'd only grazed through half the bowl.

But as evening came on, the itch got to be too much for her. She went upstairs. In the boys' room, the game lay calling out to connect with another console. It was fully charged, so she pulled the plug on it and powered it down.

There. If only it could always be like this, nothing but a few of the neighbors' e-things beeping and bopping off in the distance.

She ambled back toward the stairs, past her own room. Her phone lay switched off on her bedside table just inside the door, and the sight of the little black rectangle made her pause. How had the exchange gone this afternoon? Did Kelsie have her father back?

Chizara hoped so. She hoped nobody'd gotten hurt—she gave a shiver, remembering the hospital groaning with tech, the pile of flowers, Officer Bright's children staring at nothing.

She picked up the phone and walked on to the top of the stairs. The first detonation of the fireworks across town gently shook the air. She walked through to her parents' room, went to the very edge of the window, and squinted sideways.

Sure enough, in the distance, between the double towers of the Cambria Central Bank, a peacock tail of blue and gold lights was spreading on the sky. As she watched them fade, the delayed thud of the explosion shook the floor, and she felt a sudden dread for Kelsie and Scam, going in to face those gangsters.

Switching the phone on was like stabbing herself in the forehead with a fork. Even as she rubbed the pain away, the device pulsed more pain out into her hand, beeping an alert.

A voice message. From Glorious Leader.

"Chizara? This is Nate." It didn't sound like Nate. And no code names?

She could hear his voice clearly in the quiet room with the phone a foot from her ear. He was in the enclosed space of a car, in traffic.

"I need you to get downtown to the Parker-Hamilton as soon as you possibly can. You know how they're going to demolish it tonight? You've got to stop that happening." His voice was harsh and dry. "Scam and Mob and her father are inside, and if I can get through these damn crowds, I'll be in there too. Please, Chizara. I don't know how else to stop this."

She was already running—back to her room for her keys and backpack, downstairs for her shoes, outside and slamming the door behind her.

There was no *point* running, but she ran. She would never get there in time—but she couldn't sit at home and do nothing, either. She thought better on her feet.

What you need, girl . . . She sped along the block, slowed to take the corner, charged toward the shopping mall. Beyond its bulk, red fountains of sparks lazily rose and fell in the downtown sky.

What you need is a car.

Well, there weren't many of those around. Most people had taken them halfway into town, just like her mom and dad had done, to catch the special Fourth of July shuttle buses to the show.

And if she did find one, what to do without keys? She didn't know how to hot-wire a car. She didn't even know how to break into one.

She slowed as a thought hit her. *A shot of that fixing power would help.*

What, break something, crash something? Just so I can—

She was already scanning the smaller shops, looking for something big to crash. If she found a car new enough, computerized enough, surely the fixing juice could do *something*?

Here was the mall, closed and empty of people, but abuzz with lights and, inside, with systems at rest.

Panting, she peered in the padlocked front doors. Yes, empty—not even cleaners. They'd be in town too, with their families. The fireworks' pops and thuds were coming thicker and faster. The display only went for half an hour. Chizara didn't have time to think up another plan.

She held on to her head with both hands and reached in, past the mini systems ticking over in their sleep in the individual shops, to the central generators and transformers, timers, master switches for lighting grids, dormant air conditioners, security alarms, and cameras.

The farther she stretched into their spinning complexity and power and sheer connectedness, the heavier she felt their weight on her shoulders.

And then, with a deep breath, Chizara let it all go. She stopped holding them up, abandoned her duty, went against everything Mom had ever said about this power of hers.

Do no harm? Forget that. Harm everything. Bust everything in there down to the last LED.

The release was fabulous. She felt like a toddler knocking down the biggest, most complicated block tower ever built, like a revolutionary in a palace slicing through the cord holding up a giant, multibranched, crystal-hung chandelier, watching it fall and shatter on the marble floor.

But she didn't have time to enjoy the crash of every crystal. She reeled away from the mall, amazed that her own hands weren't lit up like glow sticks, that she hadn't exploded like a firework herself. She staggered along the sidewalk until she could break into a run again.

Her reach was gigantic now, extending deep into the electronic forest of the neighborhood around her. And she could hang on to everything, hold everything up, keep it moving. She was the world's best juggler, juggling stars and roaring chain saws and balls of fire.

It felt wonderful to run, tossing all this stuff into the air around her. She could run and run until dawn if she needed to.

But even at this speed, she'd never reach the Parker-Hamilton in time.

Cars were parked on either side of the street, crowded together. This was the tail end of the parking for the shuttle bus.

She slowed down and pulled her senses in closer, poking and prodding at the vehicles nearby.

"Speak to me!" she whispered at this pickup, that hatchback, this Volkswagen van. None of them spoke; they were all too old, too mechanical, too low-tech. Those big manual ignition switches were useless.

But then a Camaro up ahead made a clunking noise, and its brake lights flashed.

Chizara checked around for someone with a key fob. The street was empty.

It was a new model, with a nice gold-flake paint job. New enough?

She pushed her mind in under the hood, and there! At the front, on the right, clustered all the little coils of logic and circuitry she needed. Each microchip threw its map at her. She chose the ones connected to the battery and the ignition key, and with great delicacy squeezed a little power into them.

The engine cleared its throat and rumbled quietly.

Chizara crept closer and bent over to check the driver's seat.

No one. This was her work, this unlocking, this starting.

She went around and opened the driver's-side door. This was wrong, so wrong. This was a felony. This was grand theft auto, and not the game. This was also driving without a license. Chizara had only had five lessons in Dad's truck.

But she climbed in. The seat fit her snugly, perfectly.

Seat belt. Snick.

Lights. There.

Hand brake. Uh-huh.

The dashboard was lit up, the surface layer of an elaborate 3-D plan, a miniature city of systems. The cabin was peppered with little stings of tech, phone docks and mirror adjusters and seat controls. In the engine bay the electronics raced and pulsed, prompting and monitoring everything mechanical.

None of it was strong enough to hurt Chizara while she was

still this amped up from her mall crashing. Though that theft prevention system hollering for a satellite—yeah, that could go. She let it burn, one leaf in a glowing forest.

She put the car in drive, released the hand brake.

Indicate, Dad's voice said from the passenger seat. *Check your mirrors.*

The Camaro slid out into the road, smooth as silk. And the road was empty. Everyone was in town, watching those bright sprays of fireworks, impatient for them to end and for that building to come down, crash-crumple-rumble-*crash*.

The clock on the dash read 21:14—she had sixteen minutes.

She couldn't afford to be cautious. She had to drive like the mad criminal she was.

Eyes wide, hands gripping the padded-leather wheel, Chizara put her foot down. The Camaro obeyed, steady and fast.

And she started planning.

When she got there, she'd have to be subtle. To focus. Isolate the fuses and wires set to bring down the hotel, and neutralize only them. Not lurch around like a drunken King Kong and knock out half the town. She could do it with finesse, make it look like the explosives experts made some small mistake—

Her phone buzzed as she flew along Metro Boulevard. She got it out and tucked it against her shoulder the way she'd seen drivers do. *Fool,* Dad would growl whenever he saw that. *Dangerous fool.*

"Nate?" Chizara said. "I'm on my way."

"Good to hear." She'd never heard his voice so steady and hard. Was this what his fear sounded like? "I'm past the fence they put up to keep the crowd out. I'm going in to find Ethan and Kelsie." No code names. The no-code-names thing was snapping her heart in two. "In case I don't find them in time, I'm counting on you to stop this thing."

"I'll be there! I'll be there!" she shouted, terrified, elated, inflated with her stolen power, wide-eyed with horror at all the rules she was breaking, at everything hanging on her actions. Four people's lives—that had to be worth going to jail for, didn't it? "Don't worry, Nate, I'm coming!"

She took the corner onto Mason Street with a squeal of tires and floored the accelerator. Ahead, above, close enough to almost fill the windshield, fire flared up; light rained down.

CHAPTER 76
MOB

KELSIE COULD FEEL THE CROWD OUTSIDE THE building.

They were spread in all directions, vast and rumbling like a distant storm. They were excited, enjoying this big night of spectacle and adventure from vantage points safely blocks way from the Parker-Hamilton. Their excitement rose with each spindly plume of fire and carefully designed explosion overhead.

Kelsie tried to absorb the energy out there, to take strength from it. But the crowds were too far away. Mostly what she felt was the emptiness of the hotel halls and floors. Abandoned places were even worse when there was a joyful crowd in the distance, like an oasis you could never reach.

She sank into the dull ache of knowing that the last week

had been for nothing. She hadn't saved her dad, she couldn't save herself, and she'd doomed Ethan in the bargain.

A roar went up outside. The fireworks reached a crescendo, then sputtered out.

"Is it time?" she asked.

She looked at the others. The room glowed dimly from the lights outside, lit with the occasional flare from a falling ember.

Dad glanced at her through puffy eyes. "Not yet, Kels."

She strained against her bonds, trying to pull free. It was useless.

"Then why did the fireworks stop?"

"Maybe they're reloading," Ethan said dully from the gloom to Kelsie's right.

Kelsie let herself believe that. Maybe it wasn't time for the big explosion that would vaporize them all. She didn't look up at the fat block of C4 strapped to the column over her head. But she could feel it there, a misshapen totem of death.

Dad said, "I'm so sorry, Kels."

"I know."

She could feel tears begin to run down her cheeks, cutting tracks in the grime. It was so dusty in the abandoned hotel. After two long hours of being tied up, she could feel the dust in her lungs. She shook her head to clear her eyes.

She hated being tied up. If she had to die, she wanted to be moving.

"It's all my fault," Dad snuffled. His nose had been beaten halfway into his face, and he could barely breathe.

"I tried to fix it, Dad," Kelsie said. She'd tried so hard. But it was like the ropes around her wrists. No matter how much she pulled, they wouldn't break.

"I hate everyone out there," Ethan muttered. "Why do people like to watch stuff blow up, anyway? It's so *stupid*."

Kelsie shook her head. Couldn't he feel how much *joy* there was in that crowd? That was life. But here inside this building was only death.

"Ethan," she said. "I'm really sorry for getting you into this mess."

"We got each other into this mess," Ethan said.

"You helped a little, I guess."

"Yeah, well. My voice did."

Kelsie looked up at him. "Ethan, your voice *is* you. It's part of you, and it does what you want. Maybe not the exact *way* you want it, but you're the one who starts it rolling. Take responsibility for it."

Ethan let out a breath. *Now* he looked annoyed. "Gee, I wish I had the time to really think through what you've just said. Instead of, like, fifteen minutes before I get *blown up*."

Kelsie was about to reply when her father said, "*I* got all of us into this. It's my fault. You're just kids."

"Stop, Dad." Kelsie wanted to hug him and punch him at the same time. "You're just making me feel worse."

She'd known since that time he'd gone away to prison that Dad was a danger to himself. She should have taken better care of him.

The *whump* of a firework exploding made them flinch. It broke into a series of crackles, sending wild shadows through the giant room.

"See?" Ethan said. "They were just reloading. *Lots* more show to go."

Her dad started sobbing softly.

Kelsie thought back to that moment in the Moonstruck Diner, seeing him in the passing car. Less than a week ago, but it felt like it belonged to another life. Another Kelsie, one who was a thousand years younger than she felt now.

"I know when I've done wrong, Kels," her dad said.

"Dad . . ." She didn't finish. She couldn't. She wasn't sure, anymore, what she wanted him to do or say.

"Kelsie," Ethan said softly. "The guy's trying to say the last thing he'll ever get to say to you. Maybe you should listen."

"That's right," Dad rasped. "That's it exactly, son."

Kelsie squinted at Ethan, looked for the expression on his face in the semidark. He wore that smooth, practiced gaze.

She couldn't believe it. Here they were, about to die, and Ethan was still playing around with his stupid power.

"Dad, Ethan doesn't know what he's talking about. He doesn't know us."

"Just trying to help," he wheedled. Now *that* was his real voice.

Kelsie hated being trapped here, in this abandoned, empty place. She wanted to be out there with the crowd, carried up with those swells of excitement every time the sky exploded. If she only had a few minutes, why couldn't she spend it dancing to that glorious crowd music?

But no, she was here, tied to a column of concrete and waiting to die.

"I tried to do right by you, Kels," Dad said.

"He did, you know," Ethan said.

This was like being trapped in a trash compactor. The two of them coming at her from both directions, and her tied up, unable to cover her ears.

Dad said, "I did my best."

"I know, Dad." Though really, if she was honest about it, Dad's best had always been pretty crap.

A couple of burning firework embers fluttered down past the windows, lighting the room in garish purple and orange. Kelsie's pulse quickened. With every burst the end was coming closer.

Ethan leaned forward, his face lit by the vivid colors. "I think what you're both trying to say is that you love each other. Okay?"

"Stop trying to scam me, *Scam*," Kelsie said.

She wished the two of them would just stop. She knew this

was a stupid way to die, arguing with her dad and the lying kid who'd bumbled his way into her family's mess.

But when the next set of whistles and booms overhead subsided, there was Ethan's voice again: "Some things need to be said. Right, Jerry? You know what I'm talking about."

Kelsie twisted in her ropes. "Why are you doing this, Ethan?"

"Because there's something your dad always wanted to tell you. But he thought there'd be time."

"Time?" Kelsie turned back to her father. "For what?"

"To talk about your mom," Ethan's voice said.

Kelsie didn't answer. Her mother had died a long time ago, when she was little.

She watched her dad lit into garishness by fireworks, his bruised and bloodied face like a mask. She'd given up asking about her mom before she'd even turned ten. Dad always changed the subject. She figured he was too hurt by the loss to really talk about it.

But she'd always wondered.

"Who is this guy?" her dad said. "How does he know?"

"Same way as in the bank," Kelsie said.

"He can read minds?"

"Sort of." She turned to face the smooth mask. "Why are you doing this, Ethan? What do you *want*?"

"For you to find some peace," Ethan said, his voice as soft and comforting as an ad for life insurance. "You were three years old when you guys left New Orleans. Jerry, you told Kelsie's mom never to follow you, right?"

"We didn't leave her." Kelsie closed her eyes, trying to block out sound. "She died."

She felt the crowd outside whooping and hollering. She tried to reach for that feeling out there, anything to erase the desperate need that choked her.

"Dad?" When he didn't answer, she turned to Ethan. "What really happened?"

"Your mom didn't die. He saved you from her."

"What?" Kelsie tried to look at her father, but her vision was full of pinpricks of light. She was breathing too hard, hyperventilating.

This wasn't peace. What the hell was the voice *doing*?

"She loved you," it said. "But she was violent. He thought he could protect you, until your mother broke your wrist one night. He packed up and left her right then to keep you safe. Middle of the night, he got in the car and drove west and he didn't stop until he hit ocean. He loved you both, but he chose you."

"Oh my God," Kelsie whispered.

"I'm sorry," Dad said softly. "I never knew if it was the right thing to tell you."

"So it's true?"

Dad nodded. "I was going to tell you when you got older. But I kept putting it off."

He sounded fierce and sad.

Kelsie turned back to Ethan. There was a spray of embers against the windows. The fireworks were low and close now. Kelsie could see that Ethan's smooth expression was gone. He was watching her with a look of deep sadness.

"That sucks, Kelsie," he said softly.

"Where is she now?" Kelsie asked. It turned out the voice had been right. She *did* want to know the truth, even if it was only for a few minutes.

Ethan's mouth opened and the voice said, "She still thinks of you."

A feeling went through her then. Much smaller than the glorious crowd energies outside, but vital nonetheless. Like finding something old and precious that she didn't know she'd lost.

"Is she still in New Orleans?"

Kelsie watched Ethan, waiting for the voice to answer. But his face changed from a smooth mask to a panicked boy about to die.

"Do you hear that?" he squeaked.

Kelsie listened. The excitement of the people outside was making her blood beat, crowding out the quiet in her ears.

"Someone's in the building," Ethan cried. "Help! *Help!*"

"Who are you shouting at?" Kelsie asked.

"Just yell, will you? *Help!*"

Kelsie shouted with all her might. A moment later the two

of them were shouting in unison, sending their urgent cries out to fill the empty rooms and echoing hallways.

When they paused for breath, Kelsie heard it, heavy footfalls on the staircase.

Someone was coming.

CHAPTER 77

BELLWETHER

FINALLY SOMEONE ANSWERED.

Nate staggered to a halt on the dusty concrete of the stairs, panting hard.

"Help!" came the distant call. Ethan.

Scam—he reminded himself. This was a mission. He had to stay detached, in case there were hard choices to make.

Another voice joined Scam's, high and clear. Mob.

Nate hit the stairs again, climbing toward the noise, ignoring the muscles burning in his legs. The flashlight on his phone threw wild shadows, and the walls gaped open where sledgehammers had pounded through.

The fireworks were getting lower, closer. Sprays of fire spilled from the top of the Parker-Hamilton now. The windows of the stairwell trembled with the explosions.

The finale was almost here. But he had to think of the Ultimate Goal, not failure. Failure meant dying in this filthy, forsaken building. Losing everything.

Nate didn't answer the cries above. It was a waste of breath, and his lungs were full of dust.

He followed the sound to the twelfth floor, almost the top of the doomed hotel, and there they were in a large empty room. Scam, Mob, and her father.

"Nate!" Scam yelled. "I mean Glorious—um, Bellwether!"

Nate still couldn't answer. He was panting too hard.

"Whoa," Scam went on. "I didn't think it would be *you* saving us."

Nate ignored him. The three were tied up with thick ropes. He didn't have a knife.

Glass.

He ran to the windows, but they were intact. On the floor was a piece of masonry. Nate picked it up and hurled it against the pulsing lights from outside.

The brittle sound of shattering was followed by the roar of the crowd pouring through the gap. The explosions were thundering overhead, building to a climax.

"Don't cut your hands. There's a rag five feet to your left." That was Ethan's voice, being helpful for once.

Nate snatched up the rag and took hold of a jagged peninsula of glass still in the window. It snapped off and fell inward to the floor, splitting in two.

He lifted the larger piece and ran to where Mob was tied to a supporting column.

On the way up, he had decided to save her first. She was new and unknown, full of potential. Her power had filled him with questions, and she was more like the rest of them—born of the crowd, moved by the Curve. Not like Scam.

But the ropes around her wrists were thick nylon, and the piece of glass kept slipping and cutting him. It didn't help that Mob had pulled her ropes tight by struggling. Her hands were bright red.

"Cut the piece two inches above her left hand," Scam said calmly.

Right. It was near the middle of the knot, and already frayed where Mob had rubbed it against a corner of the column. Nate started sawing there, and soon it was unraveling.

Her hands parted, and Mob fell forward with a groan, rubbing her shoulders.

Nate ran to Scam, who was second on his list.

"Where?" he asked.

"No need to cut," the voice said. "Take that loose end on your left and—not that one. Yes, *that's* it. Work it back in toward the knot."

As Mob swept over and grabbed the piece of glass, Nate saw the specks of blood on the rag. His right forefinger was bleeding fast.

The blood helped, making the rope slicker. It slipped through, but the knot still held.

"What next?" Nate said.

The voice didn't answer.

"What next?"

"Oh no," Scam said, his real voice breaking. "It's not talking. There's no point."

Mob was still sawing away at her father's bonds, but Jerry spoke up. "It's gone quiet outside."

Nate hesitated, staring at the knot before him. His mind refused to resolve its puzzle, or to understand what they all were saying.

"Maybe they're just reloading again?" Scam's real voice.

Mob stood up, her ear cocked toward the crowd. The glass dropped from her hand and shattered.

"No," she said. "I think we're done here."

Nate shook his head, staring at the knot. *Think of the Goal, not of failure.*

"Chizara," he said, half to himself. But she was on the other side of town, too far away to help.

Still, there was no point sitting here and waiting for the end.

Nate rose from his crouch and held out his hand to Mob. "We can run. We can still make it."

"I can't just leave," she said.

"Wait," Scam said. "You're leaving *without me*?"

Nate turned to him. "If your voice gave up, that means there isn't time. You *know* that, Ethan. Now use it one last time and get her to come with me!"

For a moment Ethan stared at him, astonished. But then he nodded, closed his eyes, and opened his mouth.

But nothing came out. Mob wasn't going anywhere.

She had knelt by her father. "Thanks for saving me, Dad, back then. Sorry I couldn't return the favor."

"Kelsie," Nate said, trying to focus himself at her. "We have to run—*now*. If we're going to die, let's die on the stairs."

But his power wouldn't focus. The crowd was too far away to help him.

Jerry Laszlo looked up at his daughter. "You were always proof of miracles."

Outside, a mass of voices started counting down from twenty, and Mob spread her arms toward the ceiling, the numbers rippling through her body like a pulse.

CHAPTER 78

CRASH

NOW ALL THE SKY WAS ALIGHT, THE EXPLOSIONS coming thick and fast, shaking Chizara's car, shaking the whole city around her.

This had to be the buildup to what Ikem had called the "big ka-blam." He'd said there'd be a minute's silence after the fireworks before floodlights came on and the countdown started. She had a little over a minute.

In the stolen car she shot through the empty streets lit lurid by the gold, the fuchsia, the emerald, the silver-white of the fountains and flowers and starbursts overhead.

She felt ahead furiously, sifting through the piles of tech downtown, searching with her mental tweezers for the demolition charges.

How did it even work? When you blew up a tower like

the Parker-Hamilton, was it one big bomb in the middle, or a bazillion little ones, dotted through the building? She had to do this right.

She almost saw the roadblock too late. Not just hollow plastic barriers she could have punched the Camaro through, but a string of flesh-and-blood traffic cops.

She slammed on the brakes. The car swung with a scream of rubber and skidded to a sideways stop, rocking as she shed her seat belt. Startled cops backed up against the barriers. Chizara jumped out, vaulted the roadblock.

"Hey, what the hell!"

"You can't just leave that here—"

But Chizara was already running along the near-empty street beyond.

She had to get in range, and soon, or Nate was dead, and Ethan, and the new girl, and the new girl's dad. That couldn't happen. It wasn't an option.

The ground shook with explosions. Ahead—blocks and *blocks* away!—the fireworks gushed up into the darkness, all colors, all shapes.

This was definitely the big ka-blam—they were throwing everything against the sky. Chizara raced on, feeling ahead through the electronic noise. There wasn't room for fear; she needed every drop of adrenaline for running, for hunting. If she could only get a clear signal, see through all this e-garbage in the way.

Networks beat at her from the buildings all around; buried fiber-optic lines burned underfoot. And up ahead around the Parker-Hamilton, *so* many more devices seethed. What had the news report said, that one out of every three Cambrians was here? And every one of them held a phone, snapping photos and videos, tweeting, messaging, Instagramming, sending out a million darts into the flame-swept sky.

The last of the fireworks fell and faded slowly to black, leaving only feeble streetlight to guide her. Did she have the whole minute Ikem had promised, or only seconds?

She sped up, pushing past what she'd thought was her limit. The sudden quiet was horrible. Her fear flared, and she had to swallow it, gasp it away as she ran.

White light punched up into the rolling firework smoke.

Crowd roar hammered along the street.

A sob of terror escaped Chizara, but still she ran, and the light stayed steady. That hadn't been the final explosion, just the floodlights coming on. But soon—

Now the crowd's tech was clawing her face and front, every camera lifted, a hundred thousand glowing rectangles. A galaxy of pain.

She ran against the weight of it, her body peeled back to springs and wire and a core of nauseous burning. *Give in! Go crazy!* shrieked the gnawing tech, but she had to see beyond it, feel around it, push through.

It was worse, much worse, than the CCPD's big punch-in-the-guts systems. This was death by ant bites, a trillion mandibles sinking into her flesh at once. If she hadn't crashed that mall, she couldn't have stood this, wouldn't have had the strength.

She burst out onto a slope packed with spectators. Plunged right in, pushed forward.

"Hey!"

"Watch it!"

She didn't care. She forced her way on.

The ant bites kept coming, but the crowd gave her *huge* range. Her skull felt hollow with it, like she'd just sniffed crushed peppermint leaves. Ahead she sensed a vast, sweet blank space where the doomed hotel stood, empty, useless, scoured of phones and wifi.

Now the tech-peppered crowd was too thick to move through, no matter how hard Chizara pushed.

"Twenty!" they shouted around her. "Nineteen!"

She looked up in horror. The Parker-Hamilton loomed ice white in the mega floodlights. But one face had been left dark, except for bright numbers projected there, counting down the seconds.

Chizara closed her eyes and fought to focus. Deep in the empty hotel she groped after a ghost of a network, a sparse drapery of wires through the steel-and-concrete skeleton.

Countless little bombs. And she had to crash them all.

"Ten!" shouted the crowd, a monstrous, ignorant voice. "Nine! Eight!"

Too fast. The seconds were going too fast.

She couldn't do the tweezer thing. She couldn't be subtle. She'd just have to dump the whole damn city—she could see so far, could break so much!

But she had to keep control—

"Five! Four!"

Chizara lifted her arms and spread them wide, like a demon queen throwing down a curse. She reached beyond the boiling mass of ant tech around her, protecting the phones so people wouldn't panic.

"Three!"

She sank down into the power grid, shook free everything feeding into the lattice of wires charged with bringing the old hotel down.

"Two!"

Through that fresh hole she'd made in the pain, she saw the demolition setup: the timer, the board, the remote trigger, the sensors scattered like stars through the stripped building. Each star was taped, with its charge, to a load-bearing pillar, ready to blow it to rubble, to bring the massive concrete floors pancaking down on the four people inside.

"One!"

Chizara cut it all off at the root, and with her mental fingertips pinched out the backup generator before it could cough into life.

The crowd cried, "Zeroooo!"

And then . . . nothing.

Beyond the squeal of the phones, no voices. And no bombs.

Chizara raised her head, opened her eyes to darkness.

Oops, she hadn't meant to kill the floodlights.

And that wasn't all she'd killed—a great swath of the city lay snuffed out all around—no streetlights, no window lights, the skyscrapers standing dark.

Only the hundred thousand phones glowed, recording each other's hopeful glows and the darkness beyond them, recording the glorious silence, recording Chizara's triumph.

The *magnificence* of what she'd done, the magnificence of what she *was*, hit her smack in the funny bone.

Laughter billowed up from the pit of her stomach, where the ant tech had chewed the hardest. It scrabbled in her lungs, gathering breath. And then it burst up out of her throat into the silence, and the darkness, and the doubtfulness all around.

"MwahahahaHAAAA!"—like a movie villain.

People fell back from her. Some looked nervous in the faint phone glow. Most kept their cameras raised, still expecting the big event.

Chizara spun on her heel, double punching the air.

"Not going to happen, suckers!"

She pushed uphill through the assembled shadows, staggering, cheering, laughing. The crowd was a field of grass, and she could see how every blade lay around her, where every drop of dew sparkled. Phones and cameras were no more than gnats now, no more than dust motes swirling in a sunbeam.

And *she* was the sunbeam—she was the *sun*, the source! She was full to bursting with post-crash power. She could see everything, feel everything, hold everything up forever if she wanted, let go anything she chose.

Mega- or nanosized, she was master of it.

She was a freaking Zero, man!

CHAPTER 79
SCAM

ALL OF CAMBRIA WAS DARK. INSIDE THIS HOTEL stairwell was even darker.

And Jerry Laszlo was heavy.

"Landing coming up," Ethan grunted.

"Got it!" Nate's voice came from his right. It took both of them to hold up Kelsie's dad, who had been beaten too badly and tied up too long to walk.

In front of them, Kelsie lit the landing with the light from Nate's phone. It made her pale hair luminous and turned the rest of her into a dancing silhouette.

She kept glancing back at her dad.

"Are you okay?" she asked.

Jerry let out a groan. Every movement seemed to hurt him.

Ethan didn't know if Crash's crash was permanent or only a

temporary reprieve. He didn't plan on sticking around to find out.

He and Nate had formed a kind of yoke, their arms wrapped under Jerry's shoulders to lift him upright. Ethan had his left hand on Nate's right collarbone and Nate had a firm grip on Ethan's neck. It was the most teamlike Ethan had ever felt with Glorious Leader.

But he wasn't sure it was enough. They still had a half dozen landings to go before safety.

"I hate," Ethan puffed, "this hotel."

He'd never been so scared in his life. This was worse than waiting helplessly to die, because he had a chance now. Any second he wasted might be the one that vaporized him.

They hit the next landing and careened toward another flight of stairs. Ethan went wide while Nate spun practically on the spot. By now it was almost routine. Make the landing, spin, head for the next.

There was garbage everywhere, and more than once Ethan slipped on some scrap of old wire or who-knew-what. But he stayed upright, maybe out of pure desperation.

Then he heard a rumbling, booming noise begin outside.

"Oh, crap," Ethan shouted. "What's that?"

"It's the crowd," Kelsie shouted over her shoulder. "They're chanting."

"What? Why are they chanting?"

Kelsie didn't answer, but a second later Ethan heard it over the scuffle of their footsteps.

"Blow it up! Blow it up!"

"Assholes," Ethan said.

But of *course* the people who had come for the Fourth of July fireworks were crying out for the destruction of the Parker-Hamilton and everything inside it. And no doubt the demolition experts out there were furiously poking at wires, checking connections, rebooting control systems, and generally trying to figure out what had gone wrong.

"We gotta keep moving," Ethan puffed, rounding another corner of the staircase. "This place could still blow."

"Crash knows what she's doing," Nate confirmed.

Ethan had to laugh. "Since when? Since when do *any* of us know what we're doing?"

"Scam, seriously. She just saved our asses."

Ethan didn't argue, just saved his breath for moving.

Jerry was whispering a litany of gratitude and grief. Nate kept trying to reassure the old guy, reminding him to keep going, not to fall into dead weight. But the group was too small for Nate's power to do much.

Ethan doubted there was any power on earth that could convince Jerry to work any harder. He was in a bad way. If they didn't get the old guy to a hospital soon, he might not make it through the night.

The chanting of the crowd grew stronger as more and more people joined in.

Kelsie said, "I can feel them. They're all so freaking *happy*.

Like, delirious. They want us to blow up so bad."

"Can't you make them, like, *not* want to explode this building?" Ethan asked. "It's getting on my nerves."

"I can only guide their energy, not change what they are!"

"Nate?"

"Too far away," Nate gasped.

Kelsie added, "And there's so *many* of them!"

She swung the phone's light toward the next landing, and Ethan stormed forward. He was suddenly grateful that Nate always bought the best of everything, because that phone worked better than a lot of flashlights Ethan had owned. It lit the stairwell into sharp contrasts.

"Hey, Nate?" Ethan huffed.

"Yeah?"

"In case we all die in a fiery inferno of death"—he paused for breath—"I just want to say thanks for coming for us. Even though you were going to *leave* me in there."

"Only to save Mob," Nate replied in a gasp. "Otherwise . . ."

"Right, sure," Ethan said. "And hey, we made it. I guess I owe you one."

"Sorry about last summer," Nate said. "I was wrong."

For a moment Ethan didn't understand. They'd just reached a landing with a giant 2 painted on the wall. They were almost out. Ethan's lungs were burning and he was gasping for breath, and Kelsie was a shadow in front of them, carved from the bouncing, lurching phone light.

But it had really happened—Nate had just said he was wrong last summer. In that moment just before the spray of words that had busted up the Zeroes, when Nate had told him . . .

You aren't like us, Ethan. Your power's twisted, somehow. It hates crowds, and it doesn't grow with the Curve. It's mean and small and selfish. You'll never be a superhero. You'll always be a scam.

Nate had said it with a kind of perfect certainty, almost like he'd borrowed the voice for one blinding moment. And the fact that it was *true*—that Scam was different and cursed and alone—had made him want nothing more than to destroy them all.

It was the last flight of stairs, and Ethan was pretty sure they'd all fall and break their necks, but at least if they died now, he'd lived long enough to hear Glorious Leader admit that he was wrong.

Ethan's knees buckled before he realized they were on the ground floor. His feet were still trying to find the next step down.

The phone light swung wide as Kelsie located an exit. "Over here!"

She lit the floor in front of them. Jerry dangled between Ethan and Nate, barely touching the ground.

Then they were outside. Ethan had never been so glad for Cambria's sea air. His lungs ached all the way to his stomach. He'd been breathing dust for two hours.

Nate was still pushing them forward, covering the distance between them and the waiting crowd. A couple of hundred yards and a ten-foot chain-link fence.

Ethan gasped.

By the time they got Jerry to the fence, Kelsie already had her shoes off and was climbing, toes and fingers clinging to the wire.

"Help!" she was shouting. "Help us!"

Ethan was too beat to ask who she thought would hear. The crowd was still chanting on the other side, wrapped up in the dangerous delight of the explosion they yearned for. A few people cast Kelsie confused glances, but that was it.

Nate let go of Jerry, and the old man sagged down on Ethan's shoulder. The weight dropped Ethan to his aching knees.

Kelsie had reached the top of the fence. She was teetering like a high-wire artist. Ethan wanted to shout up to her to be careful, but his lungs were burning.

"Look!" Kelsie was pointing. "There's a first-aid station."

Ethan set Jerry down and struggled to his feet to peer across the heads of the crowd. He could see it too. The top of a white tent with the District Ambulance logo billowing from its point.

Nate called up at Kelsie. "Throw me my phone! I'll tell the others to meet us at the northwest corner of the fence."

The phone tumbled down to his waiting hands.

"Nate!" Kelsie cried. "Can you focus the crowd on me?"

Nate looked up from the screen. "Um, I guess? What are you going to do?"

"Something I saw one time. Don't worry, it's easy!"

"Okay. Yell as loud as you can!"

Ethan stared up at Kelsie. She hooked a heel over the other side of the fence. The moon lit the dreamy, elated expression on her face.

She sang out, a high, clear cry that arced above the hubbub of the crowd.

More faces turned toward her, lifting up expectantly.

Nate was doing something with his hands, like drawing an invisible net in toward himself. His eyes were open, but blank and focused in the middle distance—seeing something invisible and strange.

Their little corner of the massive crowd grew still, but Scam could feel the excitement build as more and more of them looked up to see Kelsie balanced on the fence.

The crowd rippled into a new shape, a tide of attention turning her way.

Then all at once she jumped.

CHAPTER 80
MOB

SHE WAS FALLING.

She'd been falling for a week, from the moment she'd spotted her dad in a car outside the Moonstruck Diner. Now she pitched forward and fell from the fence into the crowd.

And they caught her. They always caught her.

They heaved her over their heads. Hands lifted and held and pushed her. Hands turned her so she pointed at the first-aid station like a spear. She crested that wave in full crowd-surfing mode, arms splayed, facing the sky.

Most of Cambria had come to watch the fireworks. This crowd was bigger than any dance party she'd ever been to, and more united. Less like the dumb-animal mob she was used to. Keen and driven.

She knew that that sharpness had something to do with

Nate. He was working the crowd, lending his focus to her strength.

She'd been feeling their excitement the whole way down the stairs. The whoosh and rush of energy. Even frightened, even knowing how hurt her dad was, even having discovered the awful secret he'd kept from her about her mother. Even with all that, she'd still wanted to lose herself to the impatient chant.

Blow it up!

But now they had a different focus, and it was her. Their energy coiled and spun, enveloping her like the curl of a wave around a surfer.

She skimmed over the crowd, their hands rising to support her like the steady breath of a thermal. With all the lights of Cambria crashed, she could see stars above. Millions of them, stretched out like brilliant bands of twinkling color. And thousands of phones glowing beneath her, a reflection of that galaxy above.

The crowd drove her forward, toward the medical station. She thought they might drop her, or spin and toss her, leave her airsick, throwing up like that guy in the Boom Room the night she'd lost control.

For a moment she was scared of them.

But then she realized that there was no *them*. In that moment there was only *us*.

She glanced back at the chain-link fence to see how far she'd come. Nate was halfway up, taking pictures of her.

Kelsie sank back into her crowd. People reached for her, holding her up, sending her forward. She felt a rich, deep gratitude. As she fed that into the feedback loop that supported her, it doubled and tripled. People called and cried and shouted, but they weren't shouting for explosions anymore. They wanted to be part of what Kelsie was part of—they wanted to be more than the crowd. They wanted to float and skim the way she was floating.

They wanted to fly.

She'd never felt so much a *part* of anything, so supported and carried. She'd always been afraid to let herself go like this, afraid that if she surrendered so completely to the crowd she might never find herself again.

But now it was obvious—this was where she was meant to be. Her power was *strong*, and it could fix things. It could right wrongs. It was so much bigger than she'd dreamed.

The District Ambulance tent was rushing toward her. She was off course. Not by much, but at this rate she'd end up miles away.

She felt a surge of panic—her father needed help so badly—and her fear leaked into the crowd. The hands beneath her began to falter, and Kelsie felt herself sag and slow.

She bit back on her worry about her dad, channeled fear into purpose, and the crowd responded, hurtling her toward the first-aid tent. They all wanted to correct her course. To be part of her journey.

And in their hands she forgot any fear she'd ever felt.

An endless moment later Kelsie was slowing, drifting down softly to the street before the first-aid tent. They placed her there gently, like she was precious.

People still held her, wanting to stay connected. She was hugged; her hands were enveloped by other hands; her hair was brushed away from her face. She had to push them all away carefully. Her crowd. Her people.

It was hard to step out in the open and be alone again. But she had to save her dad.

She wrenched back on the crowd connection until, with a snap, her breathing was her own again. Her body was only this five feet of skin and flesh, and not a vast gyre around her. For a split second she felt like the entire world had left her behind.

She made her way to the EMT guys on shaky legs. They were staring at her, eyes wide. They'd seen her coming, flying across the crowd.

"I need help." It was hard to speak. A waterfall was lodged in her throat.

The EMT guys looked her up and down.

"Not me, my dad." She pointed.

She could still feel the laughter and joy of the crowd around her, but it was their happiness now. Not hers. She was in the middle of the bright, hard isolation that came with being herself again.

"Northwest corner of the fence. I'll show you."

She turned and, with a single gesture that focused all her pain and fear, she cleaved the crowd to make a clear path. Her crowd. They moved aside for her; they always would.

As she led the EMT guys through to where her father lay crumpled in Ethan's arms, Kelsie felt the tears slide down her face like they might never stop.

CHAPTER 81

CRASH

THE AMBULANCE PUSHED UP THE CROWDED SLOPE toward Chizara, clearing a path for itself with little siren whoops.

She stood back, trying to think straight through the after-buzz of all she'd done, through the euphoria rattling through her veins.

Had she harmed someone? Crashed a pacemaker, an insulin pump?

Was there a Zero in that ambulance?

Nate had texted her to come to this corner of the fence to meet up with them. Had one of them gotten hurt on their way out of the tower?

The ambulance passed, and she darted down the path it had left through the crowd.

"Crash, over here!"

That was Riley's voice. There she was, her bright skirt rippling in the sea breeze, catching the last red of the ambulance taillights. She and Ethan and a tall, dark guy—yeah, *that* guy, the other Zero—were three shadows leaning against the chain links.

Chizara dodged through the crowd and squeezed Riley tight. Then she hugged Ethan. "So. Freaking. Pleased to see you."

"Oof!" Ethan patted her back warily. He was dusty and scratched, and smelled like damp cement.

Chizara let him go. "Where are the others?"

Riley pointed back up the slope, and there was Nate, looking dazedly after the ambulance.

Chizara strode up and placed herself in front of him. He startled for a moment in the darkness, until she stepped in and put her arms around him.

He hugged her right back, his cheek gritty and sweaty against hers—and *alive.*

"You did it." His voice was ragged in her ear. "I knew you would."

"Did you?" She was about to melt into tears, or laugh like a supervillain again. She grinned madly to hold in all the emotion. "Because I wasn't all that sure."

Here came the others, Riley holding that guy's hand. Yes, Chizara should hug him, too. *Anonymous,* that was his name.

But first she asked, "Where's Kelsie?"

"In the ambulance," Nate said.

"Oh." Chizara's elation tumbled into fear. "How serious?"

"She's fine," Riley said. "It's her dad. Those gangsters beat him up *really* bad."

"But he's better off than if that building had collapsed on us," Ethan said.

Chizara shuddered. "It came so freaking close!"

"We know," Nate said. "We heard the countdown. Next time, feel free to ruin the suspense."

Even in the darkness she could see that his hair was gray with cement dust, and his eyes looked old enough to match.

"But thank you," he said.

Chizara looked out at the dark city around them and swallowed some of her giddiness. "I may have overdone it."

"But you kept the phones up," Riley said, staring out into the crowd. "You should see it. They're all tweeting how bad Cambria is at demolitions."

Chizara smiled in the darkness, looking out across the thousands of glittering screens. Her bones twinged from their signals, but the afterpower of her crash shielded her from any pain.

Let 'em tweet, let 'em text, let 'em call each other as much as they wanted. She was still Queen of the Night, crammed full of almost dangerous exhilaration.

The crowd was restless too, as the wind kicked up stronger.

"I came all the way from San Diego for this!" someone shouted.

"Blow it up already!"

Nate put a hand on Chizara's shoulder. "Maybe you should go ahead. Get the lights back on. Let them blow the building."

Chizara frowned. "I don't know, Nate. Aren't there better ways to spend my fixing power?"

"It'll be safer with the streetlights on." Riley gazed into the middle distance. "There are bottlenecks all around this square. Could get testy when people start to leave."

Nate held up his hands. "It's up to you, Crash."

Was he trying his charisma on her? Leveraging the crowd's frustration? She didn't *think* so—although it was hard to register anything through the buzz of aftercrash.

"Here's the thing," Nate went on. "If that building disappears tonight, the Bagrovs will think Mob and Scam and Jerry are dead. Which is a good thing."

"Also," Riley said, "it would be totally badass to watch you blow it up."

"It sure would," Ethan said. "Come on, Crash. You can pretend I'm still in there if you want."

She sighed theatrically. "Well, I guess, for safety's sake we could use some light."

With a snap of her fingers and a little mental nudge, the floodlights flashed the world back into being, the Parker-Hamilton whitely cold at its center.

The crowd gasped, and readied themselves again.

"That didn't look too hard," Nate said.

Chizara shrugged. The floodlights had taken nothing. Maybe if she was careful, she could bring the hotel down with plenty of power to spare.

She squeezed her eyes shut and snaked her mind out past the tech buzz of the crowd, searching again for that sensor network, those wires, the trigger switch, the backup generator.

Compared to the city around her, they were *tiny*! This wouldn't take more than a—

"Oh, *crap*," Ethan said.

"Hold on a second," Chizara said. "I've almost . . ."

She felt Nate's hand on her shoulder, and opened her eyes.

A big, bald tank of a man stood glaring at the four of them, his hands closed into fists. Two solid, stubble-headed guys, in black tees and sleeved with tattoos, stood on either side of him.

"Oh right," Chizara said. "The Russians."

"No," Ethan squeaked. "The Craig."

Chizara knew she was supposed to be scared, but the supervillain part of her refused to take them seriously. Such standard-issue thugs. Did they have no imagination?

The big guy, the Craig—and what kind of hopeless thug name was *the Craig*?—grabbed a fistful of Ethan's dusty T-shirt.

"Thought so!" His spittle flew. "Saw Kelsie up on the fence, and I *knew* you'd be around here somewhere."

Ethan made goldfish mouths, but no useful words came to his aid.

"Where's my money?" the Craig said.

"Right here." Someone stepped between them and calmly brushed Ethan out of the Craig's hands. A young guy who looked vaguely . . .

Anonymous. He'd been here all along, right next to Flicker, only the crowd kept swallowing him.

He swung a duffel bag into the Craig's chest, pushing him backward with it.

The Craig stared at it, looking suspicious. He unzipped the bag, peered in, zipped it up again.

"And who the hell are you?" he growled.

Anonymous raised a hand as if to shoo off a fly, then stepped away. Not in any particular direction, just . . . *away*. And suddenly there were only four of them facing the Craig.

The Craig twitched his head, like he was shaking an insect out of his ear.

"So we're square, right?" That was Ethan's true voice, shaky and nervous. "You've got your money."

"Yeah, I've got my money." The Craig thrust the duffel at one of his men and took a fresh handful of Ethan's tee. "But I got you, too."

"Come on, now," Ethan said. "This was all a mistake. I just wanted a ride home!"

The Craig's lip curled and he laughed, low and nasty.

"Well, too bad the ambulance already left. Because that's how you're getting home tonight. *After* you get a lesson in what happens when you make a *joke* out of the Craig."

Chizara opened her mouth—and out came a voice that was a hundred percent her mom's. "Put him down *this instant.*"

Surprise loosened the guy's grip for a moment. But when he turned and saw Chizara, he only laughed.

"What if I don't?"

She drew herself up, the supervillain inside her affronted by his laughter. "Then something bad will happen."

"Something *bad*?"

She reached into the Parker-Hamilton, slipped the networked sensors on like a glove, readied mental fingertips on the fused mess inside the borked generator, on the fritzed chips under the control board.

A lick of power, and they were fixed and ready.

"Drop him right now, or I'll bring you down."

The Craig leered at her. "All by yourself, princess?"

She was supposed to cringe, and she didn't. The Craig took a step closer.

"You bet." She smiled. "Just like this."

She flung out an arm at the floodlit derelict hotel a few blocks away.

A scattering of explosions traveled through the building, sharp and sudden, and puffs of dust flung themselves from the windows, along with spumes of glittery broken glass. The Craig turned back toward her, astonished, and Chizara held his gaze, claiming the detonation as her own and daring him to deny it.

The Parker-Hamilton Hotel began to implode.

CHAPTER 82

FLICKER

IT WAS THE FUCKING COOLEST THING FLICKER HAD ever seen.

As the first crackling explosions rang out, a hundred thousand eyeballs turned toward the sound. The string of little booms sent tremors through the air, like wingbeats against her face.

Larger *whoomps* pulsed inside the building, and with endless eyes she saw the concrete structure ripple with their force, a billowing curtain in the wind. For a moment the brick facade turned liquid—a waterfall, a melting photograph. It sagged among its own smoke puffs, and then the floors began their collapse from the top down, each one pancaking into the one below. All that concrete lowered itself to the earth and shattered there, sending out a roiling bank of dust.

So much dust. Plaster and brick and mortar, stone and marble and concrete, all of it crushed into grit and powder. Towering swells of it surged in all directions, as if drawn by the roar of the crowd. The sharp scent of explosives reached Flicker, followed by the chalky smell of the building's guts.

She scanned the eyeballs around her, watched the Craig and his crew disappear, still astonished as the white floodlit cloud rolled over them. The Zeroes vanished as well.

Farther out, people in the crowd punched the air, waved like maniacs, tried to capture the unfurling demolition on their tiny screens. Riley watched from endless, riveted viewpoints.

She reached out, felt Anon's hand in hers—that always-surprising perfect fit. Following the sound of maniacal laughter, she took Chizara's as well.

"It's me," Flicker said.

Chizara laughed harder. "You see what I *did*?"

"I see. Like you wouldn't believe."

"I've got Ethan," Anon said. "And he's got Nate. Let's go!"

They started to move, the chain of them winding through the coughing, cheering crowd. Flicker let herself be drawn along, moving her view farther out, past the dust, where tens of thousands more eyeballs stared.

The collapsed hotel was gone, consumed by the cloud, but a few fireworks had been held back for the finale. They arced up and spread their generous glittering arms, weep-ing willows of gold against the black sky, and the cheering swelled again.

"Man, people *love* explosions," Ethan cried out bitterly.

From next to Flicker came Anon's laughter. At Ethan's expense, or maybe he was just being carried along by Chizara, who was still borderline hysterical about having freaked out the Craig and his minions so completely.

Flicker felt it bubbling up in her, too. It was a kind of madness, seeing the world from all those eyeballs, all of them focused on that magnificent ruination.

But then the five of them were staggering from the thinning cloud, and she found eyeballs nearby not blinded by dust. Their hands parted, except for her and Anon. Here in the crowd, he had to stay close to her to keep from disappearing.

Flicker was okay with that.

The other three turned to stare back at Chizara's work, but Anon led her a little farther, finding a private corner of the crowd.

"I'm sorry," he said softly, "for leaving you alone back at the warehouse."

Flicker shook her head. "I can take care of myself. I was more worried about you. A scooter seems like the wrong place to be invisible."

"It wasn't great. Right here is better." He held her close, until she could feel his heart beating in his chest.

Her own pulse still raced from the awesome sight of the old

hotel turning into a heap of wreckage and rubble. It was amazing what humans could do. Just ordinary humans, with only science, no superpowers.

It was amazing just standing here with him.

"That was beautiful," she said. "How it just fell out of the skyline."

"Yeah, and the best part was, none of our friends were in it."

Those words made Flicker hold him a little tighter, struck again by how close it had all been. She switched her vision off, but the blackness in her head pulsed with leftover sparks and shimmers.

"What if you'd gone in instead of Nate?" she said.

"I wasn't back in time. That scooter was a glorified lawn mower."

"No, I mean, if you *had* gotten back and gone in, and then Chizara hadn't stopped it in time."

"Then I would've been . . ." A pause. "Oh, I see what you mean."

Flicker held him tighter. Would anyone have remembered Anon? Or would he have simply vanished in the dust, fading from her thoughts when he never returned?

No body. No memories. Nothing.

He gave a dry laugh. "If I make any heroic sacrifices, it won't be for the posthumous glory, I guess."

"Maybe just skip the posthumous part altogether!"

He shrugged in her arms. "I'm not in this to win medals."

Flicker shook her head, trying to force the thoughts of his death—his *erasure*—out of her head.

"You and your stupid Zen," she said. "I think you're amazing, Anon. I think you *should* get medals, because you're this crazy-beautiful person. But you keep telling me that wisdom says you're nothing."

"It does." There was a smile in his voice. "But there's another part of that saying."

"There's more? Gee, great."

"The rest didn't mean anything to me. But now it does." Anon leaned closer to her ear. "'Wisdom tells me I'm nothing. But love tells me I'm everything.'"

"Oh," Flicker said, just as their lips met full and hard, her heart beating slantways and too fast. The smells of dust and crowd and Anon blended in her head, along with the cries of joy at the last few fireworks overhead, the feel of him against her, both of them breathing hard.

When they parted, it took a moment for her to find herself. Another moment to realize what she needed to ask.

"Was that the first time we've . . ." Flicker knew this was silly. "I mean, it's just that it felt that way. But obviously not, right? I mean, we *must* have before now. But was that our first—"

"It was," Anon said. "It always is."

CHAPTER 83

MOB

DAWN WAS BREAKING ACROSS THE WAITING-ROOM windows when the doctor said she should go in and see her dad.

Not "could." "Should."

Like there wasn't much time.

Kelsie had been sitting in the broad, beige waiting room of Cambria County General for hours, feeling the storm of energies swirl around her. A hospital was not a good place to feel the crowd. Too many people dragging her emotions around. A few happy at their test results but most of them fighting anxiety, and too many cold, hard washes of despair.

Kelsie tried to tune it out. But every time she disengaged from the pulse of the crowd, she was overwhelmed by her own fear about her dad. That fear was like a channel, carrying her back to the anxious herd.

She'd been glad when the other Zeroes had turned up. They formed their own group within the larger throng of fear and pain and boredom. All of them were buzzing with energy, a dozen times more united than at the meeting two days ago.

"We've done everything we can," the doctor was saying. "Your father's suffered a lot of internal damage. And his system was already compromised by the drugs . . ."

Kelsie nodded. For hours now she'd been nodding every time a doctor spoke. The man looked exhausted, like he'd really tried. Kelsie wished she could feel her weariness. All she felt was scared.

"You should go see him now," the doctor repeated.

But she was frozen to the chair. Nate was standing by the doctor, asking for more details. He said things like, "Is there anything more we can do? Cost is irrelevant." But he seemed to be saying them from a great distance. Over against a wall she could see Chizara and Flicker, and beside Flicker a shadow that slid in and out of focus. Anon.

Ethan was sitting beside her. He nudged her knee with his.

"You want me to come with?" he asked softly.

She looked up at him, trying to feel her way through the panic and grief. She had a question for him, the real him.

"Is it true, what you said about my mom? Back in the Parker-Hamilton? Is that all real, or . . . a scam?"

Ethan took a breath. "I never know what's true or not. The voice just says the right words to make what I want happen."

"What did you want? Can you remember exactly?"

"Well, your dad was so guilty about getting you mixed up in his troubles. I just wanted him to get a little peace before . . . you know."

Kelsie stared at the floor. She did know. In the Parker-Hamilton her dad had thought he was about to die. He hadn't made up the story about her mom; he couldn't have. There'd be no peace in lying at the end.

"So do you want me to come into the room with you?" Ethan asked. "You know, get the full story from your dad?"

He looked seriously frightened by the idea, and Kelsie felt a surge of gratitude that he would even offer. She wondered if his voice could keep her father honest, if all Ethan wanted was the truth.

But she'd never be certain. Ethan and the truth had a complicated relationship.

"It should be just us. Me and Dad."

Like it had always been. Her and her dad. Since before she could remember.

She got to her feet, and Ethan rose with her.

"I still think your power sucks," she said.

"My power still does suck," Ethan confirmed.

Nate squeezed her shoulder as she passed. "We'll be right here. Waiting for you."

Kelsie nodded, a lump in her throat. She'd never been so glad to know that someone would be waiting for her. That they all would be there when she got through whatever came next.

She left the Zeroes in that beige room and followed the doctor down a narrow hall, into a small space full of blinking machines.

"Take all the time you need," the doctor said, then left them alone.

The hospital bed was dwarfed by the equipment on either side. Her dad looked terrible. His skin was pale and gray in the harsh overhead lighting, making his bruises darker.

She crossed to the bed and stood, afraid to touch him until he reached out a hand. She grasped it, feeling how light and hollow he'd become.

"I wish you didn't have to see me like this, Kels." His voice barely made it above a whisper.

"The doctor . . ." She couldn't get the rest out.

"I know, sweetie." Dad cleared his throat. "Your old man really screwed this one up."

He'd been saying that all her life. She pressed her hand across her eyes, wishing he would say something new now.

She wanted to disconnect from the tides of anxiety around her. Not all of it was hers. Every frightened, desperate, sad person in that hospital had a direct line to Kelsie right then. She stood with the tears pouring down her face. Not just for her dad, but for everyone.

She knew everyone's pain.

"Too many mistakes," her dad was saying in a thin, raspy voice. "I got myself to a place where nobody could help me."

"Dad—"

"I only wish I hadn't taken you there with me."

"That was my decision," she said.

Tears welled in his eyes. "Who's going to take care of my little girl?"

She leaned across him, hugging him as gently as she could, careful of the tubes that fed into his arms. "Don't worry about me. I have plenty of friends now."

"Friends are everything." She heard the pride in his voice. "Friends and family."

That last word made her pull back. Her dad was crying now too, his face wet and raw. He looked exhausted and even smaller than when she'd first come into the room. Like he was shrinking.

"Dad?" she said carefully. "Was it true what Ethan said about Mom?"

Dad nodded slowly. "I don't know how that kid knew all that."

"So she's alive?"

Dad nodded again. "She's not a bad person, Kelsie. But for some people, it's too much."

"What is?"

"Being a parent," he said simply.

Kelsie sat on the edge of his bed, carefully. "Didn't she love me?"

"She loved you more than anything," Dad said. The effort of speaking was really costing him. He pulled himself up from the pillows. "But your mother, she did better alone than in a family."

She nodded, but she couldn't see it. Even in this place where anxiety pulsed from the walls around her, Kelsie knew that she was better in a family, in a group, in a crowd. And now she had one all her own.

She felt sorry for her mom then, but it was like feeling sorry for a stranger. Most people didn't have what Kelsie had. A power. A connection.

"She did the best she could," Dad said softly.

"You both did." She gave him a small smile, to let him know he'd explained everything. He didn't need to fight anymore.

Dad eased back into his pillows. His eyes lost their fevered brightness, and for a moment Kelsie thought he'd already gone.

"Dad? Not yet, okay? Please? Not yet."

But he only nodded, gently, like he was listening to something else. He closed his eyes, his breath coming in soft, rattling gasps. His hand in hers became still and slack.

Kelsie stayed with him to the end. She felt it, the moment her dad stopped being part of the flux of human life. The moment he left the crowd of humanity behind and drifted away.

For a time the world rushed in. She let it happen, all the grief in the hospital flooding through her, sinking her under its weight, filling her with hurt and hopelessness and loss.

Then she pulled back and back, until she was very small inside her own skin.

For a while she was more alone than she had ever been.

She sat with her father a long time, until his skin began to cool. By then none of the anxiety of the hospital touched her. In the end, worry and doubt and fear were beside the point.

The worst had already happened.

When she made it back to the waiting room, the sun was spilling in.

Ethan and Nate were still where she'd left them a lifetime ago. Nate was upright in a hard, beige chair, looking like he was about to conduct a board meeting. Ethan was sprawled with his legs hooked over a chair arm and his head against a vending machine.

She went over to Ethan and tapped his shoulder lightly.

He was instantly awake. "Kelsie?"

Nate joined them. "The others are downstairs. Is there anyone we can call for you?"

She thought it through. She could call Fig or Ling or Remmy. Or even Mikey. They were all her friends. They'd all try to help her now, like they'd been helping her since the robbery. But right now the people she'd shared most with in the past week were here.

She shook her head. "No. Thanks, though."

"Well, anything you need." Nate gave her a reassuring smile. "You know we're here for you. All of us."

Ethan was on his feet by then. He blinked at her, eyes puffy with sleeplessness.

"There's one thing." Kelsie turned to Ethan. "That thing inside you, the voice? The thing that's so smart that it knows everything everyone wants it to say?"

Ethan nodded. "Yeah."

"Well, it's totally messed up."

"I know."

"But thank you." She wrapped her arms around him. If he hadn't found her just in time, she'd be alone now. "Thank you for what you did in the hotel. For wanting me to find some peace with Dad."

Ethan held her awkwardly, his arms coming around her, one hand in her hair.

"Hey, I'm just—" his voice said, smooth and perfectly comforting.

But then it fell silent, finishing in a kind of strangled noise. Ethan coughed hard a couple of times. Then, in his real voice, he continued: "I wish I knew half as much as my stupid voice. I wish I knew what I could say right now to make you okay."

Kelsie squeezed him harder. "Well, that's probably close enough."

CHAPTER 84
BELLWETHER

"WE DID THE BEST WE COULD," NATE SAID.

He gave them time to absorb the words. They were all exhausted, their defenses low, their minds primed to bond with each other in defeat. He could feel the eager pattern of it in the air. All six of them were part of the group, thanks to the web spinning around Anonymous and Flicker. There was even a connection, sharp and specific, between Anon and Scam.

They were all closer now. And their attention on Nate was tinged with something new and bright, something that hadn't been there before he'd led Mob and Scam and Jerry from the Parker-Hamilton.

Almost getting killed, it turned out, could be useful.

They were in the meditation chapel of the hospital, a small room with a few wooden benches and a stained-glass window ignited by the morning sun. Mob looked as though she wasn't sure if she was welcome there, but had nowhere else to go.

Now was the time to seal her to the others.

"After this last week," he said, "I feel like we understand our powers better."

We did a lot of damage with them, he didn't say. *And we had to rescue Scam three times.*

"The Bagrovs think that Scam and Mob are dead, so we're safe from them." Nate turned with a smile toward Chizara. "And thanks to Crash's panache and superb timing, I don't think the Craig will be bothering us anytime soon."

Those words lifted the mood in the room a little. Nothing disrespectful to Kelsie's loss, just a worn glimmer of levity, like an old family joke incanted at a funeral.

"At the same time, she saved four lives," he added, and a blush came over Chizara's face. "Including mine."

That part of last night couldn't have gone better. Now that she had more than balanced the scales of Officer Bright, Chizara had no choice but to feel worthy of her power.

"We know each other better," he said. "And if we can stay connected, we can make each other stronger. Most of us can remember Anonymous now. Flicker's wrapped her vision around larger and larger crowds. And Chizara's power is evolving into something completely new."

Nate hesitated. It was a risk, mentioning Scam. But leaving him out of the list would be too obvious.

"And Ethan found a new Zero," he said, directing their attention away from Ethan and toward Kelsie, sitting near the door.

He had planned to focus all the warmth of their sympathy on her, to take it all the way, bending their exhaustion into tears. But in that instant of Kelsie staring back at him, Nate remembered how tough she was.

So he simply said, "I'm sorry we didn't find your father in time. We tried."

Her gaze dropped to the floor. "Thanks. But it's not your fault. Dad was always lost, I think."

Nate tried to answer, but Kelsie's sadness had gripped the room again. It came in waves, immense, all the death in the world pressing down on them. For a moment it was hard to breathe, even to think. It was too big for him to fight, because Mob's power wasn't just about her—it was about everyone.

There was nothing to do but let it pass.

After a while Nate managed to ask, "Is there anything we can do, Kelsie?"

"If we could all just stay here for a while," she said. "The six of us. I don't want to be alone."

Nate nodded. He didn't either.

A long time later Flicker had to head off to see her shrink.

The others were fading, in any case. They'd been up all night, and the meditation room had grown warm as the sun rose. Even Kelsie looked like she was about to fall asleep. So when Flick quietly mentioned her weekly appointment, Nate gently pulled them both from the shimmering web of friendship and walked her outside.

On the wide stone stairs of the hospital's entrance he said, "I guess you've got a lot to talk about with Dr. Bridges this week."

Flicker gave a tired laugh. "I never give him any good stuff. Besides, all he wants to talk about is braille."

"Sounds scintillating," Nate said.

"I guess. But it's cool if you *don't* call me with any exciting news during today's session. Let's take a week before the next mission, maybe."

Nate nodded, looking back at the hospital. "I think we're good for now."

"Better than we were," Flicker said. "You were right. We do make each other stronger."

"And we've only just started."

She looked up and caught the smile on his face. "Let me guess. You've got some fiendish plan. Some new Ultimate Goal?"

Nate wasn't sure how much to say yet. But this was Flick, after all. His little sister.

So he said, "We need a space. Somewhere we can set the terms and choose the crowd, like in controlled experiments. Somewhere we won't hurt anyone. Chizara's right about how dangerous we are, and we can't lose her again." He turned to Flicker and felt his power shift and slip into need, the way it sometimes did when the two of them were alone. "I can't lose any of you."

She took his hand and pulled him closer to whisper in his ear. "I don't think you will, not after last night. You make a pretty glorious action hero, *mi hermano*."

And they both had to laugh at that.

There were no cabs waiting at the curb, but Nate had mastered this trick a long time ago. He raised his hand into the air like a beacon and focused the geometries of the streets of Cambria around himself, and a few minutes later Flicker was headed off to her shrink. By then the curb was brimming with half a dozen taxis.

When he turned around to head back up the stairs, Nate heard his name.

"Mr. Saldana?"

He looked up. It was Detectives King and Fuentes coming down the steps, looking pleased to see him.

Nate sighed. "Good morning, Detectives."

"Morning," said King. She looked him up and down, taking in yesterday's wrinkled clothes. "Long night?"

"I'm afraid so. A friend of mine just died."

"I'm sorry for your loss," King said, and it sounded genuine.

Detective Fuentes didn't bother being somber. "By any chance did this friend of yours happen to be Jerry Laszlo?"

There was no point lying. "Yes."

"I see," Fuentes said. "Maybe you could help us get this straight. Here we are, coming to identify the body of a wanted bank robber, and it turns out he's your friend. And you're also friends with a kid who happened to be in the bank he robbed. Small world, huh?"

"Big world, actually," Nate said. "Which made it easy to give you guys the slip yesterday."

Fuentes didn't respond to this, but his lips pulled tight as he searched for a retort. It had actually taken Nate half an hour to shake their pursuit the night before. Creating a decent traffic snafu took time.

It was Detective King who spoke next. "Did you ever hear from Ethan Cooper? His mother's still looking."

Nate hesitated. No criminals were after Ethan anymore, and the police still couldn't connect him directly to any crime. Saying things you shouldn't know on a viral video was suspicious, but not prosecutable, especially when your mom was the prosecutor.

Maybe it was time for Ethan to go home.

Though there were probably better ways for this morning's vigil to end than Scam being dragged out by the cops.

Nate said to Detective King, "If I did know where he was, what exactly do you need him for? Is he wanted by the police?"

"He's a material witness," Fuentes said. "But thanks to his, uh, ties to the prosecutor's office, there's no warrant for his arrest. We just need to talk to him."

King nodded her agreement and said carefully, "I think his mother gets him first. In other words, at the moment we just want to give him a ride home."

Those words made Nate smile.

"I think that's what he wanted all along. Wait here, Detectives. I'll see what we can do."